Summer at the Art Café

Sue McDonagh

Where heroes are like chocolate – irresistible!

Published 2019 by Choc Lit Limited
Penrose House, Crawley Drive, Camberley, Surrey GU15 2AB, UK
www.choc-lit.com

A CIP catalogue record for this book is available
from the British Library

ISBN: 978-1-78189-438-5

Printed and bound in Great Britain by Clays Ltd, Elcograf S.p.A.

To Mum and Dad, my biggest fans and earliest motorbike memories

Acknowledgements

Writing may be a solitary occupation, but
I have never felt alone. So many people have
enriched my journey towards publication. If
I haven't mentioned you, please forgive me!

Enduring thanks to Allan, who's been living
with my characters for four years and still finds
time to listen to me talking about them.

Readers of the early drafts: Pippa from the Chocolate
Shop and biker pal Annie, and the ladies of the
Curvy Riders Committee, Emma, Linda, Kaye, Mo
and Tracey, for honest and invaluable feedback.

Simon, aka Obi-Wan, my motorbike
instructor – thank you.

My uniquely awesome writing crew – Vanessa
Savage, Jan Baynham and Catherine Burrows
– for inspiration and doubt-banishing.

Michaela, for mentoring and coloured Sharpies!

RNA NWS scheme, the Conference and local
Chapter meets – a wonderful resource for writers.

Workshops by Alison May for editing clarity
and getting it out there, and Sue Moorcroft's
outstanding tuition for everything else.

My Editor, patience and focus
throughout, thank you so much.

Choc Lit for believing in me.

The Choc Lit Tasting Panel, especially those who passed
the manuscript – Jane M, Hannah Mc, Lucy M, Melissa C,
Joy S, Susan D, Toos H, Megan C, Gill L, Heather P,
Gillian C, Hilary B, Ruth N, Elena B, Sam E, Melanie R,
Dimi E, Jo O, Jenny K, Isobel T, Carol F and Cordy S.

I couldn't have done this without any of you.

Thank you! x

Prologue

Satisfied that the hired waiting staff were doing their jobs, Lucy slipped into the audience at the Mega Bikes' Grand Fundraising night. She was delighted that the evening was turning out to be such a success, and proud that she and business partner Richard had put The Art Café's name in front of this huge gathering.

The sea of avid faces focussed on the presenter's every word, as he called out the many prizes. From cleaning kits at a few pounds to mind-bogglingly expensive helmets, everything was received with equal amounts of pleasure. The café had donated vouchers for cream teas to the cause, hoping to attract even more bikers, and she smiled as she spotted girls from the local bike club exclaiming happily over their wins. From all walks of life, they included the café in many of their ride-outs, drawn in by Richard's legendary cakes. She had them to thank for being involved tonight, and she was enjoying every minute.

But tilted on a raised platform, every polished curve caressed by glittering spotlights, was this evening's main prize – a purple motorbike that revolved slowly in tantalising view. Lucy's tickets, bought weeks ago, were tucked safely into a zipped pocket in her bag, but so many had been sold that it seemed ridiculous now to even speculate. Still, she couldn't help pulling them out to check for the millionth time that evening. She jumped, nearly dropping them as rock music blared from enormous speakers suddenly. The lights dimmed until only the purple bike remained lit, raked by flickering laser lights.

'Ooh, not long now.' Nicola, Richard's wife, drew admiring glances from all corners. Black-haired, tall and slim, and dressed head to toe in her black leather motorbike outfit, she ran the local section of the ladies' bike club.

Richard called her their 'Trouble-maker in Chief', with a wry smile. With her wicked sense of humour, she and Lucy had liked each other on sight, and Nicola often dropped into the café to catch up or help out. Richard, equally tall, but blonde and wiry and in his chequered chef's trousers and white jacket, hurried towards them.

'Got your tickets?' She fanned them like a deck of cards, and grinned at him.

'Yep. Good luck! Where's your old man tonight? I would've thought this was right up his street.'

'Gerry? I did ask him. He's at another one of his business network things. He said, why would he want to go to a "smelly old bike shop for the night"?'

Richard's head made an exaggerated sweep of the room. 'You're joking. This is ...' He shrugged. 'More like a nightclub than a bike dealer's.'

Lucy laughed. He was right; the huge monolithic building dazzled with light, colour and sound. Only the scents of leather and polish, and that indefinable tang of new vehicle, gave it away.

The crowd surged towards the stage, their faces expectant while the presenter took his time opening the winning ticket, building up the suspense. Lucy felt her body tense, told herself that of course, the winner might not even be present, could be anywhere. It wouldn't be her. What had she been thinking? She couldn't even ride a motorbike.

An excruciating sense of humiliation swept over her. She'd worked herself up into a state about something she couldn't even do. Gerry was always telling her how useless she was, how she should stick to selling her paintings, in her little café where she couldn't even work the coffee machine, as he never, ever stopped reminding her. Prickly heat swept over her. She should leave now. Sneak out, so no-one could see her face, or hear her false, careless laugh when she didn't win. Because of course she wouldn't win. She never won anything. She edged her body clockwise, planning her exit, but the crush of bodies pressed closer, until she was wedged facing away from the stage, and unable to move.

'And the winner is ...' There was a drum roll from the speakers and a final crash of cymbals. Lucy widened her eyes. Surely she hadn't heard that correctly?

'... is she here? Lucy, The Art Café? Ah, and I'm told that The Art Café provided the delicious food we've been eating tonight ...' The presenter kept up a stream of words over the hubbub of noise and a dazed Lucy watched the crowd craning their necks and twisting this way and that to see the lucky winner. Her.

'You've only gone and bloody won, woman!' Richard grabbed her arm and pulled her round. 'Get up there!'

Barely aware of the thunderous applause around her as spotlights, music and fireworks blazed simultaneously, Lucy stumbled on-stage on nerveless legs, never taking her eyes off the motorbike, resplendent and shimmering in the purple of a Cadbury chocolate wrapper. And it was hers. All hers.

'Congratulations, Lucy.' The presenter turned her towards the audience. 'A big bike for a little lady! But I'm sure the back seat is comfy.'

There was a small chorus of boos with a distinctly feminine overtone.

Lucy grinned down at them. 'I expect it is. However ...' She paused, taking a deep breath. 'The front seat is the one with my name on it.'

'Oh, I'm sorry.' The presenter inclined his head. 'And I was just about to offer you a pillion seat on my own bike. Do you ride then?'

'Not yet.' There was laughter. Her eyes slid again towards her prize. She could barely believe it. She spoke clearly into the microphone. 'But I'll be booking my lessons tomorrow!'

Chapter One

'Hey! What the hell do you think you're doing?'

The voice penetrated the window of Lucy's van, just after she heard the horrible crunching noise behind her. She slammed on the brakes, scrambled out of the cab, and clapped a hand to her mouth as she realised what she'd just done ... there was a red and black motorbike lying on the ground behind her.

Throwing herself flat, her eyes swept the expanse beneath the van for the bloodstained, broken body of her imagination. To her immense relief, there was nothing. No one. Except for a pair of tall, polished black boots, on their way around the van towards her.

'It's no good hiding. I can still see you.' The voice was deep. It demanded attention. Leaping to her feet, Lucy followed the boots upwards with her gaze, over long legs encased in black leather, a bulky black jacket, to a ferociously cross expression rimmed with a bushy black beard.

'I wasn't hi—' She hooked a finger into the neck of her thick sweater, feeling her heat rise along with the banging of her heart. 'God, I thought I'd run someone over!'

'Nope. Only one of the school bikes, luckily for you.' The laser beam from his deep-set blue eyes burned into her and, feeling guilty, she looked away, but her artist's eye caught his strong profile and aquiline nose behind the beard. Those startling eyes were the same colour as her favourite paint, cobalt. His thick black hair showed only the slightest signs of grey, which seemed to add to his air of authority. Everything about his stance spoke of decision and action.

'I'll pick it up.' Anxious to make amends, she darted in front of him, gripped the handlebars of the fallen bike and heaved upwards with all her might. The bike didn't rise but scraped horribly on the concrete instead. 'Whoa – that's heavier than I thought!' She was shocked, and filled with a new respect for Nicola and her girls, moving their much larger machines around with such ease.

'Leave it. You'll only make it worse.' Stepping in front of her, he righted it as if it were featherweight and stomped into the Better Biking office without looking back.

Lucy collected her belongings from her van, abandoned halfway into the compound. She decided to leave it there. She was already late, and didn't trust herself to park it anywhere else. Blasted thing. It wouldn't be so bad if it didn't have her name plastered all over it. *Lucy Daumier, Artist, The Art Café*, it proclaimed. She'd been really proud of it until now.

She hesitated outside the offices. Who was the bearded man? The owner? She groaned inside. She'd been desperate to explain before he'd stalked away. How could she have missed seeing that bike behind her? She was always so careful. But she knew why. She'd been ready ridiculously early so she could start the day fresh and then ... Gerry. And so she'd been late, and rushing. She pushed her husband's cruel words out of her head, or she'd never be able to concentrate.

'Great start to the day. Not.' She scrubbed her hands over her face. 'Better go and face the music.'

The premises were a set of linked porta-cabins, and Lucy knocked on the open door of the office. 'Good morning, I'm Lucy Daumier. I'm booked to do my compulsory, um ... and I, er ...' Her mouth dried up and she licked her lips. She was a disaster. She should go home now and not embarrass herself any further.

'Your CBT. Compulsory Bike Training?' The woman smiled, and Lucy nodded. 'I'm Angela. I booked you in yesterday.'

'That's the one. And, er, I'm so sorry, I seem to have ...'

She made a falling over gesture with her hand, followed by 'two hands on handlebars'. What was the matter with her? Her brain seemed to have melted and she couldn't even string a sentence together. How on earth was she going to learn to ride a bike?

'Whoopsie.' Angela raised her eyebrows and smiled lopsidedly. 'It was you that ran over one of our bikes?'

Lucy cringed. 'I'll pay for the damage, obviously.'

'Ah, well, they're pretty bombproof. I'll get it over to the Bike Palace later, they'll sort it out. Anyway – ready for your course?'

'What, you're still going to let me do it?'

'Why not? If you're up to it? Try not to let it spoil your day.'

Lucy was grateful for her kindness. 'Thank you.'

'The others are in the room to the left, having a cuppa. The Ladies' is to the right, you might want to have a bit of a brush up.'

The bathroom mirror reflected her face, pale apart from the mud smears. Grateful for the liquid hand wash, she bent over the basin, rubbing hurriedly. Finally, red-cheeked and lavender-scented, she headed to the room Angela had indicated. Her 'Sorry I'm late' died on her lips, for the room contained four men, and one of them was the black-bearded man. Surely he wasn't her trainer for the day? She might as well go home now.

Sidling in, hot with embarrassment, she cringed as she saw the only empty chair was right at the front. A mug of coffee was handed to her by the youngest of the men, who told her his name was Rhodri. She mouthed a 'thank you' at him, hoping no-one could see her hands shaking.

'I'm Ash Connor, your trainer.' The black-bearded man fixed her with his steely gaze and she nodded in his general direction, unable to meet his eye. The briefing continued and she tried hard to focus, but her mind was all over the place. Dwelling on her earlier disaster, all she could hear was the thump as she'd knocked the bike over, and the image of Ash's angry face glowering down at her was etched into her brain. How could she have been so stupid?

'Lucy.' Ash's voice broke into her gloomy preoccupations. 'Are you joining us?'

Jumping up, she saw the rest of her class were now kitting up in jackets, gloves and helmets. She was sure that barely a word he'd said had settled into her consciousness. She thought about going home and giving up altogether. Then she thought about explaining to Nicola and the girls, and how disappointed they'd be in her. How disappointed she'd be in *herself*. And how Gerry would think he'd won. Squaring her shoulders, she strode over to join her class.

Ash watched Lucy during his introduction, noting that she made no eye contact, and showed no signs that she was listening to him. She looked thoroughly downcast, and he felt a pang of guilt that he'd over-reacted. He'd been a bit surprised to see a lithe, pretty woman leap down from the cab of the van instead of a burly male driver. And yes, he knew how sexist that sounded. Completely wrong-footed by her flushed, upturned face, brown eyes staring up at him in fright, he'd been a whole lot more growly-bear, as his daughter would have said, than he meant to be.

She sat there, blonde hair fallen across her face as if she was hiding behind it, which on reflection, she probably was. He took care not to give any instruction whilst her attention was lacking, and hustled the class quickly into their gear. He'd instruct on the ground. It would be fine. Watching her wrestle her way into one of the voluminous one-size-fits-all school jackets, he made a mental note to ask Angela whether they could order a smaller size for stock.

Lucy looked like a toddler amongst grown-ups. He resolved to try and make her feel more relaxed, or she might as well cancel and come back another time.

There were four identical red and black bikes parked in the compound and Ash beckoned them around one and began to talk about them.

'This is a Honda CBF125cc, a perfect commuter and school bike. A hardy and reliable workhorse, although it has been known to take the occasional 'unscheduled' nap.' The older men laughed, which pleased Ash. He wanted Lucy and Rhodri to understand that dropping a bike happened to everyone.

'Yeah, I've dropped mine dozens of times.' One of the older men said in a self-deprecating tone, and Ash saw Lucy look at him in surprise.

'It may not look like much, but it's heavy,' Ash continued. 'If it falls away from you – let it go. Don't try to lift it, you'll damage it, and yourself.' He deliberately looked away from Lucy, so that she didn't feel targeted.

He really hoped she'd start to relax soon, or the day would be a complete waste of time for her.

Lucy chewed her lip. *Didn't she know it.* Those bikes really were heavy. How would she balance it? How did people not drop bikes all over the place? She tuned in to Ash again, who was talking about up and down and left for this hand or foot, and right for that. Since winning her bike she'd been keen to learn and watched loads of videos on the internet about how to ride, but somehow in real life, it was all different. How would she remember? Maybe she could chalk it on her jeans and cuffs or something. She looked around the small parking lot wondering where they would actually ride?

'Right, we need to get these bikes over to the practice area on the other side of the road. I'll pillion you two over on the bikes you'll be using.' Ash directed his words at Lucy and Rhodri, and Lucy's stomach bubbled with anticipation. Her very first ride on a motorbike. Pity it was Ash driving. He was a bit scary, with those blue eyes that seemed to see into your soul. Where was she meant to hold on? Not to him, surely?

'Don't worry, I'll walk,' she volunteered.

'Before you go,' he continued smoothly as if she hadn't spoken, 'these are your radios. They're one way, so you can hear me, but I can't hear you.'

'"In space, no-one can hear you scream ..."' Lucy fitted the ear-piece and dropped the receiver into the chest pocket of the jacket before pulling her helmet back on. Ash's head swivelled towards her as he put his own helmet on. *Oh God, I said that out loud, didn't I?*

'From the Alien film?' she shouted, her voice muffled inside her helmet.

'*You* can hear *me*,' Ash said slowly, startling her as she heard his voice in her ear for the first time. '*I* can't hear *you*. You're wearing a helmet.'

Lucy gave him two thumbs up with a grin, to show she understood. God, did he actually have a sense of humour?

'OK? On you get,' he said, sitting across the bike that would be hers, and starting the engine. Lucy hesitated, working out how to climb on without holding onto what was surely the grouchiest and hairiest man alive. 'In your own time. I'll steady the bike, don't worry, you won't knock me over.' Gulping, Lucy tried to maintain her personal space as she flung her leg wildly over the seat, knocking their helmets together. 'Put your feet on the foot pegs. No, that's the exhaust. Try again. You can put your hands on my shoulders to stabilise yourself.'

'Oh. Sorry. I've never been on the back of a bike before.' She didn't add that she'd never been on the front either.

But then she remembered he couldn't hear her anyway. She sat back as far as possible, shy about holding onto him. As they set off, she grabbed for his shoulders, feeling horribly unstable. It was a short distance to the practice compound, and she wished she'd walked, because now she had to work out how to dismount. Did she get off like a horse? Deciding for some reason not to, she hopped her boot over the seat in the most graceless way imaginable. Stumbling in slow motion, she found herself on the ground once again looking up at Ash.

'I'm fine!' She leapt up like a child's Jack-in-a-Box. *You are a successful businesswoman*, she reminded herself. *You can do this.*

'I don't often get women throwing themselves at my feet,' she heard in her earpiece. He dismounted. 'Twice in one day! It's a record.' With an old-fashioned bow, he waved her onto the bike in his place.

Lucy's heart thudded in her ears as she climbed onto the front seat of a motorbike for the very first time. Excitement overtook her nerves. She was about to learn how to ride. Forget about this morning, and Gerry. This was the real deal. Already, she could feel how the bike fitted to her, how her hands dropped naturally to the handlebars while her feet instinctively knew where the foot pegs were.

The practice compound was a long section of a disused runway, marked out in places with coloured cones to represent a road. They began with baby steps. How to turn the engine on. Which hand worked the brake. Lucy was gratified to feel the engine rumbling beneath her. She twisted the throttle experimentally, feeling her mouth stretch in an enormous grin as she heard and, thrillingly, felt the engine note rise and fall.

Then it was first gear, and the clutch biting point. The two older men had it perfectly in seconds, having been riding their bikes for some time. She and Rhodri stalled over and over until finally, Lucy was the only one not quite managing to reliably co-ordinate her hands and feet. She heard Ash's voice in her ear-piece.

'Less revs, Lucy. Smoooothly let the clutch out ... yes! That's ... oh, never mind.' He paused as she stalled again. 'Ok. And again.'

She swore ferociously inside her helmet, wrenching the lifeless bike upright as it lurched against her inner thigh. Then she paused and congratulated herself. Only a little while ago, she would have dropped the bike when it did that. Now that she'd got used to the weight of it, she felt more in charge. She *could* do this. Pressing the starter button again, she stamped her left foot onto the lever to get first gear, and gently let out the clutch until she was rolling slowly forward.

'Well done, Lucy, just to the bottom, big circle round, and come back, like the others.'

She whooped with glee, and twisted the throttle a little more. The bike surged forward, jolting her backwards. She clenched the handlebars, sending the engine howling and her rocketing along the runway at breakneck speed, passing the rest of the class heading decorously in the other direction on the opposite side of the runway.

'Waaaaaah!' Her shout was whipped away by the wind.

'Lucy, stay calm. Left hand, pull the clutch in.' Ash's steady voice crackled inside her earpiece. 'Right hand, loose hold, let the throttle spring back. Squeeze *gently* on the brake – that's the right-hand lever.' Eyes stretched wide, Lucy followed instructions, feeling the bike slow instantly, rolling gently to a halt. In that brief moment of flight, she realised what it was that Nicola and her girls must feel when they rode. Glee mixed in equal proportion to terror. It was exhilarating. Like riding a roller-coaster, but being in charge. Mostly. The moment of howling speed before the plane lifts off, but knowing you can shut it off. The sense of control, even at such an early stage, was intoxicating.

'Neutral, and switch off. Side-stand down.' She heard Ash's voice in her ear and did as she was told.

'Wow. That was *amaaaazing!*' She couldn't help shouting aloud.

'Lucy. We don't lease the *entire* runway.' Ash jogged to a halt alongside her, resting his hands on his knees to catch his breath. 'Just this bit. Phew. Bike boots are not designed for sprinting in.' She twisted to look over her shoulder and her view stretched towards where she'd come from.

'Oops. Sorry.'

'I'm not walking all that way back,' he said, following her gaze. 'And *I'm* driving, this time. You're on the back.' She got off, and watched as he threw his long leg over the bike, buckling his helmet. She climbed on behind him, perching as far back as possible.

'Hold onto my belt. Just go with the bike if it leans. Don't try and straighten it up, okay? I'm going to talk you through this.' She did as she was told, feeling more secure as her knees gripped him. 'Okay, switching on, listen to the engine. This is first gear ...' She concentrated, shuffling forward to see over his shoulder while he rode, explaining the gears, how the bike dipped and rose as he braked or accelerated. It was fascinating. Circling in a tight turn, he pulled up alongside the rest of the class. 'Shall we start again? Less of the rocket-man impersonations this time, please.' Lucy clambered off, eager to try again, determined to put her new-found knowledge into practice.

By lunchtime, she had progressed to riding smoothly up and down the lanes, although she showed a marked tendency to catch up rather too quickly with whoever was in front of her, earning her several 'Throttle control, Lucy' admonishments from Ash. She was having the time of her life.

Lunch was in a café on the trading estate just a few hundred yards away. Dodging straight into the Ladies', Lucy made a face as she caught sight of herself in the mirror. The bits of honey blonde, expensively layered and highlighted hair not sticking straight up were plastered flat to her skull. Pulling her mobile out of her pocket, she clicked off a quick selfie, and sent it to Nicola, with the words, 'My Biker Bird's Nest hair-do. See you after class at the café?'

'We've all ordered,' Ash told her as she joined them. 'Bacon butties.' Her stomach rumbled in response. She was starving, she realised, and joined the short queue at the counter.

Taking her seat at the table, she listened to them chatting about their reasons for being there. The two older men used their bikes to commute, and weren't at all bothered about having bigger bikes or passing their tests. Rhodri said his parents had bought him a bike to go to college on.

'What about you, Lucy?'

'I've won a motorbike.'

'Have you really?' asked Rhodri, between mouthfuls. 'Wow, awesome!'

'What does your husband think?' This from one of the older men. 'I bet he's happy, he gets a new bike!'

'He doesn't ride. He's *really* happy for me.' Aiming into her bacon roll, Lucy gave the sauce bottle a fierce squeeze, wishing it was her husband's neck. He was very far from happy for her. He'd been an absolute shit that morning. How had it taken her so long to notice how controlling he'd become? He'd accused her of having a mid-life crisis, said she should sell her beautiful Cadbury, and he'd invest the money. A mid-life crisis? She was only thirty-five, not fifty-five. She wasn't going to let him spoil this for her.

'But,' she said, looking round the table, 'it's my bike. Not his.'

Chapter Two

Parking her van in the café car park later that day, Lucy paused for a moment to admire The Art Café, its pretty gable roofs silhouetted against a sky streaked with apricot and magenta. Glowing pools of light slanted across the beach from the floor to ceiling windows. Housed in the building that had once been the Tourist Offices, before the staff had been re-housed far enough away from the high street to prevent them being assailed by real people and their queries, it was, with its nooks and crannies, a perfect display case, even if it was an occasional nightmare to police against shoplifters.

She felt exhilarated, as if every nerve in her body was set to 'receive'. Breathing deep lungfuls of the sea-salty tang, she listened to the mingled sounds of booming sea and gull shrieks as if she didn't hear it almost every day of her life. Her gaze swept over the turquoise sea at dusk, a few hardy surfers skipping over waves turned lilac by the dipping sun. You could be anywhere in the world, looking out over a view like that, but this was the Gower Peninsula, and the beaches here were some of the finest surfing venues in the country. As always, Lucy thought how lucky she was to live in Wales, but for the first time in ages, she longed for a paintbrush to record the scene.

'Hey, brand new biker-girl! How did it go?' Nicola and Richard looked up expectantly as she pushed open the front door.

She'd met Richard a dozen years ago. Straight out of catering school, ambitious and keen to make his mark, he'd catered for the launch night of an exhibition of her work, creating tiny cupcakes iced in the brilliant colours of her paintings, and arranged on giant platters in the shape of an artist's palette. The youngest of six siblings – the others all girls – he'd had years of training from his sisters, meaning he knew instinctively what women liked to eat, and it was exactly what he liked to cook: cake. Cake was his passion. He was always trying new recipes and Lucy needed no encouragement to eat them, as Gerry had unerringly pointed out the other morning.

They'd hit it off straight away and The Art Café, co-owned by Lucy and Richard, had been born a year later. The palette of cakes was their logo.

Gerry, with a degree in real estate and property management, had been as enthusiastic as they were, using his skills to negotiate the confusion of paperwork and finances. Lucy had appreciated his good head for figures, and to this day left the accounts to him to submit.

So when had the rot set in? They'd worked their socks off together to smarten up the first tatty property he'd bought to do up and sell as an investment, and she'd thoroughly enjoyed it. But somehow, his burgeoning confidence in business translated into the idea that he was not only in charge of her finances, but her too. Grateful to be relieved of the burden of overseeing the VAT returns, Lucy had spent her time sourcing artists, visiting makers in their studios and choosing pieces to delight her customers and build up her flourishing business.

'I am *wrecked!*' She pulled out a chair and collapsed onto it. 'God, it's as good as the gym. I had no idea how much of my body I had to use. My thighs are killing me.' She beamed at them. 'OMG, why have I waited this long to ride a bike? Nic, it's awesome, isn't it?'

'It is awesome.' Nicola nodded. Married to Richard for three years, and a book-keeper, Nicola had pillioned him on his motorbike for years until deciding to pass her test and ride her own, and it was her sporty red motorbike that had fired Lucy's curiosity. That, and her posse of girlfriends on bikes, who often came into the café and enjoyed the afternoon teas, while Richard enjoyed their teasing banter, giving back as good as he got. 'So come on, tell us all about it. I take it you passed?'

'God, no. I was hopeless!' Lucy laughed at their expressions. 'I didn't even get to go on the road.'

'What? You didn't pass? How come?' Nicola leaned forward, her expression kind and sympathetic. 'Were you a bit timid?'

'You'd think so, wouldn't you?' Lucy levered herself upright and headed into the kitchens for a glass of water. Her mouth was so dry. Mostly due to having grinned inside her helmet for the whole day. Her teeth had been so dry by the end of the day that her lips had stuck to them. 'No. I think I'm possessed. I was like a bloody banshee on that bike.'

Richard looked perplexed. 'How do you mean?'

'We-ell, after running over one of their bikes in the car park …' Lucy made a face.

'Nooooo! How did *that* happen?'

'Oh, Richard, you *know* how carefully I drive. I'd had a row with Gerry and he made me late. My fault entirely. I was in a stupid rush.' She sipped her water. 'After *that*, I went on to break the Land Speed Record in first gear, then …'

'What? You did what?' Nicola blinked, listening with her mouth open as Lucy explained how she'd zoomed past the surprised faces of her class.

'It got worse though. I dropped the bike twice trying to do those stupid, dratted U turns, and broke the brake lever on one side, and the clutch lever on the other. Apparently, I need more practice. I'm booked in again next Monday.'

'Okaaay. How do you feel about that?'

Lucy shrugged. 'It's a means to an end. Whatever I need to do to get my licence.'

'Good for you, Luce.' Richard knuckled her shoulder. 'I wasn't sure you'd do it.'

'Really? Why ever not?'

'Er, didn't you say Gerry wasn't too keen on you learning?'

'Oh, that!' Lucy laughed and pretended a nonchalance she was actually far from feeling. 'I don't take any notice of that. Do you know what he said to me this morning? He said I was "too fat to wear leathers".' He'd actually added, 'You're not supposed to eat the profits of the café, Lucy,' along with the flat order to, 'Sell the bike. I'll invest the money in our pensions. We're not getting any younger.' But she wasn't going to tell them that. She had a good few years to go before she was even forty. He was getting much too like the older men he associated with in his business clubs. They needed to start having fun again.

'That's ridiculous.' Nicola's eyebrows shot up in outrage. 'We have all shapes and sizes in our club! What a stupid thing to say. Plus, Lucy, you are not fat.'

'Thanks, sweetie.' Lucy stood to give her friend a hug. 'Although I am a bit fat, to be fair. I even suggested to him that we both learn. We never do anything together these days.' She perched on the edge of her chair, gazing out at the beach, turning pinky-purple as the sun sank over the cliffs. 'I had high hopes of us touring Europe by motorbike next summer. Or Route 66. Maybe the Rockies. I can't tell you how sick I am of hotels on golf resorts, where I end up spending every day by myself.' Lucy sighed and then jutted her chin. 'I tell you what though. One of these days I'm beating that coffee machine into submission.'

'Don't listen to her!' Richard ran around the counter

and embraced the gleaming chrome contraption, to their laughter.

Lucy silently blessed her friends and their positive outlooks. She really did have a lot to think about. Learning to ride a motorbike had turned out to be the tip of the iceberg.

Ash ducked into the back doorway of his parents' house and sniffed the air in appreciation. No-one cooked a roast like his Mum.

'Daddeee! You're home!' His seven-year old daughter, Daisy, thudded into his legs and he pretended to collapse with an 'oof' as she wrapped her arms round him.

'Have you been good for Nanny and Bamps?' Daisy loved being with his parents, and they insisted that his daughter was an angel at all times, although he was quite sure that wasn't always the case.

'I have been very good. I helped make pudding. I did peeling.' She nodded, emphasising each word, and he smiled down at her, his heart bursting with pride at her sparkling eyes and enthusiasm.

'Thanks for having her, Mum.' He bent to kiss his mother's cheek where she was testing the vegetables. 'What can I do to help?'

'We're nearly done here. If Daisy could set the table, Ash darling, could you go and find your father, and tell him dinner is ready? He's in the shed.'

'He's mending something. I wasn't allowed to help.' Daisy's eyes were reproachful.

Ash slipped his feet into a pair of wellies, always beside the back door, and set off down the long garden towards the shed. In reality, it was a substantial and spacious wooden structure, built by him and his Dad, and more workshop than mere shed. He opened the door quietly, not wanting to surprise his Dad in the middle of some tricky procedure. A tall, spare man, he'd been an engineer all his life, and retirement hadn't stopped his eternal fascination with machines of all types. He was forever buying up bits and pieces on local auction sites to do up and then sell. His current obsession was vintage lawn-mowers. Ash was very glad his daughter wasn't in here, helping. The blades on those things were lethal.

'Dinner's nearly ready, Dad.' He leaned over to watch the older man's fingers, thickened with age yet still strong, as they threaded nuts onto screws, and then ratcheted them tight.

'Okay. Look at that. Soon be as good as new. More people should use these. Better for their waistlines. Better for the environment.'

'You had a ride-on mower when I was a kid, Dad.'

'Mm?' He laughed. 'So I did. You're not supposed to remember stuff like that. How was your day?'

'I can't decide. Two out of four passes.'

'You're losing your touch, lad.'

'Two old guys, been riding for years on their CBTs. They ought to pass their tests proper but they can't be bothered. A youngster who's never driven. He needs more road practice.'

'Fair enough. What about the last one? What was his problem?'

'Not a he. A she.' His Dad nodded, still absorbed in his workbench. 'She was a disaster zone, basically. She reversed her Transit into a bike in the car-park! Before we'd even started the lesson.'

'She drives a Transit, eh? You can't fail her for that.'

'No Dad, I meant ...' Ash broke off and laughed as he caught his Dad's studied blank expression. Only the upward quirk of his mouth gave him away. 'If only that was all. She got into first gear eventually and took off like a bloody rocket. Frightened the shit out of me.'

'You're the instructor. That would be your fault then.'

Ash snorted a laugh. He'd thought that too. 'Yeah. Thanks for that, Dad. I was running after her like a lunatic with the whole class watching. I thought she was going to end up in the next County.'

'Keeps you fit, son. No bones broken then?'

'No. Just clutch levers, mostly. She's booked in again for my next Rest Day, in a week's time. I wonder whether she'll be back though. I get the impression she's got some opposition at home.' Her expression as she'd wrung the neck of the sauce bottle whilst talking about her husband had been a bit of a give-away.

She was so enthusiastic though, and despite the fact she'd had a terrible start and hadn't even passed, she'd been so delighted with her day that he didn't like to think that she might not persevere. He hoped he'd see her again.

Chapter Three

'I had my bike training day today, Gerry,' Lucy began, in a determinedly conversational tone, as she dished up the dinner she'd had the foresight to prepare in the slow-cooker. She couldn't remember feeling so bone-tired. Gerry hunched over the laptop which was permanently before him. 'It was bril—'

'D'you mind?' Gerry cut across her. 'I've got some paperwork to sort out.' Forking food into his mouth, he focused entirely on his screen and Lucy subsided into silence, trying not to watch him. The braised steak tasted of nothing, despite the care she'd taken with it. As she cleared the table, he stretched and stood up, clicking the laptop shut.

'All finished?' She stacked their plates in the dishwasher and began to tidy the kitchen. He yawned, rubbing his face.

'Bloody paperwork. Has to be done. You're so lucky, just colouring in for a living.'

Lucy blinked. Where had that come from? 'My "colouring in" paid for the deposit on the first property we bought at auction.'

'Yeah. And you've never let me forget it.'

'What? That's unfair, we—'

'Whatever.' Shoulders hunched, he stalked into the lounge with his laptop. Lucy watched him aim the remote at the TV and slump into his chair. It occurred to her that he'd quite like a remote to use on her. With a mute button and fast forward.

Deflated, she finished clearing up the kitchen, and sat at the dining table to research everything she could find about passing a motorcycle test. Her eyelids drooped and she decided on an early night, but sleep eluded her.

She lay listening to the television blaring downstairs, thinking about how separate hers and Gerry's lives had become. It hadn't always been like this. She mused back over the early years, when they were young and enthusiastic about everything – her café, his business, each other. He'd set up his own company in Property Management. Full of energy, they'd even bought a couple of small properties to do up and sell on – with the help of *her* earnings, as she'd said earlier. He didn't involve her in that any more, brushing her enquiries aside by telling her it was too complicated to explain. She'd hoped that they would have their own property by now, instead of living in her parents' house while they lived the dream in France. Their own house, and children. Neither of which had materialised.

These days, although she didn't want to admit it, she was more excited about finding an inspiring new jeweller or artist whose work she could sell in the café than she was about going somewhere with Gerry. He could be so charming though. She watched from the sidelines, un-included. People smiled and nodded as he spoke, and for far too long, she'd accepted this as his 'business persona'. Why couldn't he be like that with her?

And was that really how life should be?

On Wednesday, Gerry texted her to say he'd be late and would eat somewhere before going on to his business network evening. Relieved to have the house to herself, Lucy downloaded a practice sheet for the Motorbike Theory Test and worked her way through it over an omelette and salad. Then she burrowed into her studio, a dove grey painted cabin in the garden with a log-burning stove. She loved it in there. It was her real bolthole. Here were pinboards and photographs and art books and drawers full of thick, beautiful paper, and brushes standing upright in handleless mugs that were too pretty to throw away. She was exactly, completely herself here.

In a mellow mood, with Ella Fitzgerald jazz playing on her iPad, her watercolours and a glass of wine at her elbow, she nearly jumped out of her skin when the studio door crashed open and in strode Gerry, red-faced and smelling of beer.

'Ha ha – so this is what you were so desperate to tell me about. You've given us a really good laugh, I'll say that for you!' He shook a newspaper in her face. Her stomach jolted as she realised he was talking about her training day. And his glee meant that it wasn't good news for her. He'd folded it to the page, which was helpful of him.

Her pulse stilled and then pounded in her ears as she read. There, in the local paper that every single person in their small, seaside town read, in bold headlines, were the words: '*Not as Easy as it Looks?*' Beneath, a series of photographs showed Lucy winning her bike at the Mega Bike Centre, followed by the most dreadful pictures of herself she'd ever seen. Obviously taken during her bike training session, she was either lying on the ground like an upturned beetle, or bending over with her bottom in the air, or she looked like a homeless person with her hair in tangles and sticking up.

Gerry stood over her, shaking with laughter. His blunt finger tapped the photos. 'I could've *told* you what a mess you'd make of it. But you had to try it, didn't you?'

Lucy stared at the photos in horror. She listened to her husband crowing with glee over her misfortune and didn't trust herself to speak. She had loved every minute of that first day on a motorbike. She might not have passed, but she wasn't going to tell him that. She looked with loathing at his fingers tracing the dreadful photos. Why was he like this? Had he always been this awful? Or was it just that she was breaking out of the mould he'd set her in for so long now? She'd never felt more lonely in her marriage than right now. Gerry was still talking and using his forefinger for emphasis.

'So, right, that's the end of it now then. You're making me look stupid.' Stab, stab. 'No more biking. That bike's for sale as of right now.' Then, obviously baffled by her lack of response – or maybe he just didn't care – he lurched out of her studio, leaving her still staring at the newspaper.

Lucy didn't know what upset her most – her husband, or the newspaper? How had this been allowed? Surely the photographer – what was his name again? Jones? – needed permission to publish photos of her? She remembered back to the night of the raffle at the Mega Bike Centre. She was standing on the platform gazing at her purple Triumph as the crowds dispersed. The photographer, a slight, dark-haired man slung about with camera bags, had hurried up with a notebook, all smiles.

'Hi, congratulations! Beautiful bike! Can I just jot your name down for the paper?'

In a daze, Lucy had felt in her bag and handed him one of the Art Café postcards. She used her maiden name for her business, and 'Daumier' was always a tricky one to spell.

'Ok?' she'd asked, seeing him frown as he looked from it to her and back.

'Fine.' Pocketing the card, he'd spun on his heel and walked away. Lucy had watched him, troubled without knowing why, and then shrugged. It had been a long day for everyone; maybe he was just tired.

Yes, she'd signed a clause allowing publicity for the actual win – but this was more than a step too far. These nasty photos felt like stalking – they were horrible. And she wasn't going to take it lying down.

Her ears registered the dawn chorus, but her eyes remained

resolutely glued shut. Forcing her aching limbs into a sitting position, she peeled the sofa cushion off the static on her hair and rubbed her face into life. Surely she'd only just fallen asleep? Her eyes felt gritty from hours spent scouring the internet during the night. Armed with righteous indignation and her newly gathered knowledge, she was ready for battle.

Slipping silently out of the house after minimal preparations, she heard Gerry's snores reverberating down the stairs. She stopped for a takeaway coffee, parked directly outside the rather lovely, mellow old stone building which housed the offices of their local newspaper at the top of the High Street, and settled down to wait for it to open.

She'd almost dozed off several times before she saw signs of life in the offices. Yawning, she climbed out of the van, took some steadying gulps of the brisk spring air, and headed for the front door.

The editor's office was packed with the written word – on the floor to ceiling shelves, in files and folders, brick-sized hardbacks, paperbacks, magazines, photocopied sheets and hand-written scrawls – wherever Lucy's eyes fell, there was a space covered with words. The Editor, Donald Peters, a bluff, grey-haired, thick-set man in his fifties, regarded her over half-glasses.

'I'm terribly sorry you've been upset, Ms Daumier,' he said, palms up in a gesture of reconciliation following her red-faced outburst before he'd even had a chance to sip at the mug of tea steaming by his elbow. 'But, I'm afraid we don't need permission from people to print photographs taken of them in a public place. And can I remind you that you have actually signed a publicity clause with Mega Bikes regarding your win?' His tone was smooth, but his manner wasn't.

'Now look here.' Lucy leaned forward, resting her hands on a pile of papers which promptly slithered to the floor. She didn't even glance at them, not giving a damn right then. He could pick them up himself. 'Be that as it may, did you have permission to take photographs on private property? I think you'll find that the training ground is privately owned – and that is clearly where these photographs have been taken.' She stood up, hands on her hips, glaring at him. She was amazed by herself.

Donald Peters stroked his chin thoughtfully, still looking at her. After a long pause he said, 'You should know that we've had a record number of emails from women who are encouraged by the fact that you're learning to ride a motorbike.'

'You've what?'

'Yes. And not just from round here either.' He indicated his monitor. 'I was just catching up when you—'

'By making me look a complete fool?'

'Well – it seems they're not seeing it like that.' He clicked the mouse and began to read from the screen. "*Can I say how nice it is to see a normal woman not being scared of learning to ride a bike?*" Here's another: "*… she looks like she's having fun … made me think I could have a go.*" All along the same lines.'

'Really?' Lucy thought quickly, sucking the inside of her bottom lip. 'Oka-ay, how about I write an article for the paper about how my training is going? So this awful thing,' she said, flicking a derisive arm at the folded newspaper, 'can stand as the "before", with much better photos for the "after". When I pass my test. Which I will do.' *No matter how much Gerry huffs and puffs.*

Donald Peters looked thoughtful, reaching for a notepad and scrawling over a fresh page. He nodded. 'It could work. We could tie in some advertising, make it advertorial, that sort of thing.' He looked up at her. 'All right. Can you get your piece in to me by next week?'

Lucy nodded with a huge grin, her mind already whirling over how she would write up her day with a more positive spin. They thrashed out the details and then Lucy was heading along quiet roads towards The Art Café, feeling happier and more hopeful than she had felt any right to be this morning.

She was only twenty minutes late, and usually the mornings were quiet – an occasional coffee drinker with a newspaper this early – but today the hubbub hit her ears the instant the door opened. The place was packed. Mostly women, their heads swivelling towards her as she threaded her way through the tables to the kitchen where Richard was a whirlwind of solitary activity.

'Get that on, where have you been? I've been ringing you for hours!' He flung an apron at her and then sent her a wry grin. 'And yes, I saw the paper.' His face twisted in a lopsided grimace. 'But look at this lot! No publicity is bad publicity. Ok – here are the orders, off you go.'

Gathering her wits, Lucy got busy. The years of working together saw all the orders out in swift succession. Even with the part-time girl, they were rushed off their feet by lunchtime. Lucy rang Nicola and asked if she would mind helping, and at five o'clock, when they were normally clearing up and preparing for the following day, the office workers came by. Girls with long, straightened hair and immaculate make-up, ooh-ing and aah-ing over the jewellery and felted bags in jewel colours; they spotted Richard, and then his cakes, vowing to return for the following day's coffee break.

'What time do you open?' They leaned forward, false eyelashes batting, their voices breathy and giggly.

'Nine thirty,' said Richard, straight-faced. Nicola watched them with a grim half-smile and Lucy nudged her with a grin.

'We'll send someone over.' Collective hair flicking as they left *en masse*. Richard looked panicky; a night of baking ahead for him if he was to keep up. Finally, they locked the door, and Lucy put a mug of peppermint tea in front of each of them, and they sat in the empty café, staring at each other.

'This should be bubbly,' said Nicola, raising her mug to them. 'Well, that may not have been the publicity you were looking for Luce, but it's certainly put the Art Café on the map!'

'Yes, and I've got some more news to tell you.' Lucy beamed, and filled them in on her morning.

'Look at today. If that's the result of your photos, it's what these women want to see. Gerry can't argue with the takings, can he?' Richard looked at Nicola for confirmation.

Lucy remembered last night. 'Yes, you're right – and how dare he tell me what to do with my bike?' She wasn't sure quite how brave she would be when she was alone with him but this was a start.

'Have you made arrangements to collect Cadbury yet?' asked Nicola.

'They're keeping him in storage for me, free until the end of the month. After that, it's £10 a month, and they'll keep the battery topped up and check him over and stuff.'

'Him?' Richard laughed. 'Vehicles are generally female, aren't they?'

'Cadbury is very manly.'

'I don't suppose that Gerry could turn up there and sell the bike? As if he was doing it on your behalf? You know how persuasive he can be.' Richard leaned forward, frowning.

'I'll ring them and make sure they know it's not for sale.' Lucy nodded firmly. 'Anyway, it's *my* name that will be on the Log Book for the bike, when it arrives, not his.'

'Good for you, Luce!' Nicola grinned. 'And you've still got that re-take on Monday? And yes, don't worry, I'll cover for you – but if this keeps up, you're going to need more staff.'

'Mm, I was thinking that this afternoon. An art student perhaps – someone to cover the art sales and the café when needed? It would give me time to get out and paint too. I miss it. What do you think?'

Richard nodded. 'Good idea. Someone who can be flexible. Get an advert out. We're going to need a bigger café at this rate.'

The three of them made light work of clearing up and after a group hug, Lucy headed for home, wondering what kind of mood Gerry would be in. Her euphoria turned into apprehension as she parked in the driveway next to Gerry's car. She sat in the van as exhaustion swept over her. The last thing she wanted was another showdown with her husband, but she wasn't going to let him speak to her like that any longer. She was going to make sure she got in first this time.

The door opened, and Gerry was framed in the warm light from the house. Her stomach clenched. But to her relief, he didn't look angry, and the fight died out of her. Was it so awful to just want some peace?

'Sorry,' he mouthed, and gestured for her to go in.

Chapter Four

Lucy was taking no chances and arrived at Better Biking in plenty of time for her re-take. Now she also had the job of writing it up afterwards, she was less fearful of mistakes, knowing her failures would entertain and encourage her readers. She'd spent the time since her disastrous first lesson swotting up on the Highway Code ready for her Theory test, which was booked for the first week of May, and insisting that Nicola explain repeatedly the gearing and braking process. She and Gerry had reached an uneasy truce which meant they were avoiding talking about the elephant in the room, the motorbike, which she knew he still wanted her to sell. She sprang to her feet as Ash, also early, appeared in the doorway.

'I'm so sorry about the damage last week!' blurted Lucy.

'I'm sorry if I was a bit hard on you on last week,' Ash said, simultaneously.

Lucy couldn't help noticing he looked quite different as he joined in with her laughter. More approachable. A lot less scary.

'Okay,' he said, 'let's agree that we got off on the wrong foot and start again, shall we?'

'Suits me.' Lucy was over-hearty with relief and embarrassment. 'I'll get the coffee.' She hurried to the machine at the back of the room.

Over coffee, Ash outlined the areas they needed to review. He really wanted today to go well for her.

'Apart from that over-enthusiastic throttle hand, we need to look at your road positioning before going out on the road. It's not at all like being in a car,' he began. 'You have to place yourself where you are safest and have the best chance of being seen.' He watched as she bent her head over the diagrams. She'd practised all this on the compound last week, but he had judged that her machine control needed more work before she went out on the road. A bit of one to one time should sort that. She just needed some confidence.

He smiled at her little wiggle of glee when he told her she was ready to go out into the traffic.

Shepherding her out of the junction onto the busy rural lane, he watched her like a hawk, not letting her off for a single thing. He felt the weight of responsibility for all his learners at this point. Their safety after this early, simple test was based on him teaching them what they needed to stay out of danger on the road. He couldn't be there protecting her from traffic when she was out on her own, and he needed to be completely sure that she knew what she was doing.

'Stay away from the kerb, Lucy,' he told her. 'You're encouraging the drivers to push past you. Move into the middle of the road. Dominate your position.' He was pleased to see her shoulders square as she checked her mirrors and manoeuvred into a central spot. It could be unnerving for beginners, he knew, and while they watched the traffic, their gear changes and throttle control went to pot. 'Well done. Good to see you're taking control.' He smiled as he saw the decisive nod from her helmet, and kept up a continual quiet stream of instruction as they navigated from the quiet B roads into the busier town roads, moving his bike so that he could watch her using the brakes and gears properly.

After two hours, he was pleased to give her the pass certificate. She was much better than he'd expected, and from her questions, she'd clearly spent a lot of time swotting up, which was good.

'That,' Ash said, tapping the piece of paper in her hand,

'means you can ride around on a 125cc with L plates for up to two years.' He gave her an appraising look. 'And some people do that, and then eventually take their proper tests. But many others train straight away on a more powerful bike. As you already have your own bike, you could do that.'

'Really?' Lucy stared at him, her eyes bright. He was pleased that she was so keen. 'Wow. So even I could go from the 125cc to a 600cc *in a day?*'

He nodded. 'Yep. Got anything planned for this afternoon?'

She shook her head. 'Not really. I've got the day off. You?'

'Well – I was wondering, why not strike while the iron's hot, and make a start on your training? You can try out the bigger bike, and if that goes ok, get one to one training – with the best trainer on the books, obviously.' He smiled.

'Oh – are you going home then?' She laughed, her head on one side, obviously teasing him, which was a nice reminder that she was feeling more confident. 'Better introduce me to this new trainer before you go. Yes, go on then. How exciting!'

'I'll just sort it with Ange – and then a bite of lunch?' Her delight was confirmation enough, and he headed to the office.

Lucy nipped into the ladies' with the hairbrush she'd remembered this time, while Ash booked her onto the bigger bike. She felt incredibly pleased with herself. It was such an amazing achievement. She could hardly believe that she could actually ride a 125cc bike on her own, on the road. She must ask Ash or Ange to take a pic of her holding her certificate, to send to the newspaper.

Over lunch – her salad and his gigantic baguette packed with sausages and fried eggs – they chatted, mostly about bikes, and she was struck by how much more relaxed he was. The idea of the afternoon on a big bike was exciting and scary, but she was already beginning to trust Ash's tuition.

Dark clouds gathered on their way back to Better Bikes, the first drops of spitting rain becoming a torrential downpour in minutes and making them run the last fifty yards to avoid a soaking.

Lucy didn't know whether to feel relieved or disappointed when Ash tapped her shoulder, holding up the most enormous pair of over-trousers. She wrestled them on together with the now familiar jacket and waddled out, feeling over-burdened by clothing. The rain had slowed to a grey drizzle.

'I know it's not the best weather for a bike, but you'll have to do all these things in the rain anyway, so you might as well do them now.'

Lucy nodded, keen to get on. She'd never been bothered by weather, liking nothing better than a hike on the coastal path with a sketch book when the conditions were at their most dramatic. Besides, living in Wales meant that if you didn't go out in the rain, you never went out at all.

Ash showed her over her new steed. 'Exactly the same controls, in exactly the same places. Just more power. But remember that the throttle goes both ways.'

'I'll be good.' She grinned. 'No more rocket-woman.' Once she'd got over how much bulkier it felt compared to the smaller bike, to her enormous surprise, the bigger bike felt much easier to control than the smaller 125cc she'd begun with. Squeezing the petrol tank with her knees, the machine felt somehow more stable. The gears clicked into place more easily, and the throttle was smoother.

'Lots of slow riding exercise for the Module One part of your training, which you will do in a compound, away from the road. We'll start with the Figure of Eight,' he said, after pillioning her to the practice arena. She followed him to where two cones had been placed apart, curious to know what came next. He walked around them to demonstrate.

'Now I want you to ride where I just walked. You can do it.'

Lucy, with new confidence, took a long run up and headed for the cones. She circled them once, just to get her bearings. And then again, as a warm up.

'Maybe I didn't make myself clear,' Ash said calmly. 'I want you to go through the cones, Lucy. Not around them, through them.'

'I'm trying.' Still circling, Lucy was starting to feel like a Border Collie rounding up sheep, and she was very glad that Ash couldn't hear her. Her language was atrocious.

'A-and through the cones ...' Ash urged. 'Through ... go *through*!'

With each circuit, she eyed the spaces between the cones. Surely there wasn't enough room. Shouldn't they be further apart? In her earpiece, she could hear Ash's progressively louder instructions. 'Through! Go *through* the cones!'

'Stop saying that!' she shouted fruitlessly inside her helmet, knowing he couldn't hear her.

'*Stop!*' He cleared his throat and took a long breath. 'Stop. Try going round the other way.'

How would that help? Flashing a glare in his direction, Lucy swung in a wide arc, looked at the cones, and willed the bike to go between them. Instead, she looped endlessly in the opposite direction.

'It won't *go*!' she bleated.

He waved her towards him and took her place on the bike.

'Watch. You need to *look*, really turn your head, like this.' He craned his neck over his shoulder.

She'd done that, hadn't she?

'And it puts your body in the right position to make the turn.' Lucy gaped as he executed two perfect, tight loops, cruising either side of the cones.

'Oh.' She snorted, hands on hips. Well, it was fine for him, wasn't it? He'd obviously been doing it for years and years. And she was just a beginner. And when would she ever need to do a figure of eight on the road? It was just stupid.

'Obviously this is not something you're going to do in the middle of the road, but it practises the same skills that you will need to park, to do a ...' He coughed. '... U turn, and for slow speed control.'

She nodded, impatient to try again now that he'd made it look so easy. Five minutes later, she was back on her infinite loop. Her mouth was dry from screaming obscenities at herself in her helmet, and she was starting to think that the bike hated her. Maybe it was the one she'd run over.

'Look at me!' Ash's tone was imperative, abrupt. 'LOOK. AT. ME!'

Her head whipped round, her eyes searching. As she spotted him, her bike bore her easily between the cones.

'Yay. It's a miracle,' said Ash in her ear, his voice smiling. 'Well done. I knew you could do it.'

'I did it!' Her heart sang – it was the best feeling ever. It had even stopped raining. Mist was already rising from the puddled tarmac as she repeated the manoeuvre successfully several times with no problems.

'Excellent. Let's have another go at those U turns while you're on a roll.' His voice was hearty, but Lucy's spirits plummeted.

'Noooo ...' she whimpered. 'Do I have to ...?'

Ten minutes later, she was telling herself through gritted teeth, 'I can *do* this, I can *do* this, I *can* do this ...' Right up until she lay on her back staring up at the pewter sky, the fallen bike alongside her, the hot engine pinging as fat raindrops plopped onto it, the rain having started again.

'Shit.' She seethed aloud at her incompetence, as she crawled to her knees, winded. 'Shit, damn, bugger … Why can't I *do* this?'

Ash walked towards her, his black brows knitted. 'You forgot to turn your head.'

Water dripped from her helmet straight down her neck. She scrambled up and turned towards him. She was angry with herself. Mad as hell.

'I looked,' she yelled, lifting her visor, heedless of the cold rain on her hot face. 'I did!' She knew she hadn't, not really, and she was shocked as she heard her own voice contradicting him. It felt as if she was suddenly brave enough to stand up to Gerry. Except Ash wasn't Gerry.

'You yanked the handlebars round at the last minute. You nod at me when I tell you, but you're not really listening.' His voice was calm.

'I didn't! I *do* listen!' Lucy insisted, stung by his incisive and completely true summing up.

Ash directed his brilliant blue gaze her way and she met it head on. 'Are you sure you really want to do this?' His voice was patient, and Lucy felt like even more of a loser. 'It's not for everyone. There's no shame in not going any further.' He hefted the bike and checked it over as Lucy glared at his back.

Her mind whirled with unfamiliar emotions. She couldn't remember when she'd wanted something this much. She was already obsessed. The staff tested her on Highway Code questions when it was quiet in the café, and she read everything she could lay her hands on. It was exciting, thrilling, absorbing. No wonder Gerry was unsettled. She barely recognised herself lately, and she was enjoying getting to know the person she was becoming. She couldn't give up now. She sighed, feeling defeated, and trapped by her own incompetence.

'Why can't I do this blasted U Turn thing? What's wrong with me?'

'You did a tighter turn on the Figure of Eight,' Ash reminded her. 'It's just practise.'

'Oh, God. I'll still be doing it when I'm a hundred at this rate.'

'Keep at it. This will be a distant memory.' He regarded her steadily, and she was aware suddenly that she wanted to succeed for him. He believed in her, and she didn't want to keep failing in front of him. But Gerry had been right all along. She *was* useless.

'No. I'm hopeless.' She sighed, unwilling to meet his steady gaze. 'I'm not going to waste your time any more.' Circling, she searched for the direction of the office, now surely at least half a mile away. Her feet squelched inside her boots as she trudged away. She heard the bike engine start and refused to look back.

'Want a lift back then? No point in walking all that way.' He rode alongside her at a steady crawl. It was exasperating that he had so much control while she'd clearly lost hers.

'Stop doing that.' She pointed at his bike.

'What?'

'Riding so perfectly slowly. It's infuriating.'

'You're only a step away from doing it. If you keep trying.'

'I'm wasting your time. And ...' She aimed her words at the ground. 'Obviously we have ...' She hunted for the right word, settling for, '... incompatibilities.'

'We're not married.' Ash said mildly. He was clearly struggling to keep a straight face. She could hear it in his voice. 'I'm only your bike trainer.'

'Well, maybe you're not used to dealing with women,' huffed Lucy crossly, trying to walk faster.

'I so am! I know the names of all the Disney Princesses and I can sing Taylor Swift.' He sang a few bars of a song, aptly entitled *I Knew You Were Trouble* …

'Yes – and *We are Never Ever Getting Back Together*,' Lucy retorted quick as a flash, plucking a title from the same artiste from her memory. Despite her fury, a tiny bubble of laughter threatened to erupt. Perversely, it made her even crosser. She'd had no practice, arguing like this. If Ash had been Gerry, he'd have shut her up long ago with a well-placed barb.

This man was not only parrying her grouchiness, he was being *kind* to her. It made her feel like even more of a failure. Not only could she not ride a motorbike, she wasn't even a very nice person.

'I knew we'd find something in common.'

'Don't change the subject. I don't want to talk about singing. I wanted to learn to ride a bike. And you don't want to help me, obviously.' That was totally untrue, but she ignored this fact.

'I'm paid to teach people how to ride bikes,' he told her. 'And if people listen properly, and do as they're told,' he said, shooting her a glance, 'they learn.'

'Oh – you're impossible.' Lucy threw her hands in the air. 'Why do I keep falling off all the time, then? I'm not stupid. I've got a degree!'

'Have you? What in? Motor Mechanics? Engineering?' Ash sounded interested. 'Acrobatics?'

She paused, glancing at him sideways, wanting badly to laugh. 'Art.'

'Very useful for bike riding, art.'

'You're laughing at me.'

'Perish the thought. Look, just get on. There are lorry

drivers practising for their tests here. I don't want to bring you back squashed. It would ruin our kit.'

Lucy didn't fancy getting squashed by a lorry. Besides, she was getting sweaty walking this fast in helmet and heavy waterproofs. Grumbling, she climbed on, not caring that the bike bounced up and down. Despite knowing that she would be more comfortable and secure sitting close to him, she sat back primly, feeling for the pillion handles, but Ash jerked the throttle and she had to snatch at his jacket. She felt the comforting warmth of his body and was shocked at how much she suddenly wanted to wrap her arms around him, instead of just holding onto his belt.

In the office, Angela stared at her in astonishment as Lucy explained she was very sorry, but she had to cancel the rest of her training. She'd pay for her session today, but that was it.

'Well, I'm very sad to hear that. You don't want to let the weather put you off. Is there anything I can help with?'

Lucy shook her head, trying to smile through lips that were attempting to hold in her confused emotions. She didn't trust herself to speak. Angela leafed through the paperwork on the desk, and then looked up.

'It looks like you got your CBT, well done. We offer the second day free, so you don't owe us anything for today; just the last hour on the big bike. And er, would you mind popping over to The Vintage Bike Palace and settle the bill for damaging the bike you ran over? I'm presuming you didn't want to put it through your insurance?'

'Oh. No. That's fine. Thanks for everything.' Shoulders sagging, she headed for the door, jumped into the van and had her key in the ignition when there was a loud knock on the window. She jumped, and turned to see Ash, raindrops glistening on his black beard.

'Oh, what?' She pounded the steering wheel. 'I haven't run over any more bikes, I've paid – what have I done now?'

He pointed. 'You're still wearing the school jacket. And I'd like my over-trousers back too if you don't mind.'

'Oh.' *Idiot woman.* Climbing out, she hurried back into the portacabin. It was humiliating, trying to peel the wet garments off while Ash stood by, watching. Her jeans had become peculiarly saggy, and she had to hold them up with one hand whilst pulling the over-trousers off with the other.

'Sit down,' he ordered, after a moment. 'You'll tear them.' Kneeling in front of her, he eased the waterproofs carefully over her boots. As she looked down at him, she felt an unnerving urge to run her fingers through that thick black hair.

'Thank you.'

'You're most welcome. See you next time.'

'There won't be a next time. I'm giving up.'

'No, you're not. Sleep on it.'

'No. I'm no good at it. I've cancelled.'

'Leave it for twenty-four hours and then decide. If it meant nothing to you, you wouldn't be so upset about it.' He turned his back on her and hung her kit up to dry. 'The only real failure is the failure to try. Don't give up.' He gave her a long look, and strode away. She glared at his retreating back, and then leaned back thoughtfully on the bench.

Chapter Five

Fifteen minutes later, she was eyeing her bill in the Vintage Bike Palace, which backed onto Better Biking.

'We've tried to keep it as low as possible,' Ed, the owner's son explained, pointing out the parts they'd used. Nicola brought her bike here for servicing. She'd often mentioned Ed, and Lucy could see why. He was nice. Easy to talk to. Very handsome, and very young. She looked again at the bill. New brake lever, mirror and some polishing out of the scratches on the engine casing. She sighed. This biking thing was turning out to be more expensive than she'd imagined.

'How's the training going?'

'It's not. Want to buy a nice new purple Triumph?' She grinned ruefully.

Ed shook his head. 'We're all classic bikes here. What's up then?'

'Oh.' Lucy puffed her cheeks out and blew. 'I can't do a thing right, and my instructor clearly thinks I'm an idiot.' She knew that wasn't true, but it was how she felt.

'Who's your instructor?'

'Ash. Big black beard. Booming voice. Obviously thinks he's Brian Blessed.'

'Ash?' Ed looked surprised. 'He's one of the good guys! His little girl comes in when he's a bit tied up over there and we find her "jobs" to do. She loves it. She's a proper little sweetie. She's dying for me to take her out on the back.' He grinned. 'Not a chance though. Ash would kill me.'

Lucy felt even worse knowing she'd had a tantrum in front of Mr Good Guy Ash. And he had a little girl. Which explained the Disney Princesses and Taylor Swift songs.

'I should just give up now. Save myself the humiliation.' She rolled her eyes, and Ed laughed.

'Sounds like you need a bit of fun. What are you doing later – about five-ish?'

'What kind of fun?' She eyed him, wondering what he was suggesting.

'A bit of dirt biking over on the waste ground. I'm meeting a few of the lads – it's a great way to get your confidence. You can just go round and round on a flat bit of a dirt trail, we'll be doing jumps and stuff but you won't.'

'Dirt trail? I don't think I could do that ...'

'There's an old tarmac road there, you can ride along that. No traffic to worry about. Practise going up and down the gears. You'll love it, honestly.'

Lucy dithered. It was one of Gerry's charity nights tonight, and it had become customary for her to attend. They didn't actually need her; everything was organised, and it was a Men Only function. The food was delivered and the staff dealt with it. There were never any other women there. She was always confined to the kitchen, and all Gerry really wanted to do was show off that his wife obeyed his every command. That, and a lift home because he would be as drunk as a lord by the end of the evening. A bubble of resentment rose and threatened to choke her. Could she tell him she'd worked late? Wouldn't he think it was a bit strange? Although he seemed to get home later and later these days, and had frequently eaten already without letting her know. She was living on left-overs. At least she wasn't living on cake.

'Won't your friends think it's a bit weird to have me tagging along? And what if I, er, drop the bike?'

'It would be weird if you didn't drop your bike. That's what they're for. And the other guys will think it's cool that you're there.'

'Ok.' She nodded. A last-ditch attempt at riding a bike. And she wouldn't have to worry about dropping it. She glanced at her watch. Enough time to sort some jobs and get back.

She opened her mouth to tell Ed she'd be back at five, when Ash emerged from the back of the workshop. Picking up a set of bike keys from the counter, he looked over his shoulder at Lucy on his way to collect the repaired school bike.

'I think you'll find that Brian Blessed is considerably older and fatter than me.' His gaze swivelled to Ed. 'And yes, Ed, if I find Daisy anywhere near a pillion seat I *would* kill you.'

Lucy stared after him, her face flaming with embarrassment. 'Why didn't you tell me he was in there?' She rounded on Ed who raised his palms, looking unabashed. 'Ah, well. I can't make it any worse.' She groaned, and then squared her shoulders, making a decision. 'Right. I'll see you at five.'

'Laters!' Ed waved casually and turned back to his work.

Ash was still wondering what to do with his unexpected spare afternoon as his house appeared, lit by the late sunshine. He never tired of seeing it. Almost derelict and barely habitable in the beginning, it was in a beautiful sunny valley, with a bit of land, a pond, and a serenity about it they'd fallen in love with.

Of course, there was always something that needed doing on the house. He still loved it, but the jobs were endless. Little bits that seemed to take ages but never looked as if you'd done much when you finished.

So – a couple of hours tops – not enough time to get stuck into one of the big jobs, but too much time for just hanging about. Ash hated not being busy. His life was so full these days and he'd got used to rushing about. He preferred it that way. No time to dwell on things he'd rather not think about. He parked his bike in the garage and looked around, restlessly.

As if he didn't have enough to do on the house, he also had several projects on the go – amongst them an old motorbike bought as a box of bits, and a VW camper van he'd promised Daisy they'd go adventuring in. She'd called it Nellie and wanted him to paint daisies all over it.

He caught sight of his reflection in its dusty windows and stroked his beard. 'Brian Blessed indeed!' Checking his watch, he headed into the house.

First he rang Sarah, his sister-in-law. 'Listen, there's no need to collect Daisy from school – I can do it today. Got some free time unexpectedly.'

'Oh, ok.' She sounded put out. He supposed she'd had to re-organise her day, and apologised. She helped out hugely with Daisy, and he really didn't want to make her feel unappreciated.

Then he hunted for his hair trimmer. That he couldn't locate it instantly told him all he needed to know about how long ago he'd trimmed his beard. Should he shave it all off? It was looking like the likeliest option – and then he found the trimmers at the bottom of his sock drawer. He plugged them in, and stood considering his reflection in the bathroom mirror.

Lucy was back outside the Vintage Bike Palace at five o'clock. She'd gone straight to the café, hidden in a corner, made a start on her article – *Yay, I got my CBT!* – and left Gerry a text to say she was delivering work, in case he rang her mobile. She was a little worried at just how adept she was becoming at covering her tracks.

Ed was sweeping the workshop. He looked up as she

arrived. 'Yo. Dad's out the back. He's got some gear for you to wear. I'll be just a few minutes.'

Lucy headed cautiously towards the room at the back. She didn't want to bump into Ash again this soon. Griff, Ed's dad, was spooning coffee granules into cups.

Without looking up, he said, 'Milk and sugar?'

She shook her head, 'Neither thanks. Ed says you've got some stuff for me?'

'Yes, you'll need a bit more than just a borrowed school jacket. This is Lyn's, my missus's.' He handed her a mug and indicated a heap of clothing on an old easy chair. He was so like Ed. The same smiling eyes and a body that looked used to hard work, but with silver hair.

'Oh, that's really kind of her! Hope they fit me. Doesn't she go any more?'

'Now and again. It's a good laugh.'

'Is it difficult?' Lucy was worrying now.

'It's fun. No traffic to worry about, the bikes are light and built for rough use. There'll be plenty of help if you drop one. Ed will look after you.'

'He's a star.' Lucy smiled. 'I'm not doing very well at it so far, am I?'

'Maybe not, but you're keeping us in business. We've had worse.' He laughed at his own joke and Lucy joined in, feeling her tensions ease. 'Go and enjoy yourself.' He drained his mug and rinsed it under the tap. 'I'm off. Have a good one!'

'Please thank Lyn for the gear.' She picked over the heap. There were two jackets, both considerably less bulky than the ones she'd been borrowing. Several pairs of trousers, gloves, long boots, and something with a waist belt which she didn't recognise.

Holding the trousers against her, she began to try them on. She felt like Goldilocks – this one was too small, this one was too big and this one was just right. Without a mirror, she had no idea how she looked, but she felt business-like, and ready for action. When Ed came to look for her she was wearing an entire outfit.

'Looking good. Have you got the back protector on?' he asked, looking her over.

'Oh! Is that what it is?'

He laughed with her as she removed her jacket and swivelled the back protector around her body.

'Are we riding there?' she asked, her mouth dry with nerves.

'Of course. Last one there buys the ice creams!' He darted out and she rushed after him, regretting her decision to go with him already. He was so young, so irresponsible. She didn't even know where she was going, for goodness' sake. Stopping dead in her tracks in the yard she saw him swing easily into the driver's seat of a navy blue Toyota Hilux with two dirt bikes strapped into the rear. She grinned, climbing in beside him. This was going to be fun.

Daisy ran into the school playground with her friends, coat open, socks round her ankles, long dark curly hair corkscrewing free of its scrunchie. Her rucksack bounced on her back. She saw Ash and flung herself at him.

'Daddeeeee!' she yelled, leaping up and trusting him to catch her.

'Hello, my precious.' He leaned down, nuzzling into her neck and blowing a raspberry on her soft, warm skin. She giggled and pretended to wriggle away from him, trying to find his neck so she could do the same.

'Whoa! Daddy, you shaved your beard!' She stood back for a better look.

'What do you think?' asked Ash, self-conscious under her scrutiny.

Daisy tipped her head on one side, narrowing her eyes. '*Much* better,' she nodded approvingly. 'It's not so prickly now.'

'Shall I take it all off?'

'Mmm ... how about taking off ... half of it?'

'What, just a moustache?'

'Noooo. Half on, half off.' Daisy drew a line with her finger from his nose to his chin, and ran away, cackling with laughter at her own joke. He grinned, following her towards the gate, and saw Sarah, his sister-in-law standing there.

He was still jolted, even after all these years. She was so much like her sister Sophie, petite with long straight blonde hair. Same sort of age Sophie had been when they'd married. Although Daisy had inherited his looks, her bright cheeky temperament owed much to her mother.

'Takes ten years off you.' Sarah reached up and kissed his cheek. 'Much better. What made you do that?'

'Oh, er, just something someone said. Anyway, what brings you here?' He realised that sounded less than welcoming, and added, 'Not that it's not lovely to see you of course, but ...'

Sarah tossed her head. 'Oh, I was off anyway, and I never get to see you and Daisy together, so ...' She shrugged, smiling.

'Hello, Aunty Sarah,' Daisy said, standing between them. She looked up at him. 'Daddy, can we go and work on my doll's house?'

'That sounds lovely, darling,' said Sarah. 'I'd like to see it too.'

Daisy made a face. Ash, feeling trapped, had to make the best of it. He would have liked nothing better than to drive home alone with Daisy, listening to her chatter all the way back. He couldn't really complain. His childcare arrangements worked because they were scheduled so tightly. It was part and parcel of being a single dad, and for Sarah, Daisy was the living memory of her sister.

'Off we go then,' he agreed in a hearty voice. 'Have you got your car, Sarah, or …?' He tailed off.

'Oh, no, a lift would be great, thanks.' She beamed at him, linking her arm through his. Daisy scampered immediately to his other side and clung on to his hand, skipping and chatting till they reached the car. There was a brief tussle as she and Sarah battled over the front seat.

Ash was forced to intervene, relegating his daughter to the back. He moved her booster seat, kissing her grumpy face, and in his head, promised himself more time with just her. Working shifts as he did made family life difficult.

Monday night was dinner with his parents and Daisy was staying over with them as he was working an early shift the following morning. He made Daisy a drink and a snack, got her out of her school uniform and let her choose her play clothes. He didn't quite know what to do with Sarah, so he made them both a cup of tea, and took them out to the workshop where he was in the process of building a luxury dwelling for Daisy's dolls.

From its humble beginnings, it had grown two storeys, and various outbuildings for the My Little Ponies and farmyard animals currently in residence under her Princess cabin bed.

'Working on my dolls' house' actually meant Ash meticulously measuring, cutting and assembling, and Daisy inserting various dolls in parts of the house and deciding that 'this is her kitchen, she's going to have big parties here,' and 'this is the piano room. For her afternoon concerts.'

Sarah laughed. 'She's going to be very busy.'

'Piano room?' he asked with interest. 'Is that something you'd like to do, Daisy?'

She considered. 'I might. We have a man who comes and plays piano. But it looks very hard.'

'Well, yes, it is. But you can do anything if you practise

hard enough, you know. You have to keep trying. The more you try, the more you can try.' He straightened up, his thoughts tumbling over themselves. 'I'd like to take a bit of a detour on the way to Nanny's tonight, if that's ok,' he said.

'Where to?' asked Sarah.

'Oh, Ed is doing a bit of dirt biking. I want to see what they're up to.' He shrugged nonchalantly.

'I like Ed,' announced Daisy, making her dolls kiss each other.

Ash looked at her sharply. 'You're not going on the back of his motorbike.'

Daisy raised her eyebrows, pouted, and waggled her head. Ash repressed a laugh. She picked all these mannerisms up at school. At seven, she often seemed so much older. He guessed it was all the adult input from both sets of grandparents, since she was a baby.

'Sarah, are you coming to dinner at Mum's, or ...?' Ash filed a roof tile with concentration, not looking at her.

'If she'll have me. I haven't got anything planned for tonight,' said Sarah happily. 'Shall I ring?'

'No, don't worry, I'll do it now. It won't be a late night; I'm on earlies tomorrow, ok? I just need to go and fetch something from the house.' Ash had known her since she was eleven, not that much older than Daisy was now. He relied on her, as he did his own parents and hers, to provide a steady and stable support group for Daisy, but it bothered him at times that she didn't seem to have much of her own life. He probably relied on her too much. Maybe he used up so much of her life that she really didn't have time to have a social life of her own. Now he felt guilty.

He rang his mum and explained the extra guest, knowing she wouldn't mind at all; there was always more than enough food. But it seemed important that he rang, and not Sarah, for some reason.

He'd thought by now that she'd be hooked up with a boyfriend. She was undoubtedly a good-looking girl, but at twenty-four, she never mentioned anyone special. Perhaps she just didn't tell him about them.

As a teenager she'd had a massive crush on him, mooning after him as if he was a more available version of the pop-stars that peopled her bedroom walls. He remembered gently fending her off, and pretending to disapprove of her teenage fashions. At a decade and a half older, he'd felt as old as the hills compared to her. Now, those years meant less in terms of a generation gap, but when Ash looked at her, all he remembered was the stroppy teenager.

Mum was expecting them for six, an early tea designed for Daisy's small stomach. It wasn't far, about twenty minutes or so. If he wanted to stop off to watch Ed, they'd need to make a move. He sorted out Daisy's school things into the wash basket, folding pyjamas and tomorrow's play clothes into her overnight bag, and picked up the toys and socks flung into every corner.

She was a good kid – busy, bright and interested in so many things – and he tried to make sure that she didn't miss out on anything. She went to ballet and gymnastics, swimming lessons and Brownies. Her social life kept him busy – although her friends' parents, once they'd understood his position, were brilliant at collecting and delivering her.

When he could, he drove her and her friends in his estate car to competitions and parties, and brought them over for playdates as often as possible. And that's where Sarah had found her niche, taking Daisy's little friends to the toilet. Playing at Mummy. Most of the little girls thought she *was* Daisy's Mummy. In the end, it had seemed easier to let it go, rather than keep explaining – but Daisy just used to announce matter-of-factly, 'No, she's my aunty. My Mummy's dead.'

He cleaned himself up, and went downstairs to get Daisy ready.

She was conversational as he gave her a baby-wipe wash. Baby wipes – the modern, hygienic equivalent of the spit wash, he reflected.

What was Ed doing? Why were they going to see him? Where was he? When would she be old enough to go on the back of his bike?

Ash heard himself say he was curious to see how someone called Lucy was getting on, biking with Ed.

'Is Lucy having lessons with Ed then?'

'Sort of.'

'Why isn't she having lessons with you?'

'She just needed to … well,' he shrugged. 'Get a bit of confidence, I suppose. Keep still, I'm trying to brush your hair.'

Daisy absorbed this information and then said, 'Ed is quite handsome, even though he's really old. Do you think she fancies him?'

Handsome? Fancies him? Ash chuckled inwardly. Where did she pick this stuff up? He struck a pose. 'Am I old?' he demanded.

She looked at him, pretending to consider.

'Not now, you're not,' she said, reaching out to stroke his chin. 'Now you've shaved off your weirdy beardy.'

'Weirdy beardy?' he exclaimed in mock outrage, swinging her up in the air to make her giggle. 'Come on, let's go. You want to see them too, don't you?'

'I want to see this Lucy Lady!' She nodded, her eyes agog with curiosity.

Daisy joined in with her favourite Taylor Swift CD all the way to the dirt track on the waste land. Ash grinned. No wonder he knew all the words. Sarah began to sing along but Daisy shushed her.

'No, Aunty Sarah – stop singing. You're spoiling it!'

'Don't be so rude, Daisy! Say sorry or I'll turn it off.' Ash paused the CD and made his stern face at her in the driver's mirror.

'Sorree Aunty Sarah,' she sang, insincerely.

Sarah smiled, 'Don't worry sweetie. I know I can't sing.'

'Don't give in to her, Sarah. She's getting to be a proper bossy little madam.' Even if she's as cute as a button with it, he thought, trying not to smile.

The dirt track was no more than a patch of disused ground, just on the other side of the industrial estate where Better Biking was. It had been colonised by the bikers. They'd hauled logs and built ramps to make it their perfect playground, and their knobbly tyres plus the weather did the rest. Lucy would have been there for just over half an hour. Parking on the boundary road of the estate, a couple of hundred yards away, Ash squinted through the windscreen, but couldn't distinguish her from the other half a dozen or so bikers. Maybe she'd changed her mind. He hoped not. He got out of the car, opening the back door for Daisy, who was craning her neck to see.

'Which one is the Lucy Lady?'

'I don't know … ah, there.' He pointed. One of the bikers had bounced over a slight incline, and he'd spotted her long honey blonde hair streaming out of her helmet.

Sarah climbed out and stood beside them. 'What are we looking at?'

'The Lucy Lady,' supplied Daisy.

'They all look like men to me.' Sarah's voice was sharp.

'She's doing well,' muttered Ash. 'Good for her.'

Lucy was bumping along on the perimeter track, which Ash knew from his own experience 'playing out' with Ed was simply a wide path, rutted by the constant motorbike traffic, but otherwise unencumbered by obstacles. It would require concentration and balance, but the constant repetition would give her confidence, he knew. It took a few minutes for her to complete the circuit, and as she came into view again, he could see even from that distance that her posture was relaxed and that her throttle control had evened out.

He was surprised and pleased. She certainly looked as if she was having fun.

Daisy turned round eyes on him. 'Wow, Daddy! She looks like ...' She paused. 'Like – Lara Croft, only blonde.'

Beside her, Sarah made a long sniff. 'Are we going?'

Chapter Six

When Ash went to collect Daisy on his way home from work on Saturday, after yet another sleepover at his parents' house, she greeted him with her usual exuberance, walking up his legs and flipping over as she'd learned at gymnastics.

'We made an underwater scene out of a shoebox and Nanny says there's a really nice café she went to and it makes cakes that are even better than hers,' she announced in a rush.

'Better cakes than Nanny? I don't believe that for one minute.' Ash winked at his mother.

'So can we go and try them this afternoon? I've been really good, haven't I Nanny?'

'You're always good, darling. You're a perfect child all the time.'

'Are you sure?' Ash held her upside down and bounced her a little, to her joyful shrieks.

'Ash, sweetheart, she'll be sick,' said his mother.

'Yes, Ash sweetheart, I'll be sick!' Daisy, still upside down, giggled uncontrollably. 'Put me down!'

Once she'd been set upright, she held her arms out and tried her best to climb up his legs.

'Again,' she demanded.

Ash laughed.

'No, you've worn me out already. And it's Daddy to you, not Ash. Ok, where's this café then?'

His mother gave him a little card. He recognised the logo instantly as the one Lucy's van bore.

'Um ...' He wondered whether it was a good idea to meet Lucy on her home ground, as it were.

'Pleeease?' Daisy twined around his arm and he laughed again.

'Okay then. Seeing as you asked so nicely.' Maybe it would be so busy they wouldn't even meet, he hoped.

The café was situated on the beach, at one end of the smart seaside town. Crowded near the floor to ceiling windows with the incredible view over the sea, they managed to get a little table with two chairs further back.

The cakes, as beautifully decorated as his mother had assured him they would be, were arrayed in a tiered, chilled display case and you made your selection on the way to ordering your drinks.

Daisy, after much indecision, opted for a cupcake with a swirl of lemon frosting. As they queued towards their collection point, Ash spotted Lucy, cheerily assembling the customers' trays and taking their payment. Her attention was focussed on Daisy – she didn't seem to have noticed him. He surreptitiously observed her. This was a different Lucy to the one he was used to, in a colourful dress that seemed to accentuate her curves. Luscious curves, he saw now, and her blonde hair fell in glossy waves past her shoulders in contrast to the static tangle he'd become familiar with during her bike training.

'Would you like some fairy dust on your cupcake, madam? It's magical,' Lucy enquired of Daisy, treating her exactly as one would an adult customer.

Daisy nodded eagerly, 'Yes, please,' and Lucy shook some edible glitter onto the yellow frosting. They grinned at each other and as Daisy looked up at him Lucy followed her eyes and recognition dawned. He'd had more time to prepare and he watched her stare in surprise at where his beard used to be and then quickly recover her professional aplomb.

'Oh! Hello. Er … would you like some magical fairy dust on your … er, coffee?' she said, as his coffee order arrived at her elbow. Daisy's Babyccino, a tiny cup filled with frothed milk and a tiny shot of decaffeinated coffee, arrived at the same moment, and, winking at Daisy, she popped a few extra mini marshmallows on the top.

'Now she'll never sleep.' Ash smiled. 'What do you say, Daisy?'

'Thank you!' Daisy smiled up toothily, her eyes already re-focussing on the delicious looking cake.

'You're welcome, Daisy.' Lucy nodded at her.

Ash was about to introduce Lucy to his daughter and then thought better of it as he envisioned her asking guilelessly whether Lucy had run over any more bikes or whether she fancied Ed, and did she know she looked like Lara Croft? Hoping Lucy wouldn't drop him in it by introducing herself and consequently feeling rather unmannerly, he chivvied Daisy hurriedly to their table, collecting a pile of serviettes on the way.

Sitting with his back to the door and facing into the café, he sipped his coffee while Daisy nibbled her way around the generous buttercream topping on her cake.

'Mmm, this is lovely! That is an enormous cup of coffee, Daddy. I could bath my dollies in it,' she pointed out, in between observations about what a nice lady that was, and could they go and see all the pictures and necklaces and things when they'd finished.

He half listened and nodded in the practised way parents do and gazed around the café. It was cleverly done. The open space had been divided up with low tongue and groove walls which were low enough to see over when you were standing, but tall enough to afford privacy when you sat down.

The entire café was decorated in pale driftwood colours echoing the sea view, and the theme was continued through the furniture, painted in pale sages, blues and sand colours, to the panels on the walls, made up to resemble a gigantic pin board with postcards from the seaside. It was soothing but interesting at the same time.

The door was thrown open abruptly and three men strode in, dressed as if from the golf course, in outlandish trousers.

The tallest, a well-made man with thinning sandy hair, was laughing loudly in a forced way which drew immediate attention from the other customers, who grew quiet and watchful. The other two men shifted uncomfortably. The loud man stared about for an empty table, and finally dragged a chair noisily over to share a table with a white-haired couple. They glanced apprehensively at him.

'Siddown,' he slurred expansively at his two friends. 'Oi! Luce! Three coffees here for your old man and his best mates. Pahahahah, oh, no, I'm sorry, I forgot, you still don't know how to work the coffee machine, do you? Silly cow, wants to ride a motorbike but can't make a cup of coffee! Hahahah.'

The elderly couple stood up, holding their cups.

'Sorree, don't let me disturb you – I only want a coffee. *Oi!* Some service would be good here!'

Ash tensed, on alert. Daisy had stopped in mid-lick and was watching the little scene develop with round eyes. He watched as Lucy hurried over, waiting for her to have no truck with this oaf and eject him without hesitation. But her body language was appeasing: hands out, palms down, her face arranged in a tight smile. She ushered the old couple to a table further away and then turned back towards what he guessed must be her husband, now sitting back with his arms folded, regarding her with a smirk on his face.

Ash saw the staff looking over with concern on their faces, and a tall, lean man in chef's check trousers emerged, frowning, from the kitchen. Lucy bent towards her husband. Ash couldn't hear what she was saying but he got the gist of it. She was asking him to pipe down or leave. It seemed to make him worse.

'Where the hell were you last Monday night anyway?' he shouted. 'You knew it was the Network Night!' His voice rose on each word, and Ash saw Lucy's face drain of colour.

'You didn't need me there, Gerry. None of the other wives go to those functions.'

'Where the fuck were you?'

Ash was not going to have language like that in front of his daughter. He didn't swear, neither did his parents, and although he was quite sure Daisy had probably heard that word already, he wasn't going to sit there and say nothing while this obnoxious bully carried on. Also, he felt slightly guilty – he knew where Lucy had been last Monday, and it was sort of his fault.

'Stay there, and don't move,' he said quietly to Daisy.

'Are you going to arrest that horrible man, Daddy?' She jigged excitedly on her seat and he gave her a stern look, standing up.

He couldn't just leave it. It wasn't his style. Lucy glanced over at him, her eyes wide.

The smell of stale beer hit him as he closed the gap. He stood where he could still see Daisy and said in a matey, crisp tone to Gerry, 'Hey. Cut out the language. I'm here with my daughter and there are lots of children in the café. No-one wants to hear it.'

'Who the fuck do you think you are? This is my café, I'll say what I want.' Gerry's face was suffused with rage. His two friends looked uncomfortable, their eyes flicking from him to Ash and Lucy.

'Gerry! This is not your café.' Lucy's hands flew to her face. 'I'm so sorry ...' she mouthed at Ash.

Ash regarded Gerry for a long moment and then bent and spoke directly into his ear.

Gerry lurched upright, knocking over his chair. His bloodshot eyes swivelled towards his two friends as if appealing for help. Far from supporting him, they were getting up to go themselves.

'Sorry, he's a bit, you know ... not himself lately,' one of them muttered, while the other leaned over to take Gerry's arm and steer him out. Gerry yanked his arm away and blundered towards the doors, scattering chairs as he went, his face red and thunderous with rage.

'Tell me he's not driving?' Lucy caught the arm of one of the men, who shook his head at her.

'His car's at the golf club. Sorry. Gotta go. Sorry.'

Ash saw Lucy's mouth twist awkwardly into a smile that she directed around the nearest customers.

'Sorry everyone. Drama over!' Her tone was bright, reassuring. She turned to Ash. 'Thank you. I'm so sorry, I don't know what ... He's not normally like this, really. Is Daisy ok? What on earth did you say to make him go? I'm so sorry. What a terrible first visit for her. Thank you again ...'

'You've got nothing to apologise for. Daisy loves a bit of excitement, don't worry about her.' He nodded to where they could see his daughter cheerfully demolishing the remains of her cake. Lemon icing and fairy dust were spread liberally across her face.

'Let me get you another coffee.' Lucy smiled. 'Yours will be cold by now.'

'Ok,' he conceded. 'A small one though. I don't think I can manage another one of those buckets.' Lucy bustled away as he returned to Daisy. 'Show's over. How's the cake? I see you're still wearing most of it ...' He wiped the worst of the sugary residue off with the serviettes he'd collected earlier and searched his pockets in vain for a packet of baby wipes to finish the job.

'You should have slapped him in jail, Daddy. He was really nasty. I saw that nice lady's mouth go all funny like she wanted to cry. Have you arrested anyone today?'

'Yes. Lots of bad people,' nodded Ash, distractedly.

Lucy returned to their table with a steaming hot coffee for Ash, another Babyccino for Daisy, four assorted cupcakes in a takeaway pink carton, and a hot damp flannel. She handed the flannel to Ash.

'I thought you might need this.' She smiled at Daisy. 'That fairy dust goes everywhere, doesn't it?'

'You didn't need to, but thank you anyway.' Ash smiled his thanks and scoured his daughter's sticky face with the hot flannel.

'Ooh, that was lovely,' beamed Daisy, pinkly. 'I feel as if I've been in a spa!'

Ash and Lucy laughed.

'Have you ever been in a spa, Daisy?' Lucy asked.

'No!' said Daisy. 'But I bet this is just what it feels like.'

'Wow, how lovely, look Daisy.' Ash opened the box and Daisy's mouth made an 'O' of delight.

'Thank-yoooo,' she said, unprompted.

'You're most welcome.' Lucy smiled at her, then turned to Ash. 'And I'm so sorry for being a pain in the a—' She clamped her mouth shut, flicking a look at Daisy, who was still inspecting her cake windfall. 'I've decided not to give up on the biking, after all.'

'Good for you.' Ash nodded, and watched Lucy head back to the counter, feeling really bad about not introducing them to each other, or even using her name, but he knew Daisy would be unstoppable if she cottoned on.

'Are we going to see all the pictures and things?' Daisy wanted to know.

'Another time, sweetheart.'

'Ok. So we're coming back then.' She was satisfied with

that. 'Loose. That's a funny name isn't it. That's what the horrible man called her. Loose.' She waved to Lucy as she left.

Ash shepherded her out quickly, anticipating the connection as his daughter began to play with the name.

'My jeans are loose. My shoes are loose. Loose elastic,' she sang, 'Loose-y loose elastic ... Loosey?' She stopped abruptly on her way to the car, staring at Lucy's sign-written van. He could almost hear the cogs clunking into place.

'Was that ...?' She eyed Ash. 'Was that nice lady the Lucy Lady, Daddy?'

Chapter Seven

On Saturday afternoon after Gerry's dreadful outburst, Lucy didn't want to go home. She'd put a jolly face on it afterwards, even though she'd never felt more humiliated in her life. There had been absolutely no need for her to be there on Monday night, the usual staff knew exactly what to do, just like they did on every other one of these Charity Nights. He just liked bossing her about in front of all the other men – his 'little woman'. Guilt assailed her anyway, knowing that she would usually have been there, gritting her teeth and smiling through her irritation, had she not had a better offer and gone AWOL.

When the last customer left, full of cake and good humour, she scrubbed the cafe until it shone, and when the Saturday staff signed off, along with a reluctant Richard, she locked up, re-arranged the paintings and dusted the displays. If nothing else, it eased the aches in her joints from the dirt biking – she couldn't believe it still hurt after nearly a week, but it had been a tremendous success, even if it had been nothing like as skilful as what Ed and his mates were doing. She'd just gone round and round, gaining confidence with each loop. Ed showed her how to stand up on the foot-pegs and flex her knees like shock absorbers, and although she never thought she could ever be that daring, she'd done it a couple of times.

With nothing to prove, she'd just gone out determined to enjoy it. All of Ash's instructions were making sense at last, and she practised some turns, turning her head 'owl-like' and noting with delight how the bike obeyed her. Her thighs were screaming by the time the hour was up. She really didn't think she could have carried on for longer.

Ed was so sweet. He'd helped her off with the long, buckled boots, keeping up a monologue of how well she'd done, and would she like to come out with them again? Then he stared solemnly at her, and Lucy had the feeling he was going to suggest something that might embarrass both of them, so she exclaimed brightly that she would definitely like to do it again and thank you so much, and scarpered, feeling flattered but relieved at the same time.

She'd finished writing her article straightaway, and taking a deep breath, she'd emailed it to Donald Peters. It had been a self-deprecating romp, from her calamitous CBT take and re-take, to her glorious gambol on Ed's dirt bike, and it had ended: *'Will I ever do a U Turn without falling off? Will I ever get that Full Licence in my hand? Should I just stick to playing on a dirt bike?'*

Short and to the point, his reply was not long arriving:
Just right. DP. Ps. Get a photo of yourself with your pass cert and we'll print both.

After her cleaning session, she turned most of the lights off and logged on to the Curvy Riders' website. This was the site of a national ladies only motorcycling club, and was what Nicola and her biker mates belonged to. Nicola was their Area Rep and arranged their ride-outs and socials, and they'd ended up at The Art Cafe one afternoon after a ride, loved the cakes and general ambience and continued to arrive regularly ever since.

It had been Nicola who'd suggested they quote for catering for the Mega Bikes Launch Evening, and maybe throw in some afternoon teas as raffle prizes. No-one could have predicted Lucy winning the star prize.

She registered as 'Arty Cupcake' and hesitantly wrote an introductory post under the Welcome In section.

'Hello ladies, I was lucky enough to win a Triumph Street Triple in gorgeous purple in a raffle ...' And she went on

to tell an edited story of her training so far. '... *wondering whether to keep going. Has anyone else been this bad?*'

She pressed send, and made a cup of tea. It was dark outside. She could hear the sea whispering across the sands below, felt the quiet and cosy arms of the café wrap around her and was comforted, even though she was alone.

Her phone pinged. A text message. She picked it up with shaking hands, hoping it wasn't Gerry. She had no idea what she would say to him. It was Richard, in typical blokey text speak, even though his mobile phone could send a message the size of an essay.

'*R u ok?*'

'*Yes. I'm still in the Café. x*'

'*Coming over. Stay there.*'

'*No, don't worry, I'm fine, honestly! :)*'

She added a smiley. Bless him, he was a good mate.

Until today, Lucy could almost have thought about winding it up now she'd got her CBT. She would have proved her point, and yes, perhaps she could sell Cadbury and update her van or something. But then Gerry had waltzed in, obviously drunk and obnoxious, and humiliated her in front of her own customers. Which had unfortunately included Ash and his daughter.

And Ash – oh my goodness – without his beard! Well, without most of it. Longer than stubble, it was a clipped short beard that revealed a lean face and wide mouth. And enhanced his bluer than blue eyes. It had totally taken her by surprise. A surprise that had caused her stomach to leap and her hands to fumble and shake, like a gauche teenager. Thank goodness his daughter had been there to distract her. And then bloody Gerry appearing, drunk as a bloody skunk, with two of his golfing buddies in tow.

She felt her anger threaten to overwhelm her all over again as she thought about him. She had no idea what he was doing right now, and she didn't even care. What the hell was going on? This wasn't his usual style. He was normally charming with other people. His vicious side only appeared in private and made her feel as if it was she alone that provoked it and so it must be her fault. She didn't know what Ash had said to him that had made him leave, but she'd seen that ferocity on Ash's face when she'd run the school bike over and knew what it felt like to be on the receiving end of it.

The last time Gerry had got drunk and upset her terribly, over that newspaper article, he was contrite afterwards and he'd been just like the Gerry of old. She'd wound up feeling unbalanced and uncertain of her reactions. This time, she wasn't going to pretend it hadn't happened. She could stand being humiliated in private, just, but to encroach on her business – in front of everyone like that – what a total shit he was. Richard had even heard him from the kitchen and had come out in time to see Ash speaking to him. She'd had to tell him who Ash was of course, and Richard had looked at her in a funny way.

'Ash – your bike instructor? He looked like an off-duty policeman in that white shirt. I don't think I'd like to mess with him. I wonder what he said to Gerry?'

She hadn't really looked at what he was wearing. She'd been too busy noticing his newly revealed face from behind the terrible beard.

The laptop pinged. There were some answers to her post, and she leaned forward to read them.

'Hi Arty Cupcake and welcome to Curvies. I've got to tell you, I thought I'd never even pass my CBT. If it helps, I have been in a fence, almost up a tree, dropped the bike many times, been scared absolutely witless for most of my training prior to passing my tests. Take the

knocks and carry on regardless and I know for a fact there are many ladies on here who will tell you how much they struggled too. Do it for you and please do not be too hard on yourself, well done you.'

'Hi! I did my CBT years ago, turned up as an experienced pillion with 'all the gear' ... and absolutely no idea. I dropped my bike as soon as I started it – the vibration from the engine came as a bit of a shock!!'

'Evening Arty Cupcake! I took 3 or 4 one-to-one sessions to get my CBT, along with several days of going round and round local empty car park with my partner before I was even allowed on the road'

The handle on the café door jiggled and Lucy's panic that it might be Gerry looking for her turned to delight as she saw Richard holding a big bag containing what looked and smelled deliciously like an Indian takeaway, and two bottles of wine. Behind him was Nicola, waving three enormous bars of chocolate.

'I couldn't decide which one, so I bought them all.' She hugged Lucy tightly. 'I've heard all about it from Richard. You don't have to talk about it unless you want to?'

Lucy hugged Richard as he was on his way to the kitchen. With both hands full, he stooped to let her. 'Wow, has this place ever been so clean? It smells lovely, and now we're going to stink it out with takeaway.'

'I had to do something. I couldn't just sit here.'

'Well, I'm sorry I missed it.' Nicola brought out plates and cutlery. 'I'd've given his arse a good kicking if he'd spoken to me like that.'

Lucy considered her enviously, wondering why she couldn't be more like her.

'But it sounds as if your Ash is a bit of a hero, leaping to your defence,' continued Nicola.

'He's not *my* Ash,' Lucy protested.

Nicola handed Lucy a glass tumbler, filled almost to the top with wine. 'Oh, sorry, red or white?'

Lucy took the glass of red, grinning at her friend. 'Either is fine. Cheers! And, thank you, you two, you're proper good mates, you are.' Her bottom lip threatened to sabotage her jollity.

'Get it down yer neck, there's plenty more.' Nicola took a big slurp of her white and leaned forward eagerly. 'So, there's you – gorgeous – and with men falling all over you,' she continued, warming to her theme. 'And what about Handsome Ed taking you out?'

'He did what?' spluttered Richard.

Nicola pretended to wipe the table with a serviette. 'Dirt-biking, Richard.' She grinned. 'And that TV Tom took a bit of a shine to you at the Mega Bikes Night, didn't he? Gerry needs to watch his step if you ask me.'

Lucy laughed, remembering how she had felt when winning the bike. The Mega Bikes' raffle and auction had been a complete surprise to her. She'd been expecting something altogether darker and greasier, and not at all a local television presenter in the shape of TV Tom to be compèring.

'Oh, my goodness, Nic, what a night that was!'

'He definitely knows how to play a crowd, that bloke.' Richard pointed with his fork, then aping TV Tom, he chanted, 'Luc-ee, Luc-ee, Luc-ee!'

Lucy laughed.

'See,' crowed Nicola. 'I said he fancied you.'

'Don't be mad. It's just professional banter,' Lucy replied, but she felt flattered anyway, recalling TV Tom's appreciative all-over glance while she stood beside him.

'It's a gorgeous bike.' Nicola raised her tumbler of wine and inspected it. 'Lucky thing.'

'So – those photos in the paper, what was that about?' asked Richard. 'I mean, it's done us a lot of good, all in all, but they were a bit, you know—'

Nicola glared at him in disgust. 'Richard—' she said, warningly.

'What?' He put his palms up. 'Be honest. They were ...' He took a big swig of wine, peering at Lucy over the top of his glass.

'Terrible?' supplied Lucy, into the silence. 'Ghastly, awful, worst photos ever? Almost as if the photographer had looked for the least flattering way to take a picture of me?'

They nodded.

'Yes, I agree.' Lucy eyed them thoughtfully. 'It was the photographer from Mega Bikes – I recognised his name on the article. Do you remember him? He was really weird with me when I gave him my business card.'

'Oh, I do remember him.' Nicola leaned forward. 'The way he was posing you – it was almost pornographic.' She leapt to her feet, mimicking taking photos. 'Stroke it here, lean forward, lovely, lovely, bend over – bit further, yes super, do you love it? Do you?'

Despite themselves, they laughed. Nicola was a born mimic.

'You're right – it was.' Lucy slapped her hand over her eyes in embarrassment, and then groaned as a further memory surfaced of laying her face against the cool shimmering metal tank. 'And didn't he get me to hug the bike?'

Richard nodded. 'Be fair, you didn't need much encouragement, Luce.' He grinned mischievously. 'You drove the crowd wild.'

'Yeah. And that TV Tom.' Nicola smirked.

'I've got to go and see him. He wants some paintings and prints for their new studios.'

'Awesome! Get in there.' Richard raised his glass to her.

The photographer was forgotten. Lucy lifted her tumbler, chinking it with her friends', thankful for their unwavering support, but thinking back to winning the bike. What a night it had been. A life-changer.

And look where it had got her. Her marriage in meltdown. But maybe it had been already? She just hadn't seen it.

Chapter Eight

She was pulled from the fuggy depths of *après* party slumber by the unmistakeable waft of grilling bacon. As her eyelids ungummed, she regarded the sideways world visible only through a forest of chairs and the previous evening began to return to her consciousness.

An evening spent laughing, eating, drinking, playing air guitar and dancing madly to Richard's iPhone plugged through the café speakers. Pushing herself upright on one of the bench seats they'd crashed out on when it was too late to call a taxi, she groaned as her aching joints made their presence felt. Whether it was the dirt biking or the dancing she couldn't tell.

'I'm too *old* for this!'

A second recumbent figure stirred nearby. Long black hair spread like a storm across Nicola's pale face.

'Morning ladies! Tea or coffee?' called Richard from the kitchen.

Nicola mumbled something sounding like 'Bleh' and sank back onto the long bench.

'I think that's two teas please!' Lucy cranked her resistant body upright. Nicola blundered to her feet and headed straight for the loos, hand over her mouth.

'Good thing we open late on a Sunday,' Lucy called to Richard. 'I think Nicola might be a while …'

Richard was sent to the corner shop for Emergency Chocolate, paracetamol and the Sunday papers, and the three of them sat companionably catching up with the news, topping up their caffeine levels and munching on doorstep bacon butties.

'So, Luce, what's your plan?' Nicola, her complexion

restored to a healthier colour after her bout of 'morning after the night before', was still looking at her paper.

'Get my Full Licence,' Lucy replied promptly.

'And Gerry?' Nicola turned a page with practised nonchalance.

Lucy made a face. Her body language mirrored her indecision.

'Oh, chuck him!'

'It's not really that easy,' Lucy began, hesitantly.

Richard snorted but otherwise made no comment.

'Why are you with a man who makes you feel this bad?' Nicola made it sound so simple.

Lucy spread her hands in front of her and looked down at them.

Nicola lost patience with her. 'Oh, well. If this is what you think you deserve.' She flicked the printed sheets irritably.

Lucy stared at her friend. Chuck him? Ok, things had been a bit rocky lately, but it hadn't always been like this. It was a blip, surely. A baby might have glued them together, but Gerry had made one excuse after another over the years and, worn down, Lucy had stopped asking. Although it hadn't stopped her wanting. Her biological clock had a flat battery these days.

'I'm sorry.' Nicola put a hand over Lucy's. 'I'm sorry Luce, it's nothing to do with me. I'm always telling people what to do.' She combed her long dark hair with her fingers. 'I just don't like to see people I care about unhappy. Anyway, listen. You could do your training on Cadbury – once you've got the Horizontal Parking thing out of your system of course. As long as you are linked with radios to a qualified instructor, you're good to go.'

Lucy scrambled for a pen.

'Horizontal Parking,' she chortled. 'I could put that in my next article, if I get the chance.'

'And while you're here, ring up and book the rest of your training.'

Lucy obediently reached for her mobile.

'And stop doing what you're told all the time!' Nicola added sternly.

Lucy stopped dialling.

'No, not me! You can do what I tell you.' Nicola pealed with laughter at Lucy's face.

'Hello – Ange?' Lucy spoke into her phone and went on to ask haltingly if she could book her full licence training. 'Yes, I know I said I wanted to cancel, but ... Oh! Really? This afternoon?'

Nicola, listening closely, bounced up and down, grinning from ear to ear.

'Say yes!'

Lucy rolled her eyes. So much for not doing as she was told.

'Ok. Yes, please. Thank you very, very much.' She ended the call and looked down with apparent unconcern at the newspaper.

'Well?' said Nicola.

'Mmm?'

'This afternoon?' prompted Nicola, fidgeting with excitement.

Lucy laughed.

'Okay. Ash is free this afternoon and had already told Ange I might call. So – three o'clock.' She checked her watch. 11.30. Bags of time. Except she was still wearing yesterday's clothes – a smart jersey dress, and high boots. And if she went home, it was inevitable that she would get sucked into another row with Gerry, the last thing she needed before bike training.

'Squeeeeeeeeee!' yelled Nicola and then clutched her head. 'Blimey. Good job you didn't drink all that wine last night.

I might ride over later, meet your Mr Ash ... he sounds a bit of all right.'

'He's *not* my Ash,' denied Lucy hotly. 'He has a child – obviously he's married – and *I'm* married, in case you'd forgotten. So ...' Richard and Nicola exchanged a glance. 'Right. I need to change my clothes.'

They looked at her, eyebrows raised.

'But ... I don't want to go home.' She made a face at them. 'I'm not having another row with Gerry and then doing my bike training feeling in a state. Stuff him.' She jutted her bottom lip, thinking. 'I don't want to spend a fortune ...'

Nicola clicked her fingers. 'Ok, I've got it. We need to do some girlie shopping. Richard, fancy chauffeuring us in Lucy's van? I don't think you had much to drink last night, did you?'

Richard sighed heavily, but held his hand out for Lucy's keys.

'Come on then. I dunno. You women just use me.' He winked.

Nicola directed him to the nearest big superstore with a clothing range and they trooped in. Richard diverted to the food aisles. 'You've got my number, see you girls later.'

The rows of jeans looked impossibly skinny and Lucy's heart sank.

'What size?' Nicola was already hunting through them with a practised eye.

'Uhm, 16 I think, the last time I bought any jeans?' Lucy said, feeling enormous next to the rake-thin Nicola.

'Try these.' Lucy was hustled into the changing rooms with several pairs of jeans. 'I'll keep looking. Shout if you need a different size.'

Slowly Lucy undressed, avoiding as usual a cruelly lit mirror which seemed to magnify every spot of cellulite on her thighs.

She separated the first pair of jeans from the vice-like grip of the hanger and stepped into them. And looked up in surprise as the expected battle to zip them up failed to materialise.

She slid them off and checked the size. They must be an 18 or something. No, size 16. And miles too big. She tried on the next pair, and the next. All massive.

'How's it going?'

Lucy opened the door, holding the jeans out with her thumbs. 'They're too big!'

'Whoa! The incredible shrinking woman. Give me a sec …' Nicola rushed off, returning with an armful of jeans in a size 14.

'I am *never* a 14.'

'Just get them on. Let's have a look.'

They weren't all perfect, but to Lucy's astonishment she found a pair that fit beautifully. In a size 14. She wanted to cut the label out and have it framed. She couldn't remember the last time she was this small. How had she never noticed? Of course, the jersey dresses and leggings – all stretchy, with no zips and buttons – perfect camouflage for both a burgeoning and shrinking waistline. Must have been all the salads she'd had recently. And not eating full evening meals with Gerry all the time as he was out so much.

They were almost too nice to ride a motorbike in, but they were cheap so she didn't feel as if it was too much of a sacrifice if she ended up parking horizontally again.

Nicola had taken away all the wrong jeans and passed over a selection of t-shirts and tunic tops. Again, all in a size 14. Lucy looked at them doubtfully but in the face of Nicola's hard glare, didn't feel brave enough to refuse.

They discovered Richard exploring the kitchen gadgets aisle with a thoughtful look on his face. 'Spiralisers,' he explained, to their blank expressions. 'For making veggies look pretty. And spiral.'

'Lovely.' Nicola rolled her eyes. 'Come on, let's go. You, my darling ...' She kissed Richard. '... have a café to open, and Lucy's got a date with her Mr Ash.'

'He's not my ...'

'Yes, yes, we know. Come on!'

Lucy felt absurdly pleased with her new outfit, plus a toothbrush, toothpaste, and hairbrush thrown in at the last minute. Back at the café, they cleaned away all evidence and odour of takeaways and wine, and, dressed in her new jeans, Lucy hugged them both with tears in her eyes.

'Thanks guys. You two are the best.'

'Yep. Break a leg,' said Richard.

'Oh, God, don't tell her that,' groaned Nicola, nudging him with her elbow.

Lucy dropped them off at their house, smiling as she saw Nicola's red motorbike parked in the front garden. 'Thanks for last night and today guys. Speak soon!' She waved goodbye and with excitement in her heart and time to spare, turned the van towards Better Biking. Collecting herself in the car park, she pulled out her mobile to switch it off, not wanting it to distract her by buzzing in her jacket pocket. Half expecting to see a message from Gerry, or at least a missed call, she didn't know whether to feel angry or relieved that there was neither. Had he even noticed that she hadn't come home all night? She pushed down her rising irritation. She was having a lovely day. Plus, he generally spent all day Sunday golfing with his cronies, without a thought about what she was doing.

Angela looked up as she entered, hurriedly folding the newspaper Lucy recognised as the one which had contained those photographs. 'We had nothing to do with these, I hope you know that,' she said.

'Yeah, I know. Don't worry about it. It's done me a good turn really.'

'Oh? Nice article, by the way, the one you wrote.'

'Glad you enjoyed it.'

'Hilarious! That beautiful boy took you dirt biking then? Lucky you! We should think about teaming up. Adding it to our repertoire.'

'It was fun. Thank you so much for agreeing to fit me in this afternoon. I owe you one.'

'A box of your fabulous cupcakes will do it.' Angela smiled. 'I can hear Ash's car now.'

Lucy's stomach erupted in butterflies, and she felt her hands go clammy. *Calm down. He thinks you can do it. And you can do it.* Angela was still chatting.

'I expect he's brought Daisy. How nice! Bless them, it's so sad.'

'Sad?' Lucy frowned.

'Daisy's mum ...' Angela shook her head with a downturned mouth and stopped as Daisy marched straight in and up to Lucy.

'Hello, Lucy,' she said, and then, as if by rote, 'Thank-you-for-our-lovely-cakes-yesterday!'

'Have you eaten them already?'

'Yes! They were yummy. We shared them with Nanny and Grandad.'

Ash locked his car and strolled into the office. He smiled, seeing Lucy already there, chatting to Angela and his daughter.

'Ange, are you ok to have Daisy or shall I take her over to Ed?' He always asked, never wanting to seem as if he took her voluntary babysitting for granted.

'Oh no, it's lovely to see her. It'll just be us, there's no-one else booked in. We'll have fun.' She pulled open a deep drawer full of colouring pens and books and glitter stickers, clearly existing solely for the entertainment of Daisy, and

Ash left them poring happily over the contents. Lucy trotted after him, seemingly deep in thought.

'You all right?' he asked.

'Erm, yes. Thanks for this and ...' She peeped up at him from under her lashes, and blushed. 'And for yesterday.'

He waved a hand, feeling a bit embarrassed. *He would have done it for anyone. Wouldn't he? Not to mention working here on his Rest Day.*

'No problem. Right, let's get you togged up. At least it's not raining.'

In borrowed boots, plus the usual gear, Lucy listened while Ash outlined the Module 1 manoeuvres again. This time, it all went like clockwork. Her practice session with Ed had obviously stood her in good stead, and she looked a whole lot more relaxed than before.

Her Figure of Eight was more like a scenic tour of the compound, admittedly, but he chuckled at her beam of delight when she completed it. He held his breath, willing her to succeed as she scribed jerkily around the dreaded U turn. Not perfect, but it would improve with practice. He knew she'd be relieved not to have dropped it this time.

Ninety minutes passed in a whirl. Lucy parked carefully outside the Better Biking office and climbed off. Pulling off her helmet, she pushed her fingers through her mane of hair and turned her brown eyes on him in a questioning gaze.

'Not so bad, was it?' Ash was breezy as he wheeled her bike into the lock-up. 'There are a few more bits to do for the Mod 1, but I reckon you'll nail them, with a bit of practice. Let's get you booked in for the tests, shall we?' He felt his eyes crinkle at the corners as she stared up at him, happiness written across her face.

'I wonder if Ed might have a cheap 125cc bike I could buy, to practise on. You know, until I pass and can ride Cadbury.'

'That's a good idea, if you can afford it. Ed has a lot of contacts. He's sure to sort something out for you, and it might not be pretty, but at least you'll know it's mechanically sound. Pop in during the week and sound him out.'

'I will.' Lucy looked as if she was going to rush over there right now. 'I don't think I can bear the thought of not being on a bike now. It's so exciting.' She beamed up at him, twin spots of pink on her cheeks. Ash tore his glance away from her pretty face, glad to be distracted by Daisy's appearance in the doorway.

'I heard you come back. Was it good, Lucy?' Daisy wanted to know.

'It was indeed, Daisy, thanks to your patient Dad.'

'Yay!' the little girl exclaimed happily, and then dodging Ash's no doubt horrified expression, announced, 'Do you know, you look just like Lara Croft?

Leaving for home had felt more like leaving a family party than work. There had been kisses and hugs all round. What was it about women with all the hugging? It left him wondering what he was supposed to do. Was he meant to join in? Luckily, Lucy, Daisy and Angela seemed happy turning it into a private party while he watched, half out of the doorway. Lucy had laughed her socks off at Daisy's Lara Croft comment, turning some poses to make Daisy laugh too. It was great to see her looking so confident after the incident in the café. He hoped she'd carry on, pass her tests. He wanted her to succeed.

'Come on, sweet pea,' he called Daisy, eventually. 'You've got some friends coming over this afternoon, don't forget, and we're doing a Treasure Hunt.'

'Co-mmmming, Daddeee!' In a springy bounce of curls, the little girl catapulted out of the office and skipped down the steps. She turned to sing back, 'Thank you Aunty

Angela, for a lovely time.' Adding his thanks, Ash whisked his daughter away before it provoked another onslaught of hugging.

'What *is* the treasure, Daddy?'

'You'll know when you find it.' He'd thought about it yesterday, and popped out to buy bits and bobs, stickers and pens and silly things that kids liked. Anything to keep them active and entertained. And worn out. He'd made up some questions and written them on a big sheet of paper, which he was going to pin to the door of his workshop. Very Blue Peter. That way, he could enjoy a well-earned cup of coffee while they ran about. 'Shall we get the mini barbecue out and do marshmallows on sticks?'

'Yum.' She nodded. 'I bet Lucy likes marshmallows. Do you think she'd like to come and play with us?'

Ash was taken aback. 'Uh, I think Lucy has to go back to work for the rest of today.' *And I can't imagine her husband being too impressed by an invitation for Lucy to come out to play with me.*

Daisy's friends, two little girls from her class called Amy and Lily, arrived not long after he'd tacked up his questions and hidden the treasures. Regular visitors now, he was pleased to see them wearing old jeans. Amy's rather humourless mum had brought them over and handed over wellies in plastic bags.

'See you in a couple of hours.' She scanned his handiwork and nodded approvingly. 'You don't make it easy for the rest of us, y'know. We're going to have to up our game. Amy loves visiting Daisy. It's all she talks about when she gets back.'

'You can stay and play, if you like? I'm teaching them log splitting later.' He kept his face straight at her look of horror. 'Don't worry. They'll be fine. I've got an up to date First Aid Certificate.'

Amy's mum backed away with an expression that said she hoped he was joking, and Ash called his little troupe to attention in the garden. They fixed him with stares of bright anticipation, hands on hips.

'What are we doing today then, Daisy's Dad?' Amy cocked her head. She'd always called him that. It made him laugh, and he loved joshing her.

'Sums.' He sipped his coffee. 'Really hard sums. And spelling.'

'No, we're not.' Daisy nearly burst with glee. 'Daddy's done a Treasure Hunt!' Ash grinned, leading them towards his list.

Lily, the quietest and most studious of the three, read the first question out loud. 'There are three buckets for collecting your treasure. In a pen for three animals. Where is that?'

'I know! It's the sheep, quick, race you!' Amy spun on her heel with the other two close behind, shrieking and pushing.

'Come straight back here with your buckets!' Ash yelled after them, perching on a sturdy stool in the sunshine. This was the life. It couldn't be a better place to raise children. It reminded him of his own childhood.

'Hellooo! There you are.' Sarah clip-clopped unexpectedly around the side of the workshop wearing uncharacteristically high-heeled sparkly sandals and spray-on pale pink jeans. 'Your Mum said Daisy was having some friends round. I thought we could spend a bit of time together while they played.'

'Hello. Are you going somewhere nice?' Ash squinted at her in the sunshine. She was making his eyes hurt.

'No. Well, yes. I've come to see you.'

'You look, uhm ...' *What the hell? Completely impractical? You have been coming here for the past eight years, haven't you?* He rushed on. 'We've already got a bit of a game going, Sarah. Er ...' He squinted at the three small figures hurtling towards him now. 'You're welcome to join in, if you like. But you might want to change first?'

'Uhm, maybe not ...' Sarah leapt back as three buckets were hurled towards them, accompanied by gales of breathless laughter.

'I won! Hello, Aunty Sarah.' Daisy clattered into her aunt, and Ash winced as her little hands left definite prints behind. There'd be a scene. Maybe it was best to say nothing.

'Perhaps Aunty Sarah can give out the treasure.' He held out a bag of goodies to her. 'One in each bucket, please.'

Dispatching the booty delicately from pincered fingers and thumbs, Sarah excused herself to make coffee, as Lily read the next question. 'How many chickens are there? Extra prizes for finding eggs.'

'Are they chocolate eggs?' Daisy demanded.

'Maybe ...' Ash laughed as they rushed helter-skelter to the chicken coop. Sarah ventured back outside as soon as they were out of sight, carrying a mug and a kitchen chair.

'So. This is nice.' Placing the mug beside her on the ground, Sarah perched on the edge of the chair. 'How are things?'

'No plans for today then?' Ash asked after a pause, listening for the girls. Maybe he should go and check. Sarah was on her feet beside him as he stood, and he glanced down at her strappy sandals. 'There are some spare wellies in the porch, if you ...?' Maybe she hadn't heard him, as she picked her way along the grass and gravel path, tripping and resorting to hanging onto his arm.

'I just thought it would be nice to come and visit you guys,' Sarah said.

'Yes, of course. But, you know, you young things, out partying with your friends ...?' Ash craned his neck. He could see the chicken coop, but he couldn't see the girls.

Peeling Sarah's fingers off his arm, he vaulted the gate. He heard the giggling before he saw them. He'd built the hen coop to resemble a little cottage, and by the sounds coming from inside it, the chickens had been evicted, and the girls were in residence. He thrust his head into the little doorway, and summoned his scariest troll voice. 'Ah-aaaaaaa!'

Three chocolate covered faces squealed in mock horror, and he retreated quickly as they pelted him with bits of mucky straw. Wiping himself down with his hands he strolled back to join Sarah with a grin.

'They're not – in there, are they?' She blanched, 'You've got something just by ...' She tapped her own cheek to mirror his, with a little shiver of disgust.

'Yep. Goodness knows how they squeezed in.' He rubbed his hands over his face. 'I think they found all the chocolate eggs.' Raising his voice, he aimed it at the coop. 'They won't need feeding now. I might lock them in there. And then I'll light the barbecue and I'll have to eat all the marshmallows on sticks with Aunty Sarah.'

'Not for me thank you,' Sarah said quickly, adding an, 'Oh, dear ...' in a faint voice, as the girls tumbled out of the coop, and zigzagged like puppies towards them, hair in tangles and dirtied knees. Ash scratched the side of his neck, dislodging a scrap of chicken shit that the girls had thrown at him.

'Hose-pipe on you lot, before you're collected, I reckon.'

'Oh, no, really, I don't think that's a good idea, Ash.' Sarah's hands fluttered around her to reduce possible contact with the mucky trio. 'Isn't it a bit too cold for that?'

'Yesss – water fight!' Amy roared.

Ash tried not to sigh at Sarah's continual little reproaches and asides. Honestly, she was a bit joyless at times. She was sucking the fun out of this afternoon. 'Nothing a few baby-wipes can't sort out,' he muttered to her in an aside, as they trailed the girls towards the house. He tried to hurry her, concerned that Daisy would have the hose unreeled before he got there. 'Children should be allowed to get dirty now and again.' Sarah winced and tripped and tutted as she stubbed her toes, and finally, exasperated, Ash abandoned her, sprinting after his charges. 'Oi! Wait for me, you horrible lot!'

Catching up with the slower two, he swept a child under each arm and stampeded past Amy in a flurry of helpless giggles. Some of them even came from the girls, he grinned to himself. Flinging themselves on the ground, they watched Sarah tottering towards them.

'Aunty Sarah,' Daisy began in her conversational tone. 'Those trousers made you look as if you've got nothing on, from over there.'

'Daisy ...' Ash warned, clocking Sarah's painfully red blush as it spread up her neck.

'They're this summer's pastels, Daisy. It's fashion.' Her tone was crisp.

'Are those green bits part of the pattern?' Lily pointed politely, and Ash shaded his eyes with a weary hand as Sarah yelped in anguish, twisting in an effort to see the Daisy-sized hand-prints they could all see on her bottom.

'I don't know why I bother.' Sarah glared, stalking off towards the house, followed by three pairs of eyes, clearly bemused as to why a bit of dirt should bother anyone.

'I still have Treasure ...' Ash reached out and shook the bag. 'Close your eyes, count to a hundred. Slowly. I'm going to hide them.'

When all the goodies had been found and distributed, it was time to light the barbecue. Ash shooed them all indoors for a wash and brush up in the kitchen sink before they ate and was startled to find Sarah lounging on the sofa, flicking the TV remote.

'I ... thought you'd gone home?'

'Why?'

'To change your jeans?'

'I thought I'd help put Daisy to bed. And then we can have a bit of time together.'

Ash swallowed. 'That's, er, nice of you. But ...' He thought quickly. 'I've got some bike lessons to plan, for a student.' He did. He wanted to present the Mod 1 tests in a comprehensible way for Lucy, but he didn't have to do that tonight.

'Is that for the woman we saw on the bike that time? The chubby one that's a bit of a loser? Nice of you to be so interested.'

Ash narrowed his eyes. He was going to have to edit his conversations at dinner with his parents and Daisy. It was the only place he could remember talking about Lucy. 'I'm cooking fish fingers on the barbecue if you want some. Or beef burgers. That's what I'm having too.' *A clear message that I'm not cooking anything special this evening, surely.*

Sarah unfolded her skinny legs from the sofa and slung her bag over her shoulder. 'Fine. I can see you're too busy for me.'

'No, Sarah, it's just ...' Ash ran out of things to say, and Sarah raised a haughty eyebrow at him. 'Catch you later, huh?' Ash exhaled quietly as she strutted out through the kitchen, calling a goodbye to Daisy and avoiding contact along with the messy possibilities that might ensue.

It was wrong to speculate what Lucy would have made of their afternoon's escapades. But he couldn't help wondering.

Chapter Nine

Lara Croft? Lucy drove home, laughing with delight. Not 'that bird out of the vampire films, crossed with a bin liner', as Gerry had unkindly forecast she'd resemble in leathers, then. She couldn't imagine a better compliment.

What an incredible day: she'd discovered a size 14 bottom, she'd booked the first part of her bike test, and she'd been likened to Lara Croft. There was a lay-by up ahead. She pulled in and tugged out her phone.

First, she messaged Nicola and Richard with her good news. Then, while she still felt in brave mode, she read a number off a business card and rang TV Tom – whose real name was Tom Wheaton – the presenter from Mega Bikes.

His voice was laconic. "Lo …?"

'Hello – sorry to ring you on a Sunday. This is Lucy Daumier. We met at the Mega Bike Centre. I won the—'

'Purple Street Triple! I remember. Hi, Lucy.' He sounded as smooth as the chocolate from which her bike took its name, and she smiled.

'You said you're looking for some paintings for the new offices?'

'I am, yes. Could we get together sometime soon and thrash out some details? How are you fixed on, er, Wednesday morning?'

'Yes, sounds fine. About ten?' Lucy made a mental note to get either Nicola or their new art student, Ella, to cover for her if one of them was free mid-week. The café was so busy now, she couldn't just bob out for a couple of hours like she used to. Ella was flexible in her hours, which suited them and her, and was happy to work Saturdays if needed. Friendly and chatty, she was already popular with the staff, and Lucy was pleased with her choice. It had turned out that she was the daughter of someone in one of Gerry's business networks, so Lucy had to admit that they had some uses after all.

Lucy quite liked working Saturdays. They seemed to attract a different, more art-focused customer. She noticed that often, women came in during the week and earmarked paintings they liked, bringing their partners in at the weekend to confirm their choice, and pay. But having Ella on the team gave Lucy precious time alone, and she planned to use it for painting, and of course, bike training.

'Perfect. I'll see you then. Looking forward to it.' He dictated his address to her while she scrabbled for a pen in her capacious bag.

'Is that the Mary Poppins bag I can hear?'

She laughed. He'd mentioned that when she'd won the bike. 'Yes. There's a pen in here somewhere.'

He waited patiently and then gave her the address again. She wrote it in her little sketchbook with a flourish.

'Thank you. See you on Wednesday then. Bye!'

Lucy was on a roll.

So … just Gerry to deal with. She was ready for it. She tried to imagine what mood he might be in. He hadn't been in touch since the café incident yesterday, but then, neither had she. This was not at all his normal pattern of behaviour and despite her anger, she felt anxious about him.

What was going on? Was he ill? In trouble? Perhaps she should have rung him … Maybe she should have gone home last night to check on him? How drunk had he been? Maybe he'd passed out and choked on his own vomit? That would be all her fault – how would she ever deal with the guilt?

Panic pressed her foot to the accelerator and her earlier euphoria evaporated. She'd got into a complete state by the time she turned onto their street. The empty drive didn't help matters. Had he been home at all? Had he driven last night after all and had an accident? Maybe he was still in a ditch somewhere? And she hadn't bothered to find out if he was ok and so if he was seriously injured or worse, dead, it would all be her fault. With shaking hands, she unlocked the door and went up to their bedroom. It looked just as she'd left it the day before, although Gerry was quite a finicky person and often much tidier than she was, so that wasn't much of a clue.

She opened his wardrobe, trying to see what might be missing. His wardrobe was much fuller than hers – crammed with expensive designer suits and shirts that cost more than any of her dresses. He'd never been one for jeans and t-shirts. Returning downstairs, she looked around the house, as smart and clean as ever, but somehow anonymous, as if the people who lived there were just passing through, leaving no trace of themselves. It was a nice enough house in building terms, but she barely had a sense of their shared lives over the years.

She rummaged in the freezer, defrosted some chicken and ready-made pastry and made a chicken and mushroom pie. She eyed the bottle of Chardonnay in the fridge – a chilled glass of wine would have been lovely while she was cooking, but she couldn't really take the moral high ground with Gerry about him being drunk in the café if she was drinking when he came home from wherever he was. Plus, she was a terrible drunk, getting sozzled on a single glass. She'd never be able to stick up for herself.

With the chicken pie in the oven, she opened her laptop in the sitting room and typed up ideas for another article. Maybe she should start an online blog, persuade the newspaper to link to it? *'At last, I've booked my Mod 1 Test! In just over four weeks' time – better get practising!'* It cheered her to write that. The front door opened and clicked shut. Hurriedly she pressed 'save', shut the lid of the laptop and slid it amongst a stack of art magazines. Just in case.

Gerry had headed straight for the kitchen and was pouring a large glass of wine from the bottle she'd seen earlier.

'Want one?' He looked over his shoulder at her. She shook her head, willing her mouth not to be prim and disapproving.

'I'll have a cup of tea,' she said firmly, picking up the kettle. 'I've put a pie in the oven.'

'I've eaten. At the Club.' No apologies. No explanation. Her pulse thudded painfully in her chest.

What had happened to the husband who used to smile at her, tell her she looked nice, make her laugh, kiss her breathless? What had gone so badly wrong that they skirted round each other like this, point scoring? Was it really just about her wanting to ride a motorbike? What if she'd wanted to learn hang gliding, scuba diving, jet-skiing? Since when had he been so controlling?

She took a deep breath. 'Gerry. We need to talk. I'm worried about you – you're not yourself lately. Is there anything you need to tell me?'

He leaned against the worktop and looked at her over the rim of his glass, which was already nearly empty, she noticed.

'Funny you should ask.' He pinned her with a cold stare. Her legs felt shaky. To distract herself, she watched the kettle as it began to boil and took a cup from the cupboard, mechanically dropping a teabag into it. 'I'm sick with worry about you on that bike, as it happens.' He refilled his glass. 'I thought we'd agreed you were packing it in and selling it?'

'No, Gerry, that was what *you* wanted. Not what *I*

wanted. I'm planning on taking extra training after I've passed, to be as safe as I can possibly be.'

'Why do you have to do something that I'm not included in?'

Lucy gaped at the unfairness of his accusation. His life had had less and less connection to hers for years. If she didn't tag along to the business network things that no other wives attended, or put up with being a golf widow, even on holiday, she would barely see her husband. Right now, she wasn't even sure that she wanted to see him.

'You haven't even apologised for humiliating me yesterday.' Lucy squashed the teabag furiously, slopping tea onto the counter.

'Yeah, well.' Gerry gulped his wine. 'I was angry. And being threatened by that copper, for fuck's sake!'

'What copper? Oh ...' A memory of Ash in a white shirt and something Richard had said last night flashed across her memory. 'He threatened you? What did he say?'

Gerry looked away from her without replying, his mouth a thin line. 'So.' He shrugged. 'I went and had a few more jars with the lads.' The 'lads' hadn't looked very impressed with Gerry the last time she'd seen them.

'Didn't you wonder where I was when I didn't come home?'

'I knew where you were.' He swirled the wine in the glass, not looking at her. 'I drove past the café and saw the lights on.'

Lucy stared at him, her pulse hammering in her ears, a thousand thoughts jamming her brain for attention. *Do you actually care about me? Because you're making it really difficult for me to care about you ...*

His head jerked up. 'So, you're going to sell the bike then, yes? It's not as if you're any good at it, is it?'

Her stomach lurched with rage at his casual assumption,

and she heard her voice say, 'No. And Gerry, you can't get your way all the time by bullying me.' He looked at her with a startled expression and it gave her courage. She carried on. 'I mean, are you happy? Is this the way you saw our lives?'

'What's wrong with our lives?'

'Us. Did you ever think about children or anything?'

'Children? How would that fit in? We've always been so busy – we could never have afforded it for starters.'

Lucy considered his expensive gadgets, gold chains, car, but said nothing, seething.

'And you've never said. You should have said.' His voice was peevish.

'Gerry – have you ever actually listened to me?' She leaned back against the worktop. Now she'd started, she wasn't going to stop.

'What are you on about?' He stuck his head out at her bullishly. 'You're knocking on a bit now, but do you want a child?'

Lucy wavered. Did she? Not with him, she realised. Not now. Her mind floated an image of Ash and Daisy together, the protective way he was with her, but teasing, listening, interested. That wouldn't be Gerry's parenting style. The realisation scorched her, a sudden picture of their relationship as other people saw it imprinting itself horribly in her mind. She felt sad. Empty. As if all their years together had left them as husks of their former selves. Echoes.

'Well, do you?'

'I did.'

'What's that supposed to mean?' He glared at her. 'This is getting us nowhere. I can't do anything right. I look after you and your accounts – you don't have to think about anything except your arty farty stuff – and now, because I'm worrying about you on that bike, I'm the one who's wrong.

I can't want a child just because you've suddenly decided you want one, or did want one, or whatever is going on in that head of yours. It's always about you, isn't it? Don't you ever think about me?'

How had this happened? How had it turned around and was now Lucy's fault? And so unfair. She thought about him all the time, worried about him, cooked the food that he liked, kept her hair the way he liked it. Her whole life, she realised, seemed to be about her being 'a good girl' for him. Apart from him doing his actual job, what did he do for her?

'I'm ... sorry.' As if she was watching a play of their lives, she realised this was her stock response. Had she imagined the small gleam of triumph in his eyes? She knew he'd trumped her again. She also knew him well enough to know he was lying. She just didn't know what he was lying about. 'I'm tired. I haven't slept much. I'm going for a bath and then I'm having an early night.'

The oven pinged, making her jump. She took the pie out, resisting the urge to throw the whole lot at his head. Instead, she slid it onto the cooling rack and switched the oven off.

He showed no interest whatsoever, got up, taking the nearly empty bottle of wine with him and wandered into the lounge. She heard the television click on.

Upstairs, she dug out her 'hospital nightie', filled the bath with hot water scented with her favourite Molton Brown's Pink Pepperpod, and locked the door. She felt vulnerable, and she didn't want Gerry to see her naked.

She needn't have worried. By the time she got out of the bath, her husband was flat on his back, snoring and taking up most of the bed.

Chapter Ten

Lucy studied her reflection. She barely recognised the woman standing there. The worm, she decided, had definitely turned. She wasn't going to be the yes-woman who appeased Gerry and did as she was told any longer.

As a thank you to Nicola and her encouragements, she'd booked them both into her smart hairdresser's, having decided on a whim that she was fed up with the bird's nest look resulting from every training ride. Plus, she hadn't changed her hairstyle for years and years. She usually had it cut exactly how Gerry liked it. She would love to be as feisty and assertive as Nicola, but it would take time. She needed to send out some signals first.

She watched the rising sea of honey blonde hair falling to the floor – a symbol of the years and attitudes she was shedding. A long, layered crop appeared that flicked around her newly discovered cheekbones, accentuating her dark eyes and wide mouth. If she didn't like it, it would grow again. It wasn't forever. But it was *her* decision. Not Gerry's.

'Nice.' Nicola nodded. 'Very Keira Knightley, actually.' She had admitted, to Lucy's horror, that she cut her own long dark hair, and had been booked in for the works. Whilst she relaxed under the attentions of the stylist, her nails were shaped and manicured. Finally, another of the friendly team assessed her face and skin and asked what kind of make-up look she usually chose. Nicola explained she didn't bother with much; a bit of tinted moisturiser sometimes, some blusher and mascara. Her make-up bag was crammed with mistakes she either didn't know how to use, or turned out to be the wrong colour, and she was loath to throw them away as she'd bought them.

'A natural look then. What about something just a little bit more polished?'

Twenty minutes later, and her skin looked dewy and bursting with good health, the shading was subtle but cleverly focussed on her best points, and her lips looked soft and full. The make-up girl had laughed with delight at Nicola's expression. Lucy grinned at her pleasure.

'Bit better than the kitchen scissors, huh?' she winked.

'I should say. And look at you! I bet TV Tom will be impressed.'

'TV Tom?' The make-up girl squealed. 'I love him! OMG! Tell all.'

Lucy began to play down her meeting the following day but seeing their faces fall, she threw caution to the wind and enjoyed telling them how she'd won Cadbury and met Tom and how he wanted some of her paintings for the TV Production offices.

'You ride a *motorbike?* Wow!'

The hefty bill was worth every penny. It hadn't just been a haircut, it had been therapy and a giant step towards 'Self-Improvement'. It was armour for the coming week.

At home, she and Gerry were avoiding each other. Whatever he thought of her new hair style, he didn't mention it. She wondered whether he even noticed. It was almost peaceful. She was making the most of it.

On Wednesday morning, in the new jeans, teamed with high-heeled boots and one of her wrap tunic tops, carrying the smart portfolio of her images, she checked her reflection in the windows of the TV company's swanky new offices and felt confident as she approached the reception desk, announcing her meeting with Tom Wheaton.

To her immense satisfaction, he did a double take when he saw her, reaching out to shake her hand and gazing with appreciation into her eyes. He led her through the various corridors and public rooms which they wanted decorating with paintings. It was easy to forget that he was a local TV personality, he was so relaxed and easy, listening carefully to her suggestions.

Lucy asked about colour schemes and sizes, and what kind of look they were after. She'd remembered her camera and took copious photos. Finally, they ended up in Tom's own suite of offices, where he rang through for coffee.

'… or would you prefer tea?'

Lucy nodded. Her heart was pounding with anticipation already. This was a big space to fill.

'Yes, please. Would they have any camomile perhaps? Or peppermint? I'm a bit over-stimulated at the moment.'

Tom raised his eyebrows, his face teasing.

'With *coffee!* I do run a café to go with the gallery.' She laughed, opening her portfolio. Amazing how much confidence a decent hairstyle could give you, plus a pair of supermarket jeans. Lucy had added some images from the other artists she represented. She wouldn't earn as much commission as if they used her work, but she was nothing if not scrupulously fair. Her own paintings, featuring both dramatic coastal scenes in saturated earthy colours, and harbours and seaside hamlets, were full of loose brushstrokes and movement.

Until the Art Café, she'd exhibited widely and become popular with a small range of limited edition prints which still sold across the country. Selling other artists' work was fun and interesting, but she acknowledged that it also kept her away from her own creative processes. She hoped that this might give her just the motivation she needed. The rooms were bright and well lit, but bland and really needed character. She could visualise her work there, in thick white mounts and generously proportioned frames. They would be a wonderful focal point.

'Have you been into The Art Café?'

'Yes, but I also went to one of your exhibitions. It was a while back.' He turned the pages of her portfolio as he spoke, staring intently. 'I really like these. You don't seem to have them in the café when I go.'

Lucy felt too embarrassed to admit she'd never seen him there. How did these people manage to camouflage themselves when they were such recognisable faces? 'No. It's a space issue. These are big prints. I earn more commission selling lots of smaller pictures.' She shrugged. 'On the whole, people have smaller houses, and if they like to buy paintings, they end up with lots of small ones or they run out of room.'

He nodded. 'I don't think we've got that problem here. Ok. I think I've made up my mind. I'll need to run this past the budget people of course, but I think we'll need about thirty – a mixture of prints and originals, if that's ok?'

Lucy hid her trembling hands by diving into her bag and bringing out her notebook and pen. *Wow.* This was fantastic.

'So what's your best price on these and ... this type of thing?' He'd settled on her favourite themes of windswept coastlines, the sunlight just flicking over the wet sand left by an ebbing tide. Unpeopled, as if the viewer had been the first one to get up and experience it. Mostly watercolour with inks and pastels and collage and all kinds of techniques thrown in.

'What sort of sizes are you thinking?' Lucy was praying he wasn't going to ruin it by having under-sized pictures in those big rooms. He tipped his head on one side and his mouth curved upwards.

'Depends on your prices.'

She laughed. 'Ok. Here's a price list for the prints, with the sizes. More than ten and you qualify for the Trade

Prices. A full-size painting, about 45 by 35 inches, including a frame, original painting, about a grand, retail. If you're going to 'bulk buy', then I think I can manage a bit of a discount.' She held her breath. She had set out her stall, so to speak. It was up to him now. Some people hated this bargaining way of buying and selling. You wouldn't dream of going into your supermarket and doing it. But in the art and antiques world it was customary. If it was done with charm, Lucy enjoyed it.

He was thinking, tapping his pen. Finally, he spoke. 'Ok, we're going to need at least ten prints for these rooms,' he ran his pen down the list, 'so I think we can qualify for your trade discount. But I'd like about half a dozen originals. Mixed sizes. If we itemise them, can you send me an invoice and I'll get it sanctioned?'

Attempting to look business-like and as if this sort of thing happened all the time, Lucy nodded seriously and wrote carefully in her notebook. Totting it up in her head, never her strongest point as even she acknowledged, made a grand total of something in the region of – well, several thousand pounds. Or something. She was relieved he didn't want her to give him a bill there and then.

'I could do a sort of mock-up – show the buyers how the rooms would look with my paintings in if that helps?' she said, her mind in overdrive. He looked at her admiringly.

'That would be great! And once they're installed, we'll be doing some publicity of course; a bit of a re-launch, you know the sort of thing.' She tried to look as if of course, her diary was packed to the brim with 'that sort of thing'. 'So – how's the bike training coming on then?' He focussed on her directly, changing the subject so quickly that Lucy was momentarily off-balance. She made a rueful face.

'We-ell. I finally got my CBT. After wrecking nearly all the school bikes ... and driving my instructor bonkers ...'

He laughed. 'I'm sure it wasn't that bad. Put in for your test yet then?'

'Sort of. I've got my Module One training tomorrow. And I've booked my Theory already.'

'Wow. I didn't do any of that stuff. I passed in the olden days when there was only one test, on the road, and you either passed or you didn't. It's a bit of a faff these days isn't it? But I guess it's probably a good thing. You're pretty vulnerable out there. Are you enjoying it?'

'I am now. It scared the pants, er ... *life* out of me in the beginning,' she admitted. 'I've even done a bit of dirt biking.'

'Good for you. Want to see my bike?'

Lucy had mixed feelings about how she was supposed to respond. Was he flirting with her? She was so out of practice. But reluctant to spoil the ease of their buyer/customer relationship, she followed him through the winding corridors to the back of the building, where she could see a highly coloured sporty-looking machine chained to a sturdy anchor plate in the wall. It was a racehorse compared to the workmanlike look of the school bikes.

'Wow.'

'It's my baby. It's a Fireblade. Beautiful isn't she?' He ran his hands over the seat and Lucy shivered.

'And you offered me a pillion ride on that? There isn't even a back seat!'

'What do you call that then?' He pointed at the tiny vinyl-covered area which looked as if it had been tacked on as an afterthought.

'That's not a seat. That's a – a perch. For ... *Pilly Princesses.*'

He roared with laughter. 'I see you're picking up the jargon already.'

Lucy was still staring at the four inches of resting place

which was barely big enough to balance a toddler on, while also appearing to lift the passenger way higher than the rider.

'I wouldn't get on that if you paid me.'

'I'm wounded. Deeply wounded. I could just see you in a nice set of full length leathers.'

She laughed. 'Nope. I'm a front seat driver these days.'

'Good for you. Good luck with it.' He smiled down, and gestured for them to return. Gathering her portfolio, he carried it back to reception and shook her hand.

'You've got my number. Ring me if you need any more information. Oh, and here's my email. You can email over the invoice and mock-up.' He handed her his business card. 'And if you change your mind about that pillion ride ...'

'Thank you. I won't.' She grinned. 'I'll be in touch. Thanks again.'

Things were definitely looking up, she thought, as she tried not to skip out of the building. Next stop, The Vintage Bike Palace, to get a 125cc to run about on.

'You're not selling your Triumph, surely?' Ed said, his eyebrows raised.

'Certainly not. I just want something to practise on, until I pass my test. Something cheap. Have you got anything?'

'Probably. Give me your mobile number and I'll sort something out for you. It won't be anything pretty, mind.'

'That's fine. I've got a pretty bike already. I don't want to make Cadbury jealous.' Lucy smiled as Ed laughed.

'You're mad, all you girls, naming your bikes. I'll be in touch.'

Chapter Eleven

Ash and Lucy were in the café near the training centre. Lucy had told him she'd bought a tatty looking 125cc from Ed, and had borrowed a helmet from him. It lived round the back of the café now, apparently, and she took it out whenever she could, even just to run errands. It was making a huge difference to her confidence. Ash watched as she traced the diagrams with her finger. He'd contemplated this next part of her training and, realising she was a visual person, he'd downloaded and printed out the layout of the Module One test which was booked for the following week, and used highlighter pens to explain how it worked.

It was a pernickety thing, this test. One mistake and you failed, no room for error. Several students had repeated it, sometimes many times until they managed to complete it perfectly. She was murmuring and nodding. He could see the tip of her tongue peeking through her lips and hid a grin, reminded of Daisy.

She seemed different. Not just the haircut, which made him notice how large and unusual her deep brown eyes were, but in her manner. Much more focussed and positive. His day job required him to be something of a psychologist. It was a useful skill, helping him detect a lie or avoid a pasting, and was never switched off, turning its radar on everyone. It was mostly body language and probably what policemen of old used to call 'copper's nose'.

He'd seen several versions of Lucy in the short time he'd known her. She'd been terrible that first day – although she'd certainly seemed to have fun, despite failing. Then nervous, over-confident and on that weird day in the rain when she'd totally lost it, she'd been angry, but he'd sensed that somewhere deep down she'd wanted to laugh.

Then with her husband in the café – how would he describe it? Timid. As if all the air had whooshed out of her. He hadn't liked seeing her like that.

'Okay, so I start by pushing the bike into the "garage".' She glanced up at him. 'Then slalom, Figure of Eight – through the cones, *through* the cones!' She mimicked him faultlessly and then talked her way through the entire test. 'Module One, Ms Lucy Daumier.' She held up an imaginary certificate and pretended to bow around the room. 'Thank you. Thank you. I'd like to thank my producer, my agent, and my bike trainer ...' she said in the style of a BAFTA acceptance speech.

He laughed. 'Daumier. Unusual name.'

'Yes. My Dad's French. I've kept it as it's more interesting than my married name. My parents are out there now full time. Mum had cancer years ago, and the health insurance paid off the mortgage.'

'Wow. But she's ok, isn't she?'

'Yes. She's amazing.' Lucy nodded. 'It made them reassess their lives. Dad's an academic, so a lot of what he does can be done online, anywhere. Mum was a teacher, and I think she wanted a different challenge. They both loved France – well, it's where Dad is from and where they met, so—' She gazed out of the window, remembering.

'So they bought a little place in France and moved.' She laughed shortly. 'They left their scatter-brained artist daughter, with the unpredictable income, in the house, so that there was always somewhere to come back to if they needed to.' She looked rueful then added, 'Good for holidays, but I do miss them.'

'How often do you go over?'

'Once a year. Sometimes, not even that. They're not easy

to get to, it's a bit of a trek – plane and drive or ferry and drive. It's a long way south and off the beaten track. Gerry says we …' She tailed off, looking pensive, and turning her mug round and round. 'Ugh, this coffee is terrible! Even I could make a better coffee than this.'

'I heard Gerry say something about the coffee machine that time in the café – what's that about?'

She blushed, looking down into her cup.

'When we first opened the café, Richard was desperate for one of those all singing, all dancing coffee machines; they're like the size of a small *car*. But you do everything with it – grind the beans, boil the water, steam and stretch the milk so you can make those pattern things on the top. Honestly, it's like being a train driver standing in front of those controls. Anyway, we had to do a course to learn how to work it. Richard took to it straight away, but I didn't. Either I burned the coffee or myself, or I put too much coffee in, or the milk boiled over, or there was more coffee on the floor than in the cup.' She laughed ruefully. 'So Richard banned me. And I've never gone near it since. Of course, Gerry uses it to illustrate my incompetence at everything else. He thinks it's hilarious.'

'What does Gerry think about you riding?' he said into the long pause.

'Hmm. Well …' Her mouth twisted and she shrugged her eyebrows.

It was none of his business, he knew. But seeing her mood switch was like turning out the lights. He waited. Old policeman's trick. People generally filled a silence if you waited long enough.

She sighed.

'He said he was "worried sick" about me being on the bike,' she said finally. 'He wants me to sell it.'

'And what do you want to do?'

'Keep it. I want to pass my test. I want to prove to him that I can do it.' She flashed a fierce glance at him.

'Okay …' He thought for a moment. 'What about the bike, is it still at the dealer's?'

'Yep. I'm planning to ride it away in a fanfare of trumpets when I've got that Pass Certificate in my hand. I've *got* to do this!'

To his own surprise he said, 'Is your van empty?'

'Yes. Why?'

'Perfect. How about we go and collect it and you do today's practice on your own bike then?'

She was staring at him, her eyes wide.

'Collect the bike? In my van? Ride it *now*?'

He laughed at her expression.

'Well, that's what it's for. Why not? You could store it at the Bike Palace, practise on it here, it's private property – and you could even use it to take your test on. It would save you a fair bit of money, you wouldn't have to keep hiring the school bikes. Of course, the downside is, if you drop it, then you run the risk of damaging it. And you'd have to pay me privately instead of the school. But my rates are reasonable, and if you can fit in round my shifts, we could do shorter sessions, more often. What do you think?'

She stood up. 'Come on, stop lolling about. You've got a desperate learner here with a bike to collect.'

He grinned, pleased at her determination.

'You're going to need to get some bike gear too. You can't keep borrowing the school stuff if you're on your own bike. I can get you some decent discounts at the dealer's.'

'Really? Thank you so much. Oh, I am so excited!'

'Daisy persuaded Mum to try and decorate their next cupcake baking session with the giant swirly buttercream like your friend Richard's,' he told her as they walked back to Better Biking. 'Apparently more of the buttercream went into Daisy's mouth than on the cakes. She spent the rest of the day in a sugar rush and was running laps around the garden.' He snorted a laugh. 'Dad had to put her to work washing the windows.'

'All that energy. It's wasted on the young. I bet your parents love having her.' Lucy smiled. 'She seems like a great kid.'

He nodded. 'She is. Have you got kids?'

She was silent and he glanced sideways to see her shaking her head.

'No. I, er, that is, Gerry, um ...' She shrugged, chewing her lip.

He cursed himself for spoiling the mood, wondering what had happened to stop them having children. She seemed very at ease with Daisy, and he got the impression that it wasn't a mutual decision the way some couples were very happy never to have kids. Maybe she couldn't. Maybe he couldn't. He searched for something else to say and failed. They were silent for the last hundred yards.

Shedding the borrowed school gear, Lucy reflected with a pang on her childless state. She hadn't known how to answer Ash's innocent enough question, feeling that he somehow deserved more than her usual flippant-sounding response that they were too busy – as if their social whirl demanded every waking second of their lives.

But confronted with her current disquieting dissatisfaction with her life, she had just ended up saying nothing. Which had obviously left Ash feeling awkward because he'd said nothing either. She pushed her worries to the back of her mind. No point on dwelling on this stuff now.

By the time they'd been over to the Bike Palace, confirmed that she could store the bike there for a small fee, and borrowed some tie-down straps, Lucy sprang into the cab of her van feeling overwhelmed with excitement. Having started the engine, her mind went blank.

'What?' he said, looking over at her.

'I can't remember how to get there.' She flicked her eyes across to him. She was so excited at the thought of bringing Cadbury home, she couldn't think of anything else. This biking thing had taken over her entire brain.

'Want me to drive?'

'I can drive, thank you. It's just – momentarily slipped my mind,' she flashed back as she saw him suppress a grin.

As he began to direct her, it all came back to her and with relief, she accelerated harder than she meant to. The van lurched over a pot hole.

'Oof. You missed one.' Ash braced himself on the dashboard.

'Sorry. This road's awful isn't it?' Lucy was hunched forward, concentrating on steering around the worst bits.

'It's the lorries. Plus, it's private property in places so it doesn't get resurfaced by the council.' Ash's voice juddered as the empty van bounced between the deep ruts and they nosedived into another crater.

'Do you drive this all the time?' he asked, his voice bouncing along with the suspension.

'Yes. Why?' She glanced curiously at him as he stared straight ahead.

'No reason. I just wondered whether you had the use of a car as well.'

'No. Gerry's the one with the luxury car.' She recited the Lexus' list of refinements, adding, 'microwave, whirlpool bath and steam spa,' for good measure.

He didn't laugh and she flicked her gaze towards him to see him concentrating on the road, remembering in a flash that he was a policeman. Hell, was he assessing her driving as well as her riding?

Feeling under surveillance, she popped onto the main road like a cork out of a bottle, crashing the gears and leapfrogging the van in a way she hadn't since she was a learner. She felt hot with embarrassment and risked a glance at Ash, who was sitting sphinx-like in the passenger seat. He'd probably decided she was as incompetent a driver as a rider now. As her mind coiled into tight springs of self-doubt, she sailed past the right turn she meant to take. Ash lifted his hand with a pointed finger as they passed.

'I know,' she squeaked, flustered.

Checking her wing mirrors, she indicated left and whirled the van around in the gateway to a field. More scraping of gears and bumping about. She was beginning to feel hot and sweaty. Why hadn't she let him drive? He probably had some sort of policeman's insurance that meant he could drive everything anyway. That would have been so much easier. They flew out of the gateway and slewed left at the junction almost on two wheels.

She couldn't make conversation, couldn't even look at him – she knew what expression Gerry would have assumed by now, if he'd even have let her drive in the first place.

When she wasn't crunching the gear-box, she was fixated on the speedo. What was the speed limit here? A country road – was it 60 or 70? Well, 70mph in the van felt like 100mph in any other vehicle, so she was never going that fast. Would he think she drove too slowly?

Out of the corner of her eye she saw him look over at her.

'What?' she almost screamed.

'What?' He sounded puzzled.

'Stop *looking* at me!' she screeched.

He tilted his head at her. 'I was checking out that house over there. The garage was open.'

'Are you *ever* off duty?'

'There was a guy working on an old bike there,' he explained in patient tones. 'I'm interested in old bikes.'

'Oh.' She sounded like a lunatic and groaned inwardly.

'What does this run on?' he enquired casually.

'Diesel. Why?'

Looking ahead, he said, 'I just wondered if you might have put kangaroo juice in instead.'

She whipped her head round to look at him.

Straight-faced, he continued, 'It's fine. I've still got some fillings left in my teeth. Have you thought about maybe adding a neck brace for your passengers? Or perhaps an ejector seat?'

Horrified, she stared ahead, and then exploded into laughter.

'Oh! You're so cheeky ...'

'I felt like I was on a pursuit for a minute. Or an extra in one of those *Transporter* films.' He grinned sideways at her. 'Have you ever applied to join the police? You'd be great chucking the Transits about. I don't think I've ever visited a field gate at that speed before.'

Gusts of laughter overtook both of them and they were still grinning when they got out at Mega Bikes and walked into the smart showroom.

Chapter Twelve

Cadbury was in their storage area and as they waited for him to be brought out, together with the relevant paperwork, Ash shepherded her towards the helmets.

'You can get everything else second-hand on eBay – but not your helmet. Very important, heads.'

Lucy was astonished by the variety of design and colour on the enormous display of helmets. They were stunning. She wandered over to a spectacular helmet decorated with iridescent swirls and as she inspected it more closely, skulls. It was as if it had been tattooed. The price tag was not quite so alluring, however, and she was still standing with her mouth open when Ash appeared beside her with a disappointingly plain helmet in pale silver grey.

'This is a top quality helmet, but it's their entry level, so not too expensive. I've asked them for an Extra Small so you can try it on. That's the size you've been wearing.' He must have seen Lucy's eyes flicking enviously towards the colourful helmets as he added, 'Lids get a tough life when you first start riding, and you might find yourself having to replace them reasonably often. Build up to the expensive ones.'

'Lids?'

'Otherwise known as helmets.'

The assistant appeared with the boxed helmet and handed it to Lucy, who pulled it on and fiddled with the unfamiliar chin strap.

'Can I help?' Ash asked.

She nodded, feeling flustered as she felt his warm fingers under her chin feeding the strap through the d-rings and pulling it snug. Her entire head felt as if it was being cradled, and it smelled new, and not at all like the ones she'd been borrowing from Ed and the bike school.

'All right?'

'I think so.'

He stood in front of her and held the helmet in both hands, looking straight into her eyes. Her mouth dried as she stood staring at him.

'I said, can you turn your head?'

She snapped back into the present and tried to turn her head as he held the helmet immobile. He looked satisfied.

'Looks like you're one of the lucky ones. Most people have to try on the whole shop to find one that's just right.'

She was removing the helmet as the assistant returned with a pile of boxes.

'I don't know if your missus wants to try these? They're all XS.'

'Oh, we're not …' Lucy's eyes darted to Ash as he was telling the assistant that Lucy was his student. Easy mistake, she thought, remembering the way they'd come in laughing together, and the way Ash had been adjusting her chin strap and staring into her eyes.

Her stomach flipped. What was she thinking? He was a married man. She was a married woman, even if she was right off Gerry at the moment. Every couple went through 'phases', she thought. They'd just have to work harder at getting their relationship back on track. She was the one rocking the boat, after all, wasn't she? She risked a sideways glance at Ash and to her horror their eyes met and she felt her stomach somersault again.

'Let's try this one,' she said, reaching out for another helmet and attempting to look businesslike. As soon as it was on her head she knew it was wrong, but at least the awkward moment had passed. She had been hoping to try some clothing on but she felt too shy to ask now.

'The Arai lid please. Ladies' bike gear?' Ash asked the assistant as he boxed up the new lid. Lucy felt hot and a bit sick. She couldn't start trying on trousers in front of Ash.

The assistant, a thin young man with an easy manner, led them over to the clothing department. 'Leathers or Textiles?' he asked her.

Lucy looked at Ash. It was like learning a foreign language. What on earth was he talking about?

'Textiles are more versatile.' Ash nodded. 'You can't really wear leathers in the rain, but you can wear textiles in the summer and layer them up in the winter.'

'Oh, but these are so gorgeous!' blurted Lucy, unable to stop stroking the butter soft leather jackets.

'You could have leathers, but then you'd have to carry waterproofs all the time. Your choice.' Ash nodded.

'What have you got?'

He laughed. 'Both.'

'Oh. How helpful.'

The assistant, overhearing their conversation, was rooting about and handed Lucy a black and white jacket.

'This one's the best of both worlds – it's leather but with a waterproof lining, and textile panels. It's not the cheapest, but if you look on it as two jackets in one …'

Lucy hefted the jacket, reading the size on the hanger. Size 16.

'I'll try it.' She took her own jacket off and slid her arms inside the new one. The thick and soft leather smelt lovely. Connecting the zip was tricky as the jacket was unyielding and once again Ash reached over to rescue her.

'Nice,' he said approvingly. 'A bit big, maybe.'

The assistant nodded in agreement and went to get the 14.

'There's a mirror over there.'

Lucy almost skipped over to see her reflection, and once

in front of it, didn't recognise herself. *Wow!* The shoulder-padding combined with the cleverly stitched panels to emphasise her waist, and the jacket flared out slightly at the hem.

She twirled this way and that, smiling in delight. Totally worth missing all those bacon sandwiches to have a jacket like this, she decided. She was even turning down Richard's free cake samples these days.

She returned to Ash and the assistant, who was waiting with the next size down.

'It feels lovely. Why do you think it's too big?' she asked them.

'It needs to be snug so the armour stays in the correct place,' explained the assistant. 'Too loose, and the armour moves if you crash. You don't want that.'

She fumbled to unzip the jacket.

'They're all a bit stiff in the beginning. They soon ease up.' The assistant handed her the other jacket. This one felt like a second skin, and accentuated her curves like a corset. She almost felt embarrassed admiring herself like this.

She looked pleadingly at Ash and he held his hands up. 'Don't look at me like that. It's not up to me – it's your decision,' he told her.

Lucy looked at the price tag and chewed her lip.

'What's your best price for the jacket plus the lid?' Ash asked the assistant, walking him towards the tills. 'Not forgetting my discount of course.'

Lucy meandered after them, eyeing the matching trousers, picking up the funkiest looking boots and fiddling with the high tech fastenings and toggles on the gloves. Everything smelled of expensive leather. It was heaven.

Ash returned to her.

'Ok. He'll give us a 20% discount, plus, as you apparently gave them a really good price for the catering, they'll throw in a £50 voucher. How about getting the trousers to match? And you need boots and gloves.'

Lucy swallowed. She could afford it – but how was she going to pay without Gerry seeing it on her bank account? Swatting the thought away as quickly as it arrived, she decided she'd pay on her credit card, and deal with the fallout when the statement turned up in 30 days' time. She'd have her licence by then. She could stand her ground. He never discussed his golfing purchases with her, after all.

'A £50 voucher? Incredible! How did you swing that?'

'I have my uses. Come on, before he changes his mind,' he teased.

Trousers proved to be a little more problematic than the jacket and to Lucy's utter chagrin she had to go up 2 sizes to get a pair that fit properly. The assistant had returned and had been invaluable, hovering near the changing rooms and finding different styles.

'Honestly, don't worry about the sizing. They always come up small. It's ridiculous, I know. You could always cut the label out if it bothers you. Get the tightest pair you can still breathe in because they do give – you can sit on one of the bikes to check you can bend your legs.'

Eventually Lucy found a pair she liked, emerged self-consciously from the changing rooms and went in search of the bike to sit on. She swung her leather-clad leg over the seat and pushed it upright off the side-stand, while Ash held it steady with the front wheel between his knees. She squealed, staring in horror at the glossy bikes on either side of her. If she overbalanced now she'd be bankrupted.

'Don't drop me!'

'I won't drop you.' His blue eyes met hers, and her stomach danced a jig. 'Put both feet on the pegs and lean forward as if you're riding. Make sure you can bend your knees.'

The trousers were a bit gappy at the back of the waist as she bent forward, but the assistant told her they could be zipped to the jacket which meant her back wasn't exposed. By the time she'd added a pair of black and white boots, Lucy was beginning to feel like a biker.

Ash was patience personified. In fact, she began to think he was enjoying it as much as she was, tirelessly browsing for sizes and styles. He really was a good egg, she thought, watching him; to think how scared she'd been of him in the beginning. He'd turned out to be a bit of a hero really.

With gloves finally added to the pile, it was time to melt her credit card. She had never enjoyed spending so much. It felt like the passport to a new life, a new Lucy. A new, black-and-white-leather-clad Lucy on a beautiful purple bike. She would show Gerry the new her. That would make him sit up and take notice. She would also get Richard to show her how to use that wretched coffee machine next.

They'd just stashed her purchases into the van as Lucy heard a throaty roar, and turned in time to see her Cadbury being ridden around the side of the building. Her face split with glee. Now that she knew a little more about bikes she could appreciate it even more. It was muscular and yet somehow feminine with its curvy pipes and high, under-seat exhaust. The seat narrowed wasp-like to a point behind the rider, and the twin diamond-eye shaped headlights reminded her of the *Transformers* films, in which cars turned into giant robots. This bike had a personality. Lucy hoped she could live up to it.

The assistant riding it twisted the throttle with a grin, enjoying the engine note as it growled and burbled thrillingly, and then switched the engine off.

'Beautiful, these Triples. You're a lucky lady. It's already got crash bungs on it, as you're a learner. They'll give it some protection if you drop it,' he said as he climbed off and handed her the keys. She stared down at them in her hand.

'Can I sit on it?' Her mouth was dry and it came out as a whisper. The two men laughed.

'It's yours now. You can do what you want with it – wheelie it down the road if you like,' said the assistant. 'I'll go and get the paperwork and then we'll give you a hand loading it.'

Lucy carefully pivoted her leg across the bike. Her hands shook. Squeezing the brake and clutch levers she gave the throttle an experimental twist, remembering the sound of that exhaust and imagining how it would feel to ride. She was terrified and exhilarated in equal measure.

She looked down at the purple tank, glistening in the afternoon sunlight, wanting to savour this moment, to remember exactly how it felt to straddle this bike which had already changed her life in ways she couldn't have imagined.

The assistant returned with the paperwork and a ramp and Lucy almost couldn't bear to watch as Cadbury was wheeled up and into her van. What if they dropped him off the ramp? She hopped anxiously from foot to foot until the bike was tethered safely, and stared down with a sense of disbelief at the registration document which bore her name.

At the last minute she whipped out her phone, took a photo of the inside of her van, and sent it to Nicola's mobile.

'*Look what I've got! So much to tell you. Lunch tomorrow, Art Café? xx*' The reply beeped back within minutes:

'*Squeeeeeeeeeeeeeeeeeee!!!!!!!!!!! C U 2moro :) xx*'

The van doors closed, the assistant was shaking Ash's hand, and Lucy stepped forward to shake his hand, changed her mind and hugged him instead.

'Thank you so much.'

'No probs. Enjoy! Oh, hang on, back in a mo.' He dashed off, returning with a set of L plates for her. 'They're not new, but it all helps. Good luck!'

Lucy was overwhelmed by everyone's kindness. She climbed into the driver's seat with shaky legs and looked anxiously at Ash beside her. 'Do you want to drive?'

'Why?'

'I'm a bit worried about him falling over ...'

'It's not going anywhere. Go on, you'll be fine. Maybe a bit less off-roading on the way back would be good.' He grinned.

As they reached the quieter, familiar country roads she switched on the radio.

'Oh, goodness me, this is a blast from the past. It's even older than I am. My Mum and Dad always loved The Beatles, listen to this ...' She reached forward and turned the volume up a bit, as 'Ticket to Ride' came on, the sound quality tinny compared to contemporary recordings. Not remembering all the words, she sang lustily along with the simple chorus, as she always did in her van. Gerry hated her singing along if they were in his car, and would reach out and switch the radio off, leaving her voice stranded tunelessly in the silence, which he always thought funny. She belatedly flicked a glance at Ash, delighted to see him miming along, and turned up the volume in case he wanted to join in.

As the music faded out, he mused, 'That's what you have, a Ticket to Ride.'

'Oh, yeah!' Her face warmed by the afternoon spring sunshine flooding the big windscreen, Lucy couldn't remember being happier. Glancing at the clock, she realised there was only an hour left of her day.

'Sorry, I hope I haven't made you late finishing today.'

'Don't worry, I've got a good support crew. If I didn't, I wouldn't be able to do this, for starters.'

'Er ... support crew? I don't understand.' Lucy glanced across at him, warily, worried that she was prying.

He paused for a moment before saying lightly, 'I'm a widower. Daisy's mum died.'

'Oh.' She was shocked. He'd said it mechanically, as if he was used to explaining himself. Her eyes pricked with tears. She hadn't expected that, but it made sense – why Ed and Angela looked after Daisy when Ash was training. So he was a single dad of a little girl. And she'd been horrible to him, saying he hated women or something stupid. She wanted to eat her words.

'What does Daisy do when you're working late?'

'I leave her on the doorstep with a dry biscuit, she's fine,' he teased. 'No, one of the grandparents collects her. Or my sister-in-law, Sarah.'

'I'm surprised that you still do the bike training. I mean I'm glad you do because you're brilliant at it, but it must take up such a lot of your time?'

'Well yes, it does. But I enjoy it. Mostly. When people aren't throwing the bikes all over the place, or making me run the length of the runway after them.' He made a mock stern face at her. 'I can't go out in the evenings unless it's planned in advance with babysitters, which meant that all I was doing was work and home. So Mum sat me down one day and said that I needed to keep doing something that was for me, and not just about Daisy. And that is *this*.'

'Wow. Your Mum sounds fantastic.'

'She is. Anyway, I do enjoy it, and I really believe that the better your training is, the safer you are on a bike.'

'Do you know a good trainer then?' said Lucy, her expression innocent.

'Can you get this bike out of the van yourself?' he said and laughed as she turned a horrified expression on him.

Ed saw them pull up outside and came out with a ramp.

He nudged Lucy and said in a stage whisper, 'Getting on a bit better with your trainer now, I see?'

'Yes, thank you Ed,' she said crisply, nudging him back and rolling her eyes. The two men manhandled her bike out and stood admiring it for a moment.

'I'll ride it round to the school. You drive round and get changed.' Ash nodded. 'Use the school stuff for now, it'll be quicker. See you in a bit.'

Back once more at the arena, her pulse quickened in anticipation.

'I want you to just ride around the circuit, go up and down the gears. If you feel like it, try the slalom. You like that. In your own time.' He swept his arm forward in a grand gesture, and Lucy concentrated on finding the clutch point, moving forward at snail's pace. The fact that it didn't leap off like a nervous racehorse gave her confidence.

Turning her head – properly, these days – she aimed at the slalom, and slowly passed each brightly coloured cone.

'Brilliant,' said Ash. 'Figure of Eight next.'

One manoeuvre after another seemed to unroll before her tyres.

'Get on with it woman, I'm freezing over here,' he said, making a show of looking at his watch as she sailed past him with a cheeky grin on her face. She knew he would call her in when her time was up, and continued around the arena with the manoeuvres he'd taught her.

She was disappointed when she heard him say, 'Great stuff. You're well on track for your test.' He gave her a thumbs up. 'Great way to finish the day.'

Just need to pass my Theory test next. She'd booked the earliest slot available, and it was still two weeks away. If she didn't pass that, she couldn't do the Module One test two weeks later. It seemed like a long way off, but it would fly past. It had already been six weeks since she'd won

Cadbury. She cruised to a reluctant halt beside him, and climbed off, so that he could pillion her back. 'Ash?'

About to pull his helmet on, he paused.

'Thank you. I haven't enjoyed a day this much since – well ...' She shrugged eloquently.

'Me neither.' His blue eyes crinkled at the corners and butterflies danced in her stomach.

She tried to tell herself they were just nerves because of the tests. It wasn't at all that she found him extraordinarily attractive. He was just a really nice guy who was very good at his job. It was the bike effect. It made all her nerve endings stand to attention. Yes. That's what it was.

The Bike Effect. She was in love with her bike.

Chapter Thirteen

On Sunday, Gerry left as usual for his day of golf, leaving Lucy to her own devices, which was perfect, giving her plenty of time to practise for her Theory test the following Tuesday. Her new bike leathers were still a bit stiff and, taking advice from Nicola, she took every opportunity to wear them around the house, bending and stretching to mould them to her body. She'd worn them to ride in a few times since collecting Cadbury, feeling very self-conscious, but had been amazed how much more precise her actions seemed. Ash's shifts confused the heck out of her, but she was really enjoying their short, focused training sessions. She'd mastered most of the manoeuvres, except the speed test on the curve where, to Ash's amusement, she was consistently 10mph under-speed.

'What happened to Rocket-woman?'

'I'm fine in a straight line,' she ruminated. 'Just not so keen on that curve. I feel as if I'm going to fall over.'

'It's only 30mph.'

'I know. But it seems so much faster on a bend.'

'Keep practising! Once more, and we'll call it a day.' He'd shooed her away, and she'd sped off with a smile on her face, recalling her earlier failures and marvelling at how they had been overcome. Persistence was everything.

Sundays had also become a day when she met Nicola and the other bike girls from the Curvy Rider club, in the café, at the end of their ride-outs. Their confidence made her head spin, but they were so welcoming, and she couldn't wait to pass her test and go out with them. Gerry could keep his golf. She was planning to have much more fun.

As busy as she was, however, juggling her bike training

with sales and orders at the café, she'd have to be blind not to notice that her and Gerry's relationship was becoming more and more separate. He made assumptions she didn't challenge – planning boys only golf weekends and only letting her know in passing, if at all. And he ate out with clients as part of his working day without telling her she needn't cook an evening meal for him. She was starting to wonder when that had become her 'job' anyway – what happened to sharing the cooking? They both worked after all. When he was home, he hogged the remote, never asked what she wanted to watch, and she simply disappeared to her studio, her sanctuary, leaving him to it.

When she looked back, she couldn't even remember how long ago the threads of their intertwined lives had begun to unravel. They'd always had busy lives, but there hadn't been a time that they weren't interested in each other. Now though ... she seemed to have been dancing to his tune for so long. Well, it wasn't too late, she decided. It took two to make a marriage work and it seemed to her that her passivity contributed to Gerry's natural tendency towards ... she hunted for the word, refusing to use the words her mind had instantly supplied – overbearing, dominant – and settled for 'leadership'.

She kept the word 'bullying' firmly suppressed, looking forward to the moment when she could appear before him, in full regalia, with that motorcycle licence in her hand. She felt sure his view of her would change.

She'd spent so long rehearsing the Theory test on various online sites that even the journey to the test centre on Tuesday morning felt like a giant video game. The part of the test she dreaded was the Hazard Perception section. A film was played in which she was the biker, and had to click the mouse at any developing hazard. During her first practices she'd clicked wildly and way too early at any hazard, and failed, then too late. She knew her Highway Code inside out, but it was the clicking thing that worried her.

The test was held in a small plain room with glass booths, and Lucy could see candidates inside, hunched over screens, the only movement the clicking of their mouse. She joined a queue of teenagers with pinched faces, holding Provisional Licences. The elderly man who checked her driving licence looked up at her with an approving smile. 'Motorcycle Theory, eh? Good for you. Not enough ladies who bike.'

Feeling strangely disembodied, she followed him into a booth and concentrated on his instructions. Seated before the screen with the headphones on, she felt a sense of joyous wonderment that she'd got this far. Words scrolled up on the screen and she paid attention. This was it. The gateway to her full bike licence.

Nicola popped into the Art Café as they were closing. While Richard checked the fridges for stock, Lucy made them a peppermint tea, and they sat at a table overlooking the beach.

'How did today go?'

'I got 97% on the Theory test.' Lucy beamed with pride. 'I only failed three questions.'

'Congratulations!' Richard laid a small platter of tiny cupcakes before them. 'Just samples. There's no calories in samples.'

'Great stuff!' Nicola stretched out an eager hand. 'So, two weeks to go now. Who's covering you while you take your Mod One test, Luce? Not me. I'm away on a course on accountancy fraud. I know how to live on the edge, I do.'

'Ella is, our art student.'

'Oh, I've seen her – the tall, leggy one that drifts about with an eighteen-inch waist and all the hair? How's she getting on?'

'Fine actually. Does she drift about? I've never noticed.' Lucy sat forward and lowered her voice, even though there was no-one else in the building. 'I worry about her a bit; she seems terribly young sometimes. She's got a much older boyfriend by all accounts.'

Nicola shook her head. 'What on earth makes young girls go for much older blokes? I never did. I like 'em young and energetic personally!' She shrugged her eyebrows up and down, making Lucy laugh.

'I don't know. I guess boys your own age can be a bit oafish, can't they? She sounds very taken with him. I just hope she's careful, that's all.' She laughed. 'I sound more like her mother than her boss, don't I?'

'Oh, girls today are so much older than they used to be. I expect she'll dump him when his knees start giving out and he starts moaning about his back. Changing the subject – how's the TV Tom order coming along?' asked Nicola between mouthfuls.

'Good. It's all confirmed and the frames are ordered, a nice wide, chunky moulding. I'm happy with one of the paintings so far, and the prints are on order.'

'And what about Gerry, is he behaving these days?'

'Gerry? He's a law unto himself.' Lucy shrugged, beginning to feel a bit as if she was being interrogated. 'And I've been busy, what with the TV Tom order, doing the invoicing, and trying to swot up on the Highway code for my Theory test. If we're in the same room, he's channel flicking, and I've been on the laptop, doing my Hazard Perception practice, with the sound off.'

Nicola eyed her owlishly over her tea.

'I read somewhere that's the modern marriage. So, no more drunken outbursts then? And demands to sell your bike?'

Lucy shifted uncomfortably.

'We just, well, don't seem to talk about it. I mean, obviously he knows I've still got the bike. He just doesn't know when I'm riding it.' She made a noise somewhere between a snort and a laugh, and added, 'As far as I know.'

'Bloody hell Lucy, just tell him! It's your bike, and you're keeping it.'

'I will.'

'When?'

'When I get my licence.'

'Well, hurry up and get it then.'

'I will. Stop nagging me.'

Nicola slid down in her seat, looking like a naughty schoolgirl.

'Hah! Talk about role reversal.' She pretended to pout. 'Makes a change for you to tell me what to do. I like it.'

Lucy liked it too. It was as if the real her, hidden for so long, was beginning to surface. And it was about time.

'Richard says the same as you.'

Nicola's face lit up. 'Yes. He's a sweetheart. I love that he pretends to let me boss him about.'

Lucy laughed. 'He's been well brought up by all those sisters.'

'I could do with a bit of his energy. Does he ever stop?'

'And he stays so thin around all that cake. Life's not fair is it?' Lucy grinned, patting her own shrinking stomach.

'Yeah, he's getting thinner, and I'm getting fatter.'

Lucy still saw a raven-haired beanpole before her and snorted in derision. 'Still plenty of room in your leathers, I bet.'

Lucy's life was packed, between the café, painting commissions, and squeezing in as much bike training as she possibly could. Having her bike at the Bike Palace meant that if she could persuade Ed to ride it over to the private bit of waste ground near the dirt track, she could follow him in her van and practise her manoeuvres on it as often as possible, which was helping enormously.

She'd also started a blog focussing on her bike training, and was quietly thrilled to find that it was gathering readers nicely. She'd felt so miffed by the sizing on her new leather bike jeans that she'd written it up before the feelings of outrage evaporated. So many ladies had replied with similar stories that she'd followed up her blog with a flurry of letters and emails to as many bike clothing manufacturers as she could find, offering to review their ranges.

All the bike magazines she'd read were full of clothing reviews for men. There was never anything for ladies. She could feel a crusade coming on.

Two weeks passed in a whirlwind. Lucy could barely believe they were already in May. The Welsh coast basked in the late spring sunshine, turning the sea turquoise and glittering. Wildflowers bejewelled the hedgerows, and visitors to the café relaxed in the warmth, opting to have their coffees on the sunny terrace. Lucy was pleased that they'd made the decision to take on more staff. Days off like this would have been unimaginable, otherwise.

On Monday morning, she arrived ridiculously early at the not yet open Vintage Bike Palace, having told a still yawning Gerry she was going off to paint on location for the day, for the TV Tom order. Feeling guilty about lying, she swept aside the observation that Gerry hadn't really seemed very interested in what she had planned for her day in any case.

Struggling into her leathers in the confined space of her van, she jumped at the loud drumming on the side panels.

'Kettle's on!' She recognised Ed's dad's voice and breathed out in relief, breathing back in again to fasten the zip and hook on her trousers.

Ed's dad let out a long whistle of appreciation as she jumped out of the back of the van.

'Two lovely girls out together.' He nodded at Cadbury, shiny and ready to go near the front of the workshop. The bike looked like a lifestyle advert for an aspirational magazine. 'And looks like you're going to be lucky with the weather. Good luck with the test.'

'Thanks Griff.' Lucy's mouth was dry with nerves. She turned as she recognised the distinctive exhaust note of Ash's powerful Triumph Explorer.

'Morning!' He greeted them both, placing his helmet carefully on the counter, and then looking appraisingly at Lucy. 'Looking forward to it?'

Although her stomach was doing bungee jumps, she tried to nod breezily and smile.

'You'll be fine. We'll have a nice ride there today, that will relax you.' He accepted Griff's offer of coffee with a smile.

She took strength from his confidence in her, calming her breathing. He was so unruffled, he made everything seem possible. She felt that if she didn't pass, she'd be failing *him*, not herself.

She had done well in training. The only thing she still struggled with was pushing the bike about, which was right at the beginning of the test. She was terrified of dropping it and felt every gram of its two hundred or so kilos. Until trying to pick a bike up on that first, awful day, she'd had no idea motorbikes were so heavy.

Ash had thought it was the easiest part, and had thrown in that part of the test almost casually at the end of a session, to her horror.

She'd managed it eventually, by learning to balance the bike upright rather than having it lean against her as she had been doing, but she really wasn't looking forward to repeating the process under the beady eye of the examiner.

As she sipped her tea, to her surprise, Rhodri from her CBT arrived, on a snazzy 125cc that looked like a much more powerful bike. His skinny frame was newly kitted out, but unlike Lucy, he had opted for an all-weather textile outfit. He grinned at her, and jerked his head at her bike.

'You got there in the end then.'

'Eventually. It was worth waiting for.' Lucy was delighted to see a friendly face, and to have someone to share the experience with. 'This is a nice surprise, and what a lovely bike! I thought you weren't going to bother with your full test?'

'I wasn't,' conceded Rhodri, 'but that CBT made me realise how little I really knew about being on the road, so the more training I do, the safer I'll be.'

'Sensible young man.' Ash nodded, sipping his drink.

After checking their paperwork, Ash handed them each a hi-viz waistcoat, and a headset with microphone.

'These are two-way, unlike the school radios. They pick up your voice from the vibrations of your jawbone, so we can all hear you,' he explained. 'So no singing aloud.' He crinkled his eyes at Lucy and she pretended to pout at his teasing. 'If you don't hear anything for a little while, the batteries might have failed, so pull over where it's safe and we'll change them. We're going to collect Pete next from his house, he's on the way.'

The test centre was a forty-minute drive by motorway, but an hour on the A and B roads which Lucy and Rhodri had to use on 'L' plates.

The early morning lemon sunshine threw alternate long lilac shadows across the quiet country lanes until they reached the busier town, but Ash shepherded them in his unflappable manner, and by the time Lucy saw Pete standing outside his house with his bike, she felt relaxed and focussed.

Pete looked like everyone's favourite Grandad: thickset, with a mass of silver hair, a wide smile that crinkled his eyes, and a jolly demeanour. Lucy wouldn't have been at all surprised if he'd produced a tube of Werther's Originals sweets from his top pocket and offered them around.

The whole day had started to feel like a jolly outing, and although Lucy wanted to pass more than anything, Ash made it all so calm, her nerves subsided and she began to enjoy the challenge of the increasing traffic, her mind whirling with remembered instructions about positioning, shoulder checks, speed, gears.

The memory of that CBT receded further, as her foot instinctively found the gear lever, or the foot brake as they slowed for lights. She almost couldn't conceive a time when she hadn't known how to even start the engine. Ash had been right – all you needed was perseverance.

Chapter Fourteen

The Test Centre was situated on the outskirts of the city, on a greyly anonymous industrial estate, beside a wide main road thrumming with heavy goods vehicles.

'We're turning right here guys, so shoulder checks, indicators and move into the centre of the road please,' Ash instructed his little posse from the back.

In the middle of the procession, Lucy thrilled as she watched them slot smoothly into position in single file, ready to turn into the road which fed the Test Centre. She was actually here. Every nerve end tingled with anticipation. She was so ready for this.

'Turn your heads to look where you're going here folks. The entrance is a tight right again, ok?' Ash's disembodied voice crackled in her ear.

Lucy saw the line of helmets nod, and guessed that like her, they were concentrating too hard to speak. The lorries rumbled past on either side, and she felt tiny and vulnerable in the middle of the road.

Pete, in front, looked immoveable and steady as a rock astride his black bike. She realised he was waiting for a big enough gap for all of them before moving off.

Come on, come on! she willed him silently, gripping the handlebars tighter. They seemed to have been sitting there for an eternity and she heaved a sigh of relief when she heard Ash say, 'Pete, go when it's safe for you. Don't wait for us.'

Finally, Pete picked his gap and went. Lucy had her eye on the gap just behind that, leaving Rhodri and Ash.

Concentrating hard, she manoeuvred the bike into the mouth of the junction and twisted her head to aim into the car park of the Test Centre, just in time to see Pete topple over with his bike in one of the parking spaces.

Oh no! Poor Pete! was Lucy's first thought, swiftly followed by a panicked, *Please God, don't let me do that!* She must have spoken the first bit aloud, as Ash spoke immediately in calm tones.

'Focus on what you're doing guys. Pete, shit happens. We'll sort you out in a minute, don't worry.'

Lucy was grateful for his disembodied presence. She'd gone completely to pieces, sitting in the middle of the junction, no idea what gear she was in, staring at poor Pete scrambling awkwardly to his feet beside his fallen bike.

Re-shuffling her mental processes, she quickly found neutral, then first gear, shoulder-checked and, desperate not to repeat Pete's mistake, rode straight into the first parking space she saw.

As she checked and double checked the side-stand was in position, she saw Rhodri and Ash ride into the same space behind her.

'Ok, leave the bikes where they are for now, we'll sort them out later. Pete, mate, are you ok?' Ash was off first and trotting towards him.

'Yeah, I'm fine,' he answered Ash's repeated question, rubbing his elbow. 'I can't believe I did that. Great start, huh? That'll teach me to check the side-stand is down.'

'Happens to us all. I've seen coppers do it on their work bikes too.' Ash nodded at someone through the big windows of the test centre.

In a couple of moments, a tall, burly man in bike gear emerged, and Lucy watched the two men carefully right the big bike without scraping the bodywork.

'One of the other instructors,' Ash explained, checking the bike over. 'Better to get it over with now than during the test.' He nodded at Pete, who was still looking miserable.

'Ok, we've got bags of time so I suggest we walk over and get a cuppa, have a comfort stop and then go down the road for a few practice runs.' He pointed to the burger van parked on the main road.

Lucy's legs were wobbly and she welcomed the idea of a short walk.

'All right?' She joshed Rhodri's elbow, seeing his pale, wide-eyed face.

He nodded, mutely. 'When I saw Pete's bike down there, I thought I was about to drop mine too,' he confessed.

'Yep. Me too,' admitted Lucy. 'But we didn't, did we? And come on, you were much better than me on our CBT, remember? When I wasn't taking off like a rocket, I was a one-woman demolition squad.'

He chuckled. 'Yeah. I didn't want you to use my bike in case you dropped that as well.'

Pete was trudging just behind them, and Lucy slowed, turning to include him in the conversation. 'Rhodri was just reminding himself about my "horizontal parking" on our CBT,' she told him. Seeing his face open with interest, she continued to tell him about her disastrous day, flicking a glance at Ash who was ambling along at the back, looking amused.

'You're a tonic, girl.' Pete roared with laughter, wiping his eyes. 'Well, you've come a long way since then. You look like you've been biking since forever now.'

Ash sent her a small nod of approval and Lucy felt a warm glow that she'd cheered Pete up, sipping the weak tea in its polystyrene cup. They chatted amiably until their drinks were finished, and Ash quietly herded them back to the test centre. After a visit to the loo, they took their bikes down the road to a disused carpark and went through a few of the manoeuvres.

Lucy wished they hadn't. Her U turn was terrible, and her

slow ride was jerky. Pete, on the other hand, had regained his confidence, and put in a perfect rehearsal.

'Don't dwell on past mistakes. Remember that you can all do this. Concentrate on the job in hand, ok?' Ash settled them all back on their bikes, leading them back to the test centre and ensuring their bikes were parked neatly facing outwards and ready to go, this time.

The Test Centre was lined with nervous looking faces – a mixture of bike and car test candidates. After Ash booked them all in, he sat beside her on one of the long benches around the wall.

Wishing she'd brought a book as a distraction from the butterflies clamouring for attention in her stomach, Lucy watched as people of all ages were called by their examiners, their expressions varying from calm and confident to pasty white and terrified.

It was a while before she realised she was attracting curious glances. Combing her fingers through her hair self-consciously, she leaned towards Ash. 'Have I got something on my face?' she hissed.

He turned a quizzical expression on her.

'Just the usual appendages,' he judged, finally, his mouth twitching upwards. 'Why?'

'Because people are looking at me.'

He glanced around the room.

'Oh, that's easy.' He shrugged, and she frowned at him. 'Why?'

'You're the only woman in here taking a bike test.'

A further scan of the room showed her he was right. The other women, mostly much younger than Lucy, were dressed in their ordinary clothes. One or two of them met her eye and she was surprised to see a mixture of envy and admiration on their faces. She laughed, remembering her birds nest hair, rain-soaked clothes, bruises and tantrums.

Today, in her smart leathers and swingy hair, she was just like the proverbial swan – poised in appearance, and paddling like mad in reality.

One of the women rose in response to the examiners call, and her eyes swivelled across to Lucy. 'Good luck!' she mouthed, smiling.

'You too!' Lucy gave her a thumbs up and smiled back, watching as she handed over her driving licence to the unsmiling examiner.

Rhodri's name was called next and he sprang nervously to his feet, his face draining of colour. Ash stood more slowly with him. Lucy heard him murmur, 'All right, Rhodri, mate?' and her heart went out to the gangly young man. He looked terrified.

'Good luck, Rhodders!' she called, and was rewarded with a tremulous smile.

'Go on lad, show 'em how it's done!' Pete joined in.

The instructor had to wheel the bike to the gate of the compound for the candidate to begin his test, so Ash had already left the building and Rhodri was ushered into the office for his paperwork check.

'Just going to the ladies',' she muttered to Pete. Lucy headed into the loo, situated just inside the big glass entrance doors.

Counting to 40, she walked purposefully out of the building, turning a sharp left towards the test compound, and walked straight into Ash peering round the corner of the building.

'Oof, sorry!' she spluttered, clutching his arm to save herself from falling. 'I just wanted to see how he got on.'

'Me too,' muttered Ash, his eyes on the compound. 'I don't want him to see us in case it puts him off.'

He pulled her in front of him so they could both see, and it was several moments before Lucy realised he was still holding her arm. For a heart-stopping moment, she wondered what it would be like to lean back into his comforting presence, feel his arms encircle her and gather her into an embrace.

She shook herself. *Get a grip, woman!*

'Cold?' he asked, releasing her arm as if he'd only just noticed it there.

She shook her head.

'No. Nerves.' It wasn't really a lie, she thought.

'You'll be fine,' he assured her again. 'Get this pernickety little beast under your belt, and you'll sail through the rest of it.'

They watched as Rhodri was put through his paces. In contrast to Lucy's sharp intakes of breath and little squeaks of alarm as he wobbled or brushed perilously close to a cone, Ash kept up a commentary throughout, quietly urging Rhodri on and groaning as he was asked to repeat the speed test. Lucy guessed he'd already watched thousands of students on this compound. She was impressed that he was still interested enough to come and watch how they got on.

And then, as that thought settled into her brain, she twisted her neck to look up at him.

'Don't watch *me*.' She frowned.

He was standing so close, she felt rather than heard him chuckle.

'Ok then,' he agreed, insincerely, and then tugged her arm. 'Quick, it's near the end. Looks like he's done ok. Let's go so he doesn't see us.' His face broke into a grin as he hustled her around the building and they scampered like children through the glass entrance doors.

Pete looked up enquiringly. 'Where'd you two lovebirds go?' he grinned knowingly at them.

Lucy's jaw dropped. Pete was summoned to the inner office at that exact moment. Which was a very good thing, as Lucy didn't have the faintest idea what she'd have said to him. And she daren't look at Ash's face. She didn't have long to fret over whatever Pete had meant as Rhodri appeared, wreathed in smiles, waving his Module One pass certificate at them. His previously pale face was suffused with pink as Lucy jumped up and hugged him, and Ash patted his back.

'Well done! You were brilliant!' Lucy blurted.

'Were you guys watching?'

'Er ...' Lucy bared her teeth in an, 'Oops, you got me' smile, and Rhodri laughed, relief showing all over his face.

'Pete's in there now, and Lucy's last. And apparently, we're not allowed to watch her.'

'Hope Pete does ok. He was pretty shaken up after he dropped his bike.' Lucy worried.

'Mmm. This is his third attempt. He gets in a bit of a state beforehand,' Ash explained. 'Fingers crossed it's third time lucky.' He went out to watch again. Lucy sat rigidly in her seat, astonished. Pete looked like the least likely person to 'get in a state'.

She sat, fidgeting on the bench, waiting for her call, and saw Pete trudge heavily back into the waiting room to await his verdict. He shook his head at Ash on his way past.

'Kicked a cone over, right at the end,' he said sadly.

Lucy's name was called as Pete disappeared into the office, and Ash rose to push her bike to the entrance.

'Right, what have you got to remember?' he asked her as she stood up carefully. Her legs didn't seem to belong to her any more.

'I can do it,' she recited by rote, 'and don't kick any cones over.'

'Attagirl. Knock 'em dead, Lucy.'

She was held for a long moment in the endless deep blue of his gaze, and absorbed his will that she succeed. Squaring her shoulders and taking a deep breath, she headed into the office, clutching her paperwork and helmet, her hands clammy with nerves.

The compound held no fears; it looked just like a more smoothly surfaced version of what she'd been practising on at Better Biking. The only difference was that this space held a hi-viz clad examiner with a clip board and a grave expression.

The very first stage was the last she'd conquered and her least favourite, but the terror of pushing her precious bike from one marked space, 'a garage' into the next 'garage', dissolved as soon as she'd successfully completed it.

Taking a deep breath, and remembering what Ash had told her about taking her time to get settled, she scrutinised the side of the building where they'd lurked earlier, and relaxed as she saw he wasn't there, as he'd promised.

The next twenty minutes seemed to pass in a whirl. There was no time to think about anything else but the minutiae of her task – a ballet of clutch, throttle and back brake. Her body felt taut, lean, compact in the snug leathers and every part of her contributed to the bike's direction and angle. She was almost sorry when the test was over. Almost ... As she paddled Cadbury carefully backwards into the parking space, knowing the examiner was still watching her, she felt an overwhelming sense of relief that it was all over, tempered with the fear that she hadn't done enough to pass.

It had seemed to go ok. She definitely hadn't kicked a cone over. The U turn had been a bit of a worry as usual, but had she managed the speed test and hazard avoidance? It had seemed quite fast, but as on previous attempts, she'd not been able to look at her speedo as she rounded the curve.

The examiner – goodness, how did they stay so poker-faced all the time? – led her back into the building. Ash, Pete and Rhodri stared at her in mute enquiry and she shrugged helplessly as she turned into the tiny office. The walls crowded in on her as she sat down. She could even hear the clock ticking.

The examiner was concentrating on the paperwork between them. Surely, he could hear her heart thudding. It was deafening her. She looked down, trying to interpret the little upside-down ticks and squiggles on the sheet in front of him.

'Ok,' he said after what seemed to be an eternity. 'U turns need more work, and you were a bit close to some of those cones.'

Her heart sank. Damn. She'd be coming back then. Probably with Pete. To her embarrassment, she felt hot pinpricks of tears threatening in the corners of her eyes. The examiner was still talking, pen poised over the yellow sheet.

'… and I thought you were going to get your knee down on that second speed test …,' he continued in his monotone.

She tried to be positive. It had been a good experience. Lots of people failed this part of the test many times. She'd do it on the next try.

His face cleared in a momentary grin which caught her by surprise.

'So I'm pleased to tell you that you've passed.' He stood up, handing over the certificate, duly signed and dated, and like a school headmaster, held out his other hand for her to shake it. 'Well done!'

Her hand shot out to grip his. In that instant she could have leapt across the table and hugged him, she was so unutterably delighted. The tears of self-pity fell as tears of joy, and she dashed them across her cheek.

'Thank you!' she beamed.

Breezing into the waiting room, she danced a little jig as she held her pass certificate aloft with both hands.

She stopped, seeing Pete's downcast face lift in a smile, and moved in for a hug.

'I'm sorry you didn't pass, Pete,' she told him quietly.

'Aw, don't you worry about that.' He grimaced heartily. 'Next time.'

'Wicked.' Rhodri fist-bumped her, which completely threw her as she was heading for a hug and made them both laugh.

Which just left Ash, standing slightly behind the others. Her joy eclipsed his usual reservation and she grabbed him in an impulsive hug, reaching up to plant a kiss on his cheek. Somehow, the kiss, aimed somewhere near his ear, collided with half his mouth – or had he turned his head? Her brain recorded everything about him in that instant. His lips were soft on hers, his arms already returning her hug and as she inhaled his fresh, soapy smell, her insides melted. As abruptly as it had happened, it ended and they flew apart like opposite ends of a magnet.

Chapter Fifteen

Ash turned away to collect his jacket and helmet to hide his unaccustomed discomposure. His brain whirled.

What the hell happened there? The poor girl had only tried to kiss me as a thank you and I nearly swallowed her!'

It was as if his brain had finally reconnected with his body. He'd been noticing her for some time now. It was impossible not to. Her enthusiasm for the training, her earnest swotting so she'd pass the Theory test, those deep brown eyes that sparkled whenever she mastered something ... it all added up to a pretty enticing package. And apart from her looks – the neat, curvy figure that went in and out in all the right places – he also found it appealing the way she stood and watched everyone else. Completely unself-conscious; unaware of the gazes she was attracting, although he'd noticed them. It was probably a good thing she was married.

Of all the training schools in the area, and with all the instructors she could've had, she'd had to join Better Biking, be in his class. And ok, he conceded, they hadn't really got off to a very good start, not at all, but she'd bounced back and he'd liked that. A lot. She'd even bounced back from those awful newspaper shots – and that must've taken some doing.

Although he usually preferred long hair, he couldn't help being drawn to the back of her neck, newly revealed by her shorter cut, where the skin was pale, and the hair downy. When she'd snuck out to watch Rhodri earlier, he'd jockeyed her into position in front of him and caught himself staring down at the top of her head where her skin dipped into her collar. It had been an effort to watch Rhodri take his test.

For goodness' sake, at one point he'd even been holding her arm. She was married. She'd think he was a pervert at this rate. He really, really needed to get a grip. Even if her husband was a bit of a knob.

There was a curious mix of strength and vulnerability about her, as if she was unfurling, re-discovering herself. She'd practised the manoeuvres tirelessly to get to where she was now, and he appreciated the strength of mind which allowed her to focus on exactly what she was doing at that moment.

She made him laugh. And when she laughed, there was none of that false, silly flapping hand in front of the face tittering; it was a proper, earthy laugh that came up from her belly.

And now, here she was, in that fantastic leather outfit he'd helped her choose – when he'd tried to pretend he hadn't noticed her unusual tawny brown eyes in that helmet, or the swelling curve of her bottom in the leather jeans she'd paraded before him. It had been torture, but here she was, looking away from him, head down, bottom lip caught between her little white teeth.

And here he was, her instructor, in a position of trust, for Christ's sake, and all she'd done was to give him a little friendly kiss in that way women do, and he'd gone and blown it. He needed to apologise. Before she decided he was a pervert and made a complaint about him. The thought was no sooner formed than he caught up with her in the glass entrance hall.

Pete and Rhodri were already outside gearing up for the return journey. Whether they'd twigged what had happened, he didn't know, but he was grateful for the bit of space.

He averted his eyes from the vulnerable arch of her neck as she bent over the buckle of her helmet, and began, 'Lucy, I …'

'I'm so sorry,' she said stiffly, looking somewhere over his shoulder. 'That was inappropriate of me. I hope I didn't make you feel uncomfortable.' Her face flamed.

'Er … no!' he spluttered. 'No. I, er …' He stopped. He

didn't have a clue what to say anyway. He couldn't very well admit he'd enjoyed it and wished it had gone on for much longer and hadn't been in front of the whole waiting room, could he?

Pete, who Ash suspected of having seen only too clearly that Ash had intercepted Lucy's friendly peck, bantered self-deprecatingly over the shared comms as they prepared to set off.

'I'm twice your age. It takes me twice as long to learn,' Ash heard him lament. He sat across his bike for a moment, thinking.

'Well done, Rhodri and Lucy. I told you you could do it, didn't I? Commiserations Pete, mate, but it's all good experience, and you're sure to nail it next time.' The rally of cheers and boos heartened him, and he added, 'It's lunchtime. If you guys are free, there's a funky American Diner not far from here. We could stop for lunch and re-fuel the bikes too. What do you reckon?'

'Yep, sounds good.'

'You buying?'

'Yay, Road Trip!'

He grinned at the replies crackling into his ear and focussed on his job.

'Ok. Sorry to be boring, but let's have some attention back on what we're doing now. Statistics show accidents happen straight after extra training, when people think they're better than they are.' He hated putting a downer on their good mood, but the responsibility for their safety weighed heavily on his shoulders.

He put Lucy at the front as befitted her semi-qualified status – and also so he didn't have to be distracted by her alluringly curvy figure in front of him. He left that position to Rhodri. Nothing distracting about his shape whatsoever, he decided gratefully.

The traffic had built up again, and he needed all his concentration to thread his little posse safely through it.

At the front, Lucy was also glad of the concentration required to deal with the busy traffic. And she was happy not to be at the back of the line, feeling Ash's eyes boring into her shoulder blades. Goodness only knew what he was thinking about her right now.

What the hell had she been doing? Poor man. There he'd been, minding his own business at the back, and she'd just grabbed him, like one of those awful, predatory women she saw coming out of clubs late at night, drunk and leering at anything in trousers. She cringed into her jacket, feeling embarrassed and ashamed. And in front of the whole waiting room too.

Ok, it wasn't that she didn't find him attractive. You'd have to be blind not to. He was … well, he was tall, and fit, obviously, and he smelled absolutely lovely, exactly as she'd somehow expected. Not, of course, that she'd ever spent any time thinking about how he might smell. That would just be ridiculous.

It was the laser blue eyes and the feeling that, if you were to cut him in half, like a stick of rock, you'd see the words decent, honest, trustworthy written over and over all the way through. And that was a good thing to be, wasn't it? It didn't mean you had any designs on someone because you liked their smell and the way they looked and thought they were good blokes, did it.

Did it?

And for goodness' sake, she was married. And Gerry was a good bloke too, wasn't he? She didn't sound very convincing, even to her own ears.

'What's the speed limit here, Lucy?' Ash's voice broke into her thoughts. 'Don't tell her, guys.'

'Er ...' She tried to swivel her eyes and not her whole head, knowing he'd be watching to see her helmet move. Obviously she wasn't doing the speed limit anyway, but was she too fast or too slow? She couldn't see any clues – no lampposts to tell her it was a 30, no repeater signs buried in the overgrown hedges.

'It's a de-restricted road.' He put her out of her misery. 'We lost the "50" signs about a mile back. We're dawdling here and I'm starving. Get a blimmin' move on, woman!' His voice laughed and she felt relieved. Clearly he hadn't read too much into a stupid mis-kiss. Phew.

She glanced into her wing mirror and saw him, sitting out of the line, towards the centre of the road, his head cocked to one side. She couldn't see his face at that distance, but she could guess.

She laughed.

'Ok, boss. Try and keep up on that butt-ugly big bike of yours.' A bike over twice as powerful as hers she knew, but she couldn't help teasing him. Crouching forward over the tank, she knocked the gears down and throttled back, gaining the extra twenty miles an hour in seconds, and then sat up, clicking into top gear, and watching in her mirror as Pete caught her effortlessly, but Rhodri on his smaller bike had to work a bit harder, trapping Ash behind in Mother Duck mode way back, as she'd already known it would.

'Much better,' he told her. 'Now pay attention. Your Module two is coming up quickly, and you can't be caught napping then.'

This information brought her up with a jolt. When she'd finished her training, there'd be no reason to see Ash. None at all. Her stomach knotted and she saw Pete bearing down on her in the wing mirrors. Oops, obviously slowed down again. Forcing herself to concentrate, she got back up to speed and paid attention.

'There's a roundabout in a couple of miles. The fuel station and diner is on the last exit. We'll fuel up first, so go straight to a pump,' Ash instructed them.

The rural road was virtually free of traffic, but winding enough to require Lucy's full consideration. As the roundabout appeared in view, Ash reminded her again, and she ticked the points off in her head – mirror, indicator, position, speed, gear, shoulder check, accelerate – feeling pleased as she pulled up beside an empty pump and climbed off the bike without stalling it.

'Butt-ugly bike, eh?' Ash had pulled up behind her.

With the petrol pump nozzle in the tank of her bike, she glanced shyly up at him, registering with a shock how the colour of his eyes was intensified because they were the only bits of him she could see. Eyes which were twinkling down at her, she saw.

She nodded at her cute, purple bike, leaning nonchalantly on the side stand, and then at his hulking great black beast, towering over Cadbury.

'I rest my case,' she said, raising her eyebrows challengingly, trying to stay cool and friendly, just like always. And not to give anything away. Whatever that anything might possibly be.

Her hands jerked unintentionally and a thin spume of petrol squirted up and over the tank.

'Shit!' she yelled.

His hands covered hers instantly, holding the nozzle back down.

'Oops. These things have a mind of their own.'

She daren't look at him again. Her face felt hot enough to fry an egg; she was sure it must be scarlet. He let her finish re-fuelling, then wheeled her bike forward so he could use the same pump. By the time she'd paid for her petrol and got back on her bike, she had her galloping pulse back under control.

They reverse-parked their bikes in a space at the front of the adjacent diner; a squat, flat building decorated in red, white and blue.

As they pushed the door open and gazed around, she couldn't decide whether to be appalled or charmed by the decor. It really was like being transported into the fifties – a juke-box, oversized bench seats around Formica topped tables, chequer-board floor, tall chrome stools at the bar and stars and stripes everywhere. Even the waitresses were dressed in black dresses, trimmed with white collars and cuffs.

'Wow!' Rhodri pushed past and made straight for the juke box. 'Awesome. Look at this, it's a Seeburg.' He turned to beam at them. '1949!'

'I wasn't even born then,' Pete told his disbelieving face, wandering over for a gander. 'I wasn't.'

'Inside or out?' smiled the waitress, holding up her notebook.

'In, I think,' said Ash, checking with them. He nodded at a table by the window. 'We can see our bikes from there too.'

Lucy enjoyed a juicy burger, and half listening to Rhodri asking Ash some technical bike question, she sipped her coffee and gazed out of the window onto the car-park. She spotted an electric blue Lexus glide onto the forecourt of the petrol station. She stiffened slightly. It could be anyone. Gerry wasn't the only person with that particular model, she was sure. She peered out. It *was* him.

She'd passed half her test, and she looked fantastic in the leathers that *he* asserted she would always be too fat to wear. She was proud of her achievements; she wasn't going to hide it away any longer. It was time to confront him, make him see her as the person she wanted to be seen as. More mighty than meek.

'My husband is out there – I'm just going to tell him I passed,' she told Ash, Rhodri and Pete, while she checked her hair in her reflection. 'Back in a mo, guys.'

Marching across the car-park, however, she saw that Gerry wasn't alone. Her legs faltered of their own accord, as a pair of long, slim legs, under a short, flippy skirt, reversed out of the rear passenger seat. Adrenaline drove Lucy forward as she saw Gerry, clearly not concentrating on his fuel pump, pat the pert bottom wiggling towards him. As the girl unfolded herself and stood to plant a kiss on Gerry's lips, she looked over his shoulder and, in an instant, her eyes widened.

'Lucy!'

'Ella.' Lucy was astonished how calm she was. Beyond rage and suddenly feeling very strong.

Gerry's double take could have been comical. He whirled to face her. 'Lucy! What ... what are you doing here?'

'Oh, hi Gerry. I just passed the next part of my motorbike test. You know, that thing you said I'm "no good at"?' Lucy watched Ella scuttle around to the front passenger seat, and levelled a finger at her. 'Aren't you supposed to be at the café covering for me? You're fired.' She turned to look back at Gerry. 'And you and me are *over*. I can't believe I've been so stupid—' Fury rose in her throat and threatened to choke her. '—for so long, trying to make things better between us, when all this time ...'

'It wasn't me! She threw herself at me.' Gerry edged away from her towards the driver's door.

'You told me you were leaving her!' Ella yelled over the car roof.

'Were you?' Lucy glared at her husband. 'I bloody wish you'd done it sooner! You've made my life a misery for way too long.'

'At least she knows now. Come back to mine.' Ella tutted, flicking back her hair. 'Well, yes, I know it's yours, but you said...'

'Shut up!' Gerry snarled at her. He turned to Lucy. 'Look, it's not what you think—'

'Not what you think? What is *that* supposed to mean?' Ella shrieked, leaning across the seats.

'You're not wriggling out of this one, Gerry. I know exactly what it is.' Lucy could barely believe her own voice. Confident, firm, not a trace of a wobble.

'Leave this to me, Ella,' he barked, without looking at the girl. 'We can discuss this later, Lucy. It's not what you think.'

'You said that. So, what is it?' Lucy folded her arms and leaned against the car, as her legs began to tremble just a little.

'Err – it's um—' He faltered. 'Watch those zips on my paintwork!' Gerry's horrified expression was just the thing she needed. He was more interested in his bloody car than their relationship. The red mists of anger finally descended and her feet in their armoured boots needed no persuasion to land a hefty whack on his precious car. It felt great.

'Argh! What are you *doing*, woman?' Gerry shouted, and Lucy aimed another deliberate boot at the door panel. His shove caught her off-balance and sent her sprawling. Scrambling to her feet, she saw him hurry into the driving seat and lunged after him, snatching at his door as he tried to close it. How dare he just drive off in the middle of this? She wasn't nearly finished with him. Her pulse pounded in her ears as she flailed to keep her balance, catching hold of anything to give her a hand hold.

'And I want you out of my parents' house … Aaah!'

She didn't recognise her animal howl of agony as the heavy door smashed into the hand curled around the door-post.

Ash hurried across the car park, having attended enough domestic crises to recognise one unfolding in front of him. Rhodri and Pete brought up the rear at a slower pace until Lucy's howl of anguish provoked them all into a run.

He saw Gerry climb back out of the car, his hands held out in appeasement, before his attention swung their way.

Seizing on his distraction, Lucy swung a couple of vicious kicks at his crotch, and Gerry shoved her away. Ash sprinted the last few yards, as Lucy stumbled and fell awkwardly.

'Enough!' he roared, standing between them, facing Gerry. 'Stop it now before someone gets really hurt. I'm looking at you. Get away from her.'

'You again!' Gerry's eyes flicked from him to Lucy, and he sneered. 'Uh-huh. So that's how it is. You're no better than I am.'

'He's my Bike Instructor, you idiot!' Lucy snapped. Ash was tempted to add that she deserved better than both of them, but held his tongue and sent him his most menacing frown. Gerry backed into his car without a word, and screeched out of the car park.

'And your fucking golf clubs are going on eBay!' Lucy screamed after him, from the ground. 'For 99p!' She looked up at Ash, her lips white. 'And I'm taking the scissors to all those designer suits. Bastard!'

Half of Ash was relieved to see Gerry leave. The other half was wishing he'd been able to punch his lights out. Unaccustomed rage had engulfed him as soon as he'd seen diminutive Lucy knocked to the ground by her bullying oaf of a husband.

His emotions were roller-coastering between horror, anger and now pity as she sagged against him, jelly-legged, all fight gone. She clutched her hand against her chest, clearly in pain, sobbing raggedly.

They walked her off the forecourt back to the diner, where there was a low wall alongside their bikes. He lowered her onto it, using Rhodri and Pete as bookends. She sat awkwardly, clutching at her left hand.

'What happened?' he nodded at her hand.

'I wanted to hit him.' She gave him a ghost of a smile. 'But he slammed the door on my hand.'

He winced. Bloody hell. He hadn't seen that part. No wonder she was in pain. 'Can you wiggle your fingers?'

She tried. 'No. I should get rid of these before they amputate my finger.' Grimacing, she wound the rings from her third finger, and handed them to him. 'I don't care what you do with those.'

'Keep 'em. You can sell them.' Pete stood. 'That hand is swelling already. I'll get you some ice.'

Ash went to his bike for first aid supplies. He pushed the thought of how they were going to get Lucy and her bike home to the back of his mind. Hospital was going to be their next port of call.

Settling Lucy's hand high up on her opposite shoulder with a tea-towel wrapped ice-bag over it, he finished tying a sling, and then opened the wet wipes and wiped her face just as he would have done had it been Daisy sitting there. She blew her nose messily, and he collected the snotty tissues and wipes without comment, shoving them amongst the bandage packaging and putting the whole lot into the bin outside the entrance.

Time to inject some calm into the proceedings. He needed to sort out the practicalities of getting Lucy to the hospital and everyone else home.

'If the guys help you, do you think you can pillion me, Lucy?'

She looked up at him, nodding doubtfully.

'No point waiting around for an ambulance, the hospital's not far. But it means you two tagging along – is that ok?'

'I'm so sorry.' Lucy looked glum. 'I've messed everything up.'

'Don't be mad girl. It's the most excitement I've had since I retired,' said Pete, patting her knee.

'What about her bike?' Rhodri said.

'I'll get Ed or his dad to collect it. I'll just go and leave the key with the manager.' He felt carefully in Lucy's pockets for her key, feeling concerned for her. She'd subsided into silence again and was leaning heavily against Pete's solid bulk. He strode into the diner and came out moments later.

'What did you say to the manager?' Rhodri was agog.

'I told her the bike was part of an ongoing investigation, and no-one was to go near it until it was collected,' said Ash, straddling the Triumph and making sure the steering lock was on.

'Wow,' sighed Rhodri. 'All that power. You can do anything really, can't you?'

Yes, thought Ash. *All that power – and all that responsibility* ... 'Right, let's get this show on the road.'

While they turned their bikes to face the right way, he replaced Lucy's helmet, buckled her chin strap and squeezed her good arm gently.

'It's not far, I promise. Ten minutes tops, ok?'

She nodded mechanically.

Getting her on the pillion seat was a bit of a palaver, as she had to contend with his top box too.

'What if I use a roll of bandage and tie her to you?' suggested Pete, looking at Lucy's slumped form.

Ash agreed, and Pete unrolled a wide bandage around them both, securing them together. Lucy had one arm around him, and her knees were clamped against his thighs. He could feel her shivering and patted her knee.

'No jerking this time,' she said through chattering teeth.

'No,' he agreed, pulling away gently with Rhodri and Pete as his outriders.

He remembered how he'd yanked the clutch just a little to make her hold on properly that first day. 'I could sing. Take your mind off it?'

'No. I'm in enough pain as it is.' She squeezed him with her good hand to show it was a joke, and he laughed.

Chapter Sixteen

Ash was impressed. He'd rung Ed to arrange collection of Lucy's bike on his headset on the way, and they'd worked like a well-oiled team at their arrival at the hospital. Pete unravelled them from their bandage, and Rhodri rushed off, returning moments later with a wheelchair.

'I did work experience in a hospital once.' He beamed.

Lucy sank into it without argument, to his surprise. She must be feeling pretty ropey, he guessed.

At the Casualty Reception, the unsmiling receptionist swept Lucy and her posse with an icy glare. 'Bike accident I suppose?' she said, her mouth a thin line.

To Ash's surprise, Lucy stood up and said clearly, 'No. I caught my cheating shi— sorry, my cheating husband with some tart, tried to hit him and he slammed the door on my hand instead.'

The receptionist looked taken aback and a ghost of a smile chased across her face. 'Respect. I'll get someone to see you right away.' She booked Lucy in.

The four of them sat in the waiting room, Lucy leaning against Ash's shoulder. He had to fight the urge to put his arm round her. Just to comfort her, he told himself as his nerve failed.

'I'm sorry I spoiled the day,' Lucy muttered through gritted teeth.

'It wasn't your fault.' Pete leaned across, his expression sympathetic. 'And just so's you know, not all blokes are like him. You might not think so now, but you're better off without him.'

'I might apply for the police next year,' mused Rhodri. 'It looks like more fun than plumbing.'

'The world will always need plumbers, lad.' Pete nudged his arm.

'You did good today Rhodri, mate. Well done on your passes today, and Pete, you'll smash it next time, I'm sure.' Ash glanced at the clock. 'Look, I need to get you two back home. Lucy – have you got anywhere to go tonight?'

'Oh no, Nicola is away, and—' She stared at him, her eyes stricken, and he made another snap decision in this day of snap decisions.

'Ok, I'll sort something, don't worry.'

Lucy's name was called. 'Can you help me get this jacket off, please?' Her voice sounded small. 'I don't want them to cut it off me, not after what I paid for it.' She smiled tremulously, and he knew she was making a huge effort to be brave.

Eyeing her poor swollen hand peeping over the top of the sling, he was about to shake his head.

'Please?'

Against his better judgement, they manipulated the jacket off her good arm, then disassembled her sling, and by unzipping the cuff and holding it as wide open as possible, eased her hand out. She bit her lip so hard she almost drew blood, he saw, and her teeth were chattering.

'I'll be back as soon as I can, with the car. You've got my number in your phone.' She nodded, standing up as the nurse arrived. He wavered. He didn't really want to leave her there, but he didn't have a choice. Pete bent and hugged her gently on her good side.

'Chin up, darlin'. Hope it all goes ok. Nice to meet you.' He kissed her cheek, adding, 'Well done with that pass. Maybe we'll get to take our Mod Twos together, when your hand's better.'

Rhodri followed suit, and Ash felt envious of their easy rapport. He was having trouble analysing his feelings for

Lucy, and he knew he was camouflaging them by being busy and practical, and 'in charge', as usual. He also knew if he kissed her – even on the cheek – here, in public, in the waiting room, he would be exposed, vulnerable. All his carefully built defences would come tumbling down. He had nearly blown it when she'd reached up to kiss his cheek earlier in the day. She was a married woman, for God's sake, no matter what had just happened with her shit of a husband. He'd handled enough domestic disputes to know it was never a foregone conclusion that she would leave the man.

She was a married woman, moreover, who had not given him the slightest encouragement or indication that she felt any more for him than she did for, say, Pete, or Rhodri.

'Right.' He jiggled his keys. 'I'll take your helmet, it can go in my top box. Okay? I'll see you later. Good luck.'

His eyes met her trusting brown ones and, confused, he turned hurriedly and led the way out. Rhodri and Pete clowned at her as she disappeared through the double doors and blew kisses as she fingertip-waved with her good hand.

He looked back and saw, just before she dipped her head, her eyes dark in her pale face, her mouth trembling, and once again he questioned his decision to leave her there. They returned home via the most direct route he knew without using the motorway, knowing their concentration would be all over the place after the day's events. To be fair, his own concentration wasn't very much better.

He rang his parents on his headset.

'Hi, Dad. Something's come up – can you keep Daisy overnight, please?'

'Of course. Is everything ok? Is it work?'

'Yes. No. It's just, er, a bit awkward.' He sounded false even to his own ears.

'Who is she?' It was his mother, on the other line.

'What?' He sighed. There was no point lying; she could read him like a book.

'You can't fool me, Ashley Connor. I've already spotted the signs – tidying yourself up, getting rid of that awful beard. Daisy says she's heard you singing.'

Ash was silent, thinking. Was he really that transparent? Even Daisy noticed? He couldn't even understand his own feelings. He had no idea what to tell his parents. There wasn't really anything to tell.

'No,' he began, 'I've got to collect a ... a friend from the hospital. And er, they're staying over so I can look after, er, them.' He cringed, knowing his evasion of the words 'she' and 'her' was a dead giveaway.

'Hospital? Not an accident on the bikes today?' His dad sounded concerned.

'No, not on the bikes.' *Don't wish that one on me as well.*

'Sarah's here, by the way.'

'Is she? Why?'

'She just dropped by to say hello.'

'Look, I have to go. Thanks guys. Give my love to Daisy. And, er, Sarah. Speak soon.'

He sighed with relief as he dropped Pete off first and Rhodri a few miles further on, and turned off for home.

He was back on the road, changed out of his bike gear and in his car within minutes. It was almost two hours since he'd left the hospital, and when he walked back into the Casualty waiting room, Lucy was nowhere to be seen. He rubbed his hands across his face. He felt exhausted. He should have rung the hospital. What if she had been admitted? He hadn't thought of that. Maybe she'd just got a taxi – to where?

He marched up to the Reception desk and was about to enquire as to Lucy's whereabouts when he heard her laugh, and turned to see her emerging from the double doors of the treatment rooms, wearing a much more professional version of his hasty sling.

'Ash!'

'This isn't your husband, is it?' The nurse holding the door open looked at Ash sternly as he closed the gap between them.

'Nooo,' said Lucy. 'This is my hero.'

She stepped straight into the circle of his arms and leaned her face against his chest. The nurse handed him a white paper bag.

'She's on some really strong painkillers. It's a hairline fracture. Good thing she's right-handed. Look after her.'

'Oh, I will, don't worry.' Holding her against him, he dropped a kiss on top of her tousled head. It felt like the most natural thing in the world.

It was pitch black by the time Ash parked outside his house. He looked over at Lucy, who'd been girlie and giggly until sinking into the front passenger seat of his comfortable estate. Then she'd simply said, 'Thank you,' closed her eyes and fallen asleep.

He guessed it was shock, plus the effects of the painkillers, and hoped what they'd given her to take home was just as strong.

Home. His home, not hers. What was going to happen to her now? Well, he'd meant what he said, that he'd look after her. If that was what she wanted of course. He reached over and patted her knee gently to wake her. She looked peaceful, lost in an untroubled sleep. She probably wasn't going to have many of those for some time to come, but at least right now, she had somewhere to stay. He didn't think about how long that would be for. It didn't really matter right now.

She was awake, her eyes unfocussed.

'Welcome to my humble abode,' he said, quietly.

She climbed out stiffly, yawning, her leathers creaking. He remembered she didn't even have a change of clothes. The security lights flooded the path around to the door they all used, the side door into the big farmhouse kitchen. No-one ever used the front door.

'Oh. This is lovely!' She blinked, looking around the room, with its oversized pine table and mismatched chairs that Ash was always planning to rub down and paint, but never seemed to get around to. He pulled one of them out for her and waved her into it with a grand gesture that produced a small smile. While he filled the kettle, she took in the array of hand painted ceramic mugs on the open-shelved dresser.

'I feel like I've fallen asleep and woken up in an episode of The Archers,' she said, and then her face flamed as she continued. 'Sorry, I really need the loo and I can't undo this stupid hook thing on my trousers. I had to get one of the nurses to help at the hospital. Would you mind?'

'You only want me for my undressing skills.' He laughed and then trailed off, not looking at her as he released the fastening.

'How's that?' He turned away, feeling awkward. It had been a very long time since he'd had a strange woman in his kitchen. She obviously trusted him enough to be here, and he was making pervy jokes. Shut up, he told himself.

'How do you like your tea?' he said over his shoulder, still without looking at her.

'Really weak, gnats pee, no milk please. And ...' She looked around her. '... where am I going?'

He directed her to the loo through the dining room, lounge and tv room. There was another room which he used as an office when he needed to. They lived in the kitchen really, unless they were watching tv, and he didn't do much of that. There was always a bit of engine to clean and strip down, or something to repair. Daisy liked to sit in there with him, drawing or chatting or bossing her dolls about. Lucy returned ages later just as he was wondering whether she needed any help.

He pulled a face at her tea.

'I can see the bottom of the cup. Is that really how you like it?'

She nodded. 'Perfect, thank you.'

'Did you manage ok?'

'It was a bit awkward, to be honest. I don't suppose you've got a pair of tracky bottoms I could borrow? Just for tonight? Tomorrow I can ...' She stopped, her mouth twisting.

'Yes, I'm sure I've got something,' he said hurriedly, turning to go.

'Ash ...'

He stopped, looked back at her.

Her mouth was wobbly but her voice was oddly formal. 'I'm so, so sorry about today. I know you must be furious with me for messing everyone about. And I do appreciate everything you're doing for me ... all this.' She waved her good hand around the kitchen. 'I don't know what I would have done if you hadn't—' Her eyes were bright with tears. 'It's all such a mess. I haven't even rung Richard.'

'Do you want to? You can use the phone – go into the office.'

'No, I don't want to. I know it sounds stupid, but I don't want to have to tell it all over again tonight. You were there. I mean, you know, so I don't have to keep explaining. I'll tell him tomorrow. I need to think.'

He nodded. 'I'll get those trousers.'

Riffling through his wardrobe he held up pair after pair. They would all be enormous on her. He was at least six inches taller than her, and although lean, still heftier around the middle than she was. He selected a pair with a drawstring, pulled out a sweater and t-shirt in case she wanted them, and presented them to her.

'Are you hungry?'

'I don't know. Are you?'

'I feel a bit empty, yes. I could rustle up some pasta while you put those on, if you like. Whatever we don't eat can go in the fridge for tomorrow.'

She laughed gently.

'You're a proper Mum, you are.' And then stopped, her expression aghast. 'Oh, I'm so sorry, I didn't think ...'

'Stop apologising for everything. Yes, I am a proper Mum, luckily for you.' He laughed and she joined in, and the tension between them began to dissipate.

'Do you ... want to talk about ... what happened today?' He threw the words behind him as he pulled the things he needed out of the fridge.

There was a long pause, and he looked over at her, slumped at the table, her face a mask of anguish.

'Bloody hell. Haven't you got enough of your own troubles?' She made a rueful face. 'You don't want to have to listen to mine.'

'Try me.'

She frowned unseeingly at the table, tracing the knot holes in the pine with her hand, her lips pressed together. He could almost see her mind chasing.

'D'you mind if I get changed?' she said at last.

'Oh, of course, I'll show you your room.'

He led the way upstairs, to the jumble of rooms that were the result of the many extensions and adaptations to the house over the years before he had it.

'Mine is on the right, and this is Daisy's.' He threw open a door into a pretty room crammed with colour, pattern and dolls. 'And this is the guest room.'

It was a nice room, decorated in restful creams and duck egg blues, the softly flowered duvet piled with cushions.

'There's a bit of an en suite too. Just a shower, loo and sink but I'm guessing baths are off the agenda anyway. Are you allowed to shower?' he asked.

'I don't really know. I guess so. I haven't got a plaster on, just a splint thing, and some sort of strapping. I didn't pay all that much attention to be honest. I was a bit out of it.'

'We'll have a look in the morning. Ok, I'll leave you to it.' He looked at her doubtfully. 'Can you manage?'

'I'm sure I can.' She closed the door on him firmly, and he stood outside in the corridor for a moment or two in case she changed her mind.

Maybe he should have dropped her off at his parents' house. At least his mum could have helped her undress. He cursed his thoughtlessness. He'd got to the bottom of the stairs when he heard the thump and muffled curse from upstairs. He hovered, halfway back up the stairs, and then there was more swearing and a series of bumps, and then: 'I can't bloody do it!' she shouted.

He took the stairs two at a time. Her door was open and he stopped outside, mindful of her privacy. There was nothing worse than feeling helpless. He should know.

'Can I help?'

She groaned loudly.

'Are you hurt?'

'No! I'm bloody stuck!'

'Er, ok – I'm coming in.'

He walked in, and despite his good intentions, barely suppressed a grin. Lucy was standing with her tight leathers halfway down her thighs, and was making a futile attempt at pushing them down one-handedly.

'Don't look.' She glared up at him. 'Bastard things!'

'Don't worry. I've undressed a sleeping Daisy, drunks and dead people. I think I can manage a pair of leathers.'

'Oh, thanks.' She waddled with difficulty towards the bed and toppled onto it, her expression murderous.

'It's a hat trick isn't it. Waterproofs, the jacket and now these. Not that I'm counting or anything.'

She snorted by way of a response.

Re-arranging his features into his professional face, he tried not to look at her exposed, creamy white thighs.

She tugged her t-shirt down with her good hand. Obviously, he'd failed.

He'd dragged the leathers past her knees before realising his error.

'You've still got your boots on.'

'Oops!'

She sat up, reaching forward one-handedly to grip her waistband, and lay down again, bouncing, caterpillar-like, to pull them back up. Even he could see this wasn't going to work, but she seemed determined so he left her to it, and set to work on her boots. With them out of the way, the jeans ought to come off with no problem. But all the writhing about had made Lucy hot and the leather seemed to be glued to her skin.

'Nope.' He stood up, rubbing his back and moved to the door. 'I was wrong. This is much harder than undressing drunks and dead people. You'll just have to sleep in them.'

'You can't go!' Lucy stared at him. 'You can't just leave me like this.'

She looked down at her legs in their leather manacles, with a horrified expression. He looked too, although he knew his expression was the exact opposite of hers. Her eyes flicked from his face to the unyielding trousers and back, and he was aghast as he saw her body tremble violently.

'I wouldn't really lea—!' He stopped as he saw her

convulse with silent, shuddering mirth, her eyes closed and tears streaming down her face. He couldn't help joining in, reaching down to yank the jeans off from the hems.

'Aha! Fiendishly hidden ankle zips.' He hammed, lifting a leg to inspect the zips at close quarters whilst she wheezed with laughter.

Giving a mighty heave, he was taken by surprise as they released their grip and he tripped backwards with them in his hands. He bounced off the wall behind and straight back onto the bed, narrowly missing her.

'Here.' He threw the leathers across her legs, panting. 'I think you should try talcum powder next time.' It made her laugh even harder.

He propped himself up on one arm, watching her as she snorted between breaths, wiping the tears from her cheeks. Where her hair wasn't stuck to her head it stood up in tufts, there was not a scrap of make-up left after her earlier wet wipe wash, she was bruised and bandaged and half naked. She looked absolutely perfect to him. He decided he should leave now. Before he couldn't.

Her giggles subsided. She drew in a ragged breath and let out a long shuddering sob. He rolled the duvet over her, bolstering it between them and tucking her in, just as he would Daisy. Her shoulders heaved and she curled into him like a child. Finally the crying abated.

'Sorry,' she hiccuped, burying her face into the pillow.

'Don't be sorry. I'm sure there'll be a few more of those.' He clambered off the bed and brought back an unused loo roll, unwinding several sheets and handing them to her. She blew mightily and once again he collected the soggy tissues, flushing them down the loo.

'Do you want me to leave you alone now?'

She shook her head, still not quite looking at him.

He climbed back onto the bed, leaving a chaste gap

between them, when really, he wanted to reach around her, pull her towards him and comfort her. She was the one to close the gap, shuffling awkwardly into him, her small body still encased in the duvet, lying full length against his.

'Lucy, I ...' he began, and then lifted his head, listening.

'Hellooooo! Where are you?'

He recognised that voice. He sprang off the bed.

'It's Sarah.' He strode to the door, pulling it firmly closed behind him. 'I won't be long.'

Chapter Seventeen

Lucy stared at the closed door, her mind whirling. What had just happened there? And who the hell was Sarah? She sat up, grabbing the borrowed track pants and began with difficulty to loop them over her feet, and up her legs. It was harder than she'd thought, even though her right hand was okay. It began to dawn on her just what this meant, apart from the obvious dressing and washing difficulties.

She could still paint, thank goodness. She had only just started the TV Tom order. But there was her bike test – she'd have to put that off now. She could still work in the café, still sell stuff, but she'd be hopeless helping with serving for several weeks. And driving. That was going to be tricky. Bloody Gerry. *Bloody Ella!*

She wanted to kill them both.

She wanted not to have to think about them.

Wanted not to have to be a grown-up. Wanted someone else to sort it all out for her. Until she remembered that that's exactly what Gerry had been doing for most of their married lives. Unbidden, her mind projected a picture of him and Ella smooching by his car. She couldn't help comparing herself unfavourably with Ella's endless legs and tiny waist.

She blamed him, of course she did, and her, but a tiny part of her demanded to know if it would have happened if she, Lucy, had lost weight earlier, tidied up her look sooner. Not made such a thing about learning to ride a motorbike. Maybe that's what had pushed him into the affair. Had it all been her fault?

She'd got the trousers on, and by hooking the draw cord over the door handles, she managed to pull them into her waist, but the knot eluded her.

The dressing table mirror confirmed that she looked like a sack not quite tied up in the middle just as the door burst open and admitted a tiny, glacially blonde young woman, wearing a skin tight mini dress which accentuated her perfect curves.

'Oh.' She halted in her tracks and raked Lucy with a glance that left her feeling as if she was something surprising and distasteful found under a stone. Ash appeared in the doorway.

'Lucy, this is Sarah,' he said. 'My sister-in-law.'

Holding up the comedy trousers, with her hair sticking up all over the place and eyes that felt grittier than sandpaper after her marathon weep, Lucy felt at a distinct disadvantage. Even more so as Sarah shot out a hand in greeting.

'Oh, sorry!' said Sarah insincerely, looking down at her hand. 'Shall I do that for you?'

Without waiting for Lucy to answer, she yanked the baggy black fleecy trousers up as far as they would go and tied them tightly like a parcel, just under her boobs, in a secure double knot. Lucy's voice and will seemed to have taken a holiday and she opened her mouth in dismay, about to say she'd never get it undone with one hand, when Sarah interrupted.

'I could see if I have anything you could borrow. What size are you?'

'A fourteen,' said Lucy faintly.

'Really? Looks can be so deceptive, can't they?' Lucy was just about to smile when Sarah added, 'I thought you were bigger than that.' Turning on her heel, she bobbed her head at Lucy. 'Well, nice to meet you. Come along, Ash.' She caught his arm and turned him towards the door. 'Did you say you're doing your special pasta? Lovely.'

To Lucy's astonishment, Ash allowed himself to be dragged away.

'Sorry,' he mouthed over his shoulder at her, and made a face.

Lucy collapsed onto the bed. Bloody hell, she thought. *What a solid gold bitch!* Like a malevolent fairy. Obviously she had Ash right where she wanted him. And now she was expected to have a meal with her? It was a sign. She shouldn't be here.

She could ring for a taxi; book into a Travelodge or something. She felt in her jacket pocket and was relieved when she located her bank cards.

By sucking in her stomach, she managed to force the trousers down to her waist and pulled her t-shirt out a bit. Her hair was a lost cause, but she fluffed it up as best she could and headed warily downstairs.

Sarah was chatting airily about this and that, clearly at home in the kitchen. She opened the fridge, brought out a bottle of white wine and reached into a cupboard for two glasses.

'Oh, do you want a glass?' she said as she saw Lucy.

Lucy licked her lips. She would have loved a glass of wine. Ash opened his mouth to speak but Sarah got there first.

'Oh, but you must be on tablets, you poor thing. Still, you don't mind if we do, do you?'

She poured a glass sloppily, but Ash put his hand over the second glass.

'You're driving,' he said.

Sarah pouted. 'Oh, can't I just stay over as usual?'

'Don't worry on my account.' Lucy seized her chance. 'Look, I'll just get a taxi and a hotel. You've done more than enough for me, Ash. I can't thank you enough. Can you just point me at the phone?'

'There we are, that's sorted then,' said Sarah, brightly, regarding Lucy with an almost friendly expression.

'You don't need to go,' Ash told Lucy. He frowned at Sarah.

'She could share with me, in my bed?' Sarah said, putting her head on one side and looking up at him coquettishly. 'She'll need someone to help her undress—?'

'No,' Lucy said firmly. She could just imagine this little minx's idea of 'helping' her. 'No, thanks.'

'No, Sarah,' said Ash quietly. 'I'm looking after Lucy. She's had a terrible day. So she'll be sleeping in the spare bed, on her own, for as long as she needs it. You have your own home to go to. Lucy doesn't, right now. You're welcome to stay for food, but you'll be going home afterwards. Ok?'

'Fine.' Sarah squeezed a thin smile onto her chiselled face. 'You shouldn't eat carbs in the evening anyway. They make you fat.' Lucy leaned tiredly against the table, half listening to them. She would have done anything for her own bed right then, and although she was grateful for Ash's offer to stay, she felt disorientated and faintly sick, and wished that she was staying over with Nicola instead.

'He's always trying to fix things,' Sarah told her in a conversational voice. 'Loves a hopeless case, he does. All waifs and strays. Well, bye then.' She gripped Ash's arm, and tugged down so she could kiss his cheek. He remained upright and her kiss met only air, somewhere near his shoulder. She swished her sleek blonde hair, swung an expensive, designer looking bag over her shoulder, and clattered off on her teetering heels without looking back.

Lucy hadn't realised she'd been holding her breath until the door crashed shut.

'You didn't have to—,' she began, not wanting to look at Ash. He'd just virtually thrown out a member of his family for her.

Ash rubbed his face ruefully. 'Sorry about that. She's lovely really. Just a bit … full on sometimes. And I suppose she's a bit proprietorial about me and Daisy now, after ... everything.'

A bit! His 'everything' hung in the air. Lucy knew he wanted to tell her something, but right now she felt completely drained. She still couldn't quite believe what had happened today.

'Do you mind if I don't eat? I'm so tired. I think I just want to go to bed now. And, I'm sorry, but I'm going to need a hand to get out of this knot she's tied.'

'Of course.' He picked up the paper bag of drugs given to her by the hospital. 'You're probably ready for another one of these anyway.' He shook out the appropriate drug, and poured her a glass of water, watching while she took them. 'Would you really have gone to look for a room?'

'Yes. Sorry.'

'Hah. You don't have to apologise to me. I'm very glad you didn't.'

They walked up the stairs to her room.

'You're a very surprising person, Lucy.'

'In a good way?'

He nodded, peeling off her socks as she sat on the edge of the bed. 'Oh, yes.'

He went into the bathroom, returning with a hot, wrung out flannel. He handed it to her.

'Returning the compliment.'

'Ooh, I feel as if I've just had a spa,' she said, mimicking Daisy's words in the café, while he unwrapped a new toothbrush, squeezed a blob of paste on it and handed it to her. 'Thank you,' she said indistinctly, scrubbing at her mouth. It was amazing how much more human a clean face and clean teeth could make you feel. Finally, he unhooked her sling, and threaded her bra out from underneath her t-shirt. He did it so impersonally that she couldn't feel awkward, and she was grateful. Her skin tingled as if his warm fingers were red hot. 'Is this your 'undressing dead people' skill again?' Making a joke eased the tension, and she liked hearing him laugh.

He helped her into the clean, cool sheets, before undoing the savagely tied drawstring knot, and leaving her to decide whether she wanted to wear the track pants as pyjamas. She couldn't imagine anyone else being kinder than he was and felt enormously comforted by his presence. However, she acknowledged in confusion, she fancied the pants off him. Which left her feeling very muddled about her marriage. But, she decided, it was one thing to think it, and another to actually plan it, and do it. Like Gerry had.

Ash bent over the bed, and chastely kissed her cheek. She couldn't help it, this time she knew she was the one to turn her head in time to catch half his mouth. He dropped instantly to his knees beside the bed, his lips still on hers. With her eyes closed, she reached out and stroked his jaw, feeling the soft, short cropped beard, just a bit longer than stubble. Her hand crept around to the back of his neck, pulling him closer and his lips opened over hers. She breathed in his fresh, soapy, clean smell and was lost in the moment.

She could feel his hands cradling her head, hear his uneven breathing, feel the pulse jumping in his neck. She wanted to fold back the duvet and pull it round them both, and make the world go away. Folding her hands in his, he returned them to her and drew away gently.

'Good night, lovely girl,' he said, tucking the duvet around her chin. 'Sleep tight.'

She closed her eyes obediently, like a child. As soon as she heard the door close, she opened them again as the day's events reeled through her mind like an old film. Unable to find a comfortable position, she lay, sleeplessly, her hand throbbing and her mind whirring. It was a long time before sleep finally claimed her, and when it did, it was full of dreams of looking for something.

She woke early, the morning sun streaming through the curtains, her attention caught by a child's piping voice outside calling for 'Harry!' That must be Daisy. Either Ash had gone to collect her or her grandparents had delivered her. She was a guest and ought to get up, she thought, aching in every joint, as her eyelids drooped over eyes gritty from tears, and she was almost drifting off when she heard a scuffling noise. Followed by a grunting noise. It must be outside, she decided, not opening her eyes. The window was open – and sounds travelled in the country, didn't they?

There it was again. A definite scuffling. From inside the room. Was it a mouse? Trying to get into her nice warm bed?

Her eyelids flew open and she sat upright. Clutching the duvet up to her neck she patted it tightly down all around her to prevent a mouse-attack and listened again. Maybe it would get bored and go away, she hoped.

Squeak! Scuffle, grunt. Bit on the loud side for a mouse, maybe. Taking a deep breath, she leaned awkwardly down to peer over the edge of the bed.

Eek! She jumped. Not a mouse then. Much bigger than a mouse. Bigger than a rat … bigger than a cat … She started to feel as if she was in a Dr Seuss book – *'bigger than a cat or a rat in a hat …'*

The grunting began again, and her duvet started to slither inexorably off the bed. Gathering up the bit of duvet she still had, she scrambled to her feet.

'Oh, no, you don't!' Dropping to her knees she scooped the duvet firmly to one side. A hairy black and white spotted face stared back at her, its mouth curved into a comical smile.

'Hello – who might you be?' said Lucy softly, smiling back.

Tousled, corkscrew curls of dark hair appeared around the door, followed by the rest of Daisy, dressed in brightly patterned leggings, a coral and white striped hoody, and buttercup yellow wellies.

'Harry!' she cried, relief flooding her face, and then clapped her hand over her mouth as her eyes met Lucy's. 'Oops ...'

'So, this is Harry.' Lucy looked down at the pig which was currently snuggling up in the puddled duvet. Tiny by pig standards, but considerably larger than a cat.

'Hello, Lucy. Sorry. He's a teacup pig.' Daisy cocked her head at her, gauging her reaction. 'He's named after Harry Styles. *One Direction?*' She sighed dramatically, like the mini pop fan she clearly was.

Ash appeared at the door.

'Lucy, now, don't panic, but have you seen a ... oh. I see you've met.'

'Another rescue project?' asked Lucy.

Ash nodded. 'Yes. People have them as miniature pets and then they grow. We've got all his brothers and sisters too. They escaped and were going to be shot by the local authorities. So we rescued them, didn't we Daisy? They have a palatial piggy pen, but Harry seems to prefer our house for some reason. Houdini might be a better name for him. He's usually safely under lock and key.' He narrowed his eyes at his daughter as she scrambled under the bed. 'Daisy! We have a guest. Why is Harry in the house?'

'I don't know!' replied Daisy, hotly, wheedling the little spotty pig off the duvet and trying to herd him out of the room. 'He was locked up – I'm sure he was!'

'Say sorry to Lucy. He may be small, but he's still a pig. And look at that duvet now!' Ash flicked a glance at Lucy, rolling his eyes and shaking his head slightly as a warning not to laugh. She straightened her face with difficulty and stood up.

'That's ok. I've just discovered I've been sleeping with a pig for years,' she deadpanned, trying not to grin as Daisy turned a round-eyed gaze on her.

'No, Daisy, not a real pig, it's a ... oh, never mind. Come on, jobs to do.' He chivvied her out with Harry in front, smiling at Lucy on the way out. 'Sorry about that. Um, don't feel you have to get up...I put breakfast things out in the kitchen for you.'

'You can have my Rice Krispies if you like,' Daisy called from the corridor.

'Thank you. Bye, Harry! Bye, Daisy! Bye, Ash.' Lucy shut the door behind them, and laughed until her eyes ran.

Wide awake now, she pulled the duvet out of the cover, awkward with one hand, but unwilling to leave it as it was, patterned with mini muddy trotters. Pulling her socks on, she splashed cold water on her face and wriggled her way into Ash's sweater, before making her way downstairs, carrying the duvet cover.

Arrayed on the worktop was a selection of cereals, and bread, jams and marmalades. Filling the kettle, she popped a teabag into one of the colourful mugs and gazed through the kitchen window, appreciating how rurally the house was situated. The early sun cast long, pale lilac shadows across the tree-edged fields, which were every shade of green, gold and rich, purplish brown.

Adjacent to the house were a number of outbuildings – some with rickety, leaning doors, cracked window panes with ivy growing out of them – and a selection of old containers that looked as if they'd been painted a long time ago, and where they might have once contained geraniums, were now the sad repositories for weeds. It was picturesque in the slanting sunlight, and she instinctively thought about how she might paint it.

She jumped as Ash strode in, wearing a pair of battered khaki work trousers and a faded t-shirt. He placed five beautiful pale eggs on the worktop, took down a second mug and put a teabag in it.

'Morning – again. Daisy's just feeding the chickens. Sorry about the pig thing.' He filled both their mugs when the kettle boiled.

'Don't be. Cheered me up no end.' Lucy smiled up at him. 'I brought the duvet cover down, but I don't know where your laundry basket is.'

'Oh, you didn't have to do that. Sorry – I should have thought.'

'Thank you so much for letting me stay. And thank you so much for this, although I can't actually eat a thing this morning.' She waved her hand over the array of food arranged on the worktop. 'But please, don't let me stop you doing anything. Are you at work today?'

'As luck would have it, no. This is my once a month, long weekend off.'

'Then I'm sure you have a million things to do. I won't impose on your hospitality any longer.' As the formality of her voice reached her ears, she dipped her head in embarrassment, blowing on her tea. After the unexpected and lovely intimacy of last night, she felt shy and awkward here in his kitchen, wearing his clothes. Her fraying marriage was finally in tatters. She felt hollow, sad, in pain, and torn between hunting Gerry down and disembowelling him with a spoon, and burrowing back into the comfort of Ash's arms and hoping the world would go away. But Ash deserved better than to be used simply as a shelter. She wasn't at all sure what their relationship was, whether it was an instinctive response to the upheaval in her life, or whether there was anything deeper. Besides, she didn't have the emotional resources to deal with it right now, and she didn't want to jeopardise it by being neurotic and needy.

'It's fine, honestly.' Ash's expression was wary, and she felt the need to explain some of her dilemmas.

'It's my parents' house we've been living in, and I have to let them know what's happened. Bit complicated – they rent it to me on a peppercorn rent, I think to stop Gerry getting his hands on it.' She sighed. "My Dad never liked him, but do Dads ever think anyone is good enough for their little girls?' She watched Ash's brow furrow, and almost felt sorry for the first boy who knocked for Daisy.

'Sure, no problem. You do whatever you need to.' He nodded, his blue eyes lingering on hers. Lucy felt the now familiar tug in her stomach and her resolve to be independent and strong almost crumbled, just as Daisy burst into the kitchen, her cheeks rosy, her smile wide.

'Can I show Lucy our chickens?' She turned to Lucy, and added, 'They're rescue chickens. They'd never been outside in their lives. That's so terrible, isn't it?'

Lucy nodded. 'It is.'

'I think Lucy was about to leave, Daisy. She has things to do...'

'I can spare a few minutes to see these chickens.' Lucy looked enquiringly up at Ash and was pleased to see him nod, despite her protestations that she had to leave immediately.

Daisy trotted ahead and waited for her to catch up. It was like walking a puppy.

'What did you do to your hand?' she wanted to know.

'The car door slammed on it.'

'Ouch.' Daisy made a face. 'I slammed my finger in the door once, and I cried and cried. Did you cry?'

Lucy nodded with feeling. 'Oh yes.'

'Look.' Daisy flung an arm towards a small paddock, fenced in with chicken wire, containing a brightly painted hen-house.

From a distance, Lucy guessed they were a rather resplendently coloured breed. As she neared, a great bubble of laughter overtook her as she realised that what she'd thought were feathers were, in fact, knitted jumpers. Tiny knitted jumpers, in a rainbow of colours.

'They don't have many feathers, poor things, when they arrive,' explained Daisy, laughing along with her. 'Nanna knits them for us. She's teaching me to make them too.'

'Does Daddy rescue a lot of animals?'

'Yes.' Daisy nodded and her curls bounced. Using her hand for emphasis she listed them. 'We've got Reggie the Ram, and we've got sheep, and we've got teacup pigs, and we've got the chickens.'

'Maybe you could use the wool from the sheep to knit the chicken jumpers?' Lucy smiled.

'Maybe.' Daisy grinned.

'Your Daddy rescued me too,' mused Lucy. *Maybe I am just another one of his rescue projects, as Sarah said last night.*

'Are you his girlfriend?'

'No. I'm just Daddy's friend.'

'Daddy's shaved off his beard and he sings a lot now.' Daisy climbed over the gate to the paddock, and the chickens hurried towards her, clucking softly. 'I've just fed you! Funny things. Nanny and Bampy said that means he's happy. And that's a good thing, isn't it? I like your bike. It's a lovely colour.'

'When did you see my bike, Daisy?'

'It's at Ed's, isn't it? Ed told me it was yours.'

Lucy nodded. 'You like bikes, don't you?'

'Yes, Daddy says he's going to buy me a dirt bike for Christmas. Or maybe my birthday, if I'm really lucky.'

'Wow – do they do them for children?'

'Yes. They're really cute. I'm having one in blue. I'll be able to go out with Ed then.'

'And you'll need all the gear as well, helmet and stuff.'

'Nanny and Bampy are getting me that. I can't wait! I'm so excited!'

Lucy could have spent the whole day watching Daisy and listening to her chatter. Bright and animated, she scooped a chicken up and held it aloft so Lucy could see the poor plucked skin. Smoothing it, she settled it on the grass, and Lucy laughed as it followed the little girl round the henhouse.

'I had no idea they could be so friendly,' Lucy said, resolving never to eat chicken again. 'Thank you for showing me. I'd love to see your sheep and the rest of your little pigs one day, but as your Dad says, I've got things to do.'

Chapter Eighteen

The taxi bumped along the lane towards them. Ash had wanted to take her home, but Lucy had insisted. She didn't want to put him out any more than she had, and she didn't want Daisy involved in any domestics involving Gerry.

'I can't thank you enough, Ash.' Her voice was husky. His house felt like more of a home than hers ever had since her parents had left.

'I'd like to say it's been a pleasure, but—' His eyes burned into hers. 'Lucy. If you need me at all, if Gerry makes trouble for you, you know where to find me. I mean that.'

'Thank you. Nicola is better than a Rottweiler though, and she's offered to come over and help me sort the house out. You should feel sorry for him.' She spoke lightly, but could see he wasn't fooled. 'Please say thank you to Ed for collecting my bike. Obviously, I'll settle up with him for that. And as soon as this is healed, I'll be wanting to get training for that Mod 2. If you can bear it.'

'I look forward to it.' He bent and kissed her chastely on the cheek, and every fibre of her body wanted him to gather her up in his arms and take her away from all this. Like he'd done yesterday. But she needed to be strong, to clear up the mess of her life. And then, maybe, just maybe, she could begin the foundations of a new life. A better one. He squeezed her shoulder, and she guessed that he was having trouble letting go too. 'Heal well. I'll see you soon.'

'You most certainly will. Bye Daisy, see you both soon.' She waved goodbye to them as she climbed into the taxi, directing the driver to the café. As brave as she'd pretended to be in front of Ash, she didn't really want to go straight home and face Gerry if he was there, in her current state.

She at least needed a painkiller, and a long chat with her parents. And she longed for a shower.

The café was busy on a sunny Saturday, and Lucy felt grubby, useless and in the way, but she was able to find a bench in the sunshine and ring her parents. It was a long call. Nicola materialised at her elbow as she slumped, holding a coffee gone cold, staring unseeingly over the crowded beach.

'I wondered where you'd gone. Come back with us so I can collect some clothes, Luce. And then let's go parteee back at yours!'

Lucy allowed herself to be ferried back and forth from their house to hers. Richard came back with them, 'just to check that everything is okay,' and after inspecting every room and the studio, left for home in her van, along with admonishments to call if there was any trouble.

After they'd waved him off, Lucy flopped onto one of the sofas, her head spinning.

'Ok?' Nicola's face was sympathetic. 'Painkiller? Tea? Coffee? Wine?'

'Hell, yeah.' Lucy gazed at her friend. 'I can't believe I've really done it. We've been married all this time. But he drove the love out of me.' She chewed her lip and then exhaled gustily. 'I am starving. I haven't eaten all day.' Ash's offer of breakfast seemed a lifetime ago. 'Shall we get a takeaway?'

'Awesome.' Nicola jumped up and fetched the takeaway menus magnetised to the fridge. 'What do you fancy?'

'Pizza,' decided Lucy promptly. 'With olives and mushrooms. Gerry hated them, and we always shared, so I always ended up with what he wanted. This time, I'm having one to myself. And I'm having it delivered.'

'Good call. Me too. And chips.'

'Diet chips.'

Lucy licked her fingers, her eyes closed with relish. 'That

was the best pizza I have ever had.' They shared the sofa, the pizzas on a coffee table between them. 'I think my eyes were bigger than my belly though. I can't eat another thing.' She patted her tummy. 'I might have to eat pizza every day until I lose the sling. At least I don't have to cook it or cut it up.'

'Or wash up.' Nicola settled back on the sofa with a smile.

'Nic. I need some advice.'

'Shag him.' Nicola winked at her.

Lucy burst out laughing. 'Not that kind of advice. I mean, accountant type advice. After yesterday, it's made me realise that not only do I not know enough about my own business, I know even less about Gerry's. And I don't trust him an inch. How can I find out exactly what he's earning?'

'You can't. Unless you're a partner in the business?'

Lucy thought back. 'I remember signing some paperwork, way back. Maybe I am. That would be helpful.'

'If you're not, then you'll find out during the financial settlement for the divorce. I can give you a hand with your accounts, if you like?'

'That would be wonderful, yes please. I need to make an appointment with a solicitor next.' It was a simple enough job to check the internet for some local solicitors and Lucy made a note to ring round for an appointment first thing Monday morning. It felt good to be taking some control back already.

'So, how much stuff has he taken here, from the house?' Nicola wanted to know.

'I don't know. It can all go on the barbecue for all I care.'

'How about we move his stuff out of your bedroom? Claim back your space. Got plenty of bin bags?'

'Under the sink.' They trekked upstairs, and Nicola gave a long whistle as Lucy opened Gerry's wardrobe door.

'If you hadn't caught him with that skinny bint, I'd've said he was gay, judging by the amount of designer suits in here.'

Lucy laughed suddenly. 'I threatened to cut them up.'

'Well, why don't you?'

'I couldn't!'

'You know you want to. Look, I'll do the first one.'

'No, don't!'

'No, you're right. Actually, it would empower you to do it. Here's the scissors. Go girl! Just do the crotch. Or maybe the arm.'

'No. I can't. Two wrongs don't make a right.'

'He spends a fortune on designer stuff and you're dressed in charity shop finds.'

'I am not!'

'Well, it looks like you are. I'm your friend. I can say these things. What else does he spend his money on?'

'Golf clubs. Weekends away with his golf cronies.'

'Bloody hell. That's a fortune. Don't you ever pay any attention to what he spends? He's kept you short all this time.'

'Mmm.'

'So, are you really going to sell them on eBay?'

'I might.'

'You can't let him get away with it. Where are they?'

'If they're not in his boot, they're in the garage.'

They unlocked the garage, and stared at the gleaming array, mounted on an electric trolley. 'Christ, he could open a golf shop in here. Why does he need so many?'

Lucy stared at them and anger flooded, slowly but surely, into her veins. How stupid had she been not to see how much he spent? And all the while, begrudging her a bike that she'd won.

Nicola was poking around the shelves. 'How about this?' She held up a tin of PVA glue.

'What the hell are you going to do with that?'

'They do rattle about in these bags, have you noticed?' Nicola asked with a sly grin, giving it a shake. 'I think they need some help to stop them moving around.' She yanked the clubs out and threw them viciously on the floor. Lucy gasped in horror.

'What are you going to do with that glue?'

Nicola looked around. 'Got it.' She dug a screwdriver into the rusting lid, and pried it open. 'I know you've got a bad hand, so I can do this for you if you like …'

'Give it here.' Lucy poured it into the base of the bag.

'Good girl. Lucky you didn't bust your right hand.'

'What about this, too?' She tapped a tin of white gloss paint. She remembered painting skirting boards in one of their first properties. Hours on her knees, and he'd swanned off to the pub with his mates. 'Open it, Nic.' She poured it in carefully, making sure that none of it dripped down the outside of the bag. She didn't want to spoil the surprise.

Giggling like naughty schoolchildren, they replaced all the clubs, pushing them firmly into the sticky syrup at the bottom of the bag and locked up.

'More wine.' Nicola reached into the fridge. 'And music. And the scissors.'

'I've got a better idea.' Lucy headed into her studio, returning moments later with her decorative hole punches. She spread them on the table. There were flower shapes, and hearts and stars, and butterflies. 'I'm thinking they'd look quite pretty along the hems of his trousers.'

Nicola stared at her and burst into laughter. 'Now you're getting the idea. You're worse than I am!'

'He'll think I've done nothing to them, until he wears them.'

'Nah. Too discreet. Cut the crotch out. Or the legs off.'

Lucy stopped laughing. This was getting out of hand and

they were being childish. 'What if he does something to the café?' She sighed. 'I'd better go and pour white spirit into that golf bag.'

'You could always tell him the pots just fell off the shelf …'

But Lucy realised enough was enough, and went to put the hole punches away. She had a feeling that divorcing Gerry would be punishment enough.

Lucy awoke heavy-eyed and stiff from sleeping awkwardly to avoid her throbbing hand. Her brain had wound itself into knots in her dreams, and this morning, as sunshine beamed through the gap in the curtains, and the birds sang in the trees, the events of the last days seemed unreal.

Threading her hand carefully through her dressing gown sleeve, and back into her sling, she padded downstairs to the kitchen and made tea for them. Glancing at the clock, she was startled to see how late it was. Nearly nine. Should she go and see if Nicola was awake? As she dithered, the back door opened and Nicola strolled in, looking pink and fresh.

'You're up! I let you sleep. I thought you probably needed it.' She waved a paper bag. 'I've been for a run and I bought us some *pains au chocolat*, fresh from your local deli.'

'You put me to shame, you do.' Lucy blinked. 'Hang a banger. We haven't got a local deli.'

'Busted.' Nicola grinned. 'Richard brought them round.'

Lucy laughed. 'You minx. Have you really been for a run?'

'Nope. I thought about it, but I didn't like to, er … In case Gerry called on the off-chance. You know …' She waggled her head and shrugged. 'I'll warm these in the oven, shall I?' She switched the oven on and busied herself in Lucy's cupboards.

'If he calls in, I'll bop him with my splint,' Lucy said in a hearty voice, although with the multi-coloured bruise extending to her finger-tips, nothing could be less likely. It throbbed almost constantly. She sank into a chair beside the table. 'Ash offered to change the locks. Apparently, he used to be a carpenter, and he says it's a simple matter of replacing the barrel. I wish I'd taken him up on the offer, now. I'm not scared of Gerry. But it's so much nicer here without him. He's like a big black cloud. I don't want him here.'

Nicola gazed around her in silence for a moment, and Lucy's mouth began to water as the scent of buttery, chocolatey croissant filled the kitchen.

'Didn't your parents tell you to change the locks?'

Lucy sighed. 'It never occurred to me to ask.'

'Ash'd probably do it now if you ask.'

'I can always ring a locksmith. I think I might have worn Ash's good nature out. God, I've been so needy. I feel embarrassed.'

'Don't be. He could've said no.' Nicola blew on her hot croissant.

'I wonder where Gerry is?'

'Do you care?'

Lucy stretched her shoulders, willing her hand to heal quickly. 'It was something that Ella blurted, during our row. I've just remembered. About him moving in with her, except that it was his.'

'I don't get it.'

'He's a property manager. He got Ella the job in the café, and I reckon he's pulled some strings to get her a place to live ...'

'... for free. You've been paying her wages. And her rent.' Nicola finished her sentence, and Lucy nodded.

They said together, 'Bastard.'

They ate in silence for a moment, then Lucy said, 'Nicola, it was lovely of you to come over last night, but I don't want to spoil your weekend.'

'You've got me for the rest of today – Richard's working anyway. How about we carry on with the Gerry-removal plan? That way, when he comes to collect his stuff, it's all in one place. We'll put it all in the garage.'

'Thanks, that'll be great. No creative revenge ideas this time, though.'

Empty plastic storage boxes were pressed into service for his countless bottles of after-shaves and shower gels, watches and other paraphernalia, and they moved on into the other rooms, where their possessions were intermingled. DVDs, CDs, books, magazines. As she thumbed through them, Lucy began to realise, with a heavy heart, that they were virtually all his. Except for most of the books. She'd been a visitor in his life. Her life was in her studio. In the kitchen. In the Art Café. In Better Biking and the Vintage Bike Palace. Bitterness swept over her, rising in her mouth like bile, and she stomped out into the kitchen, fighting the urge to stamp and yell. What a waste of love.

'I found a few more empty boxes.' Nicola, black hair cobwebby from her constant forays back and forth to the garage, discovered her putting on the kettle.

'Time out.' Mugs crashed onto the worktop, followed by clattering spoons. 'Bastard. He held me down for so long. And I let him. I've wasted all this time with him.'

'Aw, Luce, no.' Nicola turned a sympathetic smile on her. 'It's early days. Don't look on it as a waste. You had happy times, didn't you?'

'I suppose.' Lucy watched the plume of steam spouting from the kettle. 'It's hard to remember when I feel so betrayed.' She exhaled with a snort. 'Ok. I'm cancelling my pity party for one. Let's crack on. The sooner it's sorted, the quicker he'll be in and out and I won't have to look at him any longer than I have to.'

'Yes, and then you can start your life afresh.' Nicola bore their mugs into the lounge, and added over her shoulder, 'Maybe with your nice Ash.' Lucy's stomach fizzed at the mention of his name. For a brief moment, she wondered what his marriage had been like.

'I should think my "nice Ash" is running a mile right now, away from me and my messy life issues.' Sitting on the floor, she swept the paraphernalia towards her to begin stacking them into a box. 'I'll text Gerry to come and collect this stuff. Or arrange for storage. The sooner he understands that I'm serious, the better.' She jumped as the doorbell rang. 'Oh God – I bet that's him – I've conjured him up, haven't I?'

'I'll get it. The café's shut now, it might be Richard.' Nicola was already on her feet. 'If it's Gerry, he better be wearing a cricket box, that's all I can say. No-one messes with my mate.'

Lucy clambered to her feet and followed her down the passage. 'If anyone's kicking him, it's going to be me.' She squinted through the frosted glass beside the front door. There wasn't just one shadowy figure on the step, there were two. As Nicola threw the door open, Lucy burst into tears.

'Mum! Dad! How, when ...? I mean – oh!' She was enveloped in a double hug on the doorstep. 'It's so lovely to see you!' She led them into the kitchen, lifting down the big teapot and putting fresh mugs out. 'I'm so sorry the place is such a mess, we've been sorting out Gerry's stuff. This is Nicola, my best friend in the world. Goodness me, you must have been driving all night!'

Her Dad, a tall bear of a man whose only nod to ageing was that his thick black hair had greyed to white, whilst his bushy eyebrows remained dark, looked up from sorting their bags out. 'We were. But it was fine, we shared the driving, caught up on some sleep ...' He shrugged. 'Easier than we thought. We should've done it more often. But ...' He stopped, his mouth shutting like a clam.

'Gerry?' Lucy supplied.

'Bastard,' Nicola said, ferrying everything into the sunny conservatory, so far untouched by their sorting attentions.

'Couldn't have put it better myself,' said Lucy's mum. 'Hello, I'm Vanessa, and Lucy's dad is Pascal.'

'We have heard a lot about you.' Lucy noticed that her Dad's accent sounded much stronger these days and she smiled. It was wonderful to see them looking so fit and healthy. 'Lucy is very lucky to have friends like you and your husband.'

'I know.' Nicola grinned, shaking their hands and Lucy began to feel as if she was back at her school parents' evening, being discussed in her hearing. The doorbell rang again, and Nicola answered the door, this time to Richard. Introductions were made, and more tea was poured. Richard had brought a selection of 'leftover' cakes, which made him even more welcome.

'We'll go, Lucy,' said Nicola, as they stacked the dishwasher with mugs and plates, leaving Richard being interrogated by her cuisine-keen parents. 'I can help you make up the spare bed again, and if you need us, you know where we are.'

'Thank you so much, Nic.' The friends hugged, and made short work of the spare room. Lucy was reminded of the trotter-printed duvet she'd stripped only the day before, and she wondered what Ash and Daisy were doing on this sunny Sunday afternoon. Should she text him, just to say thanks? Again?

Lucy and her parents waved Richard and Nicola off, and

Lucy sensed that it was time to get down to business. She filled in any gaps left over from their phone call.

'So where is Gerry now?' Vanessa raised her eyebrows.

'We thought you were him earlier. I don't know, and I don't care. With his bint, I imagine.' Lucy shrugged. 'I'll have to text him and find out, so I can serve the divorce papers on him. How long will you be staying?'

'A few days,' said her Dad.

Her Mum frowned. 'Long enough to make sure that hand will be okay. It looks terrible.'

'It was an accident. Really.' Her parents didn't look convinced. 'And I was taken straight to the hospital, by my bike instructor.'

'Well.' Her Dad rested a beady eye on her. 'I'm glad there's someone sensible around to look out for you. Where is this bike? I want to see it. I haven't been on a motorbike in years, but it's made me think about getting back on again.'

'It's in the Vintage Bike Palace. You'd like it, Dad. Lots of old bikes.'

'Excellent. I need to have the locks changed tomorrow too.' He yawned and stretched. 'I'm stiff as a board after sitting in that car. It's a lovely evening. Shall we go and have a walk by the sea, and then find a nice pub for a meal? I miss proper pubs. And beer. And bacon. And chips.'

Lucy laughed. 'No-one would ever think you were French.'

Chapter Nineteen

On Tuesday morning, Ash drove slowly along Lucy's road in the patrol car. Should he knock and see how she was? It was probably too early. And anyway, what if she and Gerry had made up? It happened far too often for him to dismiss that possibility. He scanned ahead, seeing that her van was back, along with a newish Peugeot saloon with French plates. So, her parents had come home. That was good. He told himself that she didn't need him, and wasn't sure he liked that idea.

Reaching the junction, he paused. He couldn't drive past again now without people noticing. Quiet, well-to-do streets like this always had more than their fair share of Neighbourhood Watch members, who noticed strange comings and goings. Seeing a patrol car cruising past several times would provoke a flurry of calls to the local station, wondering what was going on, who amongst them was growing cannabis plants in the attic.

He wanted to see her again. The thought that she might pass her test and just fade out of his life made his pulse pound. If he gave her too much time, someone else would snap her up. He could just text her. That would be less invasive. To say… what? That he was around to help? No. He *was* around to help, of course, but that wasn't what he really wanted to say to her. Even if she was standing right there in her drive, he wasn't sure that he could tell her what he wanted to say. The past two days were etched brightly into his mind. Had it only been two days? Lucy, in the spare room bed, turning towards him, reaching for him, her soft lips beneath his …

He fidgeted in the seat as his groin tightened, relieved to be single crewed in the car. He couldn't text that. He didn't want to come across as some kind of a stalker. Besides, she'd been high on painkillers and emotions. For all he knew, she was regretting that kiss already.

She'd let him into so many corners of her life during those couple of days. Allowed him to see her at her worst. She probably regretted that too. She had enough to think about right now. No. He'd text her that her bike was safely at Ed's. He'd do it now, in a minute. He laughed at the Welsh-ism.

The radio crackled to life and he listened as one of his patrols was sent to a traffic collision on the other side of town. If they'd been called, there had to be an injury. The radio controller told him the ambulance was on its way. As he always did, he hoped it didn't include a child. Or a bike. It was the busiest time of the day, the school drop-offs. At times like this, he wished he was on motorbike patrol. He'd be able to cut through the traffic with no problems. Except that would mean only dealing with traffic related incidents. As it was, he enjoyed the variety of his work, never knowing what the day might bring. And he liked working with his young, enthusiastic shift. Calculating his route, he informed Control that he was ten minutes away, or less. The text to Lucy would have to wait.

By the time the traffic collision had been unravelled, there was a list of incidents that needed attention, and the day flew past. On his way back from some enquiries, he nipped into the Vintage Bike Palace to collect some parts. And bumped straight into Lucy with a well-dressed couple he assumed were her parents – the likeness to her mother was astonishing. Her father, inspecting the rows of vintage bikes, made Ed look short.

Lucy looked so much better than when he saw her last, despite still wearing the sling. Her eyes lit up as she saw him, and a blush rose from her neck, colouring her pretty face.

He didn't know whether to shake her hand, kiss her cheek, do both or neither of those things. She compounded his dilemma by stopping just short of him.

'Mum and Dad, er, Vanessa and Pascal, are over for a few days.' She turned to them. 'This is Ash, my bike instructor.'

'Ah – so you are responsible for my daughter zooming around the countryside on that enormous machine.' With lowered brows, Pascal jerked his head towards her purple Triumph. Before Ash could respond, the man continued, 'Thank you. About time she came to her senses and had some fun. And dumped that idiot at the same time.'

'Dad!' Lucy rolled her eyes with a grin that included her mother. 'Thanks again for letting me stay over on Friday night, Ash, that was so kind of you. How was your weekend, did you do anything exciting? How is Daisy?' Her words tumbled over themselves and he smiled. It was lovely to see her looking so happy. He hoped that Gerry didn't start making her life awkward again. Divorces weren't easy.

'Daisy hasn't stopped talking about your visit,' he told her. 'She's done some drawings she wants to show you. Maybe, when you're feeling up to it, you'd like to come over for dinner? Or a restaurant?' The words were out of his mouth before he'd had a chance to edit them. *Had he been rude, not including her parents? Should he invite them all now? Wouldn't they think it was a bit sudden? Hell, he was so out of the dating game. They weren't even dating!* He wasn't used to dithering like this, he was a man of action. He made decisions, and he stuck to them. Usually. Her brown eyes rested steadily on his face.

'Dinner at yours would be lovely. Thank you.' She wiggled the fingers of her splinted hand. 'Once I'm ambidextrous again, I'll return the compliment.'

Lucy's heart sank as she saw the hired van parked in the

drive on their return. Slumped in the driver's seat, Gerry scowled as she approached.

'I've been waiting for ages. This van's cost me a fortune. Where have you been? Your van is here. I could have had everything loaded by now.'

'Hello? I'm out of action, remember?' Lucy indicated her bruised fingers. 'Why didn't you say you were coming, Gerry?'

'You changed the locks.'

'No. Actually, I did.' Her Dad loomed behind her. 'Gerry. I take it you've come to collect your stuff at last?'

Gerry blanched, his lips thinning. 'Pascal.'

Lucy could hear from his tone what an effort her father was making. 'I'll give you a hand to load everything. Have you got far to go with it?'

'No. Not that it's any of your business,' Gerry snapped. 'It's all going in storage.'

Lucy couldn't resist her snipe. 'Ella doesn't want it all cluttering up her cute, girly space then?'

Gerry mumbled something and she frowned as her brain translated. She hid a grin. Barely. 'What was that?' she said, loud enough for her dad to overhear. 'She's chucked you out? Already?'

'Oh, just shut it, will you? You've got what you wanted.'

Unlocking the garage door, Lucy watched, feeling crosser and crosser as her father loaded the carefully packed boxes into the hire van. Gerry somehow managed to do hardly any of the lifting but kept up a stream of complaint. 'My suits will all need dry-cleaning now, squashed into boxes like this. I've a good mind to send you the bill. And what the hell's happened to my golf clubs?' His voice rose into a panicked screech. 'They won't bloody come out! What the ...? If you've tampered with my stuff, I'm going to sue you for damages and—'

Her dad, silent until that moment, said, 'I think not. You're lucky the arms and legs are still on those suits. If I'd been here, I would have cut them all off.' Lucy stared at her usually mild-mannered father, as he glowered at Gerry. *Go, Dad!* 'And I wouldn't have stopped at the suits. So think yourself lucky, young man, that I wasn't here. And just for once in your life, get on with something without blaming everything on my daughter. I'm not surprised she's had enough of you.' He paused for breath. 'Frankly, I don't know how she's put up with you for this long. The sooner you are out of her life, the better, as far as I'm concerned. *Comprenez?*' The accented final word told Lucy all she needed to know about her Dad's thoughts where Gerry was concerned. Mouth open, Gerry looked as if he'd been slapped.

While he was in his state of shock, Lucy threw the last few items into the van and said with a flourish, 'I hope that Ella is actually paying rent now you've moved out. On the house that I believe you and I jointly own?'

Gerry swallowed without closing his mouth. It wasn't a pretty sight. 'She's, she's ... How did you know about that?'

Lucy raised her eyebrows. 'She gave her address when she worked in the café. It's easy enough to check the Land Registry, y'know. Once I started looking, I found a whole lot more properties that you and I seem to own. So you owe me rent on them for all these years.' She faced him, hand on hip. 'I know so much more about you now than I did when we lived together. When I was stupid enough to trust you. And let me tell you, Gerry, I don't appreciate being taken for a fool.' She watched his mouth working soundlessly as his eyes flicked from her to her Dad. She forged on. 'By the way, we have a mediation appointment coming up, to discuss the finances. Bring your cheque book.'

'Mediation?'

'Well, it's that, or court. A forensic examination of the

accounts, and someone independent tells you what will happen with our money. I think you'll find that court will cost you considerably more. Don't even think about lying. I've already spoken to 'our' accountant. Funny that. I have learned so much. I suppose I ought to thank you. Did you really never think that I would check this stuff out?' She blessed Nicola and her amazing financial knowledge for helping her thread her way through the tangled net of Gerry's finances during the last few days. 'Where shall I send the paperwork, if you're not staying at Ella's? To your office?'

He nodded. Lucy had never seen him so lacking in bluster. She wondered if she should be enjoying it this much, but oh, it did feel good. If the accountant was correct, and she had no reason to think that he wasn't, the division of finances would be heavily weighted against her sneaky, conniving, lying bastard of a nearly ex-husband.

'Right. That's all your personal stuff. We can sort out furniture later. No point rushing, as you have nowhere to put it anyway, is there?'

'Oh, you think you're so clever, don't you?' Gerry's face was scarlet. 'You've got it all – you've never wanted for a bloody thing. Your parents even gave you a house, for fuck's sake! My parents have never given me anything. I've had to work for everything.'

Lucy pursed her lips at his outburst. 'Everything. Really? That includes free lodgings here, does it? That includes my earnings which you used as a deposit on the first two houses, does it? And the profits from my exhibitions that you apparently 'invested' into a 'pension' that's turned out to be another two houses which you've been renting out and I haven't seen a penny for?' She took a deep breath. 'And for your information, I've been paying my parents rent since we lived here. So you can just fuck off with your self-pitying shit. Go and find someone else to brainwash.'

The hire van lurched off the drive, gears crashing. Lucy and her father linked arms and went into the house.

'And good bloody riddance.' Her Mum turned towards them from her stance at the window. 'I saw you having words.' She reached out and pulled Lucy into a hug. 'Well done, darling. I was about to go out and join in, but from the look on his face, you were winning.'

'Oh, dear. Was I a bit harsh?' Lucy stared down the road after Gerry. 'He's right, in a way. I have always been lucky. I've got lovely parents, and lovely friends.'

'You make your own luck, in the end.' Her father shoved his hands into his pockets.

Lucy smiled. 'Maybe. It's as good a time as any to have a chat about what I do next, to be honest.'

'Do you have plans?' Her parents exchanged glances.

'I do.' Lucy nodded firmly. 'It was wonderful of you to gift us – me – the house for so long. But since I've been doing my very long overdue homework on renting, I really do think it's time that you had a proper income from it. And not the measly amount I've been paying you.' She held her hand up as her parents began to protest. 'It's time I stood on my own two feet and got a place of my own. I'd like to rent first and then, well, take it from there. The café is earning well, and there should be enough left over from the divorce for me to find somewhere. I might have to sell my bike to put towards it. I'll still have my little 125 to buzz about on.' She swallowed back a sudden lump in her throat at the idea of selling Cadbury, but steeled herself. It might not come to that. 'What do you think?'

'We're not rushing you,' her Dad said. 'Don't make any rash decisions.'

'I think it's very brave of you.' Her Mum squeezed her hand. 'You know we'll support you however we can. But your Dad's right, no rush, okay?'

'The only thing I'll miss is my studio.' Lucy had to

straighten her lip to stop it wobbling. *It was weird the things she'd miss. Not her husband. Her studio.* 'But I'll have my space all to myself when I move, so I can just use that instead. It will be fine.' She fired up her laptop. 'In fact, how about making a start right now? Maybe you could help me choose somewhere?'

'Somewhere close to the café could be good.' Her father's finger pointed at the screen. A smart modern apartment near the sea. Tiny, but really, she didn't need much. 'Something like this?' Somewhere deep down, a bubble of excitement began to rise at the possibilities of a new beginning. Away from Gerry. She looked at the rent payable and compressed her lips. That reminded her. That two-faced little bitch Ella was living rent free.

'Dad – could you give me a lift, please? I've just got one more thing to sort out.' She told them what she meant to do.

'Ooh, this sounds exciting.' Her Mum rubbed her hands together. 'Count me in.'

'I'm doing this myself though, ok?' Lucy warned them. Lovely as it was to know she had back-up in the car, this was all part of her toughening up process. Bundling back into the car, they made a quick stop off at a stationery shop on the way. Lucy rehearsed what she was going to say all the way to the address that Ella had given. They parked a little way along the leafy street.

'Go girl!' Her Mum leaned out of the car window and blew her a kiss. 'Our phones are on, if she kicks off.'

'Uhm, ok.' Lucy blinked. *Kicks off? Her Mum was so down with the kids these days.* 'Back shortly.'

She rapped on the smart front door. To be fair, the property was in good condition. But then, she couldn't imagine Gerry wanting to live anywhere that wasn't. He must be seething, in his hotel room. The thought made her want to laugh aloud.

The front door opened and then flew almost shut. Almost, as Lucy had wedged her armoured motorcycle boot, worn for just this purpose, into the gap. She was practically nose to nose with the girl.

'Lucy. How did you know I was ...' Ella flicked back her long hair. 'What do you want?'

'I brought you this.' Lucy held out a small package. 'It's a Rent Book. I don't believe you have one.'

Ella didn't even look. 'He's not here.' She gave the door another shove.

'I know. I've just seen him and he told me everything. You're finished. And that means that if you want to remain here, you need to be paying rent. So I brought you a rent book. Here you go.'

'No. Private arrangement. Nothing to do with you. Piss off.'

'In case you weren't aware from your boyfriend – my husband – he and I are partners in his business. Which, in an almost hilarious turn of events as I'm sure you'll agree, makes me, ta-daaah – your landlady. Either you pay up, or *you* piss off.'

'How can I afford rent? I haven't got a job.'

'Oh, yes, let me think, I fired you, didn't I? Ella, if you can't pay, you have to leave. I'll be fair – I'll give you a week to find somewhere else or find a job. Which is more than you deserve.'

'I could report you. Take you to a rent tribunal.'

'Oh, please do. I'm sure they'd be interested to know that you've been living rent free in exchange for services, I think they call it?'

Ella's sour expression collapsed like a bowl of un-set custard. 'I'm so sorry, Lucy,' she wailed. 'My parents threw me out. They told me to get a job. Gerry found me the job in the café. He was the only one who seemed to want to look after me. He just seemed so clever and sophisticated, and when he got me this place, I, well ...' Strands of her long hair drifted across her face, wet with tears, and stuck there.

'Really?' Lucy exhaled a bitter snort. 'Don't be fooled, Ella. He's only interested when it's all going his way. Do yourself a favour, girl, and find someone your own age. And while you're doing that, finish your education.'

'I need somewhere to live to do that. And a job.'

Exasperated, Lucy snapped, 'Oh, grow up! I'm having to do the exact same thing.'

'But you've got the café! I've got nothing.'

'I finished my degree. And look, I'm not your careers advisor, Ella. Have a look for flat shares on the student notice-board. Ask around. I'm sure you can find something if you look hard enough.' Taking pity on the forlorn girl, Lucy added, 'And look, you were good at your job.'

Ella looked hopeful. 'Does that mean you'll give me my job back?'

'Are you having a laugh?'

'Is that a yes or a no?'

'It's a bloody no! God, Ella, talk about thick-skinned.' Lucy rolled her eyes. 'Right. You have exactly one week. By that time, I want either your rent, or your key. Got it?' She watched as the girl nodded, cuffing her nose. 'I'll be back to check up. It's not the end of the world. It's the start of something better. Ok?'

'O-kkkaay.' Ella retreated, but Lucy was astonished to hear her snivel a 'Tha-ank-you,' just as the door closed with a click. She lingered on the doorstep, feeling as if she'd just kicked a bag of puppies abandoned by the road. Bloody Gerry. He was a master of sly deception. She'd been taken in by it all these years, she could hardly blame Ella for strolling the same path. She mentally added enquiries about flat shares to her list of To Do's. Maybe she could put a card up in the café. She told herself that the sooner Ella was ensconced elsewhere, the sooner this place would start earning rent again.

'Did you punch her lights out?' her Mum wanted to know. 'Chuck all her stuff in the garden and jump up and down on it?'

'Hell yeah,' Lucy lied, with a grin. 'I did good, Mum.'

Lucy's parents stayed for more than a fortnight, in a flurry of activity. The weather was glorious, as this part of Wales often was in early summer.

They registered the house with a letting agency, and between them they packed away as much of the contents as possible in preparation for renting it out. Any repairs were sorted out, and some fresh emulsion applied where necessary. They decided, when the time came, to let the house unfurnished, so Lucy could take anything she might need to help her out in her new place. There were only a few pieces of furniture that belonged to Gerry – the rest would go into storage until it was sold or shipped back to France.

While her parents visited old haunts and caught up with friends, Lucy found time to finish off the original paintings for TV Tom's order. There was going to be a party at the TV studios to celebrate the make-over, and Tom said he was sure her paintings would draw a lot of attention. She couldn't wait to see them all in situ. It was so good to be spending more time on her own art, rather than focussing primarily on selling other people's.

She found a little ground floor apartment. Converted from a Victorian, pink-painted house, it wasn't quite as high spec as the one her dad had pointed out, but it was affordable and convenient. There was a little sunny spot in a sheltered courtyard for a cuppa or glass of wine, and although there was no parking on the narrow road, she could walk to work in moments. She took her parents along to view it with her.

'It's lovely,' they agreed. She was glad that they were there. She'd missed them, these past few years. She consoled herself that she would be seeing them much more often from now on, as she wouldn't have Gerry in tow, making faces and moaning about the long journey. She was even thinking about motor-biking down to them. Now that was an adventure to plan.

It seemed never-ending, but eventually the house was packed up and given a final clean in preparation for the new tenants. As they locked up the house that represented so much of her past, her childhood, and her marriage, Lucy had a distinct sense of winding up her old life and embarking on a new one.

Her sunny little flat was ready. It contained the entire contents of her studio, and a new bed, plus a few small items of furniture from the house, and she already loved the sense of expectation that was in the atmosphere there. She waved her parents off from her new address, which felt like completely the right thing to have done. Even though she'd shed tears as soon as the car was out of sight, she knew it had given them peace of mind to see her settled.

She still had some way to go to iron out the financial details of her divorce, but the groundwork was going ahead. It would just take time, and she would have to be patient. Gerry wasn't contesting the basis of the settlement, which was something, and she'd stuck to her guns at the first mediation meeting.

Ella was still in the house, but she'd found somewhere to live, promising to be out in another week. It was irritating to have to keep going back to check, but Lucy felt strangely responsible for the girl. Perhaps she saw echoes of her own younger self.

Wandering out to her little courtyard early one evening, she lifted her face to the sun and listened to the seagulls chattering on the rooftops. It was bliss to have her own space. She would not rush into anything.

She refused to dwell on the possibilities of a relationship with Ash. If something developed, well, this time she'd retain her independence. Fresh slate, and all that. The bike-girls, who she met along with Nicola, talked about trips and ride-outs, and she looked forward to the day when she could go out with them. A tiny voice in her head piped up that ride-outs with Ash could be fun too, but she pushed it firmly away. One step at a time, she told it. Her heart, like her hand, needed time to heal and be strong.

Collecting a sketchbook and some pens and watercolours, she sat back in the sunshine, and began to doodle. Her pen made a round, smiley face, added freckles and a mop of dark, unruly curls. The shade dappled over her shoulders as she struggled to capture the image that had lurked in her mind for two weeks now. Stretching her shoulders, she tipped her painting water away and wandered into the kitchen to refill the jar, just as the doorbell rang. She took a moment to register that there was no leap of alarm in case it was Gerry. He held no power over her any more.

It was Ash, once again heart-stoppingly handsome in his uniform. She'd noticed herself registering every police car that passed, peering in to see if it was him. She smiled at him now, feeling shy and a bit flustered by his appearance, as she had the time they'd bumped into him at the Bike Palace.

'Good evening. I'm your friendly local bobby.' His hunky frame filled the doorway as he smiled down at her, his eyes crinkling at the corners. 'I understand you've just moved in, and I just wanted to check on your security.'

'Goodness me, Sergeant Connor. What a lovely personal touch.' She grinned back at him. 'Would you like to come in?' Her pulse beat a tattoo in her neck. She was sure he must be able to hear it.

'No thanks, I'm double-crewed today.' He gestured to the patrol car, parked in the road, and Lucy smiled at the WPC who waved back at her. 'I just wondered if you were free on Wednesday for an early dinner, with Daisy? It's my rest day, so we could, maybe … go out in the afternoon. She'd love to see you again.'

Daisy would love to see her? Lucy wasn't sure whether she was being asked on a play-date with the little girl, or a real date with Ash. It was naughty of her, but she rather enjoyed watching Ash flounder on. It was so unlike the 'completely in control' man she'd grown to know.

'I don't know if you're driving yet, or in the café that day? Or …?' He tailed off, and shoved his hands in his pockets, his expression hopeful but wary. She didn't need much persuading to help him out.

'Just about driving, sort of in the café when I can, love to come for afternoon 'whatever' and dinner, thank you.' She grinned up at him, her heart threshing and feeling just like a teenager on a first date. 'I can arrange a half day, does that help?'

He nodded with emphasis, and Lucy was reminded of Daisy. 'Great. I'll pick you up. At the café, Wednesday?' The door to the patrol car opened and the WPC leaned out.

'Sorry! Call for us, Sarge.'

'Oops – no peace for the wicked. See you soon.' Ash whirled away, giving her a half wave, and was gone. Lucy watched the patrol car execute a speedy turn in the road and smiled to herself as she remembered driving him to collect her Cadbury. She flexed her hand, still strapped and sore if she overdid it, but improving. She was itching to get back on her bike. Meanwhile, she had things to do. Collecting her jar of clean water, she hastened back to her drawings, the jewel-bright colours glowing beneath the late sun.

Chapter Twenty

Wednesday morning dawned sunny and blue-skied again. Lucy chose a summer dress and sandals, hooking a light jacket over her shoulders, along with a bright cotton scarf. They'd taken on extra part-time staff to cover her absences and it had been easy enough to arrange cover for that afternoon. She was glad of the many visitors as her nerves fizzed with excitement at the thought of spending the afternoon with Ash, although it felt strange not to be on their bikes. Every time the door opened, her head jerked up to see if it was him. It was worse than being a teenager again.

When she saw him stride through the sun-drenched café in an indigo shirt and jeans, her heart almost stopped. He was so handsome.

'You look lovely.' His gaze raked her from top to toes, and she had to fight the urge to fan herself.

'Thank you. You do too.' Lucy slipped her sunglasses on and settled back into the seat of his SUV. 'Am I allowed to ask what we're doing?'

'Lunch, with the best view in Gower.'

'I thought The Art Café had the best view in Gower.' Lucy turned a raised eyebrow and pout on him.

'Lunch. With *one* of the best views in Gower.' Ash grinned.

'I can't eat a big lunch *and* dinner!' Lucy blew out her cheeks.

'Ice-cream. With arguably one of the finest views in Gower.' Ash sent her a side-long glance, his eyes crinkling at the corners. 'Does it matter? It's just nice to be out in the sunshine.'

Lucy said, straight-faced, 'Maybe I can have a children's

meal ...' *I'd be happy going anywhere, as long as it was with you.* His driving was smooth and unhurried, as Lucy expected. The countryside burst with colour, and made her realise how long it had been since she'd just gone out and enjoyed it. In less than thirty minutes, they were parked on the cliff-top car park, overlooking the great sweep of the bay.

'It's ridiculous. I haven't been here in years.' She breathed in the glorious view as they walked to the end of Worm's Head.

'Next stop, America.' Ash stared out over the sea. 'Marvellous, isn't it? Also, it's bloody freezing. I forgot about the wind up here. Shall we go and find a spot of lunch?'

'Now yer talking. I'm starving.' They strolled back towards the car park, ducking into the little whitewashed hotel perched on the top of the cliff.

'Okay. You were right.' Lucy sipped her Earl Grey tea and stared through the panoramic windows. 'This *is* the best view in Wales. And these cakes are nearly as good as Richard's. I'll just check again.'

'What happened to that "child-size" portion?'

'It would have been rude not to eat them.' She laughed, enjoying their easy banter. Ash glanced at his watch, and Lucy sensed that their afternoon had drawn to a close.

'Don't rush your tea. Mum and Dad are collecting Daisy, and meeting us back at the house.'

Lucy stilled. Meeting his parents? Did that mean anything? Although, she reasoned, he'd already met hers. And although the lines between friendship and a deeper connection were blurring, he'd made no attempt to kiss her beyond a friendly peck on the cheek. He wasn't rushing her into anything.

'Will Sarah be there?' She took in the wonderful view for a final snapshot in her mind as they walked back to the car.

'Probably not. Although you can't always rely on that, to be honest. She does have a tendency to just turn up.'

Lucy pondered for a long moment as Ash navigated the narrow lanes home.

'Okay,' she said. 'Talking about honesty – you know pretty much everything there is to know about me.'

He nodded slowly.

'And I know next to nothing about you. Other than you're a policeman who does bike training in his scant spare time, you have a daughter, and you're a single dad. You have rescue chickens. And you've rescued me.' *And I'm very attracted to you. And scared about what I might be getting into.* 'And you know the words to Taylor Swift songs, and the names of all the Disney Princesses,' she said aloud, watching him show his even white teeth in a grin. 'But other than that ...'

There was a long pause. Lucy waited.

'Okay.'

He chewed his lip, and Lucy felt as if she was pulling something out of him he was unwilling to give. She was about to tell him it didn't matter, she didn't need to know, when he began to speak. She didn't interrupt.

The flow of words came haltingly at first, as if they were unfamiliar to him.

'I was an officer in the Royal Engineers when I first met Sophie, Daisy's Mum. She was a bit younger than me. We got married and everything was fine until Sophie got pregnant. She ... she didn't like me being away so much, and we argued. A lot. Anyway ...'

He shook his head as if to expunge the memory. 'I agreed to give my notice in, find something local. But it's not like civvy street; you have to give them a year. Sophie wasn't impressed about that. I thought it would all be ok once the baby was born and I was back. Her parents were around to help, and she'd made friends with the other army wives.'

Checking his mirror, he indicated and turned off onto a small country lane, stopping in the entrance to a field and switching off the engine.

'Sorry, I can't drive and talk like this,' he muttered, not looking at her. 'We'd been on the phone this one time, and she said I should ask for compassionate discharge but, well, I didn't want to. I loved my job! I didn't really want to leave. It was only because of her I was doing it. It ended in yet another row.'

He breathed in slowly and the sigh that escaped was full of emotion. His voice cracked.

'That's the last time I ever spoke to her.'

He turned his head and looked at Lucy, but she knew he wasn't seeing her. His features were rigid, set. Turning back to gaze at a spot on the far horizon, he carried on. 'She went for a drive. I still don't know where she was going, or why. It doesn't matter now.' He shrugged slightly, and then on a rush of breath continued, 'She jumped a red light at a big junction and was hit by a delivery van. It was totally her fault, I know. But I always wondered ... maybe she wasn't concentrating properly because of—'

He cleared his throat, and Lucy said hastily, 'You don't have to tell me all this. I'm sorry, I shouldn't have asked.'

'No. I need to tell you. I want to tell you. They tried to save her, I know they did. Daisy was delivered prematurely by Caesarean, but Sophie didn't make it.'

Lucy breathed in sharply. '*Oh, God! And I thought I had problems ...*'

'So. I got that compassionate discharge.' He snorted a laugh that contained no humour. 'And was flown home at the speed of light, virtually. My parents were great. I was hopeless. I didn't want to see the baby at all.'

He looked at her properly then, his expression bleak.

'I didn't want her,' he said, simply. 'I couldn't even look after myself at that point; I wasn't in a fit state to look after a premature baby.'

Lucy said nothing. She had no idea what to say. Her throat felt sore and constricted. She wanted to weep for him.

'She was shared out between both sets of parents,' he continued, rubbing his thumbnail over a speck on the windscreen. 'Mum and Dad tried to get me involved when they had her, but ...' He shrugged and shook his head. 'Then one day they brought her with them. I was ... not in a good place. And they just left her with me, with this great big bag of all her stuff. Explained what I had to do, but I wasn't listening. They just left her with me!' he repeated. His expression was disbelieving, but probably more at his own ineptitude than of his parents, she guessed.

'She was an ugly little thing. Sort of crumpled looking and with loads of sticky up black hair. I didn't go near her for ages, and she seemed quite happy just lying there. I suppose I hoped they'd just come back and collect her again, and I wouldn't have to do anything. And then she started crying. It wasn't much at first – sort of mewing, like kittens do. And I could kind of ignore it.'

Lucy's expression must have given her feeling away, as he shook his head, his mouth a thin line. 'I know. Shocking isn't it? I said I wasn't in a good place. And then the howling really started. I had no idea a baby could cry that loudly. I panicked. Ridiculous now, when I think about it. I'd dealt with men with firearm injuries, and this little scrap completely threw me. I looked out of the window to see if Mum and Dad were still there, thought they might be waiting in their car, but they weren't. I didn't have the faintest idea what to do with a crying baby. I rang and asked them to help me. I begged them. They must have heard her crying – it probably broke their hearts – but they still said no. "Try feeding her," they said.' He laughed. 'I've been doing that ever since.'

'Did that stop her crying?' Lucy felt her eyes filling up with tears. She could picture it in her mind.

'Not quite.' He eyed her. 'It makes me cringe to think how useless I was. I just sort of stuck the bottle in her mouth while she was lying there. She took a few sucks and then this look came over her face, a sort of "what the hell are you doing?" face. So, I picked her up. I didn't even know how to do that! She was so tiny. Scary. She glared at me – she still does – and went all stiff. Frightened the shit out of me, I tell you. I sat down and propped her up on my lap and had another go with the bottle, and I talked to her. And she relaxed, and that little face looked up at me, so trusting ... Well, that was it. I fell in love with her there and then.' He shook his head and then laughed. 'But I nearly sent her back with that first nappy!'

Lucy took a tissue out of the box in the passenger door and blew her nose.

'I think you're amazing,' she croaked eventually.

'Well, no, see, I'm not.' He spread his hands and stared at them. 'I've never forgiven myself for those first few weeks. I should have been there for her.' He blew out. 'For both of them. I should've been there.'

Lucy wished she had some words of wisdom to impart to make it all better.

'I'm sure if Sophie could see what a great Dad you are with Daisy, she'd forgive you.'

He patted her leg, his expression rueful. 'So, Daisy has been properly ruined by two sets of grandparents as the only grandchild. And Sarah, who was seventeen when her sister died, has doted on her since she was born. And they're all part of the support team without which Daisy and I can't function. I know Sarah is a bit ... intense ... but I rely on her an awful lot. And—' He looked away from her again. '—she's never had to share us, me, with anyone else.'

Lucy stared at him as the import of this sank in. 'There's not been anyone in your life since Sophie?'

Ash drummed the dashboard with his fingertips.

'There's never really been time. And er, I've never looked.' He glanced at her and looked quickly away. 'I didn't want to get involved with someone ... someone who might ...' He shrugged helplessly and stopped speaking.

Someone who might break his heart again? Lucy guessed it was something along those lines.

'I've had offers. I'm not a complete social hermit. But I never wanted Daisy caught up in my potential love life, getting attached to someone who might leave.' He stopped and then said, 'But then, suddenly, there was you. And no-one else has ever made me laugh like you.'

'I make you laugh?' she said, flatly, as his words sank in. And there she'd been almost throwing herself at him.

'Yes, you do.' He looked at her properly for the first time since they'd stopped, and those intense blue eyes did funny things to her stomach as always. 'And the way you sang in your van that day, it was great!' He carried on in an un-Ash-like rush. 'And er, look, I really, really, erm, like you. Okay?' He reached across the bulky console and took her hand, turning his body to face her. 'I like everything about you. I liked your messy hair, and the fact that you tried to pick up that bike on the first day and shouted at me when you couldn't do a U turn. There was so much energy fizzing out of you that day. I was so pleased when you came back.'

Lucy's heart sang but she looked at him reproachfully.

She wasn't ready to rush in yet. 'You didn't seem that enamoured of me when you first met me.'

'I'm sorry. I know. I wasn't. I just … I just imagined Daisy standing behind your van and—' He swallowed, and then looked sharply at her. 'And excuse me – "Brian Blessed"?'

It was Lucy's turn to look shame-faced.

'Well,' she said. 'I did you a favour, didn't I? See how much better you look without that terrible face fungus.' *On second thoughts, grow it back. You look far too good without it. And I'm not in the habit of sharing my men. My man? Steady on girl …*

Chapter Twenty-One

It was as if his emotional floodgates had been opened, Lucy reflected on the remaining, short drive to his house. As if, having held back for so long, he'd thrown off his hard, outer shell, and was revealing his soft underbelly. She laughed at her mixed metaphors, covertly watching his strong hands with the neatly trimmed nails on the steering wheel, enjoying hearing him laugh as their conversation flowed.

And of course, there was the added complication of Daisy. She liked children, going regularly into primary schools as a visiting art tutor, and loved being with them, and she liked what little she'd already seen of Daisy. But what if Daisy didn't like her? That would be a deal breaker.

Maybe she should be worrying about her own feelings here – she could be the one left heart-broken. He must have sensed her inner turmoil.

'Ok?'

'What if Daisy doesn't like me?' she blurted.

His expression told her that had been the last thing on his mind. 'Not like you? She's barely stopped talking about you!' He squeezed her leg, sending shockwaves of lust through her. 'Just be your gorgeous self, Luce. Who could not love you?'

Gerry hadn't, she thought, then realised she really didn't care. And hadn't cared for rather too long a time.

It dawned on her that her life was going to be very different from now on. That she was, at last, going to be in charge of her own destiny. Perhaps Gerry had done her a favour, after all.

'Hello, I saw the car. You must be Lucy. I'm Babs.' Holding a trug full of bright lettuces, the slender older woman picked her way towards them out of the kitchen garden that Lucy hadn't spotted during her short stay. Wiping a hand on her jeans, she held Lucy's in a firm handshake. 'I heard about your poor hand. I hope Ashley is looking after you.' She gripped her son in an embrace, kissing his cheek.

'Were you lurking in the undergrowth, Mum?' enquired Ash, his mouth tweaked up at one corner, as he threw open the back door for them.

'Yes.' She bumped him out of the way with her hip and began to wash the greens in the sink. Lucy could just imagine this woman having no truck with her son's protracted self-pity.

'He's doing a great job,' nodded Lucy, smiling at Ash. 'But when he invited me to dinner, I thought *he* was cooking it ...'

Ash coughed loudly. 'She's still on painkillers, poor thing. Doesn't know what she's saying.' Lucy opened her mouth to reply and closed it as a tall man joined them, smiling, Daisy in his wake. Ash bent and wrapped his arms around his daughter from behind, making monster chomping noises on her neck while she pealed with laughter.

'Mmmm. I'm starving. This little girl looks very tasty! Yum, yum!'

'Can Lucy come and see Nellie, Daddy?' Extricating herself from her father's clutches, her curls bouncing, she turned to Lucy. 'She's going to be really pretty one day and Daddy said we can paint daisies on her.'

Lucy was intrigued. 'Can I see her?'

Ash grinned. 'Come on then. You're in charge, Daisy.'

Daisy was delighted. She led the way across uneven paths and held back the clutching, overgrown vines, and Lucy and Ash obliged by pretending to be lost.

Ash's garage was actually two outbuildings linked

together: an enormous workshop that on first view seemed to house a multitude of parts of ancient vehicles in various states of repair, plus his motorbike.

'Oh, it's a split screen camper,' breathed Lucy, standing back and letting her eyes travel along the shape. 'Fantastic. I'd've loved one of these but I had to buy something ...' She paused. *Boring*, she thought. '... sensible,' she said. 'You are lucky!'

Ash laughed. 'That's one word for it. It's a wreck.'

'And,' said Daisy, dragging her away, 'this is my ... ta-daah!' She threw her arm out theatrically. 'Doll's house!' She sent Lucy a beaming smile and turned back towards the workbench, lifting off a silk sheet with all the stage presence of a magician.

'Wow.' Lucy was properly impressed. 'That is not just any old doll's house. It's a doll's palace. A *Chateau du Doll*!' She bent to inspect it, marvelling at the interlocking rooms and careful detailing around the staircases and windows. True craftsmanship, and not cheap, she thought. 'Where did you get it from? I reckon my customers would love these. They're heirlooms.'

'Daddy made it.' Daisy hopped from foot to foot in her glee.

'Ash, did you really? This is fantastic work!'

'Like it?' He whipped away a piece of rag on the workbench Lucy could see had pink bunnies on, and guessed had once been Daisy's pyjamas. She thought it was sweet, a token of the family life he'd built after the tragedy, and a lump formed in her throat. Ash was poking about in the house. He carried on, 'Gave me something to do once Daisy had gone to bed. Started off small but it got bigger and bigger. I've always liked working with my hands.' He said it without any irony but Lucy blushed hotly. She turned quickly back to the doll's house, nodding seriously as Daisy reached for one of the many dollies lying about inside the house and gave her a guided tour to equal any estate agent's blurb.

'Reggie and his girlfriends, next?' Head tipped, she looked up at her father for confirmation.

'Go on then, you take Lucy,' said Ash. 'I'll go and see if Nanny needs a hand with dinner.'

Daisy checked to see which was Lucy's bad hand before tugging her back out of the workshop; her buttercup yellow wellies flapped against her legs in their skinny jeans.

'Who is Reggie? Why has he got more than one girlfriend? Is he your gardener?'

Daisy pealed with laughter. 'Noooooo! Come on,' she urged Lucy, guiding her once again on her overgrown mystery tour. 'It's feeding time.'

'Is he a …' Lucy hazarded a guess, pretending to be serious. '… a giraffe?'

'No!'

'A wildebeest?'

'Noooo. I don't think so, anyway. What *is* a will-dy-beast?'

'A, er, pink unicorn with blue wings and purple eyelashes?'

'Don't be silly, Lucy.' Daisy giggled. 'Look.' She pointed to a square woolly creature with curly horns who seemed as wide as it was long.

'Why do you call her Reggie?'

'She's a boy.' Daisy rolled her eyes at Lucy's townie ignorance. 'He's a "reject". And those are his girlfriends. Although …' She put her head on one side, considering. '… they're quite old now. I think they're older than me.'

'What, seven …' Lucy eyed her mischievously and finished, '… teen?'

Daisy grinned at her and trotted off to a metal locker, fishing out two handfuls of large pellets which she scattered on the field. Three other sheep in various shades of dark brown and white rushed greedily with Reggie towards them and began to hoover them up.

'What do you keep them for?' asked Lucy, not sure if she wanted to know the answer.

Daisy shrugged. 'Daddy says we won't eat them. A man comes and cuts their wool when it's ready. It's called shearing, you know. I like watching him. He lets me collect all the fleeces. A lady makes jumpers or something out of it.'

'And do Reggie and his girlfriends make lambs?' Would Daisy know about this natural occurrence? She seemed like a proper country child, but who knew?

She wrinkled her nose and shook her head sadly.

'No. Reggie's cast-rated.' She made it sound like X-rated, and Lucy bit back a giggle. 'He can't have babies.'

'Don't tell me. Daddy rescued him too.' Lucy wasn't a bit surprised by Daisy's nod. 'Mm, I can smell roasting chicken.' She sincerely hoped it hadn't been wearing a cardigan until recently. 'Shall we head back to the others?'

Babs sprang into action as they wandered back into the huge kitchen, giving them all tasks, except Lucy who was excused on the grounds of her poorly hand, and dinner was soon on the table. It was a very early dinner, Ash had explained, so that Daisy ate with them as often as possible. Lucy was very glad she'd dissuaded Ash from lunch. Tea and a couple of tiny cupcakes hadn't dimmed her appetite.

'Lucy can sit next to me,' announced Daisy, making big eyes. 'Please.'

'Lucy can sit wherever she likes,' said Ash. 'And anyway, I might want her to sit next to me.' He winked at his daughter who pretended to pout.

'How about I sit in the middle then?' Lucy laughed. 'Anyway, I'll need someone to cut my food up, you can fight over that.'

Dinner was delicious. The chicken had been roasted with garlic and herbs, there was a colourful array of vegetables and baby new potatoes, and conversation flowed easily across the table.

'Ashley is an unusual name. I don't think I've ever heard it used as a—' She stopped suddenly.

'—boy's name?' Ash raised his eyebrows, and Lucy nodded slowly, aware that Babs and John were watching. 'Shall I tell her, Mum?'

'It's from *Gone with the Wind*,' Babs stated, crisply. 'No need to make a thing out of it.'

'Mum's favourite character.' Ash threw his head back, closed his eyes and clasped his hands to his chest. 'Oh, Ashleah, Ashleah! But, I love you so!' His Southern Belle accent was enthusiastic, if hammy, and Lucy exploded with laughter. Daisy giggled at her.

'It could have been worse. You could have been Rhett. And sounded like a cat with fur balls every time someone called you.' Ash's father, John, a quiet man with a slow smile, proved to have a dry wit that almost had Lucy choking on her dinner several times. 'So how's the bike training coming along, then?' he asked her, as Ash cleared the plates and Babs put a towering Victoria sponge on the table.

'I helped to make that,' said Daisy to no-one in particular, licking her lips.

'Slowly, thanks John,' Lucy replied. 'It helped when I finally stopped throwing the bikes about, I think. It looks spectacular, Daisy.'

'Babs used to park like that, when I first met her. I was always having to pick her bike up.' John twinkled. 'She was amazing. Had an old BSA Bantam. Proper motorbikes in those days. None of this plastic everywhere.'

'Yes,' agreed Babs, handing out dessert plates and forks. 'With a kick start. Bloody, er, *blessed* thing!' She glanced quickly at Daisy who was still staring at the cake. 'I can't tell you how many bruises I used to have on my shins.'

'And she used to wheelie it. A proper daredevil, your mother.' John winked at Ash, who grinned, rolling his eyes.

'Mmm. She's not the only one. Lucy was pretty hot at lifting that front wheel too, in the beginning.'

'Yes. Not that I actually meant to.' Lucy blushed, nudging Ash with embarrassment.

'Are we cutting this cake, or just looking at it?' Daisy wanted to know in a loud whisper.

The back door opened into their laughter, and Lucy looked up to see Sarah sashaying into the kitchen.

'Hello!' she sang, shaking back her glossy blonde hair. 'I was just passing and saw John's car outside. Thought I'd just pop in and say hel— Oh!' She stopped dead, staring at Lucy. 'You're here. How – nice.'

The table fell into a tattered silence. Even Daisy turned to study Sarah. Babs sprang to her feet and gathered the girl up by her elbow.

'Come along, Sarah dear,' she said, in the same way one might speak to a snorting pony. 'Sit down and have some cake.'

Something to sweeten you up.

Ash got up to get another chair and Sarah plonked into the seat he'd vacated. Lucy caught her triumphant smile. She jumped up.

'Could I be excused for a moment?'

Babs rose. 'I'll show you where to go.'

'Are we *ever* having this cake?' wailed Daisy dramatically.

Lucy remembered where she was going from the last time she'd been there, but allowed Babs to show her. 'Here it is. Do you need any help?'

'No, I'm managing ok these days, thanks.'

'I'll see you back at the table then. But, er ...' She paused and then continued, 'Someone only has the power to hurt you if you let them. That's all I'm going to say.' She stepped back towards the kitchen, leaving Lucy staring after her. Those few moments, plus the knowledge that Ash's mum was her ally, were enough to modify Lucy's reaction to Sarah.

'Budge up!' She smiled at the girl on her return to the table, as Babs was cutting the cake. 'I'm sure you'd like to sit next to your niece, wouldn't you?'

'Finally!' Daisy eyed her cake comically and swept her eye around the table, to check portion sizes.

With Lucy standing patiently behind her, Sarah heaved a sigh and plopped onto Lucy's seat. Hoping her face didn't reflect her small victory, Lucy sank down beside Ash, comforted as he nudged his long thigh against hers.

'Cake, Lucy?'

'Lovely, yes please, it looks delicious. Richard would be proud of that!'

'Is he the clever young man who runs your cafe?' asked Babs.

'Yes. We run it together. He's catering, and I'm the arty side.'

'There's a lovely ambience in there. And those cupcakes are to die for!' She put a slice of cake in front of Sarah.

'No thank you, Babs. No carbs after six for me. It's how I keep my figure.' She patted her flat stomach. 'All those carbs just sit round your bottom.'

'Personally, I find that moderation in everything is the key.' Lucy cast what she hoped was a beatific smile in Sarah's direction, and continued, 'Richard has been thinking recently about running some children's cookery parties. Maybe you could give us some tips?'

'Can I come?' Daisy cried, her voice muffled by cake crumbs.

'I feel sorry for Richard already.' Ash grinned, earning a 'Daddeee,' from Daisy.

'Do you cook?' Lucy turned to Sarah, who shook her head vehemently.

'No, I don't, thank you very much. I don't see the point of it.'

'How do you … nurture yourself then?' asked Lucy, trying not to sound appalled.

Sarah shrugged. 'Open a tin of tuna. Salad. Cereal,' she said carelessly.

Lucy, unable to respond without feeling as if she'd preach, sat back and said nothing.

'Please can I have a tiny piece more, Nanny?' asked Daisy, wiping her plate clean with an index finger.

Babs looked over at Ash, who nodded, before replying, 'Just a sliver, darling. As you've been so good today.'

'I'm always good.'

Lucy smiled as Daisy looked around the table for confirmation with the confidence of a well-loved child.

'Can Lucy read my bedtime story tonight? And Aunty Sarah,' she said, winding around her aunt's arm, looking pleadingly into her face, 'can do my nails with that special stuff on Sunday.'

Sarah's sharp expression softened and she leaned towards Daisy, trying to find a place to kiss that wasn't sticky and giving up.

'Of course, my sweet. We can be girly together.'

That child has a career in diplomacy lined up, thought Lucy admiringly, as Ash said warningly, 'Daisy, don't boss people about. You have to ask them, not tell them, darling.'

Daisy looked imploring and made a meowing sound, pawing Sarah's arm like a kitten. It was hard not to smile.

'And on that note,' said Ash, his face mock stern, 'it's nearly bedtime for you, young lady. I'm going to take Lucy home soon, and Nanny and Bampy will be here until I get back, okay? Is everything ready for school tomorrow?'

Babs got to her feet. 'There are some reading books. I'll put everything by the door.'

'You're a very well-oiled machine,' said Lucy. 'A great support team.'

'Yes. As I said, I can't do without them.' Ash gathered plates. 'Any of them.'

Sarah stood, smoothing her clothes. 'I'll be off. See you Sunday, Daisy. Bye everyone.' She finger-tip waved Babs and John, making a show of hugging Daisy and Ash, and then after a hesitation, Lucy.

'See? He doesn't need you,' she hissed in Lucy's ear. 'Like he said, he's got us.' She released her and stood back, smiling into Lucy's shocked expression. She wasn't quick enough to respond, even if she'd been able to think of something, and was left with her mouth open, trying to hide her frown. Daisy's wheedling voice distracted her.

'But I wanted to show Lucy my drawings. Do I have to go to bed at the normal time? Can't I stay up just a little bit longer? We do have a special visitor, don't we? Please, Daddy?'

'Bedtime as normal, sweetheart. It's a school night. And,' he said, glancing at Lucy, 'you'll have lots of time to show Lucy your drawings another time. I hope she'll be coming back again soon.'

Lucy nodded, hearing the door bang behind her as Sarah crashed through it. 'I'd love to read Daisy a story.'

A speedily showered Daisy was deposited into her bedroom and from downstairs, Lucy could hear Ash doing his patient best to get her into her pyjamas.

'I'm going to count to three,' he announced finally. 'If you aren't in your pyjamas by then, Lucy won't come up, I will go downstairs and there'll be no story. One ...'

Almost an hour later, Lucy was hoarse from reading

and giggling, and Daisy was snoring in her princess bed, complete with slide and castle.

'She's hilarious,' she said to Ash on the way home, having said goodbye to his parents. 'And not at all shy.'

He nodded, crinkling his eyes at her. 'I suppose she is very confident. She's spent a lot of time being passed around like a parcel, don't forget – lots of adult association. She's terribly bossy.'

'Aren't all little girls? She seems very bright to me.'

'Mm. She's got a lot of "parents", but we all try and stick to the same rules. It wouldn't work otherwise.'

Lucy sat back. 'I feel as if I've got a lot to learn about you all.'

Ash put his hand over hers and her heart jumped at his touch. 'Lucy,' he said softly. 'It's not all about Daisy. Forgive me if I give you that impression. It must seem as if my whole life is a logistical operation. Today was probably not at all what you were expecting. Sorry.'

'You're right, it wasn't.' She looked down at his hand covering hers. 'It was much better.'

They drew up outside her apartment. Every fibre of Lucy's inner senses wanted to pull him into the house and rip his clothes off. She squashed them. This was no rebound affair. A tit for tat. Separated from Gerry, she wanted time to be herself, on her own terms. Unencumbered by bandages and divorce papers. Not a rescue case. If Ash had managed to wait all these years for the right person, then she too could be patient.

'Thank you, Ash, for today. My turn to "cook" next.' She clicked the passenger door open a notch, in case her resolve failed and she threw herself at him. Reaching across the bulky console, she determined to kiss him goodbye on the cheek. Her insides turned to melted chocolate as he took her face in both hands and kissed her slowly on the mouth. It was the hardest thing in the world to climb out of that car.

Chapter Twenty-Two

With the sunshine stretching ahead as far as could be forecast, Lucy found herself included often in Ash's plans, juggling an afternoon or evening here and there, depending on his shifts and the busy café. Thinking about her promise to 'cook next' and baulking at the idea of doing it in her tiny apartment, she decided to throw a barbecue at the café one Saturday in June, to coincide with Ash's long weekend. They had a half oil drum type barbeque in the store-shed, squashed in with her bike. It just needed a bit of elbow grease and it would be perfect. After discussing it with Richard and Nicola, she invited Ash and Daisy, and his parents if they were free.

Nicola was delighted. 'I'm dying to meet your Mr Ash.'

'No rolled eyes, no asking him if he's shagged me yet, ok?' Lucy fixed her with a stern look. 'We're "just good friends" for now.'

'Course you are.'

'I mean it. I'm taking this slow. There's no rush.' Taking a deep breath, she added, 'I've invited Sarah too. Via Ash, as I haven't got her number.'

'Eek! The evil sister-in-law?'

'Sssh – don't say that in front of Ash either!' Lucy couldn't help laughing at her friend. 'I'm thinking that if I include her in things, she won't feel like I'm trying to take Ash and Daisy away. I've asked him to invite his parents, and I'm going to ask the girls in the café if any of them want to come along as well. And what about Ed from the Vintage Bike Palace, and any of the bike girls? May as well make it a party.' It was time she celebrated dumping Gerry.

'Blimey. You don't do anything by halves, do you? What do you want me to bring?'

The 'bring what you're drinking' news circulated amongst the staff quickly and before she knew it, Lucy had a fair size party going on. She reminded herself to invite her new neighbours too. And sort out some music. She doubled her order of barbeque meats, breads and salads. The perks of running a café, she told herself.

She was beginning to wonder whether it was still a good idea by the time she'd assembled the food and drinks, put out bright table cloths, draped fairy lights everywhere and put night-lights into every jam jar she could find, finishing them off with raffia bows and little pebbles from the beach. One of the girls loaned her a hand-painted wooden cart that fitted a freezer box, and she filled it with ice-creams and soft drinks for the children. Beers went into a huge plastic barrel filled with ice. She wanted it to look like a private party, and not just the café extending its hours. Ash arrived early with Daisy and his parents, ferrying out vast quantities of foil-wrapped trays and bags of nibbles.

'Crikey, thank you! But I'm supposed to be feeding you, not the other way around.' Lucy laughed, hugging them all in turn as Ash distributed their largesse into the café kitchen.

'They're only Nachos and things.' Babs shrugged with a smile. 'How can I help?'

'Have a glass of wine and go and enjoy the sunshine, I think.' Lucy ushered her onto the terrace, where she'd spread a tablecloth over the big wooden table that had until recently lived in her studio, weighting the corners with pebbles which she'd painted. Ash busied himself with the barbecues while John wandered down onto the beach with Daisy. It was a lovely scene, and Lucy rather wished she hadn't invited anyone else.

She was pinning a note onto the café door that said 'Private Party, You Know Where We Are' as Sarah arrived, bouncing towards them wearing skinny white jeans which accentuated her perfect bottom, and a grey cropped t-shirt that looked to Lucy as if it would fit Daisy better.

Her freshly-platinumed hair swung glossily over her shoulders and she was wearing full make-up. She turned the beam of her smile on them all, throwing her arms around each of them in a flamboyant hug. Lucy did her best to reciprocate.

'Thank you so much for the invitation! I hope you don't mind me coming over early but I wondered if I could help.'

Lucy glanced down at the pristine and dazzling jeans and thought about asking her to help light the barbecue, before she realised that meant leaving her with Ash.

'Well, it's all pretty much under control, really,' she began.

'Oh, you're so organised,' Sarah shrieked. She made the word sound like a fault and Lucy felt her face frown before she forced the corners of her mouth upwards.

'But come on in and er, we can sort all this stuff out,' she said, hearing the false brightness in her tone.

Sarah's version of helping meant her reading aloud the information labels on every item of food and noting how many calories there were. 'Hummus!' she cried. 'I love hummus, but look how much fat there is in it. And coleslaw. Yuk. Crisps? Disastrous! Full fat Pepsi – bursting with calories.'

'I'm surprised you came, seeing as you don't eat,' Lucy said through gritted teeth, shoving packets of crisps and tubes of Pringles into a cupboard out of her reach.

'I do eat, but not any of that stuff. I just eat …'

'… *air*,' supplied Lucy in her head.

'… salad and tuna really,' finished Sarah. She sat back and admired herself. Lucy was overcome by an urge to squeeze a ketchup bottle near her.

'I've made chicken kebabs, you'll be ok with those.'

'Kebabs? Aren't they those things dripping with fat and have that bread stuff underneath? I don't think so.'

'No.' Lucy's laugh was brittle. 'That's a doner kebab. These are simply cubes of chicken breast threaded onto skewers with tomatoes and peppers and mushrooms. Very low fat.'

'Oh.' Sarah sounded put out. 'I suppose so. But I don't like mushrooms. Or peppers.'

'I could make you some without any of those things if you like.' Lucy plugged gamely on.

'Oh, no, don't worry. I'll just have a bit of salad or something. Clean eating. That will leave more for the rest of you. You look as if you have a good appetite.'

Lucy blinked at her. Was that an insult? She really wasn't sure. Nicola's head appeared around the kitchen door.

'Hallooo!' she called, sashaying in bearing a foil-covered tray. 'Richard and Ash are being manly over the barbie. He's got the bottles.'

'Oh, I'm so pleased to see you.' Lucy enveloped her in a huge hug. 'What have you brought here? Honestly you didn't need to, talk about coals to Newcastle … ooh, these look nice!' She lifted a corner of foil and peeped inside.

'Samosas and Filo pastry Spanakopita,' supplied Nicola. She turned to Sarah. 'Hello, I'm Nicola. And you are?' She smiled and held a hand out to Sarah who barely brushed her fingers over it.

'I'm Ash's sister-in-law. Daisy's aunt.' She shook her hair back and pursed her lips.

'Sorry ladies, I should have introduced you. Sarah, this is my friend Nicola,' Lucy said with exaggerated politeness. 'Nic, this is Sarah. She doesn't eat.'

'I don't over-eat,' corrected Sarah. 'You look very slim too,' she said to Nicola. 'You obviously don't eat much either.'

Lucy met Nicola's eye and they both spluttered with laughter.

'Fat boy breakfast here with the bike girls tomorrow morning?' Nicola asked Lucy. Sarah frowned at them and stalked away.

'So that was Sarah. Goodness me. She's weird!'

'I'm so glad you arrived when you did. She was about to model a bottle of barbecue sauce.' Lucy made a rueful face. 'I'm trying to be nicer to her. She doesn't make it easy though.'

'Never mind. We'll dilute the impact. Now, what can I do?'

'Nothing to do. Let's have a cuppa and you can fill me in on the gossip.'

The afternoon sunshine cast golden light on them all, and the food smelled divine as it browned over the hot coals. Daisy had brought a little bag which contained colouring in books, crayons and a selection of little furry creatures, and she seemed happy enough with her grandparents or mixing in with any of the other children who'd been brought along by her staff. Ash and Richard took it in turns to dispense meat from the barbecue, working together as if they'd been doing it for years.

Bab's nachos and Richard's pastries disappeared rapidly, and Lucy's glass of wine slipped down nicely. She felt relaxed and well disposed towards everyone. Even Sarah, who was behaving impeccably in Ash's company, of course. She was leaning towards Richard and hanging on his every word. Nicola looked perfectly serene and was sipping from a glass of something sparkling. Water, Lucy thought. There wasn't anything else sparkling here. Apart from beer.

'Your turn to drive, Nic?'

'Mm, yes, but um, that's not why she's not drinking,' Richard said quickly, his eyes darting towards Nicola, eyebrows raised.

'Anti-biotics?' said Lucy. Then her head swung between

her two friends as her brain logged on. 'Oh, my goodness, Nic, are you …?'

Nicola nodded. 'I am!' She grinned. 'Well, we are. We were going to tell you earlier … but we've only just had the three-month scan, so …'

Everyone within earshot leapt to their feet, hugging the prospective parents and asking all the usual questions. The news spread quickly.

'Boy or girl? Do you want to know? How are you feeling?'

'I thought you'd guessed when you laughed at Sarah telling me I was so slim!' Nicola whispered to Lucy.

'No, you are slim. Although …' Lucy looked properly at her friend, noticing now the loose summery top which camouflaged the slight bump.

'I'm not really showing yet. I'm still fitting into my ordinary clothes, but my bike leathers are starting to feel a bit tight.'

'You're still riding?'

Nicola nodded. 'No reason why not, as long as I can still get my trousers done up and climb on and off.'

Lucy clinked their glasses together. 'I hope we get to ride together at least once before you have to give up.'

'Don't worry, I won't be giving up for long. Don't forget that Richard has all those sisters. They're dying to babysit. And I've got all my bike girls. No shortage of help around here.' She grinned as said girls bore her away to quiz her. Alone, but not lonely, Lucy jumped as Ash quietly slipped his arms around her, and she leaned into him with a smile.

'Wow! One heck of a party,' he murmured in her ear. She grinned up at him, saluting him with her glass.

'Sorry, I hadn't meant for you to end up doing all the cooking!'

'I've enjoyed it.' She looked up into his relaxed

expression, seeing that he really had, and she was glad she'd gone to all the effort. 'Oops, there's a queue. Gotta go and flip a burger.'

'No, have a break, I'll do it ...' She twisted in his arms. Giving her a squeeze, he planted a kiss on the top of her head, unwound his arms and strode away to resume his cooking duties.

Lucy luxuriated in the moment, feeling the imprint of his arms around her as she watched Nicola and Richard enjoying the attention from their friends. Her friends. Virtually everyone gathered today was connected by motorbikes, she realised with amazement. Even some of her staff. How her life had changed. She thought about the valuable order she'd just completed for TV Tom, also a biker. Only waiting on framing now, then she'd be delivering that very soon. She wiggled the fingers of her left hand, flexing and squeezing as the physio had shown her. Setting up the party things had tired it, but it was improving every day. Glancing at her watch, she realised sadly that Ash would probably have to leave soon to get Daisy off to bed.

She became aware of Sarah standing alongside, and felt a bit sorry for her, realising that she probably knew no-one except for Ash and his family. It was brave of her to come along.

'Great news, huh?' She turned to include the young woman. Sarah smiled thinly.

'Don't go getting any ideas,' she said, her expression hard-boiled.

'What's that supposed to mean?'

'Catching Ash by getting pregnant.'

'Sarah. I think we need to talk.' Barely expecting the girl to follow, Lucy led the way into the cool café, thankfully empty as everyone enjoyed the golden evening sunshine outside. Her stomach churned. She didn't really know what she was going to say next, but she did know that after years of being bullied by Gerry, she was not going to be anyone's victim any longer. She took a deep breath. 'Daisy loves spending time with you, Sarah. You're a great aunty to her.' She smiled, as naturally as she could manage. 'I think a lot of her, and her father. And I'd very much like for you to carry on being a part of that, if our relationship moves on. How does that sound to you?'

A deep flush spread across Sarah's face. 'He's only interested in you because he thinks he's helping you. Don't fool yourself. There won't be any "moving on".' She rose, slowly. Every inch of her shouted insolence. Lucy's hands twitched across the table for the bottle of ketchup she'd longed to use earlier. Fortunately for Sarah's jeans, there was a commotion outside and Daisy appeared in the doorway, wet through and covered in slimy seaweed.

Her grandfather, close behind, wore an expression of guilt mixed with apology. Leaping to her feet, Lucy was on her knees beside the little girl in a moment. She pushed the dark matted hair to one side, and Daisy's huge blue eyes, so like Ash's in colour, met hers, brimming with unshed tears. Her mouth quivered. She seemed such a tough, country kid at her own house, that Lucy had almost forgotten that she was just a little girl. She wrapped an arm around her.

'Oops! Did you fall in? Have you hurt yourself?'

'No-o-o-o-o.' Daisy cuffed her nose, leaving trails of green slime over her face, and triggering the threatened tears. 'I w-w-was trying to catch the c-c-crabs.'

'Yes, my fault.' John leaned over. 'Terribly interesting down there. Did you know you have sea-spiders and Plumose Anemones on this beach?'

'I didn't even know we had crabs.' Lucy pretended, wondered what Ash would make of his daughter falling in a rock pool. Every time they met, she learned something about the two of them.

'Stupid place to have a barbecue. She could have drowned!' Sarah skirted around her niece.

'It's a beach. There are rock pools.' Lucy tried not to belittle Sarah's accusations, but honestly ...

'Ew. Daisy. Look at that nice dress now!' Sarah pursed her lips. 'I bought you that.' Daisy's face crumpled.

'I'll find you something else to wear. It won't be as pretty as your nice dress ...' Lucy paused, gritting her teeth and adding for Sarah's benefit, '... which I can pop straight into the washing machine later—'

'It's designer. Hand wash only,' Sarah said, with a tut.

Who the heck bought children hand wash only summer clothes?

'But it will do you for now. How does that sound?' Daisy's sturdy soaking wet body leaned against her, and Lucy felt rather than saw her nod. 'You'll soon dry off, sweetie.'

'I'm telling Ash.' Sarah stalked away in her strappy sandals.

'Oh, well. At least it's warm. Naughty rock pool. How big was this crab, Daisy?'

'This big,' declared the little girl, putting both her fists together.

'Goodness me. Maybe it was a handsome prince. Did you try to kiss it?'

'Nooooo!' Daisy giggled. 'That's frogs, not crabs. Yerrrk. I wouldn't kiss a frog!'

'Kissing frogs?' said Babs, joining them. 'Bit desperate, I reckon. Have you been swimming, Hazy Daisy?'

Lucy hunted round in the store-room and found what she was looking for. A spare Art Café T-shirt was always lurking there, plenty big enough to cover Daisy from neck to knees. Plus a selection of beach towels left behind by trippers. She made a point of throwing them in with the café laundry for these exact incidents. But Sarah's words were haunting her. Children could drown in a foot of water.

'Thanks, lovely.' Babs took the items from her. 'Don't worry, accidents happen. Oh, and I've spoken to Richard about a cupcake party for Daisy's birthday. It's such a lovely venue. Is that ok with you?'

'Oh, goodness me, yes, that's a lovely idea. Thank you, Babs.'

In the kitchen, Lucy ran warm water into the non-food sink, and carefully rinsed all of the seaweed out of the little dress, before adding a squirt of hand-wash to it. How could it possibly be a practical thing to dress a child in? Especially a child like Daisy.

'Was she shrimping?' Wrapping her in a bear hug, Ash rested his chin on her head.

'Oh, you made me jump.' She turned in his arms to look up into his face, holding her soapy hands out of the way. 'Crabs, apparently. And some sort of nautical flora and fauna.'

'I know, Dad told me. And Sarah hasn't stopped telling me.' He gathered her in more closely, and she felt her body flow into him. It was an exquisite torture. Did he want her as much as she wanted him? She knew that he had amazing self-control and patience – but she didn't. 'We'll have to leave soon. I hate not being here to help you clear up.'

'It's fine, you've got enough to do. Everyone here is well trained – the empties are in the re-cycling already. And you and Richard cleared as you went along. The barbecue will burn off most of what's on the grill and I can clean that up tomorrow.' *Besides, washing up and clearing would give her something to do while he was back in the bosom of his family.* 'Don't worry, honestly. I'm an independent woman.'

Chapter Twenty-Three

Ash wondered about Lucy's 'independent woman' comment, but before he could think of how to tackle it, Daisy appeared in one of Lucy's t-shirts and a silly mood, announcing in a loud voice that she wasn't wearing any pants. Over-excited and over-tired. It was time to go. He glanced round the terrace. It was the right time anyway. People were beginning to drink a bit more. But he didn't want to go. He hadn't seen much of Lucy, and his daughter's impromptu dunking had taken up the time left after his cooking duties.

He wondered what Lucy made of his family commitments. She and Daisy seemed to get on really well, but he was careful to make sure that Lucy was treated as a guest. A very welcome guest, but not someone expected to take part in all the duties that were required to maintain their little family of two. She probably didn't have the first idea how much laundry he needed to keep track of; between school uniforms that came home muddier than any boy could manage, brownie kit, swimming and gymnastics, plus the general jeans and playthings around the animals.

Lucy's life was – he brought her new flat to his mind's eye – tidy, orderly, peaceful, pet-less. It worried him that including her fully into their lives would scare her away. Was he being fair to her? Was he stopping her from having a relationship with someone without all these responsibilities? Already, he couldn't bear to think of her with someone else, but doing his best not to be selfish, he wanted the best for her. Who was he kidding? He was desperate to take their relationship to the next stage. Every time he touched her, it was an effort to pull away.

'Daisy can sleep over at ours, if you'd like to come back

here. Help clean up, that sort of thing ...' Interrupting his thoughts, his Dad, bless him, had felt terribly guilty about allowing his granddaughter to fall into the rock pool, despite Ash's protestations that no harm had been done. Sarah hadn't helped, going on and on about that bloody dress she'd bought her. She'd sloped off home already, with a face like thunder. What a drama over a dress. He could barely believe it.

Daisy wasn't a doll, to be primped up in expensive clothes. She was a proper kid, climbing gates, petting pigs and chickens and having to be nagged about washing her hands. She would have been just as happy in an inexpensive outfit that went in a washing machine. He'd been mortified to see Lucy washing his daughter's clothes in the sink at her own party. No wonder she'd dropped that line about being independent. If he wanted to keep her, and he did, he needed to let her know that their relationship was a separate entity to his role as father. If that was at all possible.

'That would be great Dad, if you don't mind? Don't tell Daisy though. She'll want to come too.'

'At least she won't need a bath before bed.' They looked over to where Lucy had the little girl on her knee at the table. Daisy was giggling at whatever Lucy was drawing for her. 'Don't let this one get away, lad.'

Ash coughed, to hide his embarrassment. Hell. He was a bit old for his Dad to be giving him relationship advice, wasn't he? Although given his parents' happy marriage and the laughter which glued them together through their ups and downs, maybe he wasn't too old to be told.

'I will try very hard not to, Dad.' He was startled when Lucy directed a soft smile his way, as if she'd heard him. Picking his way towards them, he steeled himself for his daughter's inevitable wails when informed that they were going home. Definitely over-tired. 'Come on, sweet-pea.'

He scooped her up onto his hip, her hot, tear-stained face resting against his. 'Give Lucy a kiss and say thank you for a lovely party.' He dipped her towards Lucy, who kissed her cheek and told her she'd be over soon to do some more drawing and it was her turn to do the bed-time story.

Getting his entire family out of the house was a protracted affair of kissing and waving, and having buckled Daisy into her car-seat, he dashed back to Lucy, and whispered into her ear as he hugged her. 'I'll be back in an hour.' She beamed up at him, two spots of pink rising on her tanned cheeks, and instinctively he bent to kiss her soft mouth.

It was a little over an hour before he returned, as his Mum had insisted on going through Daisy's birthday party arrangements. He thought it was a terrific idea, although having had experience of children's birthday parties, even the better behaved ones, he thought Richard was a saint for suggesting he actually get them cooking. It would be a baptism of fire for Lucy.

She'd sent him a text saying that they'd locked up the café and gone over to her flat. He hesitated outside for a moment, listening for the music from the back, and hearing none. Had everyone gone? Would she think he wasn't coming? Might he look a bit too keen? For goodness' sake, he was never this indecisive at work, or anywhere else. The side gate opened and a couple came out, calling their goodbyes. They smiled and nodded as they passed.

'I've come back to help clear up,' he told them, heading towards the gate. He cursed himself for feeling the need to explain. He barely remembered the last time he'd felt this nervous. He could hear the music now, much quieter. In the gathering dusk, he recognised Nicola and Richard and some of the bike girls and their partners, although he couldn't see Lucy. There was a low murmur of conversation, punctuated with laughter and the chink of glasses. It was a good sound.

Fairy lights were draped over the flowerpots, and she'd put those little candles in glass jars and grouped them about. The little courtyard looked like a fairy tale, and he thought how Daisy would have loved to see it. Lucy was so clever at making somewhere look special with apparently no effort. She made people feel special too. In general. Except Sarah. He sighed. His sister-in-law was very possessive over Daisy. He hoped that it would wear off as time went on.

Lucy appeared, loaded down with blankets. As she caught sight of him, she tripped on a trailing corner and when he plunged forward to catch her, she fell into his arms. Exactly where he wanted her. Sometimes, he thought, you just had to trust in fate.

Curled into his lap on the patio, Lucy wanted the evening to never end. Her new place, her best friends, and this man who set her body aflame, but made her feel secure and admired and wanted. He'd hardly let her go since he returned, and she so appreciated the effort he'd made to arrange that. She wondered whether he would leave at the end of the evening, or ... her body trembled with anticipation. His arms tightened around her.

'Cold?' he whispered into her ear, and she shook her head, despite her thin summer dress. She enjoyed listening to him joining in naturally with everyone's conversation, mostly about motorbikes. There was none of the pompousness that Gerry had used around her friends. Her friends who no longer visited her, because they didn't like Gerry. It would be wonderful to seek them out again, pick up the threads of her old life. She saw Nicola smother a yawn, and Richard leap to his feet.

'Time to go.' He smiled through Nicola's protests that she was fine, and Lucy hugged them both goodbye, watching them leave hand in hand. Their lives would change beyond all recognition, with a baby in the house, she thought. It was an exciting step. And Richard would need some kind of paternity leave. They should think about getting him an assistant for those times. She wondered whether Babs, Ash's Mum, might be interested, and filed the thought away to discuss it later.

The remaining stragglers drifted away with hugs and promises of ride-outs together when she'd passed her test.

'I'll get some bin liners to sort this lot out,' Ash began as she locked the garden gate, sending a conflicting signal by maintaining his warm arm around her waist, and inclining his head so that his lips found hers.

'Sod that.' Turning into him so that her body pressed against his, she murmured into his mouth. 'We'll do it in the morning.'

He needed no more encouragement, sweeping her off her feet and into the flat. When he put her down, she held his hand, guiding him through the rooms, both of them tripping and giggling as they tried to navigate around the furniture without letting go of each other.

'In here.' Lucy pushed the door open to her new bedroom, so glad that she'd splashed out on a new bed. They collapsed onto it now, their giggles subsiding into lust as they rolled together. Their lips met, slowly, tentatively at first, and then with more urgency, his arms enfolding her, their bodies arching towards each other. She could feel the heat rising from him, feel the urgency in his groin, and tugged his shirt up, leaning into him, rocking her hips against him, wanting to feel his skin against hers. She wanted to bite him, possess him, feel every inch of him inside her, beside her, around her. He groaned, catching at her hands as they began their descent on his jeans.

'Slow down, rocket-woman,' he whispered into her ear. 'We've got all night.' He kissed her neck and bare shoulders, gently persuading her out of her dress. Any anxieties she had about her body were quelled by the dark lust in his eyes as he gazed at her. She trailed her fingertips and then her lips over Ash's lean torso and muscular arms. Not too muscular, she decided, just exactly right, as her fingertip traced the line of chest hair down over his flat stomach, to the buckle of his belt.

He moved away to hurriedly remove his socks, kicked off his jeans and underpants in one go, and gathered her into his arms. The only thing between them was the thinnest sheen of sweat, and Lucy's inhibitions dissolved as he caressed her naked body, her hips arching towards him as he finally, slowly slid into her.

She had forgotten it could feel so incredible. Sex with Gerry had become, at best, perfunctory, and had tailed off to nothing during the last year. She wasn't sure it had ever been as amazing as sex with Ash, so unhurried, slow, powerful.

It was the most natural thing ever to snuggle under the duvet and go to sleep, curled into each other as if they would never, ever let go.

Waking up the following morning, Lucy self-consciously raked her hair with her fingers, worrying what she must look like, squash-faced from sleep. She peeped at Ash's dark head on the pillow beside her, her fingers trailing over his smooth muscles, and laughed with shock as his eyes snapped open, the beam of sapphire blue pinning her. He reached out for her, a long, lazy smile on his face.

'Come here, gorgeous girl.' His strong arm scooped her body into him, and she giggled as she felt his arousal.

'Don't you want a cup of tea first?' She teased him, her hands making it clear that she applauded his intentions.

'Tea can wait,' he growled. 'I can't.'

By the end of June, Lucy's hand was healed. The cogs of her life were settling back into place and making her whole again. And she and Gerry had had a final meeting with the solicitors – the divorce was progressing nicely and the Decree Nisi would be coming through soon. They'd agreed that Lucy would divorce him on the grounds of adultery – there had to be a reason if you wanted to do things quickly – and all the financial stuff was settled. Not that Gerry was happy about any of it, but that wasn't her problem any longer. She just wanted it over and done with.

She texted Ash. *'Fancy a bike ride?'*

'Your bike or mine?'

'Both. If I can remember how to do it. Know a decent bike instructor?'

They made plans for Ash's next Rest Day, which was a Monday. Wales was in full and glorious technicolour, but Lucy knew it wouldn't last. The peninsula had a tendency to dissolve into rain as the rest of the UK basked in sunshine.

She climbed aboard Cadbury with her heart knocking against her ribcage. So anxious, she couldn't even remember which hand operated the throttle and which the clutch. She felt sure she would kangaroo hop down the road and look like a complete idiot. To her relief, as soon as she was sitting astride her beautiful purple bike, everything flooded back to her and as the bike pulled smoothly away, she felt her shoulders return to their normal position. Her body was stiff and jerky to begin with, but she soon began to loosen up and feel just as she had on the last day she'd ridden, weeks ago. Almost the same anyway.

She giggled aloud as she heard Ash say, 'Nice arse. Have I told you how great you look in leather?' She waggled her head in her wing mirrors at him and he laughed in her earpiece.

Lucy laughed aloud with pure joy as she breathed the air rushing past her visor. She felt alive on this motorbike.

Nothing existed but her and this engine and two wheels. And Ash, behind her, imposing and bulky on his bigger bike, a comforting presence, shielding her from traffic approaching too fast from behind, talking her through her gearing around the bends in the road.

They threaded their way along sun-dappled country lanes towards the coast, and then stopped for coffee, parking up and sitting where they could admire their steeds against the backdrop of the sparkling sea.

'How's the hand?' Ash reached out and gently stroked his thumb against her palm, sending her heart rate rocketing.

'A tiny bit twangy, but really, nothing I didn't expect.' She smiled. 'And totally worth it to be out on the bike again.'

'Time to put in for the final part of your test. You ride well.'

She wished she could freeze-frame the moment right there, and keep it forever in one of those snow-globe things. Only instead of snow there would be dust motes glittering in the rays of the sun, with two motorbikes parked up against the hazy backdrop of the turquoise sea.

Throughout the following week, they went out on their bikes as often as possible; an hour here and there made a huge difference to her confidence and skill levels. She felt a bit guilty about not being in the café occasionally, but made sure she'd arranged cover. What was the point of being the boss if you couldn't play hooky now and then?

Luckily, Jo, the sensible, competent single mum who'd turned out to be a godsend after Ella, was only too willing to earn some extra money, and the customers responded to her enthusiasm for the designer jewellery and desirable ceramics which Lucy hunted out.

Lucy enjoyed the training. Ash allowed no slacking and she began to think she was never going to live up to his high expectations, but it made her work hard. She read his copy of Roadcraft, the police manual, exhaustively, and she heard his voice intoning what he called 'the system' as a mantra in her sleep:

Information (signals) Position, Speed, Gear, Accelerate once the hazard is clear. She studied his diagrams for roundabout positioning and remembered thinking it didn't apply to her, when she was on her CBT. How far she'd progressed. How much her life had altered. Sometimes she felt like a different person altogether.

'I'm only going to give you directions now, just like the examiner would,' he told her before one session. 'No instruction. Nothing. You won't hear me at all. Go for it!'

Lucy had become used to hearing his voice in her ear, keeping her on track. Without that, it was weirdly like having a stranger following her, and quite unsettling. Getting a grip on her thoughts, she talked quietly into her helmet, reciting the mantra as she approached junctions and hazards. They rode for around forty minutes like this, and she became used to being told where to go, and making her own decisions.

'Take the next turning left please, and pull up behind the bus stop.'

Lucy smiled at his formality, knowing he was behaving exactly as her examiner would. It did sound odd though. It made her remember just what he did for a living. Somehow, although he often regaled her with stories of his day, she couldn't quite equate the kind, animal-rescuing Ash she knew with the authoritative policeman he was. She pulled up as directed, waiting for her next instruction.

'Switch off the engine and get off please.' Ash was parked behind her.

Lucy's heart began to thud. Goodness – it was just like having the real exam. How had she done? Had she done enough to pass? She climbed off and stood nervously, waiting for his pronouncement.

'Lucy.' He removed his helmet and indicated for her to remove hers. 'If you ride like that on your test ...' he said, seriously. Lucy gulped. 'You'll pass with flying colours, you clever girl!' He reached out and grabbed her in a bear hug. 'I'm so proud of you! Well done. I could hear you talking. That's fine. Shows you're thinking.'

Lucy beamed and did a little jig, locked in their embrace. A car hooted as it passed and they both laughed. And then Ash's mobile buzzed into life.

'Yes. Ok. No, no, I get it. Yes.' Ash nodded into his mobile as he listened. Lucy, gazing carefully away, knew it was Sarah on the other end. There was something about Ash's manner that gave him away when she rang. A kind of self-consciousness.

She wondered what drama would be revealed this time, and whether they would be required to turn around and go straight home so Ash could don his superhero outfit.

'Er, yes, I'll ask, hold on.'

What would it be this time? Light bulb blown? Straighteners blown a fuse? Broken nail?

'Sarah can't collect Daisy from school tomorrow. Any chance you could do it?' Ash said. 'I'm working days, and Mum and Dad are on a gardening trip.'

Lucy thought for a moment and said, 'No problem, I'll work from home in the morning. I've got something I want to finish.' She smiled and made a thumbs up sign. Ash mouthed a thank you and turned back to the phone. There was a whole lot more, 'No, really, it's fine, don't worry, she said it's fine,' from Ash before he finally hung up. 'Thank you, Lucy, you're a star.'

'What's the problem with Sarah?' Lucy wanted to know. It was the first time the girl had ever changed a plan that was to do with Daisy. It must be something serious.

'As I understand it, she wasn't going to be allowed to

leave work early as she'd arranged. They're a bit short, or there's someone new in, or something like that. She sounded terribly upset and kept repeating herself. I didn't quite get the reason, but the upshot of it was, she couldn't collect Daisy.' He looked at her. 'You're sure it's ok? Maybe I could ring one of the other parents, if you've changed your mind. I don't want you to think I'm taking advantage ... I'll be home an hour or so after.'

'Ash,' said Lucy firmly, 'it's fine. I'm happy to help. And it's good that Sarah is including me now. She's been a bit awkward at times.'

'I suppose,' he said slowly, 'I suppose Daisy is all she has left of her sister.'

'I understand.' Lucy nodded. 'I really do, but ... oh, Ash! Do I have to spell it out?' His face told her that she did. 'You must know she's in love with you.'

His face was a mask of shock. 'Of course she isn't. She's not much older than Daisy.'

'She's not looking at you as a father figure, trust me.'

'No. I think you've misread her. She loves Daisy, of course she does. I'm just part of the package.'

'Hmm. Well. I'm just warning you.' She didn't want the day to be spoiled so she changed the subject. 'Come on. I want to go and book that test.'

Chapter Twenty-Four

Lucy stood back and looked down at her paintings. Very different to her usual work, she'd enjoyed creating them, and she already had plans for them. She checked her watch for the thousandth time that day. It was only just after lunch. Daisy finished school at 3.15. It was a twenty-minute drive, so she had ages yet. She smiled ruefully at her anxiety. It wasn't a difficult task – she was looking forward to it – but it was assuming a much bigger importance as it marked the first time she'd been asked to help with what she privately called The Daisy Team. Until now, she'd been very careful not to get involved for fear of fanning Sarah's flames of jealousy.

She'd nipped straight down to the 'open all night' supermarket the previous night and bought terracotta plant pots which she planned to paint with Daisy until Ash came home, and then cook for all of them. It was lovely to think about including Daisy in making things for her new space. Her new life. Packing away all her paints, she spread out the things she'd bought for their play date. A cute little red painting pinny, a packet of baby-wipes and kitchen roll, and an array of brightly coloured emulsion tester pots with the brushes in the lids. She'd stayed up late and put a coat of white paint on the pots already, so they were all ready to be decorated. It would be fun to plant up some summer bedding in them when they were dry. Cleaning up the little kitchen she checked the fridge again for the ingredients she needed for the evening meal. Finally, walking aimlessly from room to room to kill time, she decided to leave early anyway. She'd need to find somewhere to park her van near the school. It was always clogged up with yummy mummies in 4×4s.

Locking up, she swung her bag over her shoulder and strolled down to collect her van from the café car park. She stopped dead. The van was listing at an odd angle. Running towards it, she could see that both offside tyres were as flat as they could possibly be. She clutched her head in a panic. *No!* How could that have happened? How could they have both deflated during the day? She hadn't even been out in it.

And more to the point, how on earth was she going to collect Daisy? Daisy, who had been on the phone last night, so excited at the prospect of being collected by Lucy and would soon be standing forlornly at the school gates as one by one, all her friends' parents and grandparents and aunties and nannies disappeared. Leaving just her. On her own.

'Shit, shit, shit!' she yelled, feeling hot and nauseous. Her mind was whirling. If it had just been one tyre, maybe she could have got the spare on. No. Who was she kidding? Her hand would never cope with that. And two? No one ever had two flat tyres.

Was it worth inflating them and hoping they wouldn't both deflate until they'd got safely home again? She dismissed that idea instantly, imagining herself and Daisy stuck halfway home in a van with two flat tyres. *Think, woman.* She ran into the café to see if there was anyone whose car she could borrow for the journey.

'Nic's on a course,' Richard told her. 'What's up?' Lucy told him, running her eye down the taxi business cards they kept on the counter. The third call was successful. She gave them her address, and then rang the school to ask them to hang onto Daisy for a few minutes in case the taxi was late.

'According to my list,' said the school secretary, 'Daisy's aunt is collecting her.'

'No, she couldn't make it today, she asked me to do it instead.'

'I'm sorry, she rang the school at lunchtime to confirm it.'

'Oh. Thank you …' Lucy hung up. She cancelled the taxi. Then, doubting herself, she checked the calendar on her mobile. She'd spoken to Daisy last night. It was definitely the right day. What was Sarah playing at? Unless … unless Sarah had been the one who'd punctured her tyres? Knowing that she was working at home that day.

Anger burned white hot in her stomach. The more she re-lived it, the angrier she became. It had to be her. How else would she have known that Lucy wouldn't be able to make it to the school on time? What on earth was wrong with the girl?

Wondering how to explain to Ash that she hadn't collected Daisy, she rang her breakdown insurance, explaining that she might need two new tyres. While she waited, she stared at her phone. How would she word this? *Your bitch SiL sabotaged my van?* Despite her well-grounded suspicions, she had no proof that it had been her. Eventually, she settled for:

Two flat tyres?? Sarah collected Daisy. AA en route.

The reply came back: *Ok. No probs. xx*

The breakdown van arrived in a couple of hours, during which Lucy fidgeted restlessly, checking her phone or out of the window to see if Ash might arrive with Daisy anyway, and oscillating between irritation and anger and anxiety that he hadn't.

The breakdown man squatted alongside the flat tyres.

'You've been pranked.' He pointed at the valve. 'Look. Oldest trick in the book. Matchstick.' She bent closer. There was a matchstick rammed into the valve. 'It makes the tyre go down quite slowly. People don't always notice at first. Naughty though. Very dangerous. Should just re-inflate now, with a bit of luck. You haven't driven it, have you?' Lucy shook her head. 'Seaside car-park. I suppose it goes with the territory, really.' He shook his head.

'Mm.' Lucy was non-committal. It had never happened

before, it wasn't that kind of seaside. But then, she supposed, she hadn't been leaving the van overnight there before. 'Would you like a cup of tea?' Ferrying the tea tray back outside, along with a plate of cakes, she was pleased to see that one of her tyres was looking almost back to normal. The noise was deafening, and she could see the customers peering out of the windows.

Richard came out, wiping his hands on his apron. 'Have you checked the CCTV?'

'Have I what?' Lucy stared at him with her mouth open. How had she not thought of that?'

'Yeah – if we've got a problem with kids hanging round out here in the night, maybe we need to speak to Ash.' Richard walked back with her to the café. 'See if he can send a patrol round now and again.'

Lucy thought she would be only too pleased to discover that it was kids who had let her tyres down. She was soon peering intently at the little monitor, pausing and re-winding. The noise from the compressor stopped, and the breakdown man appeared in the café, bearing his mug and the plate of cakes.

'Both inflated. We'll just give 'em a few minutes and check the pressures again, before I go.' He peered over her shoulder at the screen. 'Looks like a girl. Unusual.' He straightened, draining his tea and taking a bite out of one of the cakes. 'Mm. Delicious. Me and the missus have been in here loads of times. Fabulous view, cakes to die for.'

'Thank you. That's so kind of you to say.' Lucy spoke automatically, her mind on autopilot. Although she'd had her suspicions, she felt sick that she was looking at proof on the screen. Ash would be furious with Sarah. Was that what she wanted?

By the time the breakdown man had left, along with a voucher for free afternoon tea for two at The Art Café, Lucy had formulated a plan. Taking some steadying breaths, she rang Ash on his mobile. He sounded pleased to hear her voice.

'Hello, sweetheart. You okay? We're just at Sarah's flat. Lucky she was home early with Daisy, her loo was over-flowing. I've been fixing it for her.'

'That's nice. Can I speak to Sarah, please?'

Her mouth dried as she heard voices and the muffled handling noises which meant the mobile was being passed over. She sipped some water.

'Hello, Lucy.' Sarah sounded smug, and Lucy's resolve hardened.

'Sarah. I know you let my tyres down. I've got evidence from our CCTV cameras and you rang the school to cancel me, which was a bit silly.' She waited, expecting some rebuttal, but there was nothing. She continued, 'You will put Ash in a very difficult position if I press charges against you for tampering with a motor vehicle, and I'm sure you don't want that. I would never stop you seeing Daisy, but Ash and I have a relationship now, and nothing you do can interfere with that, ok?' She listened hard, and could just hear the sound of breathing on the other end. 'And we had plans for tonight. I expect you've already fed Daisy, which is fine, but if you'd just like to say thank you to Ash for mending your overflow, which I suspect you set up in the first place, you can say a nice goodbye to them both, and send them home. So, nod and smile now, and hang up. All right?'

'Whatever.' Sarah managed to mumble the one word before the line went dead. Lucy stared at the phone, burdened by the fear that she'd just made everything much worse, but not knowing what else she could have done.

Her mobile pinged again. *'Dropping Daisy off to M&D. On my way over.'* She smiled. It would all work out, she was sure.

She hoped so, anyway.

'Thanks for having Daisy again, Mum.' Ash kissed his mother's cheek, as she stood preparing vegetables in the kitchen. 'Sorry. It's not quite gone according to plan tonight.'

'What happened?'

'Sarah had an overflow issue.' He shrugged. 'Easy enough fix.'

'Couldn't her father have sorted it for her, then?'

Ash shrugged. 'Maybe she didn't like to bother him. And as she had Daisy anyway, and I was there ...'

'I thought Lucy was having Daisy?'

'Car problems.'

'That's a shame. Daisy was so excited about them spending some time together.'

Ash paused, alerted to his mother's sharp tone. With her back to him though, he couldn't read her expression. He said, carefully, 'I don't want Lucy to think I'm treating her as an unpaid babysitter.'

'But it's okay for Sarah to treat you as an unpaid seven-days-a-week handyman?'

'Huh?' He was taken aback. For a ghastly moment, he thought she was about to say that he treated *her* as an unpaid babysitter.

'Ash, that girl has you at her beck and call. Don't think I haven't noticed.'

'She does not. She's always been there to help me with Daisy, and I'm just ...' He shrugged. '... returning the favour. That's all.' His mother turned and fixed him with a long, silent look, which took him straight back to his childhood.

'Really? And have you actually discussed this with Lucy?'

'Have I what?' He was wary now, his mind flicking back over Lucy's comment the previous night.

'How much she wants to be involved with Daisy?'

He hadn't. Did he want to? What if she told him she didn't want that much involvement? How would he deal with that?

'Don't just make assumptions, Ash. Talk to her. And let someone else sort out Sarah's little dramas once in a while.'

He lifted his hands, at a loss for words. 'Right, I'm off. Thanks again.' He pecked her cheek and, waving goodbye at his daughter in the garden with her grandad, swung behind the wheel of his car with relief. He was already looking forward to Lucy's cheery and uncomplicated personality.

He drove slowly past the café on the way to her flat, spotting her van, still in the car park and now resting on four perfectly inflated tyres. He didn't doubt that someone had let the tyres down, it was an old trick. But it could have been anyone.

Lucy said the same, after he'd covered her with kisses and then let her come up for air. She looked fresh and sexy in a summery skirt and top, her tanned legs bare.

'Kids, I expect.' She shrugged a shoulder dismissively. 'I've put a chicken traybake in the oven. Is that ok?'

'Lovely, thank you.' He opened the wine he'd brought with him. Sod the traybake, whatever that was. He just wanted to take her to bed. 'Could Gerry have done it, maybe?' He wouldn't put it past the man to do something that spiteful, just to be annoying.

'Oh, who knows. It's sorted now, anyway. No harm done.'

'Well, maybe you and Richard should have a look at some security lighting.' Bending, he nibbled her ears. 'And I can put a note in the patrol book to keep an eye on the place.' His lips trailed along her neck. 'Nothing on the CCTV, I take it?'

'Nah, nothing I could make out. Salad?' She opened the fridge door, leaving his lips hanging where her neck had been moments before.

'If that's what you want ...'

'You're probably right about the lighting. We've never left any vehicles out there overnight before, so it's never come up.'

Ash pulled her onto his lap, relieved that she seemed not to be fazed by the incident. 'And the bonus is that you and me can spend a bit more time together, on our own.' Wrapping his arms around her, he pulled her closer. 'Good thing Sarah was able to pick Daisy up after all.' She sprang off him and peered into the glass oven door, fiddling with the timer. 'Garlic bread? I can get it out of the freezer.'

'I don't mind.' *I don't care. I just want to peel you out of that little top and ...* A thought struck him, and he swallowed. 'You didn't, er, feel like I was imposing on you today, asking you to collect Daisy?'

'Of course not. I was looking forward to it.' She frowned. 'What makes you say that?'

God, his women were prickly today. 'Er, I just want to make sure that you don't think I'm using you as an unpaid babysitter, or anything like that. You know. At all.'

'What on earth are you talking about?'

'I, er ...' The timer pinged on the oven and made them both jump.

'Ash.' She flicked the timer button and silence reigned. 'Just take me to bed, will you?' She squealed as he covered the short distance between them in a couple of long strides, wrapping his arms around her and lifting her, fireman-style, straight into the bedroom.

Later, they ate the chicken straight out of the oven dish, their fingers sticky with the still warm juices.

'Your Mum said she's booked the café for Daisy's birthday party.' Lucy licked her fingers, getting up to take the garlic bread out of the oven. 'Have you decided what to buy her for her birthday?'

'I've bought her a bike helmet. In pink, of course. And boots and gloves. Mum and Dad have bought her jacket and trousers. She's thrilled. I don't think she's ever going to take them off.'

'Are they as good as the adult stuff?'

Ash nodded. 'They are. All the armour, just like ours, only smaller. Very impressive. Only difference is, she'll grow out of hers.'

'So, a bike outfit, but no bike? Isn't that a bit mean?' Lucy cocked her head at him.

'It does sound a bit mean when you put it like that.' Tearing a piece off the baguette, he leaned over to steal the juices on her side of the dish. 'But we thought she could start out by pillioning me, and then she can decide whether she still wants to learn to ride her own little bike.'

'Oh, trust me, riding your own is wa-ay better than pillioning.' Lucy grinned cheekily at him, pushing his stealthy hand away from her food, and pulling the dish towards her. He wanted to take her to bed all over again. Luckily, he could.

Chapter Twenty-Five

Birthday Party Day. The Art Café looked lovely, lit up and festooned inside with the bunting, birthday banners and balloons that she and Nicola had put up, and Lucy was pleased with it. She wanted it to look perfect for Daisy. They'd closed the café to the public a little early, at four o'clock, ready for the party at 4.30. She was also pleased with her gifts to Daisy. She couldn't wait to give them to her.

Richard, enthusiastic almost-dad, had everything organised. There were ten mixing bowls and wooden spoons laid out, each with pre-weighed ingredients beside them. All the party bags of food were made and ready on trays, with jugs of squash, following consultation with Ash and Babs.

Fifteen minutes later, a gaggle of children burst through the doors, the little girls dazzling in their sparkly dresses and shoes and hair accessories, all bearing brightly wrapped gifts. Lucy barely recognised Daisy in her party dress. Her dark curly hair had been swept up in elaborate ringlets, and secured with a sequinned headband, and Lucy suspected Sarah's handiwork. Even at eight, it was possible to see how beautiful she would be when she grew up.

'Lucy!' Daisy ran towards her, throwing her arms around her.

'Happy Birthday, sweetheart!' Lucy bent to kiss her cheek. 'You look beautiful. Like a princess. Give me a twirl.' She clapped as Daisy pirouetted like a ballerina. Ash, Babs and John brought up the rear, their arms loaded with gifts, and another, elderly couple, who Lucy assumed were the other grandparents. Sarah's parents. They seemed much older than Babs and John, and although they smiled at the children, they moved stiffly, and didn't get involved with the party capers. Sarah looked, as usual, immaculate in black trousers and a black shell top.

Within minutes, the noise had reached deafening levels, as the children shrieked at each other. The boys ran around the chairs, and the girls compared dresses. Most of them had one or two parents in tow, for which Lucy was grateful. She couldn't imagine how teachers ever got control of their classes. And there were only ten children here.

Richard clapped his hands and then rapped a huge wooden spoon on the counter.

'Hands up, who likes cake?' he yelled. Hands were thrust into the air, several of them belonging to parents.

'Right, well, you're going to have to earn yours. Line up behind Daisy to get your pinnies, and then over to the sinks for some major hand-washing.'

Ash sidled up to Lucy, and they watched as the children queued obediently.

'I'm impressed. Was he ever in the army?'

Lucy linked her arm through his, smiling up at him as he kissed her. They laughed as they heard Richard supervising the children.

'No nose picking, no scratching of bums or earholes, yours or anyone else's, ok?' he told them all, earning a chorus of giggles and 'Euwwws!'

'Awww.' Nicola had a soppy smile on her face. 'Isn't he cute? He's going to be the best daddy, ever.'

'Right, let's join them, shall we? Otherwise they'll be eating all the mixture before it gets as far as the oven,' Lucy said, although she was enjoying the feeling of Ash's firm muscles and was reluctant to let go of him.

They and the other parents helped out with some of the beating, but mainly the children mixed their own cakes, particularly enjoying cracking the eggs. There was a good dusting of flour over every surface, and Lucy thought ruefully of the amount of clearing up there would be once they'd all gone home. It was worth it, she thought, watching Daisy laughing with her friends. She looked so happy.

As Richard slid their creations into the ovens, the children washed their hands and filed into the café for games and present opening. After *Pass the Parcel, Statues* and *Musical Chairs*, during which Nicola was a game DJ and Lucy refereed, Lucy gave Daisy her gifts. Both of which bore prints of the paintings she'd been working on for weeks. A small girl with a cloud of dark corkscrew curls and freckles, on a little blue motorbike, and a tiny, happy, spotty pig riding pillion. The little girl was delighted, staring at the images printed on the colourful watch and sequin-encrusted backpack.

'It's me!' An enormous smile spread across her face. 'And Harry! Look Aunty Sarah!'

'It *is* you, Daisy!' Lucy was beyond thrilled that the little girl liked her gifts. It was the seal of approval she needed.

'Lucy, these are amazing.' Babs reached over to inspect the bag. 'You are clever.'

'Not really. I was inspired by your granddaughter. I hope you don't mind.' She turned to Ash, who was also turning the items over in his hands. 'And I know it's not your birthday, Ash, but I framed the original drawing for you.' She handed over the flat parcel, studying him as he opened it. 'And if you like it, could I have permission to call the series Daisy and Harry?'

Head down, he said nothing as he gripped the painting in his hands, and Lucy held her breath. *Would he like it?*

'It's ...' He cleared his throat, and Lucy stared at him, her pulse pounding. 'It's so *Daisy*. How have you done that? I mean, it's not realistic, but it's exactly *her*.' When he looked up, his blue eyes looked ever so slightly moist, and Lucy's heart bumped painfully against her ribs in relief.

After the rest of the presents had been unwrapped and admired, and Babs had written down who the donor was so that Thank You cards could be dispatched, the children donned their plastic aprons again and got busy with the fat, sticky icing bags of buttercream. The parents helped to re-organise the chairs and tables after the games, ready for the children to eat. Babs had ordered a giant cupcake-shaped birthday cake from Richard, which took centre stage on a separate table, adjacent to the mountain of gifts.

There were gales of laughter from the kitchen. Lucy went in to collect the trays of food, and laughed too, seeing the wonky, towering icing on each cupcake, liberally encrusted with tiny smarties, chocolate stars and hundreds and thousands.

'They look, um, lovely,' she lied, grateful she wasn't eating them. They made her teeth ache just looking at them. Each child was also decorated with icing and Lucy went to get a couple of kitchen rolls to add to the tables along with the food.

In the momentary lull while the children ate, Lucy swallowed a couple of paracetamol. Her skull was thumping. Sitting on the periphery of the party, she sipped water and watched the children. The parents moved and swooped amongst their charges, mopping spills, moving sandwiches perilously close to table edges and whisking away food items which provoked cries of 'don't like this.' Thankfully, there weren't many of the latter, but the whole thing was a revelation to Lucy. It was exhausting.

The tide was out, and it was a balmy evening, so Ash and some of the others took the children onto the sunny beach to play *Follow my Leader* and other running around games, while teas and coffees were dispensed to weary parents sprawled in the café. Sarah and her parents sat on the balcony and watched the children, and Lucy made sure to bring them out a tray with a teapot and a cafetière so they had a choice. Lucy and Richard took the opportunity to start the clean up in the kitchen, scrubbing at clouds of icing sugar that seemed to have landed everywhere.

'Fancy doing this again?' Lucy asked Richard, pouring hot water and detergent into the sink for the umpteenth time.

'Um, let me think.' Richard mopped energetically at the floor. 'How about when my own kid is the same age? It'll take me that long to recover. I had no idea little girls could be so ...'

'... loud? Messy?' chuckled Lucy. 'They were just excited. You did an amazing job. So amazing that some of the parents are considering having one for their children.'

'Uhh.' Richard looked horrified, but his eyes twinkled, and Lucy made a mental note to factor the idea into their forward planning. She'd be ready for it next time.

Finally, it was time to usher the tired children out of the door and into the arms of waiting parents.

'Coming back to Ash's after?' Babs asked Lucy. 'Tea, wine, whatever. The grandparents get to put the birthday girl to bed, and the rest of you can have a break.'

'Sounds lovely. I'll see you there later, once we've finished tidying.' There was still the tables and chairs to clean, and the bunting and balloons to take down. She made Nicola put her feet up on the sunny terrace with a pot of peppermint tea, while she and Richard returned the café to normal, ready for the following day.

Daisy, the Birthday Princess in the front seat, chattered all the way home to the house. Ash winked at his parents in his rear-view mirror, where they had been relegated to the back seats. He guessed that they were actually enjoying the breather. It had become an annual custom that Daisy was handed over to the grandparents next for the long drawn out birthday present appraisal, bath, story and bed tradition.

Personally, he was looking forward to a cold lager, and catching the last rays of the sun in the garden with Lucy, later. At the house, Daisy knew perfectly well how the evening would unfold. Beckoning her grandparents bossily up the stairs, along with her gifts, she scampered in front of them, flinging herself onto the bed in preparation to tell them everything they never knew they needed to know about her gifts.

Ash set some chairs into her bedroom for Sarah's parents, whose aching joints weren't designed for lounging on the little girl's bed, or the floor. He opened his mouth to admonish her about being bossy, and then shut it again. It was her day, after all. He sneaked silently away.

Sarah was still standing in the kitchen when he got to the bottom of the stairs. He could see her, staring down, Lucy's painting of Daisy in her hands.

'Great, isn't it?' Ash said as he wandered in. 'She's really caught her, I think. She's done lots of different designs, she was telling me, and had them taken on by quite a big manufacturer. There's going to be Daisy and Harry stuff everywhere. Bedding, bags, kids' plates and cups, as well as ...'

Sarah held the painting level for a moment and then dropped it, quite deliberately, onto the stone tiles. The glass scattered across the floor.

'What the hell did you do that for?' Ash stared at his sister-in-law, stunned.

'How come everything is about her all the time? It's Lucy this, Lucy that, and we even had to have Daisy's birthday party in her bloody café.' Sarah folded her arms and glared at him. 'We were fine until she came along. Then she turned up and took over.'

'I don't know what you're talking about, Sarah.'

'What do you see in her?'

'She's beautiful, and smart. And kind. And I love her.'

'You loved my sister.' Sarah's voice was harsh. 'And look what you did to her. Have you forgotten that it's not just Daisy's birthday?' She took a ragged breath. 'My sister died too. Eight years ago. She'll never see Daisy grow up, never go to her birthday parties.' Her voice caught on a sob.

'I would never forget Sophie.' Ash's movements were measured and careful, just as he'd learned from dealing with over-wrought witnesses. He pulled out a chair and sat down. 'What do you mean, look what I did to her, Sarah?' he said slowly, wary now, and very glad that Daisy was upstairs and nowhere in earshot.

Sarah trembled. 'The accident. She went out after you had a big row. She was upset … that's why she crashed.'

'How did you know about the row?' Ash was completely focussed on her. *He'd always wondered why Sophie had gone out that night. How had this not come out before now?*

'Because she told me.'

'Before she went out? Why did she go out?' She hesitated, and he leaned forward. 'You know, don't you?'

Sarah inhaled a long, shuddering breath. 'That was my fault. I was out with a boy. On a motorbike.' Sarah glanced up quickly and then down. 'I wanted a boyfriend like you.' Her face twisted. 'But he wasn't like you at all! He rode like a lunatic – I was so scared – I thought we were going to crash. As soon as he stopped, I jumped off and said I wasn't getting on again.' She paused, her eyes unseeing. 'He just laughed and rode off. Left me in the middle of nowhere. So

I rang Sophie to come and get me. I couldn't ask Mum and Dad, they'd have been furious.' Tears poured unchecked down her thin, pale cheeks, and Ash stared at her in horror, visualising the scene only too well. 'I was crying and upset. She told me she'd had a big row with you and she didn't want to drive. She said you were a bastard and she was going to divorce you. I told her not to be silly, you'd make it up to her, but anyway ... I made her!' She covered her face with her hands, and her voice dropped to a whisper. 'I made her drive out and get me.'

'Sophie was going to divorce me?' Ash was stunned. He knew his wife had been angry, but they'd had rows before and always made it up afterwards. This was much more serious. He couldn't take it in.

'Yes! No. Well, maybe ... I guess. Whatever, it was both your fault and mine that she died. Me because I forced her to drive when she didn't want to, and you because you'd argued with her and made her so mad. I ... I heard the crash. I was on the phone when she crashed.' She sobbed. 'I miss her so much! I miss her ... and I look at Daisy ... and Sophie is in there. And I can't let her get on a motorbike, I can't bear to think of her being hurt. And there's you now with *her*, who's on a bike, and Daisy is having her own bike. What the hell are you thinking?'

Ash handed her a sheet of kitchen roll.

'All this time ...' His voice was hoarse. '... you've been living with this? All these secrets and worries?' And he'd felt guilt too, but he hadn't known the full extent of Sophie's state of mind that night. Now everything suddenly seemed so much worse.

Sarah nodded miserably. 'And I thought if you and me got together, I could stop you getting her a bike. I could stop you putting her on the back of your bike. And ...' She hiccupped. '... and I've always loved you, Ash, you know I have, since I was a teenager. We could have been a family. And Daisy would've been mine.'

Ash sat back, reeling as the words rolled into his brain. He said reflexively, 'Daisy will always be partly yours. She loves you.'

Sarah broke into racking sobs again. 'I'm sorry. I'm so sorry.' She blew her nose in the sodden tissues. Ash couldn't look at her. Overcome by her revelations, he didn't know what to say to her. A need for some kind of action made him get up for the dustpan and brush and begin to carefully brush the jagged pieces of picture glass into the pan. He picked up the drawing, and stared down at it.

'Oh, look, here she is now.' Sarah's head swivelled towards the door. 'Come to deliver another one of her little tellings-off, I imagine.'

On her way to Ash's house, Lucy bowled along in her van, singing along to the radio, pleased with the way the party had gone and thinking about possible different scenarios for her 'Daisy and Harry' series. The branding merchandising company were enthusiastic about the possibilities. She'd just held off on the name until she'd spoken to Ash. It still didn't seem quite right to profit from his daughter, but equally, she felt it would be a shame for Daisy not to get the recognition for being the inspiration behind it.

Ash's farmhouse was painted pale vermilion by the sinking sun. She parked in the spacious yard, sniffing appreciatively at the honeysuckle blossom which clambered riotously across the sunny walls, and strolled towards the kitchen, with a smile on her face, looking forward to a glass of chilled white wine.

And walked straight into a kitchen sink drama between Ash and Sarah.

'What?' She looked warily between the two of them.

Ash was frowning at his sister-in-law. 'Did you let Lucy's tyres down the day she was supposed to collect Daisy?'

Sarah stared at him with reddened eyes, and Lucy saw her expression hardening.

'Oh, yeah. She's been blackmailing me with that.'

'I what?' Lucy stared at her. 'I have not!'

'Honestly, it was just meant to be a prank, you know? I wanted to see if she could take a joke. But she's been threatening me with the police and restraining orders and stuff. She told me to stay away from you and Daisy or else ...' Sarah glared at Lucy now, and snarled at Ash, 'That day, she told me to feed Daisy and then send you away, so you could come and see her instead. And to stay out of your way from then on.'

'I never ...' Lucy's mouth dried up. *What a bitch! She's totally twisted everything.*

Ash held up his hands, looking unutterably weary. 'Let's not do this now, Lucy, ok? Sarah and I have just had a rather ... harrowing discussion about her sister and, well, I need some time to process things.'

'But ...' Lucy had caught the smug expression on Sarah's face as the girl hid behind a soggy tissue, ostensibly wiping her eyes.

'I said, not now! Please.' Ash's voice was firm and his blue eyes flashed. He sighed and dry-washed his face, and while his eyes were shut, Sarah sent Lucy a fleeting, but triumphant smile.

Something inside Lucy snapped. She had a horrible sense of *déjà vu* – it was Gerry all over again, never allowing her to have her say or get the last word in any argument. Always having to give in, have people walk all over her. Well, she was so done with that. She wasn't a doormat any longer. She was strong and independent, and she didn't need all this hassle. Sarah wasn't going to go away, and even if they sorted this blackmailing accusation out, the girl would come up with something else, over and over again, until eventually all Lucy's newfound confidence was eroded. No, thanks.

I am never *going to let myself be bullied again. Ever.*

Picking up the handbag she'd only just put down on a chair, she turned and headed for the door. 'I can see there's never going to be a good time for this discussion, so I'll leave you to it,' she threw over her shoulder.

'No, Lucy, wait, I ...'

But she didn't want to hear whatever Ash had to say. She didn't need a man who couldn't listen to her point of view or see what was right in front of his nose. Sarah was welcome to him.

Chapter Twenty-Six

'You know, for someone who's normally pretty intelligent, that was incredibly stupid.'

Ash swivelled round and saw his mother standing in the door to the kitchen. Sarah had just left on another flurry of sobs, after she'd clung to him for ages while saying goodbye, making his shirt wet with her tears. He'd still been in shock at her revelations about the night Sophie died, and just let her get on with it. He hadn't had the strength to push her away, and she'd obviously needed to cry after keeping her secret for so long. Poor girl, to carry around so much guilt for seven years. Well, he knew how that felt and she'd been right – he was partly to blame.

'What?' He frowned at his mum, not really following.

'You've just lost Lucy because you got caught up in that little minx's schemes again. Don't you remember what I told you? And I heard her admit it too – she's been in love with you for years. Still is. And she'll stop at nothing to get you. Honestly, are you completely blind?'

'That's not what this is about, Mum,' Ash started saying, but to his surprise she held up a hand and sent him an icy glare.

'Spare me. You bloody well deserve to be dumped!' She went to call his father, then stalked past Ash to the door without saying goodbye.

Ash stared after her, and his father, who gave him a half-hearted hug before leaving too. What the hell? He hadn't lost Lucy. He'd talk to her tomorrow. When he explained, she'd understand that he needed to process things; that after such a long day, the last thing he'd wanted was to referee a fight between her and Sarah.

But when he tried to call Lucy the following day, all his messages went to voicemail and she never replied to any text messages either.

His mother had, as always, been right.

A few weeks after Daisy's party, it was the open evening to show off the newly refurbished TV studios. Lucy's paintings were exciting a lot of attention, and although she was her own harshest critic, she had to admit she was proud of them.

'Penny for them?' said a voice in her ear. Pinning a phoney smile on her face she relaxed a little as she turned to see the urbane figure of TV Tom.

'Oh, hi Tom. Good turnout tonight!' She nodded at the crowd of people drinking and chatting loudly over the music in the TV studios.

Tom chinked his glass against hers. 'Ok, the paintings look great and you look fantastic, so why the glum face?'

'I'm sorry. Just … thinking.' She had no intention of discussing her thoughts with him. Hoping he would immediately begin to talk about himself, she said, 'Tell me about your exciting life on TV.'

Tom wasn't to be deflected. 'How's the biking going?' he said, bending his head near to her ear. The music was deafening.

'It's not.' She laughed lightly, hoping he wouldn't notice there wasn't much humour in it.

'Why's that?'

She tried not to sigh. Her bike was tucked away in the Vintage Bike Palace, and had been since that awful day when she'd left Ash and Daisy. She couldn't think about her bike without conjuring Ash up in her head too. The two things were inexorably linked. It was too painful to think about it – so she didn't.

It wasn't that she didn't want to ride her bike. Just that

the memory of their last ride out had represented the best day of their relationship. Also, she couldn't imagine taking her test with anyone other than Ash. He'd been there since the beginning. Biking *was* Ash.

Tom was still looking at her speculatively over the top of his beer. He raised his eyebrows. She refused to be drawn in, and said nothing.

'You look sad,' he said. 'This is an evening for celebration. Look how fantastic your paintings are – you're a star! Let me get you a top up.'

Lucy looked into her almost empty glass. She barely remembered drinking it. She was about to ask for an orange juice and then decided, sod it. She had a taxi booked. She was on her own now, there was no one at home, no one to look disapproving the following morning when she had a hangover.

'Lovely. White please.'

'Shall we find somewhere a bit quieter? Maybe I can persuade you back onto your bike.' Tom moved towards the bar, then looked back over his shoulder at her and winked. 'Or mine ...'

'On that perch thing you call a pillion seat?' said Lucy. 'Not a chance!'

Tom laughed. 'I like a challenge.'

He carried their drinks out onto the glass-walled balcony. There was a gas heater out there, and a few knots of people sitting chatting quietly. The music was audible but it was possible to talk without shouting, at least.

She forestalled his interrogation by asking him about his job. He was happy to oblige, perhaps realising Lucy didn't want to talk about herself, and proved to be an entertaining companion with a fund of interesting stories. Lucy relaxed a little for the first time in weeks.

'Well, I'm afraid I have to go and mingle some more,' he

said. 'Would you like me to introduce you to some more art lovers first?'

Lucy nodded. She still didn't feel sociable, but she knew she should make an effort, after he'd been so attentive. And it would be good for business too – she couldn't afford to pass up a chance like this for some networking.

'Thanks, Tom. And then I'm leaving. My taxi's booked for eleven.'

He nodded. 'Maybe you'd like to go out for a drink one evening?'

She frowned a little and chewed her lip.

'Are you off men as well as bikes?' he said with a glimmer of a smile.

She nodded. 'Sorry.'

'It's just a drink.' He looked into his glass. 'I know it sounds weird, but I don't meet many people I can just be myself with. People expect you to be on duty I suppose, all the time. You don't seem like that.'

'Ok. You've made it sound as if I'm doing you a favour now. And I owe you one for this.' She waved her hand around the walls.

'Great. I'll text you. Now, let me introduce you to Mike. He's an art collector, and I saw him paying particular attention to your seascapes.'

Lucy was more at ease amongst the crowd with Tom beside her. She was almost sorry when it was time to go, and waved around the room as she left. Tom bent and kissed her cheek.

'I'll be in touch,' he said.

Lucy smiled. She thought he probably wouldn't be. But he'd lifted her spirits and she was grateful.

The text arrived as she unlocked the door. She filled the kettle, plopping a peppermint teabag into a mug just as her phone pinged.

Thursday 7PM? I can collect you. Tom

He was keen. Did she want to go? He was nice enough, and a million women would walk over hot coals to be in her shoes right now, she knew. But she really didn't want to be involved. She wasn't ready to have another relationship.

She thought she'd probably *never* feel ready to have another relationship. As she stared at her phone, debating how to reply, another text appeared.

Don't worry, not on the bike!

She smiled, pushing the green leafy teabag round the mug.

Or you can meet me there …?

Sipping her tea, she pondered a reply. '*Ok. Where?*' Meeting him would feel less like a date. And goodness only knew, she didn't want to go on a date. Ever again.

The Three Cups. On the coast – do you know it?

She did know it. An unpretentious little pub, popular with walkers and foodie types. Sounded ok. She still didn't know whether she wanted to go there though, with Tom. Surely he had lots of impossibly glamorous girlfriends to call on?

Her phone beeped again.

Go on. You know you want to …

She laughed, and surprised herself. What else was she going to do next Thursday? It would be just her and the TV for company. It wasn't a date – she was just being friendly.

Taking a deep breath, she texted back a '*Yes, see you there*', and flopped onto the sofa with the TV remote in her hand.

She'd been the one to walk away from Ash, but she missed so much about their lives together. His big cosy kitchen. Cooking for them, drawing with Daisy, folding up her pretty little clothes, seeing all their wellington boots lined up by the back door after a long walk. Missed snuggling up to Ash's lean body in the warm bed. She shrugged irritably and tried to concentrate on the movie she'd tuned into. Some vampire horror thing. Not really her style, and her mind wandered.

It was hopeless. She missed Ash with every fibre of her being. Every blood vessel in her body yearned to be with him. She dashed a stray tear away. It was ridiculous to feel like this. Ash wasn't ready for a relationship. Not a relationship which meant him severing his support crew. Perhaps not all of the support crew. Just the one who threatened their relationship most: Sarah. As she had a million times already, she wondered whether she'd done the right thing by leaving.

Had she just left the field open for Sarah to move in on Ash? If she'd stayed, would things have improved? She answered herself, knowing she couldn't have stayed, remembering Ash's plea for her to leave it, his inability to tackle the issue then and there and listen to Lucy's viewpoint. That had told her everything she needed to know.

She'd had no choice, she'd had to leave. It had been the worst thing she'd ever had to do. Leaving Gerry had been a piece of cake by comparison and had made her realise how she'd fallen out of love with him a long time ago. Sometimes she wondered if she'd ever really loved him. She'd certainly never had feelings for Gerry as strong as those she'd had for Ash. Feelings she acknowledged she still had. She dared not admit how much she missed Daisy. Stupidly, she'd begun to imagine her and Ash having a child together, a sibling for Daisy, and being a family.

Thinking about Richard and Nicola and their 'bump' brought it all into sharp focus.

She was all alone. What a mess she'd made of her life. She switched off the television, and washed up her mug. The double bed felt too big as usual and she pushed away the memories that demanded attention.

Sleep was a long time coming, and when it did, was full of disjointed dreams about cardigan-wearing chickens with soft, short beards, in camper vans called Nellie.

Chapter Twenty-Seven

Nicola made a rare appearance at The Art Cafe a few afternoons later. Lucy hugged her gently and stood back to take stock of her friend. Pregnancy was not suiting her. Her face was thinner than ever, which made her bump seem bigger by comparison. She waved away the offer of tea or coffee.

'Hot water and lemon please. I can't stand the smell of tea or coffee. Which is why I've been keeping away from this place.'

Lucy carried their hot water and lemons to a quiet table as far away from the kitchen as possible. 'Gosh Nic, you look terribly thin. Are you eating?'

Nicola made a face. 'I *am* eating, but this baby's eating me! I swear it's going to be bigger than I am.' She leaned forward awkwardly. 'Anyway, you're one to talk. How much weight have you lost now?'

Lucy waved a hand dismissively. 'Dunno. Don't feel much like eating these days.' She blushed under Nicola's fierce glare. 'Ok, I promise to eat properly, Mum.'

'Quite right too,' said Nicola. 'So, what's this about a date with TV Tom? You are a fast worker.'

Lucy grimaced. 'It's not a date. I told you, I'm never going on a date ever again. In fact, I might sign up to be a nun.'

Nicola laughed. 'I don't think it works like that. So come on, spill.'

Lucy explained about the party at the TV studios and Nicola nodded. 'Yes, I'm sorry, I wanted to come but The Bump didn't want me to. I spent most of the night with my head down the loo.'

Lucy patted her hand, glad to be off the subject of TV Tom. 'Poor you. How is Richard coping?'

'Oh, he's brilliant, of course. Holding my hair back and everything.' She laughed. 'If the tables were turned, he wouldn't get that sympathy off me. I can't stand sick.' Her eyes widened. 'And stop trying to throw me off the scent. Is he really as nice as he seems on the telly?'

Lucy nodded. 'I think so. I've never seen him much on the TV, to be honest.'

'That's why you're not star-struck. You're probably a breath of fresh air for him. You are going on this "non-date", aren't you?'

'Yes, but I don't fancy him, Nic.' Lucy bent her head and took a sip of her hot water. There was a pause while she felt her friend regarding her.

'Oh, well,' Nicola said finally. 'It's a night out, with entertaining company. What's not to like?'

'I just don't know how to do this dating thing. I didn't do it with Ash because I'd already got to know him.'

'I thought you said it wasn't a date?' Nicola smirked.

'Yeah. Well. It's not.'

'So just talk to the man for goodness' sake! Like you'd talk to me and Richard.' She sat back, thoughtful for a moment. 'Well, maybe not me but Richard. Just be your normal self. You'll be fine.'

Lucy slumped in her seat. 'Sorry. Just feeling a bit fed up. Two relationships gone pear-shaped in such a short space of time. I can't help feeling like it must be my fault. Whether I should have done something different.'

'I don't think you had any choice. Gerry is a two-timing slimy worm who never deserved you, and Ash ... well, Ash has things to sort out. Don't give up on him. He loves you.' She paused for a moment. 'It's whether you want to pursue it.'

Squeezing her eyes shut for an instant, Lucy reached over for a napkin and swiftly blotted her face.

'I guess that's answered that, then.' Nicola narrowed her eyes as Lucy tried a weak smile, her throat croaking with unshed tears.

'So ... names for The Bump?' Lucy managed finally when she could speak.

'Engelbert if it's a boy, and Evangeline for a girl.'

'Oh!' Lucy blinked. 'How ... interesting! Are they family names or something?'

Nicola guffawed. 'Oh, Luce, you are so polite. God, no. If they were I'd have to leave the country. Could you imagine?' She laughed and after a moment Lucy joined in.

Richard wandered over. 'Lovely to hear you girls laughing.' He bent and dropped a kiss on Nicola's upturned lips, and Lucy looked away, feeling the sharp pang of loss all over again. Would this feeling ever go away? She'd had it all with Ash. She couldn't imagine having it again with anyone else, and she didn't want to either.

She would go to The Three Cups on Thursday, and be friendly and polite to TV Tom, why not? But that was all.

She stuffed a handbag with her phone, lipstick and money, locked the front door and left, driving slowly and hoping to arrive later than him. She didn't feel excited, she didn't feel anxious. She didn't feel anything. It was a dreary existence, she noted, wondering if she'd ever get back to normal.

Tom was sitting just inside the door and rose as she entered. Kissing her chastely on the cheek, he said, 'I've got us a table behind one of those settles. Nice and quiet.'

Privately, Lucy would rather be in the middle of the pub, where there would be no opportunity for any kind of romantic interlude, but she nodded and smiled.

'Thanks. Sorry to be late – have you been waiting long?'

'Aages! I was beginning to think you'd stood me up.'

She laughed. 'I did think about it ...'

'Nice to know I'm so irresistible.'

'I thought you'd have a million girlfriends to choose from to take out tonight.' Lucy fiddled with the menu, not really reading it, feeling on edge. Meeting Tom in connection with her job was different, and she was in control. She couldn't work out how to behave here in this cosy little pub, where having recognised Tom, people were glancing over at them. It would only be a matter of time until their smartphones emerged and photos of them together would be all over social media, with her cast as his mystery woman. She groaned inwardly. What would Ash think if he saw them?

'Who says I haven't got a million girlfriends?' said Tom.

'Well, where are they all tonight then?'

'Oh, well, you know, they're great, but they're all a bit high maintenance, as I said to you. We have to be seen in the right places, that kind of thing. I don't mind doing it as part of my public persona, but I like a bit of down time now and again. Are you ready to order?'

'I'll have the steak and ale pie. And chips,' she added firmly.

'Good choice. Me too.' He nodded, getting up to order at the bar.

She turned to watch him chatting easily with the regulars while he waited to be served. They seemed to be quite at home in his presence. He obviously came here a lot. Maybe he did just like a bit of down time now and again. She supposed you couldn't be in the limelight every minute of the day.

Returning with knives and forks wrapped in napkins, and a flowerpot with a numbered wooden spoon, he sat down and turned towards her. 'Ok, I'm going to be honest with you – I didn't invite you out in order to hit on you. Not that you're not gorgeous and everything, but like you, I'm actually off dating at the moment. No, what I wanted to do was run something by you. How would you like to work on a little project with me? On TV?'

'A what?' Lucy blinked, relieved that he'd let her off the hook about the whole dating thing, but taken completely by surprise that he'd had another motive for asking her out.

'Not a chat show, perish the thought. It's a much more exciting idea than that. But you need to pass your test. And soon.'

'Oh, why's that then?'

As food arrived – simple, honest and completely delicious – Tom outlined his idea.

'I love your paintings – they really do capture the spirit of our coastline. I've got this idea that we film you painting them. But more than that, we film you riding your wonderful purple bike to the locations. Then maybe riding off to meet other artists, art groups, schools ...' He paused for breath.

Lucy could barely believe her ears. Had she heard this properly? Was he really talking about her, or some other artist?

'Other biking artists, craftspeople, stuff like that.. Get you all together to paint and chat about your bikes. How you network, link together. You know that's what happens. Get a bunch of bikers together, and they never stop talking. And obviously, I'll be presenting it. From my own bike.' He sipped his pint. 'I'd like to set up a pilot. A taster. Pitch it to a TV channel I think would go for it. I've already got a camera crew standing by, and a camera drone. So we're just waiting on you.' He grinned at her, boyish excitement written all across his face. 'What do you reckon?'

'My test is booked, actually,' Lucy admitted, when she could finally string a sentence together. Her brain crowded with ideas and questions. When? Where? How? 'It's in a few days' time. But I don't know how I'm going to do it. I'm not allowed to ride my bike without my instructor present, and I don't have an instructor any more.' She made it sound flippant, careless, even though an invisible hand squeezed her heart.

'You might not need an instructor. Are you ready for the test?'

She nodded, a memory of that day when Ash had told her she was ready springing up to unseat her emotions yet again.

'Well, I could ride your bike to the test centre and pillion you, or you follow in my car. I go on to work or whatever and you pass, then ride your own bike home. No problem.'

Lucy looked at him, eyes round. 'Would you really do that for me?'

He laughed. 'Are you kidding? That is one hell of a funky bike. I've been dying to give it a good thrashing since I saw it on the podium.'

'You will not! My lovely Cadbury? He's not used to that sort of treatment.' Lucy glared at him.

'Only joking. I will be a perfect gentleman. Although I'm not sure about riding a boy bike. They're usually female, you know.'

She laughed. 'Looks as if I'm leading you into bad ways.'

Tom picked up his glass and chinked it with hers.

'Yes, and there was me hoping it was going to be the other way round ...' He held up his other hand. 'Joke! It's a joke, I swear. Let's just be friends, ok? And possibly work partners.'

Lucy was happy to toast to that.

The following Saturday she was in the big local supermarket and happened to pass the toy aisle. Since she'd moved, there had always been the possibility she might run into Ash and his family when out shopping, but she was still jolted when she suddenly came face to face with Sarah and Daisy.

'Lucy!' the little girl cried, throwing her arms round Lucy's legs without warning. 'Where have you been?'

'Er, hi, Daisy. Sarah.' She nodded at the older girl, but kept her eyes firmly fixed on Daisy. This was awkward. 'I've been a bit busy, sweetheart. Are you buying anything special?'

'I dunno. Aunty Sarah wanted some stuff so we came in here, but I want to look at the toys.'

'Yes, why don't you check out those new My Little Ponies down there?' Sarah pointed. 'I think I can see one you don't have. If you're good, I'll buy it for you.'

'Okay.' Daisy skipped away, scanning the shelves, although she didn't go very far.

Sarah turned to face Lucy. 'I'm glad you finally got the message. Ash is much happier now you're gone.'

Lucy kept her cool and didn't reply to that. What was the point? 'Sorry, but I'm going to have to get on. Lots to do,' she said airily.

Sarah grabbed her arm. 'Ash and I are going to have a baby,' she announced.

'What?' Lucy froze in shock, her eyes going automatically to Sarah's slim waist.

'Well, not right this minute, but soon, you know? We've talked about it. No point leaving it too long or Daisy will be very much an older sister.'

'I see.' Lucy swallowed hard. Was Sarah telling the truth or just winding her up? She could never be sure. Whatever. It didn't matter now.

'And just so you know – he prefers women who aren't fat.'

'Excuse me?' Lucy narrowed her eyes at Sarah and sent her a death glare. That comment didn't really merit a proper reply either. It was more dignified to just walk away, so she did.

But oh, it was tempting to grab the nearest bottle of something-or-other and dump it on Sarah's head.

Ash was in the kitchen when Sarah and Daisy came back

from their shopping trip. He knew he should have gone with them, but he couldn't muster up the enthusiasm today. Or any other day, for that matter. He had lost all his former energy and envied Daisy who came skipping in through the door. She was clutching a box with a new My Little Pony. Ash frowned. He'd told Sarah not to buy any more toys unless there was a special reason. He didn't want Daisy to become too spoiled. He was just about to say something about that when Daisy forestalled him.

'Daddy, why don't you like fat ladies?' she asked, starting to rip open the packaging.

'I'm sorry, what?'

'We met Lucy and Sarah said you like women who aren't fat.'

Ash felt as if someone had dumped an ice bucket over his head. He looked over at Sarah, who had gone very still and pale, but then she forced a smile.

'That's not what I said, Daisy. Anyway, what have I told you about listening to other people's conversations? Now why don't you show Daddy your pony? Isn't he gorgeous?'

'It's a *she*.' Daisy glared at Sarah. 'And you *did* say that. I heard you. And Daddy, when is the new baby coming? Aunty Sarah said you're having one soon. Will I be a big sister? I want a little brother. My friend Alice has one and he's so cute!'

The ice in Ash's stomach turned to hot coals of rage. He took some deep breaths, persuaded Daisy to go and play in her room for a bit without answering her questions, and rounded on Sarah. 'What exactly did you say to Lucy?'

Sarah's chin went up. 'Nothing! Honestly, that child has such an imagination ...'

Ash wanted to shake her, but restrained himself. His mother's words of warning ticker-taped across his mind. 'What. Did. You. Say. To. *Lucy?*'

Sarah started pacing around the kitchen. 'Ok, fine. I just warned her off a bit, that's all. Just in case she had any ideas of coming back. We don't need her. *You* don't need her. You've got us, me – *you said that* – and these last few weeks have been so much better—'

'Sarah, just shut up!'

She stopped and stared at him, her eyes wide. He saw the instant tears start welling up into the corners, but they were crocodile tears, he could see that now. How stupid he'd been.

Through gritted teeth, he said, 'I thank you from the bottom of my heart for all the help you've given me over the years with Daisy, but I really think it's time you went and found friends your own age. Go and travel. See the world. Am I making myself clear?'

'But Ash ...'

'I wanted to give you the benefit of the doubt, but you know what? You've just proved to me that I was wrong. I should have listened to Mum, to Lucy, and most of all, to my own daughter, who always, *always* tells the truth. She may have an imagination, but she does not tell lies. Please get it into your head – I don't fancy you. I never have, and I never will. And the way you've come between me and Lucy is unforgiveable.'

Sarah's tears stopped abruptly and were replaced with a frozen expression. 'You can't mean that ... I only ever wanted ...'

'Yes, Sarah. It's only ever been about you, hasn't it? Not any more.'

She stormed out of the kitchen, slamming the door so hard the units shook.

Ash gripped the nearest one, wanting to slam something himself. But he had a daughter to talk to and, possibly, a relationship to salvage. He needed to calm down and think.

Chapter Twenty-Eight

As summer drifted lazily to an end, the Art café was busier than ever. There was a softness in the air that heralded the start of autumn, and the horizon was hazy against the sky.

Lucy threw her energies into organising the big event she and Tom were planning to kick-start the publicity for their joint venture. They'd decided the café was the perfect venue and were hoping for good weather so they could put up a gazebo to house a bigger audience, but there was still a lot to do. When she wasn't thinking about that, she was busy sourcing new work and she persuaded Richard that they needed better lighting for on-the-wall stuff and another display case for some sensational enamel jewellery she'd discovered. The walls were filled with more of her own work too. Now that she spent her evenings alone, she painted more. In the beginning it was a distraction, but then she'd found it increasingly involving and she looked forward to her uninterrupted creative time. Best of all, she could leave her paints and papers out, safe in the knowledge that they would be undisturbed in her absence.

It was also a way of reclaiming her identity. She hadn't seen Ash since the day after she'd stormed out. She'd ignored all his messages, mainly because she hadn't known what to say – and certainly not in the truncated form of a text – and there had been nothing from him since.

She wondered whether he might try and visit her or whether she ought to go back and see him and when she weakened, which was often, she'd remind herself that Sarah would simply continue her games and they would be back to square one in no time. Her thoughts just went round and round in circles.

Although she was so excited about the filming idea, she'd always visualised taking her bike test with Ash, had always anticipated the solid comfort of his calmness with her. Getting Tom to take her felt strange, as if she was wrong-footed to start with. Flattering and exciting, but somehow disloyal. Had she done the right thing accepting Tom's help? Nicola thought she'd gone mad when she rang to mull it over with her.

'I can't believe you are even discussing this with me! Do you know how lucky you are?' she screeched down the phone. 'Just bloody do it, for goodness' sake. Eurgh, I'm going to be sick …' Lucy grimaced at her phone as Nicola's retching reached her before cutting off. Poor girl, she thought guiltily, turning back to unpacking the latest box of ceramic and felted wool pendants to arrive from a new maker.

One of the deep drawers in the filing cabinet was sticking out, as it had been for some time, and Lucy kicked it viciously shut, wishing it was Sarah's backside. It remained stubbornly out of line and she yanked it open, furious with it and herself. Using her mobile as a torch, she could see something was stuck behind it, a folder or envelope. Yanking all the files and brochures out of the drawer, she piled them up on the floor and reached into the back of the cabinet, her fingers searching.

The plain buff folder had torn on one corner where it had slid to the back, and the business card clipped to the top was crumpled. Lucy frowned over the name on the card. Where had she seen that before? Ignoring the files she'd emptied onto the floor, she sat at her desk and opened the folder.

'Wow!' she breathed, staring down at a sheaf of black and white photos. Mostly ten inches by eight, they were stunning. Lined character faces in sharp focus against blurry backgrounds; a group of young men loitering, their short-sleeved t-shirts tight around muscular biceps; a row of old women knitting – Lucy laughed aloud in delight.

Then two women on motorbikes, under a brick archway. The women, in bike gear, helmets swinging from their elbows – Lucy peered closely to see if she knew them – were leaning against the wall, the bikes reflected in a puddle. It was powerful and sexy, but not in the usual way of naked women draped over motorbikes as beloved by bike manufacturers. Lucy let out a long breath as she realised where she recognised the name from. He had been the photographer at the raffle, when she'd won Cadbury. She'd seen his expression change when he read her card, and wondered why. She groaned, realising what must have happened. He'd submitted these fantastic photos to her for exhibition and she, to all intents and purposes, had ignored them. No wonder he'd taken those hideous photos of her at Better Biking. And she'd probably got him fired over that.

'Drat, drat and double drat!' she cursed aloud, slapping the folder on the desk.

But maybe it wasn't too late to fix this? She dialled the photographer's number.

Having ticked one job off her list, the one which scratched most insistently just below the surface rose to the top again. She decided. She'd ring Ash and ask him if he'd take her to the test. But what if he agreed, and was all 'professional'? That would be unbearable. She couldn't do it.

Seeing her standing chewing her lip in a quiet moment, Richard picked up the phone. 'I'm going to ring him if you don't,' he warned.

'No, I can't do it. I'll be fine without him.' She snatched the phone off him and put it back. It would be too embarrassing. Better to let Tom take her and be done with it. 'Anyway, he'll think I'm deranged,' she told Richard. 'Dumping him one minute, then asking for favours the next.'

'He'll think you want him to take you for your test. Us blokes don't go in for all that soul-searching stuff. We're simple creatures.'

'Who's a simple creature?'

Lucy turned to see Gerry at the counter. He looked as smart as ever, in a dark charcoal designer suit, his blonde hair neatly cut.

'What do you want, Gerry?'

'Aw, don't be like that, Luce. I just popped in to see how the old place was doing without me. Richard.' He nodded.

Richard glanced a query at Lucy, and she nodded back. 'It's fine Rich. Gerry and I have nothing to discuss.'

'Well, actually, that's not quite true.' Gerry cut across her. 'Is there somewhere quiet we could go?'

Lucy looked around the cafe. It was the pause between lunches and afternoon teas. There were several tables empty. Feeling put on the spot, she led the way to one of them.

'Any chance of a coffee?'

Not bothering to disguise her irritation, she marched back up to the counter, but then her anger turned to amusement as she remembered something. One good thing about having had so much time on her hands was that she'd learned to use the blessed coffee machine. While Gerry watched with growing amazement, she set about making them both the most complicated coffee in the history of coffees. With knobs on. And she didn't spill a single drop.

'There you go.' She presented Gerry with an immaculate cup, complete with an arty swirl pattern in the frothy milk. 'It's on the house.'

Gerry just stared, the wind obviously taken out of his sails momentarily.

Lucy sat down opposite him and picked up her own cup. 'So what is it you want?'

But he wouldn't be rushed, stirring his coffee slowly without looking at her. She wanted to scream.

'Gerry ...'

'Still playing Happy Families with Mr Lover Boy Policeman?'

Her hesitation gave her away and his smug expression enraged her. 'What has that got to do with you?'

'The thing is,' he interrupted. 'I've been wondering whether we've done the right thing.'

She frowned at him. 'About what?'

'Well, you know, the Decree Absolute is due any day now, and that will be that, and I wondered—'

'Gerry – just get on with it!'

'Whether we could start again.'

'At what?'

'You and me! Start afresh, somewhere else. Just us.'

'You and me?' she echoed in disbelief.

'Yes. You know, move somewhere – abroad maybe. Have an adventure. Like they do on the telly. We've always been a good team, haven't we? We did up those houses, and we had fun, didn't we?'

Lucy eyed him. 'Ella not been replaced then?' He looked away, but she knew him well.

'We could start again, now you've got it out of your system. You've had your fling, I can forgive you.'

Lucy leapt to her feet, so outraged she almost couldn't get her breath. She looked at the hot coffee in the cup she was holding and contemplated the mess it would make of Gerry's suit. If it had been cold, she wouldn't have hesitated.

Gritting her teeth, she said, 'Goodbye, Gerry.'

'It's your last chance. You'll be penniless without me.'

'Actually, I think not.'

'What do you mean?' Gerry's demeanour changed from pleading to purposeful. If he'd been a dog, he'd have pricked up his ears. Lucy smirked. She sat down, twirling her coffee cup and playing for time.

'I do have ... other fish to fry, you know. Opportunities, you might say.'

Gerry stared at her, his chin pushed forward. She could almost sense him straining not to ask. 'What opportunities? Only, if you need any investment advice ...'

She laughed. 'Gerry. If I wanted any investment advice, you'd be ...'

He cocked his head at her, waiting.

'... the last person I'd ask.' She stood again. 'Bye, Gerry. Thanks for calling. Don't rush back.'

Her mobile rang. She whipped it out of her pocket and strode away from Gerry without looking back, pressing Accept on the screen. She didn't usually accept calls from unrecognised numbers, it was all too often marketing calls, but it had provided a timely escape – and it might be Ash.

'Hello!' she said into the receiver, trying not to sound over-enthusiastic.

'Hello. This is Phil Jones. The photographer. You rang me.'

'I did! And I have a huge apology to make to you ...' She carried on chatting, glad to be distracted from Gerry.

As soon as Daisy had finished her breakfast, Ash chivvied her out the door.

'We're going to Nanny and Bampy,' he said. 'I might need you to stay there for a little while because I have to go and talk to someone.'

'Who? Daddy, why are you rushing? And I thought we were going to work on Nellie today?'

'Not right now. Maybe later. Come on, sweet-pea.'

His mother had been extremely frosty with him of late, so he almost tiptoed into his parents' kitchen. Luckily Babs would never dream of showing Daisy that she was displeased with her son, so his daughter at least received a warm greeting.

'What brings you here so early? It's lovely to see you! Why don't you go and help Bampy – he's picking strawberries I think.'

'Oh, strawberries! Yum!' Daisy set off down the garden quite happily.

Babs turned to Ash, the glacial look back in her eyes. 'I hadn't expected to see you today.'

'No, well, actually ...' He took a deep breath. 'Look, I want to apologise, Mum. You were right and I was wrong. I've, uhm, told Sarah that she needs to, well, travel, maybe. Round the world. Anywhere but here. You know, get a life, hang out with friends her own age. She ... well, she did something unforgiveable yesterday.'

'Oh?' Babs' expression had only thawed a little, but she listened as he told her what had happened.

He spread his hands. 'So, you see, I need to go and talk to Lucy and I wondered if Daisy could stay here, please? I'll try not to be too long. I—'

His mum interrupted him. 'Ash, I think it's too late. I'm so sorry.'

'What do you mean?' He stared at her and she pointed at the newspaper she'd had open on the table in front of her. It was the local rag, the one that had printed those awful pictures of Lucy. His stomach churned. Had they done it again? But when he looked down, he saw a completely different photo of her – and she wasn't alone.

'I think she's moved on,' Babs said quietly. 'That's TV Tom, you know, the presenter. It says here that Lucy did some artwork for the TV company's new offices and during the opening party she and Tom were seen together quite a lot.' She pointed at a second photo, slightly grainier. 'This one was taken a few days later when they apparently went out to dinner.' She shook her head. 'I did tell you ...'

Ash tried to keep breathing, even though his chest felt as though a vice was squeezing it. No, this couldn't be happening. Lucy wouldn't go out with someone else just a few weeks after breaking up with him. Would she?

But this guy, this TV Tom, was obviously handsome, rich and famous. What was not to like? And what woman wouldn't fall for that? Plus, Ash had heard the guy had oodles of charm. A real ladies' man.

Fuck!

'I'm not saying you shouldn't try, Ash. I just wanted to warn you that it might be too late.' Babs sounded sad and Ash realised how well Lucy had fitted into his family. Everyone had loved her. Everyone except Sarah ...

He sighed. 'No, I should probably just leave her alone. She's been through a lot. She deserves better than me – I come with a lot of baggage, don't I.' It wasn't a question. He knew he did. How could he possibly measure up to this TV Tom guy who was footloose and fancy-free? He couldn't.

So what was the point in trying?

Lucy ticked off the days to her test. Less than a week. She read her copy of Roadcraft and the Highway Code at every opportunity, practised as often as she could on her 125cc, and felt ready for the test.

What she wasn't ready for was the phone call from Tom a few days later saying he couldn't take her bike to the test centre.

'I'm so sorry it's such short notice, Luce – I'm being sent off to Scotland for some Celtic arts festival thing. I'm really, really sorry. Is there someone else who could take your bike?'

Lucy rang Nicola.

'Bugger – I've got clients booked in. I can't change it,' said Nicola. 'You could try some of the other girls, but they're pretty much all working during the day as far as I know.'

Lucy took a deep breath and dialled the number for Better Biking. 'Hi, Angela, it's Lucy Daumi—' she began.

'Lucy! How are you? Ready for your test then?'

'Oh, well, that's what I wanted to talk to you about. Is there any chance someone could take me?'

'Oh! Not Ash? I thought you two were …'

'Erm, well, er, he's not, er, available. He's not working with you that day, is he?

'No, not as far as I know, but—'

'So,' Lucy cut across her quickly, 'is there anyone else?'

'Oka-ay. I'll ask. When is it exactly?'

Lucy told her and waited, hearing the murmuring voices indistinctly. Angela came back to the phone.

'My husband says he'll take you, especially as you've given us such great publicity from your blog, but you'll have to use one of our bikes. We're not covered by insurance on yours. Is that ok?'

'Oh, yes! That's fine, thank you. I'll get used to the bike on the way to the test, and I did ride it for a little while before we picked mine up.' Her voice choked off as she was assailed by the memory of that afternoon, going to the dealer's to collect Cadbury, when Ash had helped her shop for bike gear and they'd sung in her van on the way home.

'Are you ok, Lucy?'

'Sorry, yes, just … Er, what's your husband's name?'

'Brian. We were going to call it Brian's Bikes, but we called it Better Biking so we could sell the business when we retired.'

'Thank you so much Ange, and please thank Brian too. I'll see you on Friday!'

Chapter Twenty-Nine

The instant the photographer appeared in the doorway of the café the following morning, Lucy knew who he was, and he didn't even have a camera slung around his neck. Not too tall, slight in stature, with pale hair and a pale complexion, she realised how he was able to blend into the surroundings and capture the candid photographs she'd seen in that folder. He was almost transparent.

'Mr Jones!' She hurried forward, and held out her hand. 'Thank you so much for coming. Would you like a coffee? Or tea maybe?' She knew she was gabbling but couldn't stop. He was so low-key that she felt the need to make up for his lack of enthusiasm.

'It's Phil. Tea, please.' His eyes travelled around the café.

'Er, this is our main exhibition area,' she said, waving an arm towards her own paintings on the way to the counter to get their drinks, 'but we can use the whole café. We just take down everything else. How many photographs do you think you can lay your hands on? I'm sorry, this must seem terribly short notice. I expect you have exhibitions all over the place, don't you?' *Let the man speak, Lucy!*

Putting their teas on a tray, she led the way through to her office, where she'd laid out his folder in preparation for their meeting. She had never felt so nervous before meeting a client. He sat down.

'Look – I think I owe you an apology,' he began, lifting the lid from his tea pot and poking the tea bag with a spoon.

'Oh, no, I think it's me that ...'

'No, I ... I shouldn't have taken those photos of you. I was going through a bad patch at the time. My dad was ill and my wife ... well, the less said about her the better. And I just wasn't myself. My confidence was at an all-time low, and when I heard nothing from you after submitting what I hoped were my best shots, I, well, I was going to give it all up.'

'Oh, no! I'm so sorry! You haven't, have you?'

'And then I saw you, splashing the cash at that bike show, and I felt really angry. So ...' He looked uncomfortable. 'I wanted to get back at you. As I say, I really wasn't myself. So unprofessional of me.'

'Let's call it quits, shall we?' Lucy was quite shocked at the idea she'd been seen 'splashing the cash'. She certainly didn't remember doing any such thing. And Gerry would have had a fit anyway ... 'So we're having a big event. We've got TV Tom opening it, and quite a lot of other media names will be there, and I thought it might be a good idea to use it as a preview night for your work too? What do you think?'

'It sounds marvellous. I've got a stack of photographs you might like – you can see them on my iPad here.' He drew the device from his jacket pocket and Lucy leaned forward eagerly to see them. 'They're not all framed. Is that a problem?'

'Can you get them framed?' Lucy looked up from the photographs, all of which were as amazing as the examples he'd first sent her.

'Erm, well, I can't really afford to do them all at the moment.' He sipped his tea and looked away from her.

'How big are they?'

'All the same size, 10 by 8 inches.'

Lucy thought for a moment. 'Ok, we're on good terms with a local framer. How about we pay for say, a dozen frames? If they sell, you can pay us back. If they don't, we'll have the frames back and I'll re-use them.'

'Oh, I couldn't possibly expect you to ...' His hair looked paler than ever against his beetroot red face.

'I think you can. Right, that's settled,' Lucy said firmly.

They discussed the finer details of delivery times, and said goodbye. Lucy went back to her To Do list feeling happier than she had for a long time. Social Media was next on her list.

On her laptop, she opened Photoshop, and began to design a poster. *'Big Night at The Art Cafe!'* she typed, and inserted one of Phil Jones' incredible photos. Underneath she added *'Big Announcement! Celebrate with us and share our Exciting News!'* Tom had emailed her a file of portraits of himself. She selected one and slotted it into place on her poster, and added a recent one of herself. Between ticking everything off her list and the many customers who came to browse and buy, the day flew past.

Her stomach rolled with nerves when she thought about taking her test. It now represented so much, with what TV Tom was offering her. If she failed, he might just offer the part to some other artist ...

On test day, she was up, breakfasted and ready to go with bags of time to spare. She was amazed at how much more organised she seemed to be now she was on her own. There was none of the last-minute panicking that had characterised her life with Gerry.

She was relaxed as she drove to Better Biking. Reversing carefully into a space in the car-park, she remembered ruefully her helter-skelter dash for her CBT on her very first visit.

Taking a deep breath, she made herself stroll into the office. Look calm, and you'll feel calm, she repeated to herself. 'Morning!'

Angela looked a bit flustered, not her usual serene self. She hurried round the desk to hug her.

'Lucy! Hi, hello, morning! So, all ready for it then? Nice and early this time, remember that first time, ha ha?'

'Ye-es, I was thinking that,' Lucy said, eyeing her

curiously. 'Everything ok, Ange? Am I too early? Is Brian here yet? Do I need to sign anything?'

'Er, let me check.' Angela began to riffle through the papers on her desk. 'Lovely morning for it, no rain forecast or anything,' she prattled on, 'very lucky.'

Lucy watched her in bemusement, and heard a bike pull up. The engine note sounded like Ash's, another Triumph. That must be Brian. Maybe he'd been late and that was what Angela was worrying about. What would he be like, she wondered?

She heard the tread of the heavy bike boots as they entered the portacabin and as they approached the office, she half turned, curious to meet him.

It wasn't Brian. Filling the doorway, expression uncertain, arms hanging loosely – it was Ash.

Lucy caught her breath and her stomach went into freefall. She could hardly believe her eyes.

'Are you ... taking me?' Please, please say yes, she thought, mentally crossing her fingers.

He nodded. 'If that's okay?' His eyes flicked doubtfully over to Angela and back to Lucy. 'You don't have to, you can still have Br—'

The remainder of his sentence was knocked out of him as Lucy cannoned gleefully into his arms.

'Oh, yes, please, I do want you to! I wanted to ring you, but ...'

'I wanted to see you but ...' they said simultaneously, drawing apart a little and searching each other's faces.

She suddenly felt awkward. Nothing had changed really, so what was she doing throwing herself into his arms? 'I'm sorry. I should have asked about, er, your family. Everyone all right? Daisy? Uhm, Sarah?'

He stared at the floor. 'They're fine. At least, Daisy is. As for Sarah ... I don't know. I'm hoping she's somewhere in Asia by now.'

'What?'

Ash looked up and shrugged. 'I'm sorry Lucy. I should have realised just how bad she ... but I was a moron. I should have put my foot down. But she shocked the hell out of me that day and I couldn't think straight for ages. Can you forgive me?'

Lucy nodded slowly. 'Of course.' She meant it. They both had so much to learn about each other. 'Anyway, I shouldn't have let her get to me, so I'm to blame too. Your mum told me as much, right at the start.'

'Really? Hmm, I guess she sees a lot more than you or me. Oh, Lucy, I missed you so much,' said Ash, pulling her in again and wrapping his arms around her.

'I missed you more,' Lucy said into his jacket, not wanting to lose the slightest contact with him. She lifted her face, staring into the brilliant blue of his eyes. His hands moved up to cradle her jaw, his thumbs brushed her cheekbones and he dipped his head hesitantly. She closed her eyes, waiting joyfully for his lips to meet hers.

Angela blew her nose and they jerked apart.

'Sorry! Sorry – carry on!' she sniffed, fanning her face with her tissue. 'I'm so soppy, sorry!'

'Did you set this up, Ange?' asked Lucy, still holding onto Ash and knowing the answer already.

'*Moi*?' Ange was all innocence. 'I'm just an old romantic, me. Anyway. Go and get your bike.'

'My bike? My Cadbury? I can do the test on my bike?' Lucy's face split into a beam of happiness.

'I think she's happier about that than seeing me.' Ash laughed.

Lucy punched him lightly on the arm and hurried around the counter to Angela, hugging her tightly. 'Thank you so much,' she said, squeezing her.

'After all the great publicity you give us? Go on. Knock

'em dead. Well,' she said, looking horrified, 'no, don't do that – oh look, you know what I mean … begone, you two!' She waved them away, and shuffled her papers, pretending to work. 'Shoo!' They heard her humming happily as they left.

Lucy felt as if she was in a dream as she hopped onto the back of Ash's bike and squeezed him tightly. He patted her hands where they were clasped around his waist and they rode the short distance around to the Bike Palace to collect her bike. Ed and his dad came out to see her off and wished her luck.

'Glad to see you two have sorted yourselves out,' Ed murmured to her as he wheeled her bike outside. 'He's been as miserable as … the most miserable person I've ever met …'

'He's not the only one.' Lucy grinned. 'Thanks, Ed.'

The ride to the Test Centre took about forty-five minutes on the smaller A roads, but gave Lucy a chance to get her head into test mode.

'Concentrate, Lucy!' Ash said in her earpiece. She waggled her head in a biker's version of poking out her tongue and heard him laugh. Ever the professional, he reminded her about her positioning and shoulder checks, and she was soon in the zone again. She reversed her bike carefully into a parking space at the test centre, so she was ready to ride straight out.

After she'd booked in, they had almost an hour to wait, and wandered around to the burger van to get a coffee. Lucy was pleased to walk; her legs felt a bit rubbery.

'Have you shrunk out of your leathers? Ash asked. 'There's a lot more room in that jacket than there used to be.' He grabbed a handful of spare leather around her middle to demonstrate his point.

'Oi – pack it in!' Lucy brushed his hand away, pretending to frown. 'More room for jumpers now. And apparently you don't like fat girls.'

'Oh, God.' Ash shook his head, his expression rueful. 'She's a mixed-up person, she really is. I must've been blind.' He joined the short queue at the van and smiled down at her. 'Better get you a doughnut to go with your coffee, I think.'

Ambling slowly back to the waiting room and blowing on their hot drinks, they chatted about this and that. Lucy told him about her discovery of the photographs, and the upcoming exhibition.

'Tom is going to open it,' she said, 'and ...' She clamped her mouth shut. She'd almost divulged Tom's big news, which he'd specifically told her to keep secret. But would it be so bad if she told Ash? She trusted him to keep quiet.

Ash glanced across at her. 'Should draw a good crowd then. He's very popular. Tom, I mean.'

She nodded, still indecisive. 'Yes, he's been a good mate. I've had a lot of commissioned work since the launch of the new TV studios.' *Stop talking!* she berated herself.

'Mmm. I heard you two had been out a few times ...'

'Yes.' Lucy gaped at him. 'How did you know that?'

'Don't you read the paper? There were pictures of you.'

'Oh,' said Lucy. 'No, I've been too busy. But as I said, he's a mate.' She shrugged, then made up her mind. 'Can you keep a secret?' When he nodded, she filled him in.

His expression went from wary to joyful. 'Is that all? Phew! That's a relief. I won't have to fight him for you after all.'

She punched him on the arm for the second time that day. 'Of course not, silly. Why would I want him when I have you?'

'Well, he's rich, handsome, famous and he doesn't come with an eight-year old daughter, rescued escape pigs, a bunny-boiling sister-in-law—' Ash was counting on his fingers, but Lucy grabbed his hand.

'And wouldn't life be dull without them! They're what make you unique, and I *love* Daisy. Seriously, there's nothing between me and Tom and there never will be.'

He leaned over to kiss her. 'I am very glad to hear that. And we really do need to have some proper talks about everything. But not now. Right now, you wonderful, clever, brave girl, you are going to totally nail this test.'

By the time they arrived back at the Test Centre, Lucy barely had time to visit the loo when her name was called.

'Show him what you can do, Luce.' Ash winked at her as she wobbled to her feet, rubber-legged again. 'Go girl.'

Collecting her helmet and gloves, and clutching her paperwork, she smiled tremulously back at Ash and headed off. Her mind looped in a mantra. *You can do it!* She committed her feelings to memory for her blog. Her examiner was standing outside waiting for her, unsmiling.

'Can you stand here please?'

She did as she was told, feeling as if she was in the headmaster's office again.

'Now, before we go out, I need to check your eyesight,' he said.

Crikey, thought Lucy. *Bit late now to discover I can't see properly, surely?*

'If you can just read that number plate for me?' the examiner repeated.

Lucy looked wildly around. What number plate? Maybe her eyesight was that bad. There was a car driving out of the gate. He must mean that.

'LG61 ... er ..., S ... er,' she began, squinting.

The examiner's head whirled around.

'What? What are you looking at?'

'That!' Lucy pointed at the car disappearing towards the junction.

The examiner shouted with laughter. 'Not that. Those!'

He pointed at a set of number plates fixed to the wire fence of the compound.

'Oh! EJ58 TGB.' Lucy reeled the numbers off.

'Yes, that's it. Goodness me – nothing like making it harder than it already is.' The examiner was still chuckling.

Lucy laughed too. So he was human, she thought, realising how much less tense she was now. To her amazement, the next hour passed in a flash. Seeing the examiner in Hi-Viz tailing her on his big bike was just like being followed by Ash, and she wasn't fazed at all.

She thought of nothing except the task in hand, following his directions. It was as if every nerve in her body was tuned to her surroundings. She noticed everything – every person about to step off the pavement, every child with a football, every loose dog, every driver about to change lanes without indicating. It was like playing a giant, real-life video game. She had no idea where she was, and was surprised as the Test Centre re-appeared. Had that really been an hour? It was the moment of truth. She thought she'd done ok, but ...

Her nerves returned as she parked her bike, her brain shrieking, *'Don't drop it, don't drop it here!'*, and switched the engine off with relief. It was only once she was upright that she realised how much she'd been holding her body in a state of tension.

'Don't take off your helmet. Go straight into the office, please,' she heard the examiner intone.

Ash's eyes met hers the minute she walked into the waiting room, his eyebrows raised in query. She shrugged minutely, her eyes wide, as the examiner shepherded her into the little office. It felt terribly hot in there after being out in the cold air, and Lucy's nervous fingers fumbled at her zips and fastenings while the examiner pulled the paperwork in front of him.

She watched anxiously while he ticked boxes and wrote. Finally, he looked up at her.

'Ok, you left your indicator on for too long as we approached the first roundabout, and then you didn't indicate at all as you left it.'

Lucy gulped. How had she done that?

'But the rest of the test was ok. Apart from that hill-start …' He looked at her with a glimmer of a smile, 'I thought you were going to take off!'

'Oh. I was terrified I'd stall it,' she remembered.

'Those indicators are what tell other road users where you're going, and misinformation and not using them is very dangerous.'

'Yes.' Lucy hung her head. So, did that mean she'd failed? Ash would be so disappointed – failing on not using her indicators? After he'd drummed it into her over and over again?

'But as you settled down so quickly, I put it down to nerves. Which leaves you with three faults. Well done.'

Lucy looked down at the form in disbelief.

He held out his hand and began to stand.

'What – I passed?' she said, shaking his hand on auto-pilot.

'Yes.' He chuckled. 'Off you go, and don't forget those indicators! Well done.'

'Thank you!' She pumped his hand with more enthusiasm this time and gathered all her bits and pieces. 'Thank you again!' she threw over her shoulder, hurrying into the waiting room to share her good news.

Ash was still sitting in the now empty waiting room, looking as anxious as an expectant father. He jumped to his feet as he saw her.

Her beam of delight told him everything and he swept her up in his arms, lifting her effortlessly and whirling her around. 'Well done!' he said, over and over again. 'I'm so proud of you!'

'Thank you so much for taking me today. I couldn't have done it without you,' she said, when she got her breath back. 'You've changed my life, Ash.'

'You've changed mine, too. But you did this all by yourself, sweetheart. You wanted it, and you worked at it. I just ... facilitated. Let's go and have a ceremonial removal of the L-plates, shall we, and then a nice café for lunch?'

'Ooh, yes – and I need photos for my blog!' she squealed. 'I can't believe it. I'm so happy!'

He dropped his lips onto hers, squeezing her against him. 'I couldn't bear the thought of *not* being here. When Ange called, I jumped at the chance.'

Their kiss seemed to go on for ever, but eventually they headed outside and ripped off her L-plates. It was one of the proudest moments of Lucy's life and sharing it with Ash was just the icing on the cake.

Epilogue

The Art Café was filling up rapidly, and the giant TV screen was set on a loop of photos of Lucy winning her motorbike, and then, courtesy of Phil Jones, photographs of her training – thankfully better than the ones that had appeared in the newspaper – plus others of her with the biker girls from the Curvy Riders club.

Lucy's eyes scanned the enthusiastic crowd, taking a mental snapshot. So many people, their faces lit by thousands of sparkling lights. Her parents, bless them, had arrived that day and were staying in a local hotel, mingling like pros amongst the throng. They knew what was going on, she'd had to tell them, but she knew they wouldn't breathe a word of it. Angela, smiling with her husband Brian – so that's what he looked like – Ed and his parents, plus a whole posse of Curvy girls, dressed up or in their leathers. Rhodri, from her very first training day, and Pete, who'd also finally passed his test.

She would remember this night. It was another beginning. But what on earth was keeping Ash so long? Had something happened to Daisy?

She recognised people from the TV studio launch, and newspaper editor Don Peters, now a firm friend, raised a glass to her as she passed. People she didn't know at all smiled at her, and commented on how lovely her dress was. People she did know pulled her to one side and congratulated her.

'Wow, this is quite an event, but what's the big secret?'

'All will be revealed soon.' She smiled mysteriously, and sidled away as soon as she could, only to be embroiled in a similar predicament straight afterwards.

Tom's ability to smile and shake people's hands without pause was amazing. She had the beginnings of a headache already, and it had barely been an hour.

Babs and John had arrived early, offering assistance as was their usual way, but where was Ash? He'd promised to be here and she couldn't wait to see him again, even though they'd spent the last few days virtually joined at the hip.

'You look absolutely wonderful!' Babs looked her up and down. 'I love that dress on you, it's fabulous.' Lucy thanked her with a hug, but couldn't help looking over her shoulder.

'He's coming, don't worry. Probably just Daisy playing up.' Babs gave her arm a squeeze. 'And Lucy, I hope you know how pleased we are that you ... well, found each other again.'

Lucy smiled. 'Not half as pleased as I am.'

She escaped into the relative calm of the kitchen, where she found her wonderful staff assembling tray after tray of mouth-watering appetisers under Richard's beady eye. She tried to help but they gently and firmly elbowed her out of the way, until she hovered at the edges, feeling like a fish out of water.

'Better get used to this,' Tom muttered to her in a swift aside as he winkled her out of her hiding place. 'Any more of those delicious filo parcels?'

'When are we doing the announcement?' Lucy asked, grabbing one of the loaded trays and holding it out to him before heading back towards the café.

'You can't hand those round!' Tom looked shocked. 'You're the star!'

'I'm still a working girl, y'know. And I can't handle all that small talk like you do.' She grinned, slipping away with the tray. 'May as well be useful.'

'Ok. Give it another half an hour and then get miked up, ok?' Tom tutted. 'We go live in forty-five minutes.'

Ash smiled at his daughter, who looked like a miniature version of Lucy standing before him. He'd carefully tucked her ponytail into her jacket so it didn't fly out and become tangled, and zipped her jacket to her trousers. Buckling her helmet reminded him of performing the same task for Lucy.

'Warm enough?' he said, into her open visor.

She nodded, her tongue out like a dog, her eyes bright and excited.

'Ok, we've practised this lots of times already. You'll be able to talk to me through that little microphone inside your helmet and you're going to be wedged in with the top box behind you and the panniers by your legs, like a big armchair. Now you tell me what you're supposed to do.'

'I put my feet here, and I hold on tight to those,' she pointed at the attachment he wore around his waist, comically called, 'Love Handles'. 'And I don't fidget, or try to get off until you tell me to. And when you go round corners, I hold on and just lean with you.'

'And?' he prompted.

'And if I'm scared or want you to stop, I tap you with my hand, or shout,' Daisy recited. 'I won't be scared.'

'I won't be going very fast.'

Daisy pouted, and he rolled his eyes.

'I've created a monster,' he muttered.

She climbed on first so he could check she was ok, and then he hopped his leg between her and the petrol tank, feeling behind him to make sure she was holding tightly to the handles at his waist. In the gathering twilight, his headlights threw a bright beam along the lane, and he concentrated on giving her an easy ride across the shallow pot holes.

'Ok?' He turned his head and spoke into his microphone, stopping at the junction at the end of the lane.

He got the shock of his life as her helmet appeared over his shoulder, and he looked behind to see her standing up on the foot-pegs. Her head curved towards him and he saw her sparkling eyes behind her visor, as she nodded vigorously and jabbered excitedly into her mouthpiece.

'Oi! Sit down you little minx!' Little daredevil, he thought, stifling a grin.

'Let's go, Daddy!' she yelled, bouncing back into her seat. He felt her bony little knees squeeze him and he patted her leg.

'Not far to go,' he called and turned onto the main road, towards the Art Café – and Lucy.

Tom seemed casual and relaxed beside the crew, nodding as he heard the TV studio in his earpiece and winking at Lucy as she re-appeared wearing a neat, flesh-coloured headset and mic, the radio part discreetly clipped behind her. She could sense the atmosphere changing subtly as the sound and camera crews did their checks, moving themselves discreetly into position.

Cameras and mobile phones were in evidence everywhere as the masses jostled for the best view, and there was a loud, excited hubbub of voices.

'One, two, one two.' Microphone in hand, Tom had shed his 'bloke next door' persona and turned into the professional, smooth TV presenter, doing his sound checks.

Standing beside the stage, Lucy's heart pounded. Could she do this? As the thought sped through her mind, she knew she could. She'd passed her test – she could ride a motorbike. And she had Ash back. She could do anything now. A quiet confidence swept through her, like cool water on a hot day.

She saw Tom nod, and jerk his chin at Richard, who clapped his hands and called for quiet.

'Ladies and gentlemen,' he began, looking thoroughly at home on the stage, his blonde hair a halo under the lights. Lucy could see Nicola on one of the few chairs, gazing up at him adoringly, and smiled. How she loved her friends. 'Ladies and gentlemen, thank you all for coming to The Art Café tonight. I hope you are all enjoying the wonderful exhibition of photographs by Phil Jones, who is here tonight ...'

Richard swept his arm towards a pink-faced Phil, and continued, 'And I am delighted to pass you on to someone who needs no introduction at all – Tom Wheaton, known to us all as TV Tom!'

Leaping onto the stage, Tom smiled round over the head of the cameraman at an audience that Lucy could see were already star struck. The TV screen segued from photos of her to live TV and she laughed at the ragged cheers as people began to see themselves.

'Good evening everyone!' roared Tom, lifting his hands and encouraging them to yell back. Lucy knew he was in touch with the production team via his earpiece, and once he'd got an animated crowd, he launched into his spiel.

The few miles had been torture for Ash. His instinct to get to the café as soon as possible had fought with his need to ride slowly and carefully with the precious cargo of his daughter on the back. It didn't help that she was digging him with her knees and yelling, 'Faster Daddy, faster!' into his earpiece.

He exhaled with relief as they turned into the overflowing car park. It seemed as if the whole world was there – cars were parked right down the surrounding roads. Circling slowly, he spotted Ed's pick-up near the entrance and pulled up directly in front of it.

Abruptly, nerves overtook him and his legs felt leaden as he parked the bike onto its side stand. He was about to do something monumental, and he was worried it might be the worst idea he'd ever had ...

Daisy wasn't suffering from nerves at all and, without waiting to be told, clambered off the bike like a monkey. He saw the café doors open, and a long shard of bright light illuminated her before she was swallowed up inside.

'Hey! Wait!' he yelled, snatching the key out of the ignition and giving chase to his daughter.

He burst through the doors, dragging off his helmet and sweeping his gaze over the café, taking in the thickly packed crowd and the stage on which he could see TV Tom talking on the mike, alongside Lucy's purple bike, gleaming under the lights. But where was Lucy?

'... As some of you know, amongst my other duties, I've recently been made arts correspondent, and it was my interest in the arts, plus a shared passion for motorbiking which has led to this amazing relationship with Lucy.' Tom was saying, into the flurry of clapping and wolf whistles.

'Aw, they make such a lovely couple.' Ash heard someone say, as Tom's words thudded into his brain. His stomach lurched.

Like wheat parting, he could see Daisy's progress, but there was no room for him to follow through the throng, who were either staring at the stage or watching the giant TV screen high on the wall.

He was well and truly wedged at the back. *Damn! If I'd stuck to Plan A, we would have been here much earlier.* He and Daisy had been ready, both of them scrubbed and smart, and then a thought had struck him like a physical blow. Since he'd found her again, those thoughts had been coming thick and fast. Call himself a copper? He'd missed every single clue about Sarah. It was not going to happen again. He might not have been great at talking through all the things that worried him, but he *was* a man of action. With all his heart, he was going to send Lucy a clear message that he wanted her in his life. And he wanted Daisy to be as much a part of it as he was. He'd knelt beside her, pulling her into a big hug.

'Daisy, sweetheart. I think I need a bit of daughterly advice ...'

Lucy's eyes snapped towards the little pink-helmeted figure, muffled up in armoured clothing, as it made its determined way towards her.

'Daisy?' she said in astonishment and delight as the little girl finally stood before her, flapping her hands urgently and gesturing back into the crowd.

Lucy bent towards her, frowning in concentration as Daisy hopped up and down, eyes blazing and evidently shouting at the top of her voice. Lucy pushed back the visor on the cute pink helmet, knelt down and unbuckled the chin strap.

'I didn't quite catch that,' she laughed. 'You look awesome!'

'I came on the back of Daddy's bike!' Daisy repeated. 'It was wicked! But he wouldn't go fast enough ... oh, and he wants me to ask you something ...' She trailed off as Lucy snapped upright, searching over the heads of the crowd for Ash.

What had happened to send them both here on his bike? *Don't say Sarah had sabotaged his car!*

Tom caught her arm to draw her towards the stage, still speaking. '... and our relationship has led to this opportunity, which will combine both Lucy's incredible artistic talent, and also her biking skills. We will be ...' He paused for dramatic effect, his eyes flicking at the camera crew and at Lucy, counting down to the great announcement.

'Just a minute, Tom,' she murmured.

'Lucy, we're live on TV here! What's up?' Tom hissed.

'Can't you ... play a song or something?'

'This isn't radio. It's TV and we're live!'

She sent him a look. They weren't really live. It was recorded and would go out later. The audience didn't need to know that though. Still holding Daisy's hand, Lucy searched on tip toe for Ash.

Lucy looked, Ash decided, like a goddess, just by the stage in that gold, figure-hugging dress. The gathering was thickest there and in a moment of inspiration, Ash yanked his helmet back on and spoke urgently to his daughter.

'Daisy, I want you to tell Lucy something. I want you to say, um ... Actually, no, I'll tell her myself, if ... I. Can. Just ...' He pushed more urgently towards the stage, earning frowns and return shoves.

Tom, frantically trying to get Lucy's attention although her eyes were raking the crowd, wasn't giving up. 'I am thrilled to announce,' he battled on, 'that Lucy and I ...'

Ash heard Daisy just then in his ear-piece. 'Daddy said,' said Daisy, in her 'important voice'. 'That—'

'Hang on!' cried Ash, finally reaching the stage. 'Not yet!' But Daisy, clearly impatient with her father, carried on regardless. Lucy knelt beside her, and her mic picked up Daisy's clear, piping voice.

'Daddy said, that if you were my Mummy then we'd be a proper biking family. Would you like to be my Mummy?'

Ash groaned. His child had no idea of timing. How had he thought this was a good idea? He took off his helmet, raking a hand through his hair, and bent to take Daisy's off too.

Lucy's face was unreadable. He'd blown it, surely. Tom stared down at him with a look of astonishment, but he saw him whirl his fingers at the cameras in an unmistakeable signal to 'keep rolling'. He visualised himself on video bloopers on a never-ending reel. Maybe he could just take Daisy now, and sidle away. Do it another time.

'Go on, Daddy.' Daisy was unrepentant. 'Say the words. Like you said.'

Ash swallowed as his heart rose into his neck. He was never going to live this down at the station. He fumbled through the many pockets of his motorbike jacket. *Damn!* Where had he put the thing? It had been such a rush in the end, and he remembered zipping it into one of the really safe pockets …

'So …' Daisy put her hands on her hips and looked up at the speechless Lucy, every inch of her impatient to get on. '… Daddy says, will you m—'

'Marry me, Lucy?' Ash interjected the words before his daughter stole every single bit of his thunder. This was a disaster. It was meant to have happened *after* the broadcast. Not instead of. He hadn't meant to hijack her big moment. He fixed his gaze on Lucy's face.

'No, you said it wrong. Marry *us*.' Daisy tugged on his sleeve. 'You said, Daddy. She has to have both of us. Ask her again!'

Laughter rippled gently from the audience as the camera focused on Daisy's little face, serious and adorable.

'Quite right too.' Tom laughed as well, obviously deciding to play along with this as if it had all been scripted beforehand.

'Oh, right, well …' Ash decided he'd already made such a spectacle of himself, he might as well do it properly. He went down on one knee, and heard the crowd cheer. 'Lucy, please will you marry *us*? We love you!' Hearing his own voice coming out of the enormous TV screen wasn't helping, but he'd done it now. There was no going back. But God, this was embarrassing.

'Yaay! Go Daddy!' Daisy yelled. The crowd laughed even more.

'Hold on – shouldn't there be a ring?' Tom appealed to the gathering, getting another cheer.

'Yes, I know, it's in here. Somewhere …' Ash shot him a look, still hunting through his many pockets, while Daisy burrowed into hers.

'Here you are!' she cried. 'And there's no fluff on it!' She held aloft a pink and white Haribo ring, and added, after closer inspection, 'Well, not much, anyway,' to the delight of the audience. Ash was about to reject her kind offer, when he stopped. This was, after all, as much about Daisy as it was about him and Lucy, and so far, she was taking a whole lot more charge of the situation than he was. And wasn't that exactly what he wanted? They were never going to be an ordinary family.

'Thank you, darling.' He took the sweet from his daughter. He couldn't begin to imagine what Lucy was making of it all, but he had never been more serious. Taking a deep breath, he stood before her, holding out the sticky sweet ring.

'Somewhere, in this infernal jacket, I have a more expensive, and much less soluble version of this. If you'll have me … us …'

'Yes! Oh, yes!' Lucy squealed, throwing her arms around Ash's neck just as he was starting to wish the stage would open up and swallow him whole.

He grinned and bent to kiss her, oblivious of the cheers, claps and whistles.

TV Tom tapped him on the shoulder. 'Congratulations to the happy couple, but if I might interrupt for a second, we have another rather important announcement. The reason we are here tonight, in fact.'

'Sorry,' Ash mouthed, grateful the man was such a pro.

He'd had every right to push Ash off the stage really. His eyes ran across the audience, and he groaned inwardly as he spotted Lucy's parents.

'Lucy and I ...' Tom paused once more for effect, '... are making a TV series together!' He nodded at Richard, who tugged up the pull-up banner which showed a huge photograph of Lucy in leathers on her purple bike. Superimposed over one of her coastal landscape paintings was the wording:

'Ticket to Ride – coming soon on your TV!'

The crowd were struggling to keep up with the turn of events, their heads flicking from Tom to Lucy and Ash and back.

'Beginning from this very café,' said Tom, grinning, 'Lucy will be biking around the country, painting the coastline and other areas of interest, and meeting up with other motorcyclists and artists along the way, some of whom, like Lucy, do both!' He waved an arm at Lucy to come forward and Ash let her go. But Daisy didn't.

'A year ago,' Lucy began hesitantly, squeezing Daisy's hand. 'I was a very different person. And then I won a motorbike – that I couldn't ride! But I learned, although ...' She laughed, glancing back at Ash. 'I was pretty terrible in the beginning, actually ... and it wasn't the only thing I learned. My life has changed, in ways I could never have imagined. And whatever happens next, I will cherish the experiences I've had.' Her voice choked as she looked around at the smiling faces of the crowd. Tom whirled his fingers at her and she hurried on, 'And I am thrilled to have this opportunity to be able to combine two of my great passions in this way. Huge thanks to Tom for coming up with this idea!'

There was more applause, but as Lucy turned back towards Ash, she was the only thing he could see.

They stood together, hands clasped tightly in the velvet dark outside the café. On the beach below, the waves whispered lazily onto the sand, gilded by car headlights. It had been the most incredible night. Lucy and Ash had been mobbed by their parents and friends and their good wishes still rang in their ears. After all the excitement had died down a little, Daisy had been whisked home with Babs and John. Her eyelids were heavy and she made only a token protest. Except to murmur that she'd like a baby brother or sister, but could she possibly have a puppy first?

Richard and Nicola switched off the lights and locked the door, standing with them for a few moments. The last few stragglers making for cars and taxis wished them all a good night and 'Congratulations!'

'New starts all round then.' Lucy's parents were about to leave too, arms about each other, their faces wreathed in smiles.

'Yes. A perfect Summer Snow Globe moment,' said Lucy, looking up at the stars.

'You what?' Nicola looked perplexed.

'You know, those snow globe things, that you shake and it snows? What if you could save a perfect moment, and shake it up and have sunbeams instead. Or stars, like now? I try to paint them in my head, so I can shake them up and remember them forever.' She turned to Ash. 'I've got quite a few lined up on the mantelpiece inside my head, now.'

'O-kaaay,' Richard said, his teeth white in the dark. 'She's all yours, mate. Good luck!'

Ash wrapped his arms around Lucy, smiling. 'She is.'

'Couldn't have done it without you guys,' Lucy said. They reached out for a group hug before peeling away.

'Home – mine? Or home – yours?' Ash asked, when they were alone.

'Yours. Let's start the way we mean to go on. I love you, Ashley Connor!'

'I love you too, Lucy Daumier! Here's to a lifetime of summer snow globes!'

Thank you

Dear Reader,

Thank you for reading my debut novel, *Summer at the Art Café*. I do hope you enjoyed meeting my characters and following their story.

Ash, Lucy and Daisy were born from the experiences of my life, although they found their own personalities as time went on. They surprised me with laughter and occasionally exasperated me, but I love them all, and still expect to bump into them in real life when I'm on the beach.

It's exciting and terrifying in equal measure to share them with the world. I would be thrilled if you took the time to leave a review on the retail site where you made your purchase. Reviews really do help to improve a book's profile and sales and are very much appreciated.

My contact details are given at the end of my author profile, and if I've encouraged you to learn to ride a motorbike, details of how to do that are there too!

Much love,
Sue X

About the Author

 Sue McDonagh's career as a policewoman for Essex Police was cut short when she was diagnosed at the age of twenty-four with ovarian cancer. After a successful recovery and a stint working as a Press Officer she moved to Wales.

In Wales her love of art evolved into a full-time occupation and she made a living teaching and sketching portraits at shows. In 2014 she was a regional finalist for the Sky Arts Portrait Artist of the Year. She now works exclusively to commissions from her art gallery.

In 2009 she learned to ride a motorbike, and now helps run Curvy Riders, a national, women only, motorbike club. Her joy of motorbikes and her love of writing inspired her to write the Art Café series.

Sue, granny of three little girls and proud to be owned by a clutch of stepchildren, lives a mile from the sea in Wales. She can often be found with her border terrier, Scribbles, at her art gallery. Scribble thinks the customers only come in to see him. Sometimes, Sue thinks that too.

When she's not painting, she's writing or on her motorbike. She belongs to a local writing group and the Romantic Novelist's Association.

Summer at the Art Café is Sue's debut novel and the first in her Art Café series.

You can find more about Sue here:
Website: http://suemcdonagh.co.uk/
Facebook: https://www.facebook.com/SueMcDonaghWriter/
Twitter: https://twitter.com/SueMcDonaghLit

More Choc Lit

From Sue McDonagh

Meet Me at the Art Café

Would you take a chance on a bad boy with a leather jacket and a vintage motorbike?

That's the question single mum Jo Morris has to ask herself when she collides with local bike mechanic Ed Griffiths on a rainy Welsh hillside. Working at the Art Café, Jo hears the gossip and is all too aware of Ed's reputation.

But whilst he's certainly no angel, there is something about Ed's daredevil antics that Jo can't ignore. And as she gets to know him better and watches the kind way he deals with her young son Liam, she begins to wonder – is there more to this 'bad boy' than meets the eye?

More from Choc Lit

Why not try something else from our selection:

Too Damn Nice
Kathryn Freeman

Do nice guys stand a chance?

Nick Templeton has been in love with Lizzie Donavue for what seems like forever. Just as he summons the courage to make his move, she's offered a modelling contract which takes her across the Atlantic to the glamorous locations of New York and Los Angeles. And far away from him.

Nick is forced to watch from the sidelines as the gawky teenager he knew is transformed into Elizabeth Donavue: top model and the ultimate elegant English rose pin-up, seemingly forever caught in a whirlwind of celebrity parties with the next up-and-coming Hollywood bad boy by her side.

But then Lizzie's star-studded life comes crashing down around her, and a nice guy like Nick seems just what she needs. Will she take a chance on him? Or is he too damn nice?

Available in paperback from all good bookshops and online stores. Visit www.choc-lit.com for details.

Little Pink Taxi
Marie Laval

Take a ride with Love Taxis, the cab company with a Heart …

Rosalie Heart is a well-known face in Irlwick – well, if you drive a bright pink taxi and your signature style is a pink anorak, you're going to draw a bit of attention! But Rosalie's company Love Taxis is more than just a gimmick – for many people in the remote Scottish village, it's a lifeline.

Which is something that Marc Petersen will never understand. Marc's ruthless approach to business doesn't extend to pink taxi companies running at a loss. When he arrives in Irlwick to see to a new acquisition – Raventhorn, a rundown castle – it's apparent he poses a threat to Rosalie's entire existence; not just her business, but her childhood home too.

On the face of it Marc and Rosalie should loathe each other, but what they didn't count on was somebody playing cupid …

Available as an eBook on all platforms.
Visit www.choc-lit.com for details.

Introducing Choc Lit